SPIDER'S WEB

GLENMORE PARK BOOK 1

MIKE OMER

For Liora

ONE

When Kendele selected the songs for her jogging playlist, she didn't pause to think "What if I die hearing this?" It wasn't a question that normally occurred to her, though perhaps on that day it should have. She thought Taylor Swift's *Shake It Off* would be a fun song to jog with.

It played as she ran through the park, toward a thick cluster of trees.

The park was mostly empty this early in the morning. Thin mist hovered above the grass, covering the ground in a forlorn gray blanket. A long, paved path circled the park, twisting around Buttermere Pond, and then led into a small grove. This was the path Kendele now followed on her early morning jog, listening to Taylor Swift, thinking about her growing clientele and income. By the time she reached the artificial pond in the middle of the park, she had broken a sweat. The chilly morning breeze was pleasantly cool on her skin. She watched the calm, dark water as she ran, noticing the way the trees reflected in it, warped into strange shapes. She was cautiously happy. Kendele treated happiness like a toddler learning to walk. She approached it gently, taking careful, tentative steps. She didn't want to rush into happiness. That was how you got hurt.

She didn't want to get hurt again.

What she loved most about her new life was the complete control. She had control over herself, over her financial situation, over her schedule. She had complete control over the people in her life.

She kept those to a bare minimum.

She rounded a corner, following the path as it moved closer to the pond, when something exploded against her right temple. Her vision darkened for a moment, and then she could see again. Everything seemed fuzzy. She was on her knees, one hand on the ground and one hand against her head, trying to understand what had just happened.

Taylor Swift was singing about haters.

Someone grabbed her arm, twisting it behind her back. She screamed as he pulled her to her feet. She tried to look backwards, but turning her head was hard, and the world was an unfocused blur. Her attacker shoved her forward and she stumbled, nearly fell, the person behind her holding her up by her twisted arm. It felt as if he was about to rip it out of its socket. She cried in pain, begged him to stop, whoever it was. She tried to make sense of things. Who was it? What did he want from her?

She realized where he was taking her, and she struggled, trying to twist away. Something—a rough hand—smacked her on the back of her head. She knew it was a hand; she knew how it felt, being beaten. But it wasn't supposed to happen anymore. Not here.

Two more steps, and she felt the cold against her legs. Her attacker forced her into the pond, the water's surface a blurry thing, sparkling in the early sun. Her eyesight slowly focused and she realized that, in the background, Taylor Swift was still singing, telling her to shake it off.

And then, another sharp pain, her arm twisted even higher. She screamed again, tears filling her eyes. She was forced to bend forward, stumbling to her knees, the water lapping against her, drenching her shorts. She babbled, pleading, she didn't know what was happening, couldn't see her attacker, who never let up pulling harder, and harder, and she felt dizzy, nauseated, about to faint.

And then everything was cold. She inhaled in shock, and her mouth and throat filled with water. A hand held her head under; she panicked, twisting, not caring about the pain in her arm anymore, just trying to breathe. Spots danced around her field of view as it darkened, the muddy water's swirling cloud patterns growing dimmer. The hand was relentless, crushing her head against the pond's sandy bottom, wet sand clogging her nose, brushing against her teeth—and still the music played.

It was getting dark, her mind foggy, and her lungs exploding with pain. She had just one reflex left, telling her she had to break through, screaming that she had to get away, had to breathe.

But she was weak, and helpless, and she couldn't.

———

Detective Mitchell Lonnie walked down the paved path that snaked through the park, approaching the crime scene. The rain pattered around him, a light drizzle, but enough to make him regret his decision to leave the umbrella at home. He hunched his shoulders and pulled the collar of his jacket closer as the raindrops crawled down his neck. The sky was gray, matching his mood as he thought of Pauline's face when he told her that he'd gotten a call, that they would have to cancel their plans for lunch. She'd had that spark in her eyes, the kind she had when she knew she shouldn't be angry but was anyway. They hardly had any time together lately, and though people could be murdered anytime, she would have appreciated it if they wouldn't do so on a weekend.

Candace, the dispatcher, had told him on the phone that a body had been found buried near Buttermere Pond. He could see the crime scene now; several people were already there, near the path by the grove of trees. He'd already seen his partner's car parked in the parking lot next to the patrol car that had originally been dispatched to the scene. It was a good thing it was raining. On a sunny August weekend, the park would have been full of people, and they'd have had to handle the gaggle of onlookers that would invariably flock to the scene. As things stood, the park was empty, and the scene held only five—no, six—people, and he recognized almost all of them.

He stopped for a moment, trying to take in the entire scene. Kate and Noel, the patrol officers, were talking to a young, scared-looking Hispanic teenager. He wore a yellow raincoat and a backpack, and clutched the leash of a wet golden retriever. The two crime scene investigators, Matt Lowery and Violet Todd, were hunched by a shallow hole. Matt dug carefully with a small shovel while Violet took pictures with a small camera. Next to them stood Mitchell's partner, Detective Jacob Cooper, wearing his iconic fedora over his completely bald head and holding a black umbrella. He was a wide-shouldered man, his presence authoritative and imposing. His eyes were icy blue, always alert, and missed nothing. He'd spent the last twenty-five years on the force, and was one of the sharpest detectives ever to work for the Glenmore Park detective squad.

Mitchell approached Jacob, who shook his hand.

"What do we have?" Mitchell asked.

"The kid's dog found the body," Jacob said, indicating the teenager. "It was buried about two feet deep. He called us as soon as he realized what it was."

"He just happened to be walking in the park on a rainy day?" Mitchell asked.

Jacob shrugged. "I haven't talked to him yet," he said.

Mitchell approached the grave. It was only partially uncovered, with the body's feet and head visible, and the rest of the body still buried. Matt, his dark-skinned neck glistening in the rain, slowly scratched away the soil, careful not to disrupt the evidence in any way. Kneeling, he looked even shorter than usual. Matt was one of the shortest people Mitchell knew, and his surname, Lowery, had probably caused him infinite grief over the years.

The air was rank with the smell of rot and death, and Mitchell found himself taking quick, short breaths through his mouth. The body was far from fresh; the blackened, glistening skin made Mitchell's stomach turn. It was, as far as he could tell, a woman, her eyes and tongue protruding gruesomely. Her hair was partially detached from her scalp. He took a step back, an involuntary gasp escaping his mouth.

"Watch your step," Matt said, without turning around.

Mitchell looked at the ground by his feet. A splash of yellow sludge was only inches from his left foot. "What is that?" he asked in a muffled voice, holding his wet shirt to his mouth and nose.

"A partially digested breakfast, contributed by the kid who found the body," Matt answered.

Vomit. Stood to reason. A few feet from the puddle of vomit was another splash. "That one as well?" Mitchell asked, pointing.

"That one belongs to Noel," Matt said.

"Right," Mitchell said, and considered adding his own contribution to the lot. His empty stomach was rebelling against the whole thing.

There was a pile of evidence bags by Matt's feet, most holding dirt. Next to them were several containers in which Mitchell spotted some insects crawling.

"How long do you think you'll be here?" Mitchell asked.

"Well," Matt said. "I'll uncover the body and take some additional insect and soil samples. I'll scan the surrounding area, but I wouldn't hold my breath for any evidence I find here. Hundreds of people walk here every day, and this isn't a fresh crime."

"Any idea how long ago?" Mitchell asked. "Just an approximation?"

"No," Matt said shortly.

"Yeah, okay," Mitchell said. He walked away to join Jacob, who was approaching Noel and the teenager. Noel nodded at Mitchell and Jacob, his eyes serious. Mitchell liked Noel; he was a solid cop and never showed any of the resentment some of the other patrol cops displayed toward detectives.

"I'm Detective Jacob Cooper," Jacob told the kid. "This is my partner, Detective Mitchell Lonnie. What's your name?"

"Daniel. Daniel Hernandez," the kid said. His light brown face was wet from the rain, his black hair flat on his head. His eyes were a bit red, and Mitchell suspected he had cried earlier. His golden retriever sat on the ground glumly, its head on its front paws, its fur a soggy mess.

"Can you please tell us how you found this body?"

"It was my dog that found it," Daniel said. "Not me."

"Did you pick up anything, or touch anything before or after you found the body?" Jacob asked, narrowing his eyes.

"No, I mean... maybe I touched some things but not the body. I think. I might have touched it once, accidentally. I'm sorry." The boy began sobbing again, his eyes on the ground.

Mitchell knelt by the boy, and touched his arm gently. Daniel lifted his gaze, and met Mitchell's compassionate stare. Mitchell saw the boy's shoulders sag as he relaxed a bit, identifying a perceived friend. It was a cheap trick. Both detectives knew well that people reflexively liked Mitchell. Jacob would establish the role of the hard, no-nonsense detective, and then Mitchell would swoop in and earn their trust. Though probably, in this case, it was hardly needed. This was just a kid who was in the wrong place at the wrong time.

"Don't worry, Daniel," Mitchell said, his voice soft. "You did nothing wrong."

Daniel nodded, sniffling.

"How did your dog find the body?" Mitchell asked.

"She's like a stench magnet. If there's anything rotting or stinking within a mile, she immediately homes in on it. She likes to roll in dead animals."

"I see," Mitchell said, queasy at the thought. "So she smelled it?"

"I guess," Daniel said, looking at the dog in irritation. "She pulled me over there and started digging. I let her dig—I was just messaging with my girl, so I didn't really mind stopping for a bit. But then I noticed something in the ground. It… it was the head. I called the police right away."

"Do you live nearby, Daniel?" Mitchell asked.

"Yeah. I mean, about fifteen minutes from the park."

"Do you often come here to walk your dog?"

"Sometimes, on weekends," Daniel said, shrugging.

"Even when it rains?"

"Dog's gotta do what a dog's gotta do."

"Okay, so you found the body, and called us. What did you do then?"

"Nothing. I just waited. The cops got here about twenty minutes later."

"Did you see anything unusual while you were waiting?"

"No."

"Did anyone go by?"

"No."

"Okay. Thanks, Daniel."

"Can I go?"

"Sure," Jacob said. "Just give us your details so we can contact you if we need anything."

Daniel gave them his address and phone number and turned to leave.

"Hang on," Mitchell said.

"What?"

"Give me your phone for a second, Daniel."

"Why?"

"Just do it."

Glumly, Daniel handed Mitchell the phone. Mitchell opened the picture gallery and looked at the most recent pictures. He sighed. The last three images were selfies that Daniel had taken, the head of the uncovered body prominent in the background. Mitchell showed the images to Jacob, who shook his head.

"Daniel, a selfie with a dead body? Seriously?" Jacob said.

"I was just going to—"

"No," Mitchell said, "you weren't." He deleted the images.

"Did you share these images?" Jacob asked.

"No."

"Are you sure? We'll check."

"No! I didn't share them with anyone."

"Okay," Mitchell handed the phone back to Daniel.

"Look," Daniel said, "can I take a selfie with one of you, then? I just want something to show my friends."

"Sure," Jacob said. "Take a picture with Detective Lonnie."

Mitchell sent Jacob a scathing look, but Daniel was already happily edging next to Mitchell, tapping his phone. He slung his arm around Mitchell's neck as if they were long-lost friends and took some photos, all the while trying to make Mitchell act a bit more "detective-y."

Finally, to Mitchell's relief, Daniel left, the dog plodding after him.

Mitchell approached Violet, who was pacing around the scene now, examining the ground carefully. "Found anything interesting yet?" he asked.

"A used condom," she said, raising her eyes to meet his. "And two beer bottles."

Mitchell made a mental note of the condom and wondered briefly if this was a sex crime. He turned around and looked at the grave again.

Matt still knelt next to it, his face grim, patiently scraping the dirt off the body. He turned toward Jacob. "Strange place to hide a body," he said.

"Yeah," Jacob said. "This area is usually full of people." He stared into the distance, and Mitchell followed his eyes. Three figures drew nearer, two men carrying a stretcher and a woman by their side.

"Assuming the killer came here with the body," Mitchell said, "he'd have to carry it all the way over to the grove, dig a hole in the ground, dump it, and cover it without anyone noticing."

"And why would he even do that?" Jacob answered. "There are a million better places and ways to get rid of a body."

The three figures were close now. Mitchell recognized Annie Turner, her red hair completely soaked.

"Hello, Detectives," Annie said as she reached them. Annie was Glenmore Park's medical examiner. She was easy to work with, and did her best to explain any medical findings until even the thickest of detectives could follow what she said.

She wore a yellow raincoat over her white pants and shirt. The square eyeglasses she always wore were spattered with rain drops, and Mitchell wondered if she could really see anything through them. He showed her the way to the grave. Matt had removed most of the soil from the body's torso. Tatters of what had probably once been a sports bra covered very little of the woman's decaying flesh. Despite his nine years on the force, Mitchell found the sight distressing, and averted his eyes, looking at Annie instead. She approached the grave hesitantly, her steps small and careful.

"Uh… hello Matt," she said.

Matt cleared his throat. "Hello Annie," he said.

Annie crouched next to the body and looked at it intently.

"I see you already bagged her hands," she said softly.

"Well… yes," Matt said. "Do you want me to wait for you next time? I can definitely do that. You're right, I should have waited—"

"No, no, it's okay. No need to wait. You did what you were supposed to." Annie's voice became a bit choked.

Mitchell stared at them both, his eyebrows raised. It was like watching two teenagers try to gather the courage to ask each other to the prom. What was up with them?

"You didn't have to come," Matt said. "I mean, it's not like you had to pronounce the death here, right? You're just getting wet."

"No, it's okay. I wanted to see… the body." Annie bent to touch one of the body's hands just as Matt cleaned some dirt off it. Their fingers touched and they both withdrew quickly.

"I'll be done in a minute," Matt blurted.

"Right! Right." Annie stood up and turned to the two men who accompanied her. "Let's open the stretcher," she said. "Matt will be done soon."

Mitchell circled the grave, then turned to Jacob once more.

"Looks like she was wearing running clothes," he said.

"So she was probably jogging," Jacob said.

"Probably."

"She went jogging in the park, and the killer waited for her here."

"I'm guessing it was very early in the morning, or late in the evening," Mitchell said. "There weren't many people in the park."

"And after she was killed, he buried her in the same spot," Jacob said.

"Right."

They stayed on the scene while Annie collected the body, placing it in a black body bag. Matt bagged a car key found in the body's back pocket and gathered some additional samples. The two detectives and two crime scene technicians canvassed the crime scene. In addition to the beer bottles and the condom, they found an old dry pen, a cigarette stub and a candy bar wrap, all within fifty feet of the grave.

There was no ID on the body.

———

There was no reason to rush the investigation. The crime wasn't fresh—Annie had quickly determined it was committed at least a week before—and there was no easy way to identify the body, no family to notify. In short, there was no excuse for paid overtime. The chief was quick to inform Captain Bailey that his squad could wait and start working the case on Monday.

Unsurprisingly, no one argued.

What was left of the weekend passed uneventfully. Though they had seen the dead, buried, decaying body, the detectives and the crime scene crew refused to let the incident mar their weekend plans.

But death can trickle in during quiet, thoughtful moments. It doesn't ask for permission, often sneaking into people's minds before they notice it is there.

During Saturday dinner, Jacob's daughter Amy asked him to pass the salad bowl. She repeated the request three times; each time her father stared through her, as if she had turned invisible. Finally, he cleared his throat and passed over the salt shaker. Amy exchanged a look with Marissa, Jacob's wife. The rest of the dinner was a silent affair.

Matt was driving down the highway when a huge surge of loneliness hit him. He got off at the next exit, and stopped at the side of the road, tears springing from his eyes. He took out his phone and thought about calling someone. He scrolled down the contact list, seeing only one name he really wanted to call. But he didn't. Instead he opened Twitter, tried to think of something witty or thoughtful to say, found nothing, and eventually retweeted a tweet from the Oatmeal. For some reason, this made him feel better, and he got back on the road.

Mitchell and Pauline were kissing, naked in bed. Pauline's hand snaked along the back of his leg, her fingers lightly touching his thigh, and suddenly he moved away.

"What's wrong?" she asked.

"Nothing," he said, unable to explain that her body suddenly reminded him of the dead body he had seen earlier, the remnants of the sports bra failing to cover the girl's decomposing flesh. He kissed her lightly on the lips and she smiled, her eyes concerned.

She fell asleep with Mitchell hugging her from behind, listening intently to her deep breaths, wondering if the dead girl had someone who missed her body, her warmth, her love.

Annie, who had seen more death than any of the others, was mostly undisturbed. But there was a moment, just a tiny moment while she was in the shower, that a flashing memory of the girl's face invaded her thoughts.

She brushed it aside, got out of the shower, dressed, and went to see a movie.

On Monday morning she autopsied the dead woman's body. She did it by herself, preferring the solitude. She didn't like using assistants for murder autopsies, though she couldn't say why. Once she was done, she called Jacob and informed him that she had some conclusions she wanted to share.

TWO

To avoid any embarrassing moments in the morgue, Mitchell decided to smear some VapoRub under his nostrils to mask the body's smell. As he stood by the metal gurney on which their Jane Doe lay, it occurred to him that VapoRub was supposed to open up his nasal passageways even more, and that it might have not been the best idea he ever had. The smell was overpowering, and his stomach turned.

He tried to push the feeling away and pay attention to what Annie was telling him and Jacob. She gestured at the body as she talked, the harsh white light in the morgue emphasizing the corpse's discolored skin.

"The deceased was twenty-one years old," Annie said. "She was Caucasian, five foot seven, red hair. It's difficult to determine exact weight, but she was quite thin. I can't really give you an accurate time of death yet. The ground at the burial site was moist, and summer temperatures fluctuate wildly. However, Matt extracted several larvae from her cavities and from the surrounding dirt, and we're consulting a forensic entomologist this afternoon. I think we'll be able to give you an approximate time of death this evening."

"Okay," Jacob said.

"The stomach and intestines were already liquefied when we uncovered the body, so I can't really tell you anything about their contents. However, I did find some interesting samples in the body's sinuses." She walked over to a shelf which held several jars and picked one of them up to show them.

"What is it?" Mitchell asked, squinting at the small patch of black matter.

"It's some sort of vegetation," Annie said.

"She inhaled it?" Jacob asked.

"So it appears," Annie said. "This could have happened for several reasons, but one of the most likely possibilities is drowning. Victims of drowning sometimes inhale aquatic vegetation when they are trying to breathe. She also had some sand particles in her mouth that didn't match the soil she was buried in, which I collected in the jar over there." She indicated a different container. "But that doesn't tell us much, since she would have inhaled the particles if she was running during a windy day with some dust in the air. I also checked her bone marrow and found some diatoms there—"

"What's that?" Mitchell asked.

"I'm getting there," Annie said testily. "Diatoms are one-celled phytoplankton that sometimes live in water. When people drown, they inhale these organisms, which later collect in the bone marrow."

"But wouldn't a drowning victim have water in her lungs?" Mitchell asked.

"Not necessarily," Annie said. "About fifteen percent of drowning cases are dry drownings, which leave the lungs completely dry."

"So she drowned?" Jacob asked.

"Well…" Annie hesitated. "The diatom test is not exactly conclusive. But it does indicate a likely possibility of drowning. Couple that with the plant I found in her sinuses, and we have high likelihood for drowning."

"How high?"

Annie shrugged.

"Could the vegetation and the dust have come from the pond water in the park?"

"Absolutely," Annie said.

"Can you check if they match?"

"I think so. I'll contact an expert I know."

"Okay," Jacob said. "A twenty-one-year old female who probably died from drowning. What else do you have for us?"

"I sent DNA samples to the lab to check in CODIS," Annie said. "Unfortunately, I couldn't recover any finger-prints. I did find a root canal which seems to be quite old. Probably from childhood. If we do have a suspicion for a match, we can check against dental records."

Jacob and Mitchell both nodded. This was helpful, though they had hoped for more.

"Anything else?" Mitchell asked.

"I think she was abused as a child," Annie said.

"What makes you say that?" Jacob asked.

"See here?" Annie said, and walked toward one of the walls where some X-ray images hung. "Two old fractures on the third left rib, and one additional fracture on the fourth. Her left hand was broken twice, and there were several fractures in the fingers as well."

"Maybe she was involved in some sort of accident," Mitchell suggested.

Annie shook her head. "The fractures occurred at different times. No, this was a case of someone who for some reason got her bones broken over and over. I see this sometimes with people who do extreme sports, but these are really old fractures, so she had to be about ten or eleven when some of them occurred. This makes me doubt the extreme sports theory."

"Okay," Jacob nodded.

"Is there a way to know if she was sexually assaulted before she was killed?" Mitchell asked.

Annie shook her head. "No way to know for sure, but I didn't find any traces to indicate she was. And her shorts and underwear were mostly intact."

"Okay," Jacob nodded, "Thanks, Annie."

So far their Jane Doe remained anonymous.

———

As soon as they returned to the squad room, Mitchell made his way to the filing cabinet. He was not interested in anything inside; these days almost all their files could be accessed digitally. But the file cabinet held the important position of pedestal for the coffee maker. He made a pot of strong, black coffee and poured two cups, handing one to Jacob, who was already typing furiously on his keyboard. The coffee maker, a ridiculously expensive model bought a year before by Captain Fred Bailey, was the squad's most treasured possession. As far as Mitchell was concerned, it was more important than any of the detectives.

He leaned against Jacob's desk, one of four desks in the room. The Glenmore Park police department had four detectives and a captain. They'd once had a lieutenant as well but, due to budget problems, the chief had decided they could do without, a decision that still inspired controversy and criticism.

"Once you're done writing the report, send it over to me and I'll submit it to the system," Mitchell said.

Jacob sent him a look overcome with gratitude. His relationship with the department's internal report program was fraught with distrust and downright hatred. He sometimes reminded Mitchell of his mother, who called him regularly with complaints like, "The internet won't play the song I clicked on the desktop," or "I wrote an e-mail but then the computer made it disappear, and now I can't find my pictures."

Mitchell crossed the room to one of the whiteboards. The room had two of them, used for brainstorm sessions or to collect info on major cases. Both were currently covered with doodles, mostly of ducks. He erased all of it, ducks included, and wrote at the top: *Jane Doe Murder*

- *Buttermere Park*. Then he headed to the captain's office, to see if he was in and give him an update.

The captain's office was adjacent to the squad room, separated by a rickety wooden door that was always on the verge of collapsing, due to the captain's tendency to slam it when irritated. Mitchell knocked on the door several times, then went to sit by his computer. They could update Captain Bailey later.

Mitchell opened NAMUS, the National Missing and Unidentified Persons System, on his computer. He searched for missing females in Massachusetts, and received five results from the past year. Two of those were aged forty six and eighty nine. Mitchell ignored those and focused on the rest. Of the three left, one was African-American, so he could ignore her as well. That left only two. Their descriptions didn't exactly match the dead girl's, but Mitchell had seen descriptions that ended up being wildly different from the actual person's appearance. He preferred to check for himself.

He picked up the phone, then hesitated. After a second, he put down the phone, took out his mobile, and called Pauline instead. The call went unanswered, as it usually did. Pauline hardly ever answered calls during work, but he'd been hoping she'd answer anyway. It seemed as if they rarely had time together lately, with him working at all hours, and her going to night classes in the evening and working during the day. He missed talking to her. The more he thought about it, the more he realized how much happier he was in those few minutes they managed to occasionally steal together. He was determined to try harder to find extra time to be with her, or at the very least talk to her.

A moment later, the inevitable message blinked on his phone screen. *Can't talk now, sry*. She almost never shortened any word while texting except *Sorry* and *Goodnight*, which invariably turned to *sry* and *gnight*. He sighed and put the phone back in his pocket, then picked up his office phone and called the number on the first missing female.

A female voice answered the phone. "Hello?"

"Hi," Mitchell said. "I'm Detective Lonnie from the Glenmore Park police. Is this Mrs. Brody?"

"Yes, that's me."

"Mrs. Brody, I'm calling about your daughter, Patricia."

"Why?" the woman asked. "What happened to Patricia?"

"I understand you reported her missing two months ago?"

"That's right."

"Well, we've had some recent developments and we think that we may have new leads—"

"My daughter returned two days after she went missing," the woman said.

"Oh." Mitchell drummed his fingers on the table. "Why didn't you inform us?"

"We didn't think about it."

"I see. When was the last time you saw your daughter?"

"Fifteen minutes ago. She went to her boyfriend's house."

"Uh-huh. Okay, thanks Mrs. Brody. Next time, please—"

"It's the same boyfriend she ran off with last time."

"Yes, I see. Well, next time, please let us know if—"

"He's up to no good, that one."

"Thank you, Mrs. Brody," Mitchell said, and hung up.

He called the second number. A gruff, impatient voice answered the call.

"This is Bob Vern."

"Hello, Mr. Vern, this is Detective Lonnie from the Glenmore Park police department. I understand that your daughter went missing three months ago."

A moment's pause. "Yeah?"

"Well, we've had some recent developments, and we wanted to check if they were relevant to your daughter's case."

"What kind of leads?" The voice became soft, more urgent. "Do you know where she is?"

"I would like to ask you some questions about your daughter."

"Go ahead."

"Her height, according to the missing person's report, is—"

"Five foot six. She has red hair—kind of strawberry-blonde—and green eyes. A scar behind her right knee. Do you know where she is?"

Annie hadn't mentioned a scar, and the Jane Doe's hair was a dark red, not even close to blonde. Still, Mitchell had to ask: "Did she have a root canal at some point?"

"No."

"You might not remember; it might have been when she was a small child. I—"

"I'm a dentist, Detective. I do all of my children's dental procedures."

"I see."

"I take it that the new developments are no longer relevant?"

"I'm sorry."

"I should have learned by now." The man's voice became bitter. "I should never get my hopes up when you people call. But I still do it, every time."

"I'm really sorry, Mr. Vern."

The man hung up.

"Missing persons is a dead end," Mitchell told Jacob.

"Okay then," Jacob said. "We'll have to go with the car key."

"Right," Mitchell said. "If she lived near the park, she wouldn't have taken the car key with her. She probably parked her car in the vicinity."

"Sounds likely," Jacob said, nodding. "Since there was no apartment key on the body, or anything else for that matter, she probably left whatever she was carrying in the car and went for a jog."

"Okay, then," Mitchell said, and opened a map of the city on his browser. "Here's Buttermere Park. If she parked on the southern side, on Valley Vista Road, it would have been in one of those parking lots." He pointed at two parking lots on the map. "There are no other parking spots on Vista Road."

"Okay," Jacob looked over Mitchell's shoulder. "If she parked east of the park, she would have had to run through some unpleasant terrain to get there, so for now let's assume her car's not there. But she could have parked anywhere on Firestone Drive. It's a quiet street, and there's lots of parking space there."

"If she did, and her car was left there for a week or more, it might have been towed."

"Good point," Jacob said. "Let's start with that."

He stood up and put on his hat.

"Where are you going?" Mitchell asked.

"To Traffic," Jacob said.

"The Traffic division is inside the building," Mitchell pointed out. "Why are you taking your hat?"

"It's my hat," Jacob said. He looked offended. "It's part of my uniform. Do you go down to Traffic without your pants?"

"Sometimes," Mitchell said. "When I want them to take me seriously."

"Okay. Keep your pants on, please, I'll be right back. That report is waiting on my computer to be submitted."

———

When Jacob walked into the Traffic division, it was empty except for Sergeant Wallace. Jacob had known Wallace for a very long time. They'd joined the force the same year, and had been at the police academy together.

Though they were on friendly terms, Jacob secretly thought Wallace was one of the most useless cops in the station. He'd been useless at the academy, always one step from being discharged, and he continued to be useless once he became a cop. During their academy days, their entire room disliked Wallace because he snored at night. Each snore was a long, ever-changing buzzing sound, rising high, then dropping low, only to suddenly stop completely. Anyone nearby would feel himself tense up, certain Wallace's breathing had finally stopped altogether, and he was about to choke to death. Seconds would tick by—one... two... three—and then another buzzing snore would emerge from the man's twisted sinuses. It was a sound that was impossible to ignore, impossible to get used to, and it kept them awake at night when every second of sleep was precious. In the morning, when Wallace woke up, his bed was surrounded by shoes that had been lobbed at him during the night by his irate roommates.

Wallace was a medium-sized man, a bit chubby, with tanned brown skin. He was balding; unlike Jacob, however, he still had a crown of gray hair surrounding the bald spot on his head. His nose, despite the snoring, was quite wide and took up a large part of his face. As he saw Jacob, he smiled and leaned back; his belly made a brief appearance.

"Cooper!" he said. "What brings you to our humble division?"

"Hey, Wallace," Jacob said. "I'm trying to locate a car. It might have been towed from Firestone Drive sometime."

"Okey dokey," Wallace said cheerfully. "Do you have a description or license plate?"

"No."

"Do you know when it was towed?"

"I'm not even sure it was towed," Jacob said.

"Well, that might make it difficult," Wallace sighed. "I mean, there could have been dozens of cars towed from Firestone Drive in the past year. How will we be able to tell which one you're looking for?"

"That's my job," Jacob said.

"It's just that if I had a more accurate description, I could save you some time."

"I know, but I don't have a description."

"Not even part of the license plate number? Maybe a witness saw some of the numbers. Sometimes people notice the strangest things. Did you ask the residents if they saw the car's license plates?"

"No, Wallace. No license plate."

"Tricky one, huh? Doesn't make our life easier. Who knows how many cars were towed during—"

"Can you check?"

"Sure, sure. It might be difficult, but I'll check. I mean… it would save us some time if you tried to find some details. But let's see, maybe we can figure something out." Wallace swiveled his chair to face his computer. "How is Melissa?"

"*Marissa* is fine," Jacob said. "Doing great, actually."

"Glad to hear, glad to hear," Wallace said, typing slowly with one finger. He was twice divorced, and loved to tell anyone who cared to listen about his divorce woes. "A nice catch, that one."

"Thanks. I think so too."

"Okay, there were no cars towed from Firestone Drive in the past six months."

"None?"

"Nope."

Jacob was incredibly proud of himself for thanking Wallace politely. He returned to the squad room, dragged his chair to Mitchell's desk and sat down. Mitchell was lost in thought, staring at the screen, and didn't turn to look at him.

Mitchell always made Jacob feel a bit old. The young detective was thirty-two, which was *twenty four* years younger than Jacob. When Jacob had become a detective, Mitchell had been learning to draw with crayons instead of eat them. He was good-looking too, as Jacob had repeatedly been told by his wife, his teenage daughter, and several coworkers. He was tall, wide-shouldered, skinny and muscular, his skin tawny. Unlike Jacob, he had hair, and it was infuriatingly rich and thick.

And, of course, he had the Lonnie eyes, which all the Lonnie siblings were blessed with: jade green, deep, and perfect. Mitchell's eyes gave a constant impression of wisdom and sorrow, the eyes of an old soul, well acquainted with humanity's evil ways. Once, Mitchell had told Jacob this was no accident. He trimmed his eyebrows to make himself look more sorrowful. Jacob wouldn't have known how to trim his eyebrows even if his beloved wife's life depended on it.

Then again, as Jacob had repeatedly proven, he could outdrink the young shrimp three pints to one.

He cleared his throat. "No car towed from Firestone Drive in the past six months," he said.

"Okay," Mitchell said, turning to face him. "Let's check the parking lots on Valley Vista Road."

They got into their car and drove off. Traffic being what it was, it took them almost half an hour to get to the first parking lot on Valley Vista Road. There were fourteen cars parked there. The key matched the fourth one they checked, a battered blue Chevrolet Cobalt.

According to the registration, it belonged to Kendele Byers.

THREE

Kendele Byers's car had a small handbag in the trunk, and inside it Jacob and Mitchell found a keychain with two keys, and a wallet containing fifty-seven dollars, a driver's license, and a credit card. They drove to the station, processed the car and its contents, and signed the keychain out.

Kendele's address was registered as 76 Halifax Drive, which was an address in the Halifax Gardens Mobile Home Park, the city's only trailer park. Though it housed some of Glenmore Park's more impoverished citizens, Halifax Drive was a clean, quiet street. The trailers were small, beige-colored homes that hid their mobile infrastructure with white wooden bases. At first glance, they all looked the same. Same walls, same windows, same roofs. But on closer examination, the differences popped immediately. One was surrounded by circular pots containing various small trees. Another had custom-made red drapes on its windows. Most of them had tiny front yards, which ranged from *immaculately tidy* to *jungle of death*.

Kendele's trailer was pretty much bare, and looked as if it had just been bought and placed, except it was a bit dirtier than the trailers that surrounded it.

The smell inside was slightly stuffy. It reminded Mitchell of the way his own apartment had smelled once, after he had returned from a long vacation. The space was surprisingly roomy. The open-concept kitchen had a breakfast bar over which one could look out onto the living room. In the living room, a worn gray couch faced a small television set, with a battered coffee table between them.

The sink was mercifully empty. Mitchell had once entered the house of a woman who'd gone missing two months before. A few dirty plates had been left in the sink with some food leftovers. By the time the police had gotten there, the entire thing was infested by maggots and flies to the extent that it was hard to look at—not to mention the smell.

There was a small black laptop on the coffee table. It was unplugged, and when Mitchell tried to turn it on the screen remained dark. He located the laptop's cable under the table and plugged it in, then followed Jacob into the bedroom.

Kendele seemed to have been quite orderly. Her clothes were hung neatly inside her closet, a small shabby dresser sitting underneath them. A red sweatshirt lay on the bed, and Mitchell guessed that she used to wear it at night when she went to sleep. He noticed her phone on the bedside table. Like the laptop, it was unplugged and dark. The charger lay on the same table. Mitchell plugged it in as well. He had a moment of unease, as he always did when he went through a dead person's things. What would Kendele have felt, knowing two strange men would be pawing through her meager belongings after she died, prying into her life? Mitchell doubted she'd like it.

Jacob was checking the bathroom. He opened the small closet above the sink and scanned the interior.

"Cymbalta," he said. "That's an antidepressant, right?"

"Yeah," Mitchell said.

"Several boxes here."

Mitchell glanced inside. The bathroom was small and didn't really have room for both detectives to stand in it comfortably. Like the rest of the trailer, there was a layer of dust and dirt on everything, but in the white Fluorescent light of the bathroom it was a lot more pronounced. He noticed a small laundry basket with some shirts, pants, and socks on top.

Mitchell turned away. He wanted to check the phone and the laptop. If there was interesting information to be found, it would be on them. He made sure both were really charging, then went to the kitchen, where he methodically checked all the cupboards and drawers, but found nothing of note. He opened the fridge, and the situation there was not as horrid as it could have been. There were some rotting vegetables in the vegetable drawer, and a distinct smell of food gone bad, but it didn't look like this fridge had been abandoned for months. He glanced at the milk's expiration date. Three weeks ago. When would Kendele have bought this? Five weeks ago?

He returned to the bedroom. Jacob was looking at the open closet, frowning.

"What?" Mitchell asked.

"Pants," Jacob pointed. "Shirts, short-sleeved and long-sleeved. Some skirts. Three dresses. Sock drawer. Another drawer with bras and two pairs of pantyhose. The shoes are on the bottom. See anything strange?"

It took Mitchell a few seconds. "No underpants," he finally said.

"Right."

Mitchell thought about the laundry basket. He went to the bathroom and emptied the basket on the floor. No underpants there, either. He returned to the bedroom.

"Weird," he said. "Maybe she went commando."

Jacob shook his head. "Nah," he said. "She had underpants on when we found her, Annie told us so."

Mitchell tried to think. Would someone have taken the underpants away? But the closet didn't have an empty shelf, and the drawer with the bras seemed full. He looked around the bedroom for another place to hold them.

"I think this bed opens up," he said. He went to one edge and lifted. The entire bed frame rose, revealing a small storage space. Inside were some boots, a couple of additional dresses, three handbags, and two big boxes. One was taped shut, the other was open. It was half full of underwear.

"That's… interesting," Jacob said. He got the open box out of the bed, put it on the floor, and sifted through the contents. "There are maybe a hundred pairs here," he said.

Mitchell started looking as well. The underwear were in all colors and all shapes. There were bikini briefs, G-strings, thongs, boyshorts, and even several that looked as if they belonged in someone's grandmother's closet. He got the second box and tore open the lid. More underpants. All of them were brand new.

"Who the hell needs so many underpants?" he asked.

Jacob shrugged. "Maybe she had a weird phobia. Didn't want to wear the same pair twice."

"Could be," Mitchell said. "I've never heard of anything like that."

"We learn something new every day."

Mitchell went over to the phone and turned it on. He waited patiently as the Android operating screen showed up. To his relief, the phone was unlocked. There was no e-mail app on it, which he found unusual. He opened the last calls. Some incoming calls from unrecognized numbers, one call from someone named Leon, some calls from Debbie, two from Vernon. Last outgoing call was to Debbie, four and a half weeks ago. He checked the contact list, which was depressingly short. Kendele did not have a very active social life.

He scanned the messages. Several "Call me" and "Why aren't you picking up, call me" messages from Debbie. A message from a tourist agency advertising a lake somewhere, with an image depicting it, and three messages from someone selling a newspaper subscription.

Finally, on July 20, four weeks before, a conversation between Kendele and Leon. Just random bits of information. Kendele asked him how he was, Leon said he was better, Kendele wrote that she would love to see him sometime soon, Leon wrote that he hoped to have some days off on Christmas. He called her "sis" in one of his messages.

Eventually the messages ended with several increasingly worried messages asking Kendele why she wasn't answering her phone, and finally a message sent a week ago, saying that if she didn't answer him right now he'd call the police

43

and report her missing. Mitchell wondered why he hadn't. Maybe because Leon knew she was actually dead, and was just covering his tracks with those messages?

Mitchell decided to check the phone more thoroughly once he returned to the office. He went back to the living room, where Jacob was checking one of the kitchen drawers. Mitchell had already checked them, but it wasn't like there was anything else to rummage through.

"I have an outgoing message from her phone on July 20," Mitchell said.

"Okay."

"She was probably alive then."

"Probably."

Mitchell turned on the laptop. After several seconds, Windows came up. Once again, no password. There was a Thunderbird icon on the desktop and he double clicked it.

"Woah," he said.

"What is it?" Jacob asked.

"She wasn't leading a very exciting life according to her phone, but her inbox is bursting with incoming e-mails. From dozens of different e-mail addresses." Mitchell scanned them. "Most are almost certainly men," he added.

He looked at the subjects. Some mentioned a package that hadn't arrived yet, or an order placed. There were several subjects which contained the word "subscription."

Two seemed incredibly desperate—all caps. One asked *WHERE IS MY PACKAGE???* and another said *PLEASE REPLY I NEED SOME MORE.*

"I think she may have been a drug dealer," Mitchell said, scrolling down. He reached the read e-mails. Last e-mail read was on July 20.

"Why?" Jacob asked.

"Just those e-mail subjects… Hang on." He clicked one of them, with the subject *Order Details.*

It was quite short.

————

Hey pantyGirl, I would like to order the following:

1. Two blue G-strings, worn for a whole day

2. One regular pair, worn at night, never mind the color, surprise me ;-)

3. One regular pair, red, worn while running, at least twice.

Please send it to the same address, and send me the invoice. I think the order totals up to 210$ right? Because last time I paid 40$ extra for every run.

Thanks, and have a lovely week!!!

Mitchell glanced at Jacob, who was inspecting the window. "She wasn't a drug dealer," he said. "She was selling her used underpants."

———

Captain Fred Bailey was leaving work early. He was supposed to pick up his son from daycare, and this time he was determined not to be late. He didn't want to face the angry stare of the daycare teacher again, not to mention his son's disappointment and sadness. Sid had a knack for asking questions like "Why did you pick me up after everyone left and I cried?" and "Why am I always the last to go home?" Which made Fred feel bad for days. Not anymore.

He left his office through the squad room. Jacob and Mitchell were there, standing by one of the whiteboards. Fred paused behind them and cleared his throat. Both detectives turned around.

"Hey, Fred," Jacob said.

"How's the case going?" Fred asked.

"The victim's name is Kendele Byers," Jacob said. "She lived in the trailer park. We came back from there about an hour ago. The trailer park manager said she moved in there in January."

"Moved in from where?"

"She didn't tell him. He said she was very quiet and kept to herself. First three months she was late to pay the rent every month, and he almost kicked her out. Then, in April, she paid four months in advance."

"So she came into some cash," Fred said.

"Well…" Jacob said. "She found a lucrative job. She was selling her used underwear online."

"Seriously? Does that pay well?"

"According to what we can see from the PayPal invoices she started receiving, she was making about a hundred and fifty a day," Mitchell said.

"Huh," Fred said. "Well, like my father used to say, there are all sorts of zebras in the herd."

"Indeed," Jacob said, and pointed at the printed map they'd taped to the whiteboard. "We found her car here. Last communication she had on her phone and her e-mail account was on July 20."

"So we assume she died afterward," Fred said.

"Annie just called to say that she and Matt pinpointed the date of death to sometime between the 19th and 22nd," Jacob said.

"All right."

"She may have been drowned in Buttermere Pond," Jacob said.

"So… drowned and then buried?"

Jacob nodded. "Yeah."

"Did we notify the family?" Fred asked

"We think we have the phone number of the brother," Jacob explained. "A guy named Leon. We didn't call him yet. She didn't seem to be in contact with her parents."

"Maybe they're dead," Fred suggested.

"Maybe," Mitchell said, "but Annie thinks Kendele was abused as a child, so that might have something to do with it."

"Any suspects?"

"Not really." Jacob shrugged. "There are some leads that we need to check. She had one friend named Debbie. And then there are her customers."

"Do her customers know where she lives?"

"Not as far as we could tell," Jacob said. "Also, most of them live pretty far away. Some don't live in the United States, one lives in Texas, one in California. But one lives in Boston."

"What a happy coincidence!" Fred said. "My father would say he was close enough to feed the neighbor's chicken."

"Right," Jacob said. "His name is Ronnie Kuperman. We plan on giving him a surprise visit tomorrow morning."

"Do you know where he works?"

Jacob shook his head. "Nah, we'll wake up early, ahead of traffic, be at his doorstep by seven."

Fred glanced at Mitchell, who seemed pretty glum at the prospect of getting up so early. "Well," he said. "You two are certainly eager to follow this thing. Do you need Bernard and Hannah's help?"

"I talked to Bernard an hour ago," Jacob said. "They're investigating the rape case down at Silverleaf Lane, right? There's no point in pulling them off the case. This murder is cold, and we don't have too much to go on right now. We'll see how it develops."

Fred nodded. "Okay. Keep me updated." He glanced at his watch. "Damn," he muttered. He could already imagine Sid's eyes as he asked, "Why are other daddies never late to pick up their sons?"

———

Jacob called Leon several times, and sent him two text messages before Leon returned his call.

"Hi," Leon said, his voice soft and slightly feminine. "This is Leon Byers? I understand you were looking for me?"

"Hello Leon, I'm glad you returned my call," Jacob said. "My name is Detective Jacob Cooper, from the Glenmore Park police department."

"Glenmore Park?"

"That's right."

"Where's that?"

"Uh... Massachusetts, sir. About twenty miles north of Boston," Jacob said, doodling thoughtfully on a piece of paper. If Leon really didn't know where Glenmore Park was, he didn't know his sister was living there.

"Okay. Why are you calling me, Detective?"

"Do you have a sister named Kendele Byers?" Jacob asked.

"That's right," Leon's voice tensed up. "Did you find her?"

"Were we supposed to be looking for her, Mr. Byers?"

"I reported her missing a week ago."

"Mr. Byers, where exactly did you report her missing?"

"The police, of course."

"There is no missing persons description that matches your sister in Glenmore Park, sir."

"Why would there be? She lived in San Francisco."

"I see. For how long has she been living in San Francisco, sir?" Jacob asked.

"For the past six months or so."

"Mr. Byers, why would you think that Kendele lives in San Francisco?"

"Because that's what she told me, of course."

Jacob glanced at Mitchell, who was listening to the call and frowning. Why would Kendele give a false address to her brother?

"Mr. Byers, I'm sorry to say that I think we have recovered your sister's body."

The seconds went by in silence. "What?" Leon finally said. "Are… Are you sure? My sister is not even close to the East Coast. I think you must be mistaken, I—"

"Was your sister about five six, Caucasian, with red hair?"

"Yes, but listen—"

"Did she have a root canal as a child?"

"Maybe, I don't know."

"Well, if you could find out, it will help us clear up this case. If your sister really does live in San Francisco, perhaps we misidentified the body."

"S… Sure. What do you need?"

"Can you give me the name and address of the dentist she went to as a child?"

"Yeah, of course," Leon said. "We've been going to the same dentist for years. His name is Doctor Harrow. Hang on, I'll get his address." Jacob waited. Finally Leon found the address and dictated it to Jacob.

"Okay," Jacob said. "We'll get a warrant for her dental records and will cross reference them with our Jane Doe's as soon as we get them."

"Okay. I'm sure you have the wrong person, Detective. Please let me know once you're sure?"

"Of course. Thank you, Mr. Byers."

Jacob hung up. A second later Kendele's phone beeped. Mitchell picked it up and glanced at it. He showed the message to Jacob. *Kendele, please call me, it's urgent!!!*

"What do you think?" Jacob asked.

Mitchell fiddled with the phone a bit. "It has a San Francisco area code," he told Jacob.

"Maybe she really did move to San Francisco at first," Jacob said.

"Or she got the phone number with this area code, to make it seem that way."

"Let's try and get that warrant," Jacob said without enthusiasm.

It was one of those days when bureaucracy didn't fight back. They had the warrant within an hour, and it took only forty five minutes more to receive the dental records from Doctor Harrow. They passed them over to Annie, who compared them to the body's teeth immediately.

The body was Kendele Byers.

FOUR

Something was beeping in the darkness. What did it want, this alien sound, its shrill pitch assaulting her ears in the middle of the night? Did it seek to destroy her? Drive her to madness? Was it the sound of pure, malignant evil?

No, Marissa slowly realized, it was the sound of her husband's alarm clock. It wasn't really the middle of the night; it was four in the morning, which was almost as bad. He had mentioned the night before that he'd be getting up very early.

"Jacob," she mumbled, and nudged him. "Jacob."

"Harummmmph," he muttered into his pillow.

"Jacob, wake up."

"No, it's okay, there's no need. I'll clean it later."

"Jacob, your alarm clock."

"It's not mine."

"Jacob!" she barked impatiently.

Jacob sat up, confused, his eyes open wide.

"What? What happened?"

"Your alarm is beeping!"

"Oh. Oh! Right!" Jacob finally turned the damn thing off. "Sorry, hon, go back to sleep."

"'kay," she mumbled and rolled to her side. "Have a nice day."

Her husband got up and quietly began to dress. Or, at least, dressing quietly was his intention. Jacob always thought of himself as a morning person, but Marissa knew well that in the first thirty minutes of the day her husband's cognitive abilities were quite similar to the abilities of a toddler—and not a bright toddler, at that.

It was even worse when he woke up early. Pants were dropped, as well as socks. He managed to somehow bump his head on the closet door, though Marissa couldn't begin to imagine how. He tried to close their bathroom door silently, and instead slammed it like an angry teenager making a point. Beyond the door she heard the cup that held their toothbrushes fall on the floor, heard her husband curse. She sighed.

Finally, he was more or less ready, but this was just the first act. Now it was time for the main event. The "Where is my stuff" show. She heard him opening drawers and cupboards. That went on for a while, then he tiptoed back to the bedroom.

"Marissa," he whispered, as if the fact that he spoke quietly would wake her up any less.

"Hmmmmm?"

"Do you know where my car keys are?"

"On the kitchen table, hon."

"Okay, sorry. Go back to sleep."

A bit of silence. Then some additional drawers and cupboards opened and closed. More muttered curses from beyond the bedroom door.

The door opened again.

"Sorry, hon," he whispered. "But I have to go and—"

"Your wallet is probably in your coat pocket. If not, it's on the small table by the front door."

"Okay. Thanks hon, you're the best."

"Go away, you oaf. I'm trying to sleep."

Even with her eyes closed, she could almost see his grin as he left the bedroom. She smiled a small, content smile. There were some hours till morning. She rolled over to his side of the bed, took a deep breath of his pillow, where his scent still lingered, and slowly fell back to sleep.

———

The detectives' careful planning fell completely apart due to unforeseen roadwork on I-93. It delayed them for forty minutes, which meant they hit heavy traffic in Boston, which in turn resulted in another delay. Mitchell nearly ground his teeth to dust in frustration as they inched ever so slowly toward Ronnie Kuperman's address. Finally, at ten to eight in the morning, they knocked on Ronnie's door, hoping that by some miracle he was still at home. To their surprise, he was.

His housekeeper led them through Kuperman's large apartment and into his study. It could have been mistaken for a low level bank manager's office, if it weren't for all the movie posters that covered the walls. These were not posters of thought-provoking and deep dramas. There were scantily clad women, blood, and corpses on the posters, in pretty much equal amounts. The movie names depicted on the posters were *The Catacombs of Sensuality*, *The Attack of the Octopus People*, and *Bloody Love Mountain*.

Ronnie Kuperman sat behind a mahogany desk, his fingers tap-dancing on his laptop's keyboard. He was dressed in a brown suit that clashed violently with his blue tie. He was a thin man, with a haircut that looked as if his mother had done it; his auburn hair circled his head like a helmet. He had a mustache that automatically made Mitchell annoyed. Mitchell didn't believe in mustaches; he called them "lip toupees." But even mustaches had better and worse versions, and this one, a sort of horizontal slug trail, was one of the worst he'd ever seen.

A few seconds after they entered the room, Ronnie lifted his eyes and looked at them.

"Gentlemen," he said. "You're early. Please sit down." His voice was high-pitched and his words wavered as if he weren't sure if he was asking a question or making a statement.

Mitchell, whose nerves were completely frayed, felt this voice was sent from hell to torture him for his sinful past. All he really wanted was to curl up in the back of their car and go to sleep. It was clear that Ronnie Kuperman had mistaken them for someone else, but Jacob said nothing, and Mitchell didn't have the energy to correct the man.

"I'll get straight to the point; I know you two are busy. Do you want some coffee? Tea? Something stronger?" He pressed on without waiting for them to respond. "The short pitch, or the long pitch? I'll start with the short pitch— ha ha—everyone wants the short pitch first, am I right? Here's the short pitch: It's *When Harry Met Sally*, but with vampires. Got your attention now, haven't I? Intrigued? So here's the thing—vampires, they're the real deal, right?

I'm talking about *Twilight*. I'm talking about *True Blood*. Do you need any more examples? No, you don't, 'cause everyone knows, they're the best. Now, vampire movies, they're always sexy, right? But you know something? People are getting old-fashioned again. They want their child-hood movies. They want romantic comedies. And we've already established that vampires are romantic, right? So there you go. You've got your vampire. You've got his best friend, maybe a neighbor or something. He always wants to drink her blood. Half the movie's jokes are based on that. And the girl has to be played by Keira Knightley. That's non-negotiable. What you need to understand—"

"I'm afraid you've mistaken us for someone else, Mr. Kuperman," Jacob said, finally. "We're not from the enter-tainment business."

"You're not?" Kuperman seemed perplexed.

"No. I'm Detective Jacob Cooper, from the Glenmore Park police department. This is my partner, Detective Mitchell Lonnie."

"Seriously?" Kuperman stared at them. "That's so weird. You look just like… I thought you were a couple of pro-ducers I was supposed to meet."

"You're a director?" Mitchell hazarded.

"A screenwriter," Ronnie said. "Detectives, huh? What are you doing here?"

"We wanted to ask you some questions."

"What about? Should I be calling my lawyer?"

"That's up to you, Mr. Kuperman," Jacob said. "We just wanted to ask about Kendele Byers."

"Who the hell is Kendele Byers?"

"You might know her as pantyGirl," Mitchell said.

There was a moment of silence.

"I might know her, huh?" Kuperman finally said. "What is it that you wanted to ask me, Detectives?"

"Can you tell us how you know pantyGirl?"

"I never said I knew her," Ronnie Kuperman said.

"I'd say you did," Mitchell said, losing his patience. "I'd say she sent you three thongs and a set of crotchless panties she wore for twenty-four hours each, two months ago. We have a PayPal invoice from your e-mail, sent to her, for three hundred dollars. Now, you can cooperate with us right now, or maybe you'd rather we let some reporter know that Ronnie Kuperman regularly orders used underpants online?"

Ronnie Kuperman looked at Mitchell, then at Jacob. He cleared his throat

"I recognize this scene," he said. "This is the scene where I start to cry and beg, right? Oh please, Officer, don't expose my dirty little secrets. I have a wife and two daughters, and they know nothing, Officer! I'll tell you everything, Officer, just don't ruin my life. I should probably burst into tears, wringing my hands in weakness. Maybe fall to my knees, clutching at the lapels of your jacket. That's what you had in mind, right? Kind of clichéd, really overused, but I guess an actor like David Paymer could make it work. Is this really what you want here?"

"Look, Mr. Kuperman—" Jacob started to say.

"I sniff used underpants, Detective," Ronnie Kuperman said sharply, interrupting him. "It's a fetish, not a mark of Cain. My wife knows about it; the people I work with know about it. I joke about it all the time. There was an article on Buzzfeed, titled *Five amazing things you didn't know about Ronnie Kuperman*, and my underpants fetish was mentioned there—and it wasn't even the top thing on the list! So if you manage to find a reporter who's interested in the story, be my guest. God knows I could do with a little publicity!"

"Mr. Kuperman, calm down," Jacob said. "My partner didn't really mean anything by what he said. We are, like you said, just playing our part in a well-known scene. But Kendele Byers has been murdered."

"Murdered?" Ronnie Kuperman said in shock, his eyes widening in alarm. "How? When?"

"We can't divulge that information. However, we would like to rule you out as a suspect. If you cooperate with us, things will be much easier."

"I… Yes. Of course. What do you need?"

"How did you meet Kendele Byers?"

"I never met her, Detective. I chatted on Reddit with someone who identified herself as pantyGirl."

"Reddit?" Jacob asked.

"It's a site… a forum," Mitchell explained to his partner. "I'll show you later."

"Anyway, that was it. I never really knew her, and all our chats were about what type of underpants she had, and how much they cost."

"Do you know her address?"

"No."

"Was there a return address on any of the packages she sent?"

"She sent two packages, and no, I don't think there was a return address."

"Can we see the boxes?"

"I threw them away. I can show you the underpants."

"That won't be necessary. Can you give us your whereabouts between the 20th and 22nd of October?"

Kuperman nodded. He tapped some keys on his laptop and then exhaled. His shoulders sagged. "Sure," he said. "I was in Canada. We were filming there."

"Any witnesses who could attest to that?"

"A full filming crew, about two dozen actors—one of them a well-known porn actress—and some of the locals."

"When did you film the movie, exactly?"

"Between the 14th and the 25th."

"I see," Jacob said. He glanced at Mitchell.

"Mr. Kuperman, did you at any time contact pantyGirl other than in e-mails?"

"Not beyond our first chat on Reddit," Kuperman said, shrugging. "It was a very professional relationship."

"We'd like a contact list of the people who were on the film set with you, as well as the subreddit in which you met Kendele Byers," Mitchell said

"No problem, I'll have my secretary send the information to you."

Mitchell handed Ronnie Kuperman a business card. "Thanks for your cooperation, Mr. Kuperman."

"Sure."

The detectives stood up. Just as they were about to leave, the door opened and two men came into the office. It was one of the strangest moments in Mitchell's life. He now understood why Ronnie Kuperman mistook them for someone else. The men were uncannily similar to Jacob and Mitchell, if the two detectives had chosen careers as movie producers. The Jacob clone was a bit chubbier, and wore an expensive black suit and a pair of black-rimmed eyeglasses. The Mitchell clone looked almost identical, except his face was happy, small laugh lines at the corner of his eyes, and his skin was completely smooth, no stubble in sight.

The four men stared at each other for a moment as confusion settled around them. There was nothing to say or do that would make sense of this peculiar encounter. Finally, Jacob strode forward, shouldering his clone on the way out of the office, almost as if he was offended by the entire thing.

Mitchell quickly followed him. As he closed the door, he heard Kuperman say "Gentleman! Do you want some coffee? Tea? Something stronger? Should I give you the short pitch, or the long pitch? Think *When Harry Met Sally*, but with vampires…"

FIVE

They decided to interview Debbie, the only girl who seemed to have talked to Kendele on a regular basis, according to Kendele's phone. They called her on the way back from Boston, and she answered her phone almost immediately. She had trouble hearing the conversation because of the background noise. She was on her way to work, she explained, and there was road construction. Mitchell said that they were detectives and they wanted to ask her some questions. He had to repeat this sentence several times, and by the end he was practically hollering into the phone, with Jacob flinching visibly as he listened. Well, she was about to start her shift, so they could meet her at work, she suggested. She worked at Paulie's Peppery Poultry.

Mitchell asked her to repeat the place's name once more, just to be sure he heard right.

They reached Paulie's Peppery Poultry, a fast food restaurant on Sun Valley Boulevard, just after noon. The exterior of the restaurant was painted in clashing yellow and red stripes, and on the roof just above the double glass doors was a huge oval sign with a picture of a manic, grinning duck and the letters PPP painted in a garish green.

They were surprised to find that the place was packed. Apparently a lot of people loved peppery poultry, at least when Paulie was involved. Each table was occupied, covered with red trays brimming with unattractive oily chicken bits. The walls were decorated by photos of meals that were not, in Mitchell's opinion, even distant family members of the things he could see on the customers' trays. On each picture the same psychotic-looking duck from the sign outside smiled at the meal.

Three young women stood behind the counter at the far end of the restaurant, taking orders from customers. They all wore the same uniform, its white and red colors matching the colors of the restaurant's mascot, and each wore a hat that looked like the top half of the duck's face. It was the worst branding Mitchell had ever seen, and he was amazed at the place's apparent success. Perhaps the food, despite its appearance, was really good.

The detectives approached the counter.

"Excuse me," Mitchell said to one of the cashiers. "Can you tell me who Debbie is?"

"I'm sorry, but there's a line," An overweight woman clutching the hand of a toddler told him in a shocked and offended tone. "I was clearly here before you."

Mitchell flipped his badge quickly hoping this would calm her down.

"Oh!" the woman said, shaking her head in indignation. "So this is what we've come to? Can the police just cut the line because they have a badge and a gun?"

"We're here on official business, ma'am," Mitchell said, his eyes following her quivering cheeks in fascination.

"I am also on official business," the woman said loudly, looking around her, clearly expecting the support of the other customers in the line. They, in turn, looked the other way. "There is a line!" Lines were obviously a big deal to her.

"I'm Debbie," interrupted one of the cashiers. She was a young girl, nineteen or twenty. She had deep brown skin and dark, alert eyes. She was the only one of the three cashiers who didn't look as if the job had completely sucked out her soul and left an empty, living husk.

"I'm Detective Mitchell Lonnie, and this is my partner, Detective Jacob Cooper," Mitchell said. "We need to ask you a few questions."

"What about?" she asked, her eyes shifting left and right. She seemed scared, but people often did when they talked to the cops.

"It's better if we talk about it sitting down," Mitchell said.

"Well, I can't right now, it's really busy," she said. "But I have a break at two thirty, if that's okay."

"It's an important matter," Mitchell said. "We really need to talk right now."

"Hang on," she said. She called the manager, a thin man whose facial expression was that of constant hysteria. There was a short whispered discussion, and finally she turned toward Mitchell and said, "It's really the busiest time of day. I can take a break at a quarter to one. Would that be okay?" Her eyes were begging him, and Mitchell had a feeling that her job was on the line. He sighed and nodded, and she breathed in relief.

"Would you like to order anything while you wait?" she asked.

They had been awake since four a.m. They were starving. Usually Mitchell wouldn't have been caught dead eating in a place like this, but now he found himself ordering the *Paradisiacal Poultry* meal. Jacob ordered a *Peppery Perfect Potato* and a small *Pineapple Pork* in barbecue sauce. The woman from the line moaned noisily as they placed their orders, and Mitchell smiled apologetically at her.

Their meals arrived quickly, which was the only thing that could be mentioned in their favor. The food was awful. Oil invaded everywhere, making Mitchell feel as if his tongue and palate were victims of the BP Gulf spill. Soon, he thought, video clips of the insides of his mouth would be shown on TV, seagulls and fish covered in barbecue sauce dying between his teeth. He looked around the restaurant in amazement, searching for the tortured eyes of the customers around him, but they were all happy with their food, eating with gusto as if they had been served the most exquisite French cuisine. He turned to Jacob, who was eating a morsel of pineapple pork. Jacob clearly looked as if he was chewing death.

"How is this place so successful?" Mitchell asked.

"Maybe it's an acquired taste," Jacob suggested, swallowing hard.

"Why would anyone try to acquire it?" Mitchell asked, but Jacob had no answer.

By the time Debbie joined them at their table, they had both managed to eat half their meals, and left the other half untouched. Mitchell's appetite was gone, and he wasn't sure it would ever return.

Debbie looked at their trays. "Didn't like the food?" she asked.

"It's ghastly," Mitchell said, his usual politeness gone in the face of this culinary atrocity.

"Yeah." Debbie nodded. "It is."

"Miss, could you please tell us how you know Kendele Byers?" Jacob asked.

"She's my friend," Debbie said, her eyes widening. "She used to work here. Is she okay?"

"When was the last time you saw Kendele?" Mitchell asked.

"About a month ago," Debbie said. "We went out. Then she stopped answering my texts and calls. Please, Detective, where is she? What happened to her?"

"I'm afraid Kendele is dead," Mitchell said softly.

"Oh," Debbie said weakly, slumping in her chair. Her eyes filled with tears, and one spilled over and trickled slowly along her cheek. She paid it no mind, turning to stare out of one of the windows.

"Was it one of her... customers?" she finally asked.

"We don't know," Mitchell said.

"She said that some of them were kind of creepy."

"Did she mention any names?" he asked. "Anyone in particular?"

"Nah." Debbie sniffed, and turned to look at Mitchell. "She didn't like to talk about it."

"But she did tell you about… her business." Mitchell said.

"Yeah. I mean, she told me all about it when she quit this place."

"And she never mentioned anyone specific who bothered her?" he pressed. "Someone she was worried about?"

"No, she just said there were one or two creepy guys, and that she wasn't selling them anything anymore."

"Debbie," Jacob said. "Did Kendele have a relationship? Did she go out with anyone?"

"No."

"Are you sure?" he said.

"Yeah, I'm sure. It was her number one complaint. That guys always wanted to fuck her, but no one wanted to stay the night."

"What guys?"

"Just random guys," Debbie shrugged and wiped her eyes. "You know how she looked."

"No," Mitchell said, "Not really."

Debbie blinked. "Then how do you know—"

"We don't really know how she looked when she was alive," Mitchell explained delicately.

Debbie pulled her phone from her pocket, fiddled with it, and showed the screen to the detectives. It was a selfie, taken by Debbie, of herself hugging another girl in a place that looked like a pub. The girl had long, smooth red hair, and a beautiful face. She smiled happily at the camera, exposing small, perfect white teeth.

"You can't see her body here but, trust me, it was gorgeous," Debbie said. "Guys were falling over each other trying to flirt with her. I never bought my own drink when I was with her, I can tell you that."

"So did she see a lot of men?" Jacob asked.

"Detective, are you trying to ask me if she fucked a lot of guys?" Debbie asked, turning to look at him.

"I meant what I said," Jacob said, unwavering.

"Fine, whatever. Nah, as far as I know only one or two. And like I said, they never stayed around afterward."

"Do you happen to know why her brother thought she lived in San Francisco?" Mitchell asked.

"Sure," Debbie said. "She didn't want him to tell their asshole of a father where she lived."

Mitchell nodded, waiting.

"Look, Kendele's dad beat her, okay? She was seriously abused as a kid. Eventually she ran away. Found a place to stay, with some friends. Then her dad went looking for her. Told her brother that he wanted Kendele to come back home. That he had seen the error of his ways, blah blah blah, he would never lay a hand on her again. So her idiot brother told him where she was staying, and what do you know, her dad barged in and beat her to a pulp. She ran away again, ended up here. But she didn't tell her brother where she was really staying because she didn't trust him anymore." She leaned back, folded her arms. "Now that she's dead, you guys finally take an interest."

"You think her father killed her?" Mitchell asked.

"How the hell should I know? All I can tell you is that the list of nice people that Kendele knew was really short."

"Do you know if Kendele used to jog regularly?" Jacob asked.

"Sure. Four times a week, at five in the morning, like clockwork. She loved running."

"Why so early?" Jacob asked.

"She liked running while the city was still sleeping," Debbie said. "She said that everything was beautiful when there weren't people in it."

"Did she always jog in the same place?"

"I think so. She jogged in a park. Not sure where."

"I see." Jacob nodded.

She stood up. "Gotta go back to work. Those chickens aren't going to serve themselves," she said.

Jacob handed her a card. "If you think of anything, let us know," he said.

She nodded and walked away.

———

The sun was beginning to set as Mitchell pulled the black Dodge Charger in and parked by Buttermere Park. He and Jacob got out and started walking down the trail.

They had spent a few frustrating hours running up against dead ends. Jacob had talked to Kendele's parents on the phone. They'd been notified by Leon about their daughter's death. They were quite cooperative until the matter of abuse came up. Then they promptly hung up the phone, after telling Jacob he could talk to their lawyer if he needed anything else.

Meanwhile, Mitchell had started calling the men on Kendele's client list, Or at least the ones where he managed to find a phone number to match their address. There were a lot of calls with claims of total ignorance, offended threats, and hysterical denials. People hung up on him a lot as well. Only a few managed to supply an alibi for the relevant dates. That suspect list was not getting slimmer anytime soon.

Eventually Jacob suggested they take a break, drive by the crime scene, and look around a bit. Mitchell suspected Jacob simply wanted a walk in the park, but seeing as his own ear was beginning to hurt, he wasn't about to argue with his partner.

As they got closer to the patch of trees where Kendele Byers had been found, Mitchell found himself imagining that morning. Kendele running down that very trail, the park completely silent, just the way she loved it. According to Matt, she had been wearing black running shorts and a purple sports bra.

She probably ran fast, to overcome the chilliness of the early morning. And then… what? Had she seen someone down the trail? Had he been waiting for her? Perhaps a familiar face? Or did he hide behind a tree and grab her when she was close enough? Had she struggled?

They reached the trees, and Jacob went over to the grave where Kendele had been buried. Mitchell stared at the pond, and a strange feeling of déjà vu struck him. He had been here many times before, but… There was something else about that pond. A thought or a memory was trying to emerge… As he tried to force it out, it dissipated; it left him frustrated, like he had been about to say something and then forgot what it was.

The water rippled in the slight afternoon wind, the surface shimmering under the setting sun's rays of light. How had the water looked that day? Mitchell tried to picture it: the man dragging Kendele to the pond, plunging her head beneath the surface. Why? Why do it like that? It seemed so unnecessarily complicated.

He walked over to Jacob.

"Doesn't this murder feel weird?" he said.

Jacob nodded

"Why here?" Mitchell said. "Why like this? Why not strangle her, or stab her, or shoot her?"

"He planned this carefully," Jacob said.

"How do you know?"

"He knew her. Knew she ran here regularly early in the morning. He was stalking her," Jacob said. He pointed at the grave. "He didn't dig this entire grave after he killed her. If he had, it would have taken too long, people would have started walking around. Someone would have seen him. No. He got here during the night, dug up the grave and waited. She showed up, just like she always did, just like he knew she would. He grabbed her when she was close enough, drowned her in the pond, then threw her into the grave and covered her up."

"Then why drown her?"

Jacob shook his head. "It was intentional. It was the way he planned it. It was important."

"Why?"

Jacob looked at him. "How the hell should I know? I don't have all the answers."

They both became quiet. This was worrying. It was all beginning to sound very obsessive, and very insane.

"Would her father do something like that, if he found out where she lived?"

Jacob thought about it. "I don't know," he said. "Doesn't sound likely. The deranged used-underpants customer sounds like the more likely scenario."

"Then we need to get cracking on that list."

"Yeah."

The two detectives stood above the grave for a minute more, then turned and walked back to the car.

———

Mitchell felt drained as he walked into his apartment. The entire day felt like one big failure. What had they managed to learn? That a paltry number of their suspects had alibis? That Kendele had been abused by her father? That she jogged regularly? Somehow all those little facts didn't feel as if they were about to amount to anything.

"Pauline?" he called.

"In here," she said from the bedroom.

He walked over, stopped in the doorway.

She lay on her stomach on the bed, staring at her laptop screen. She was watching an episode of *Shameless*, a series which she had repeatedly tried to convince him to see with her, to no avail. She wore a black tank top with spaghetti straps, and slightly translucent white shorts. She was barefoot, and her feet kept swinging up and down as she stared intently at the screen. Her long brown hair was tied back in a ponytail, as it always was. Her bare upper back, tawny beige and smooth, beckoned to him. He felt as if the entire day's weight slowly dissipated from his shoulders. Gently he got on the bed, lying on top of her, hugging her from behind.

"You're squashing me," she complained, breathless, and elbowed him.

He rolled away, laughing. "How was your day?" he asked.

"Fine," she said distractedly. "A customer at the clinic flirted with me today."

"Yeah? Did you tell him you were taken?"

"Don't be silly. I wanted to hear what he had to offer first."

"Ah," Mitchell said, his fingertips caressing the top of her back gently. "And what did he have?"

"A root canal."

"Sounds like a fantastic catch."

Pauline worked as a dental assistant. Mitchell constantly tried to convince her to try and do something better with her life. He was convinced she could be so much more. She often got angry at his attempts. There was nothing wrong with being a dental assistant, she always said.

"And then," she said, "when I rode the bus home, it had a flat tire and I had to wait for the next one, and ride it standing up, stuffed with all the other bus refugees like a can of sardines."

"The struggle is real," Mitchell said.

She glanced at him. "Are you mocking my suffering?"

"No, not at all."

"How was your day?"

"I interviewed about twenty people who like to sniff underpants today," Mitchell said.

"Really?" This made her pause the video. She rolled to her side, smiling at him. He loved her smile.

"Yeah."

"And what did you find?"

"I found that most people do not like it when you ask them about their underpants-sniffing habits."

She grinned at him. He smiled back. Her tank top was a bit crooked, exposing the top curve of her breast. He shifted closer, wrapping his arm around her, and pulled her toward him.

"Are you getting turned on by this panty-sniffing conversation?" she whispered.

"No," he said. "I'm getting turned on by being near you."

She kissed him, her hand sliding on his stomach, and Mitchell rolled to his back, pulling her on top of him.

SIX

He stood in a small clearing in Buttermere Park's grove. The police had found the body of Kendele Byers nearby, just a week before. That was not part of the plan, though he wasn't particularly disturbed by it. He had been careful.

He was looking at the ground, where just four months before he had scattered hundreds of yellow flower seeds. He was pleasantly surprised by the results. There were dozens of flowers growing all over the ground, dotting the clearing. He did it in memory of *her*. She had loved the color yellow, wore yellow shirts and dresses almost every day.

He had come to the clearing to think of a very special date. Over thirty years had passed since that occasion, and it was still the most vivid memory in his mind. He smiled as he thought of it, looking at the blossoms around him. It was a warm and sunny day, and the park teemed with people: families spending time together; couples in love walking on the paved paths, holding hands; dog walkers marching briskly, their pets padding along with their tongues lolling. And one man, traveling down memory lane. Thinking of Kendele Byers, thinking of a day long ago, thinking of another beautiful girl, and the invisible thread that tied them together.

He had been dormant for so long before his awakening. Years lost to routine, a dull job, tepid encounters with other people, a long stretch of colorless days and dreamless nights. He almost felt sorry for the people in the park, leading the same drab lives, doomed to waste their short lifespans on nothing.

They were too blind to see the truth. There was more to life than that. There were pure moments of thrill and joy. One just had to find them. Kendele had understood. Just before she'd died, she had understood; he could feel it.

He felt the growing anticipation inside him. Soon, it would be time once again. He could almost imagine the moment of impact as his next victim would die. His heart thumped a bit faster as he pictured it happening, late at night, not far from her home.

It was going to be a violent death.

Anticipation. There was almost nothing better.

———

Mitchell occasionally thought of himself as a hound dog. Sniffing at the trail, catching a scent, following it, getting ever closer. Maybe at times the scent would dissipate, and the hound would sniff around, trying to catch it once again, running into a few dead ends, finally catching a break.

Other times, when cases were vague and frustrating, he felt he was more akin to a chicken, pecking the ground for morsels, looking for anything edible. Peck peck peck. What was that? A tasty seed? Nope, just a small rock. Peck peck, hang on, found something! A paper clip? What was a paper clip doing here? Peck peck peck peck, completely random pecking, shoving its beak hopefully into the ground again and again. Peck peck. Nothing good here. And eventually, this chicken might tire, and begin to think it would never find anything worthwhile to eat.

Kendele Byers's murder investigation seemed to be more like the chicken type of investigation. For every tiny seed, the detectives would find a lot of sand, a lot of pebbles.

Kendele's father had a tight alibi for the date of her murder. He worked every morning at the grocery store he owned. Started working at six. Never missed a day. He had security tapes and customers to support his alibi. He claimed that he had never abused his daughter, and his wife and son said the same.

Peck peck peck.

Kendele had eighteen regular customers, and thirty-two additional customers who had purchased from her once or twice. Alibis trickled in. Most of the customers lived abroad. There was no hint of the so-called "creepy" e-mails Kendele had received, nor was there any indication of those customers in the subreddit Ronnie Kuperman gave them. Perhaps there were no creepy customers, and Kendele had only said it to dissuade Debbie from going down the same path. Who knew.

Peck peck.

The plants found in Kendele's lungs matched plants in the pond, but they were commonly found in other ponds and lakes in the area. It probably meant the detectives' theory about the murder was correct, but there was no way to be sure.

Peck peck peck.

There was no DNA match in CODIS, the database used by the bureau, for any of the objects found at the crime scene.

Peck peck.

They searched for other similar crimes. Other crimes in which someone was drowned, then buried nearby. Other crimes involving women who sold their underwear online. They found nothing.

Peck.

The chickens were getting tired.

SEVEN

Kenneth Baker should have known better.

Cocaine? Hell, he snorted the stuff on a daily basis. How could anyone function in this crazy world without cocaine, anyway? Who could even generate the amount of productivity modern life demanded, without resorting to a bit of snow? No, cocaine was fine.

Alcohol was also fine. No question there. Alcohol was even legal. You could walk into a store, buy a bottle of whiskey, and walk out—just like that, no questions asked. Was there any better way to go to sleep then after a glass or two of cheap whiskey? There wasn't. In fact, these days he couldn't manage to fall asleep at all without drinking first.

But mixing the two?

He really should have known better.

And now it was on. Kenneth's heart raced like crazy. He was overcome with massive waves of euphoria. When the euphoria was gone, he realized he was shaking with rage. Someone was screaming. It was him.

"—this is how you repay me?" he yelled. "After all these years that we've spent together? After all the money I invested in you? I took care of you! I did everything you asked me to do, and now… this?" Tears ran down his cheeks. How could this happen? His life… ruined.

He grabbed his helpless victim, his fingers whitening as they pressed hard. His victim emitted strange, unintelligible noises, but Kenneth ignored it.

"We're done, you and me," he growled. "This is the end of the road, darling. No! It's too late to try and make amends now. It's gone. It's all gone!"

He stomped out of the bedroom, carrying his victim with him, not hearing the panicked screeching and moaning. He paused in the kitchen, opened a drawer, and grasped the gun inside. He had never used it before, except at the firing range. He would use it tonight.

He kicked the front door open, the drug in his blood pumping him with adrenaline. There was no going back.

This relationship was about to end. Terminally.

———

Officer Tanessa Lonnie opened the front passenger's door of the patrol car and got in, handing a Styrofoam cup of coffee to her partner, Sergio Bertini.

"There you go," she said. "I asked them to make it extra strong."

"Thanks," he said, his face sagging with relief as he held the cup in his hand. He sipped from the cup and shut his eyes for a second, taking a long breath. "God, I needed that."

"Didn't sleep again?" Tanessa asked, sipping from her own cup. It was one a.m. They were parked near a small gas station, having just began their patrol shift an hour ago. Tanessa and Sergio were on the graveyard shift—midnight to eight—as they had been for the past six weeks, ever since Tanessa finished her training in the academy.

"It's Gabriella. She keeps waking me up," Sergio said, shaking his head. "She's driving me insane."

Tanessa nodded, her face full of empathy she didn't feel. The whole thing with Gabriella should never have started; it had clearly been a mistake. Tanessa had warned Sergio he would regret it. But she wasn't the type to spread salt on the open wounds of a suffering man. She squeezed Sergio's shoulder—a sympathetic touch, full of support.

He turned to face her, his eyes red and swollen, his bushy eyebrows raised in an expression of acute misery. When he wasn't so tired and morose, he was quite attractive. Tan, wide-shouldered, a nice enough face, white teeth. Teeth were important to Tanessa. She was really turned off by bad teeth. He was bald, which was a shame, but he shaved his head on a weekly basis, so it had a certain sexy appeal, if one liked that sort of thing.

"She screams," he said. "All day long. Terrible screams. Ear-shattering."

"Yeah," Tanessa nodded.

"And she bites me! When I try to calm her down she bites me! Look!" He showed her a scratch on his finger.

"Why don't you get rid of her?" Tanessa suggested.

"How? Who would take her?" Sergio asked, his voice dripping with misery.

"No one needs to take her," Tanessa said patiently. "You just… open the window, and she'll fly away."

She had told him buying a parrot was an idiotic idea. Her cousin had had a parrot once. She remembered the incessant noise that had filled his house whenever the damn thing was awake. When that parrot died, they'd nearly thrown a party.

"I can't do that," Sergio said. "She would never survive on her own."

"Who knows," Tanessa said. "Think about it—"

The radio suddenly burst to life. "Attention all units, report of shots fired at the corner of Adams and Cedar Road."

Tanessa grabbed her shoulder mic and pressed the PTT button "Four fifty-one, responding."

Sergio shoved his cup into the cup holder, and started the car. They weren't far, no more than five minutes' drive. Tanessa buckled her seat belt and took one last sip from her own cup before putting it down as well.

If there was one joy in the midnight shift, it was the absence of traffic. Rush hour was not a thing when Tanessa and Sergio drove through Glenmore Park's streets, the moon high in the sky. A few cars passed them, the drivers inside quickly making sure their seatbelts were fastened and their car lights were switched on. At one point they slowed down as a man dressed in rags crossed the street slowly, pushing a supermarket cart full of plastic bottles. Other than that, their drive was a smooth and silent affair.

They were calm as they drove, knowing well that the majority of *shots fired* calls turned out to be kids lighting firecrackers, or cars backfiring. Even in the case of actual shots fired, the people involved were often far away by the time the patrol managed to arrive on the scene. They didn't talk. Tanessa thought about her mother's upcoming birthday. She had to come up with a good gift. Last year they'd blown it, buying their mother a handbag she never used. She would have to talk to Mitchell and Richard about it tomorrow morning, before she went to sleep.

They approached the corner of Cedar and Adams and as predicted, the street appeared to be empty. It was usually a quiet neighborhood, the residents a mix of young parents and old pensioners. The right side of the street was populated by two- and three-story houses, their walls wooden in various stages of neglect. On their left was a small park, dark and abandoned, a swing, and a small slide barely visible in the pale moonlight. In the day, Tanessa thought, this park was probably full of young mothers or nannies, and their children. But now the only occupants would be homeless people, asleep on benches. The road was cracked in numerous places, weeds sprouting on its margins.

Where had the shots come from? Tanessa looked around, alert to any movement. The windows were all dark. She could see no one.

"What do you think?" Tanessa asked.

Sergio shrugged. "There's nothing here," he said. "Let's drive around a bit, make the residents feel safe."

They drove slowly. The patrol car's flickering blue lights illuminated the street, signaling to anyone who cared that the police were there, that everything was fine.

"Hang on," Tanessa said. "What's that?"

There was a tiny alley between two of the buildings, a place in which garbage cans resided. It was cast in shadow and, within, something moved. A silhouette of a man.

He stood still, facing away from them. As they came closer, the car's lights partly illuminated him. He was moving animatedly, as if talking to someone. Sergio stopped the car and Tanessa got out, walking slowly toward the man, a hand on her gun.

"Excuse me?" she said. "Sir?"

"… such a long time together," the man was saying. He sounded as if he was crying. "How could you? Two months' work, down the drain."

He was drunk, Tanessa thought. He was a bit wobbly, his stance unstable. She heard Sergio get out behind her as she got closer. Something about the man made her uneasy.

"You forced my hand!" the man said, raising his voice. "I didn't want to do it! But did you really think this would go unpunished?"

"Sir!" Tanessa said. "This is the police. Please turn around very slowly." She drew her Glock, her muscles tense.

He swerved drunkenly to face her, and the first thing she saw was the gun in his hand.

She didn't even realize as months of training took over, her arms rising to point her own gun at his chest, aiming for center mass, her lips moving, shouting at the man. Shouting at him to *drop it.*

She was surprised by how much her mind registered in a very small fragment of a second. The bewildered, unfocused stare of the man as he looked at her, the blue light flickering on his face, blinding his eyes. The way his gun hand moved, rising higher, the fingers clutching the gun fiercely, unwilling to let go. Her ears heard her partner as he yelled at the man to let go of the gun, that he was about to shoot.

His finger wasn't in the trigger guard, Tanessa realized. His five fingers were wrapped around the weapon's grip, as if he held a walking stick, or a ball.

"Sergio, don't shoot!" she shouted. "Don't fucking shoot!"

The man froze completely, his hand halfway up. Only his lips kept moving, though Tanessa couldn't hear a word.

"Sir," she said, walking even closer, blocking the patrol car's blinding lights with her body. "Put the gun down."

The man stared at her and then looked at his hand. He seemed surprised to see the weapon clutched in it. Slowly, he knelt down and laid the gun on the ground.

She was already at his side, grabbing his arms and twisting them behind his back. He didn't resist, quietly saying, "I had to do it. I had to. I had to." Her handcuffs clicked, fastening around his wrist, the metallic noise a soothing lullaby in her ears. The suspect was disarmed and restrained. No one was about to get hurt. Except…

"I think he shot someone," Tanessa told Sergio without looking back. She let go of the man, grabbed the flashlight from her belt, turned it on, and pointed it at the alley.

There was something in the dark. She aimed the beam of light at it, and caught her breath. A small, open laptop stood on the alley's floor, its screen shattered, spotted with multiple holes. It was clearly beyond saving.

———

"I had no choice, I had to do it. Two months of work, gone! Just like that. BAM. Blue screen of death. No backup." Kenneth Baker babbled in the back of their car as they drove toward the city jail. Tanessa half-listened to him, feeling exhausted. She was drained after the encounter, the adrenaline that had been pumping through her blood gone now. She wished for some peace and quiet, but it wasn't meant to be.

"I mean, you could hear the hard drive spinning. It was definitely still working, but it just wouldn't start! Do you know how that feels? The fruit of your toil consumed by a… a… machine? I was furious."

Tanessa was sure he was. His breath reeked of cheap alcohol, and she'd spotted some white powder traces under his nose, probably cocaine. With such a fun cocktail running through his blood, it was no wonder he decided to go out to the alley and shoot his computer.

"This never would have happened forty years ago. A typewriter wouldn't suddenly chew up your novel. Humanity is being enslaved by machines, and we don't even notice. People need to open their eyes, before it's too—"

"You know," Tanessa said, turning around. "I'm not sure we read you your rights. You have the right to remain silent. Anything you say can and will be used against you in a court of law…" She recited the rest of the Miranda warning. "Got that? Remain silent?"

"My novel is gone!" the man said, his voice brittle.

"Well, maybe it could have been restored, if you hadn't shot your computer eleven times!"

There was a moment of silence.

"I doubt it," the man finally said.

"Yeah, well, you keep telling yourself that. Whatever helps you sleep at night." She sighed and turned to face forward again.

"All units." The dispatcher's voice filled the patrol car. "There's a hit and run on Ambleside Drive. Ambulance needed."

"What the hell is going on tonight?" Sergio muttered.

"Turn right," Tanessa told him. "We aren't far."

"Yeah, yeah,"

"This is four fifty-one, responding," she told Dispatch.

Sergio accelerated, turning on the car's flashing lights.

"This is eight-o-one, on our way," someone said on the radio. It was the medical emergency crew.

"Hey," the drunk novelist called from the back. "Where are we going?"

"Don't worry about it," Sergio said.

"You can't just drag me along! I have rights!"

"It's research for your new novel," Sergio said sharply. "Now shut up."

The car swerved onto Ambleside Drive, and Sergio slowed down. It was a small residential area at the edge of town. The street was narrow, cars parked on both sides, the streetlights dim. Tanessa looked intently ahead, her eyes scanning the area.

"There!" she pointed.

Someone was kneeling in the middle of the road. As they got closer, they saw it was a man, kneeling by a motionless body. Sergio stopped the car on the side of the road and they both leaped out. Sergio ran for the trunk to get the temporary roadblock gear. Tanessa dashed over to the body. It was a young woman, lying in a pool of blood. The man by her side was saying, "Hang on, just hang on, the ambulance will be here any moment."

Tanessa knelt by him. "I'm Officer Lonnie," she said. "Can you tell me what happened?" She looked at the woman on the ground, who was young—nineteen or twenty—her skin dark, her black hair braided into hundreds of thin braids. She stared upwards, her eyes blinking in confusion. There was a trickle of blood at the corner of her mouth, as well as a gash on her forehead. Her body was positioned strangely, her torso twisted sideways. She wore a black tank top and black pants. Her lips moved slowly, opening and closing.

"I… I don't know what happened," the man said. "My house is across the street. I heard a large crash, and screeching tires. When I came outside, the car was driving away."

"Can you describe the car?" Tanessa asked, bending over the girl's mouth and listening intently. The girl was breathing.

"No… Square taillights. I couldn't see anything in the dark. Is she going to be okay?"

"We'll do the best we can." Tanessa said, trying to sound much calmer than she felt. They were both kneeling in a growing pool of blood. She couldn't see where it was coming from, but there was a lot of it. She didn't dare move the girl, knew she should wait for the ambulance. She caressed the girl's forehead gently.

"Hey," she said, half whispering, "Hang in there, sweetie, you're going to be okay. Can you hear me? You're going to be just fine."

The girl kept blinking. Her eyes turned toward Tanessa.

"What's your name, sweetie?"

"Tamay," the girl croaked, her eyes suddenly narrowing in pain.

"Shhhh. It's okay. Don't talk if it hurts. Tamay? That's a beautiful name. Tamay, my name is Tanessa. The ambulance is on its way, okay, sweetie? They're going to take really good care of you, don't worry." She put her hand on Tamay's cheek, her fingers brushing the girl's skin. She was cold, Tanessa realized.

"Sergio!" she called, "Can I get something to warm this girl up? She's really cold."

Her partner was by her side in seconds, handing her his uniform jacket. Tanessa spread the coat over the girl's body, whispering reassurances the entire time. She heard the ambulance stop behind her, the men inside shouting at each other as they got their gear out of the vehicle.

"Move, Officer," one of them said firmly. Tanessa got up and moved aside, grabbing the witness's arm and pulling him back. They let the emergency crew work, checking the girl, immobilizing her, putting her on a stretcher, wheeling her toward the ambulance. It took only minutes, and the ambulance was already screeching away, not a moment to lose.

Tanessa looked at the witness. He had blood on his palms and on his clothes. She realized her own pants were drenched in blood as well. She stared at the pool of blood on the road in disbelief. How much blood had the girl lost?

"Will she be okay?"

"Do you know her?" Tanessa asked him. He was about twenty-five, stubble on his face, thin glasses on his nose. He looked dazed, confused. Tanessa couldn't blame him.

"Yeah, I do. I don't know her name, but she was a waitress in *The Wild Pony*."

"The Wild Pony?"

"It's the local bar. It's a few blocks that way," he said, pointing.

"Tanessa, check this out," Sergio called.

She walked over. He stood near a dark lamppost, which leaned sideways, its base bent.

"The car crashed into it after hitting her," Tanessa said.

"Sure looks like it."

"So…" she said, trying to create a mental picture of the accident for her report. "It came from there, hit the girl over there, and then lost control, crashing into the lamppost. Then probably reversed a bit, and drove away in that direction." She pointed.

"Sounds right," Sergio said.

"Excuse me," the witness called.

Tanessa turned. "Yes?"

"It didn't drive away in that direction."

"I'm sorry?" Tanessa said.

"It drove away in the other direction."

Tanessa frowned. "That doesn't make any sense," she said.

"Maybe the car hit the lamppost first, then hit the girl and kept on driving," Sergio suggested.

"Doesn't look like it. Not the way the lamppost is leaning," Tanessa said. "It's leaning away from the spot the girl was lying in."

"Sir," Sergio said. "Was the lamppost maybe broken before the accident?"

"Well, it was fine a few hours ago."

"Are you sure?"

"Yeah, I would have noticed if it was broken when I came home from work."

Tanessa's skin crawled. "That would mean," she said slowly, "that the driver hit the girl, lost control, hit the lamppost, then reversed his car, turned it around... and fled down that way." She pointed at the pool of blood.

They all stared at the narrow street. The pool of blood was surrounded by parked cars.

"There's no way he could have gotten around her," Sergio said.

"He drove over her," Tanessa said, feeling sick. She thought of Tamay, lying motionless, her body twisted unnaturally.

"Jesus."

"We should inform dispatch."

This wasn't a random hit and run anymore. This was beginning to feel like something much more sinister.

EIGHT

A blue Honda Civic pulled in and parked by the accident scene, and Tanessa didn't need to glance inside to see who was driving. She knew that car well, had been in it numerous times. She'd ridden in the front seat to her first day at the academy, and after her graduation ceremony as well. She'd once sat in that car for forty-five minutes, crying, blowing her nose into one tissue after the other, as her brother consoled her, telling her there would be other guys. And, on a memorable night, she had thrown up all over the backseat after drinking six vodka shots on a stupid dare.

Mitchell got out of his car and walked over. Tanessa stood by the temporary roadblock they had raised, prepared to intercept any car that might want to drive through.

"Hey, Mitch," she said, trying to sound casual.

"Hey, Sis," he replied, smiling at her. "So what do we have here?"

"A hit and run," she said, and cleared her throat. "Except it looks like the car turned around and ran over the victim again as it was escaping."

"Any witnesses?"

"A guy named Troy, he's over there. He didn't see it happening, just saw the car driving away."

"Then how do you know what happened?"

She walked him through their reasoning, the angle and location of the lamppost, the corresponding location of the pool of blood. When she finished, her brother just looked at her. He said nothing, but she could see a tiny spark in his eye. She knew that look well, and was filled with relief, knowing he was proud of her.

"Okay," he nodded. "We'll need to go door to door, see if someone maybe saw—" He suddenly paused. "Who's that in your patrol car?"

Tanessa looked, and was surprised to see that Kenneth, the laptopcidal novelist, was still in the backseat. He suddenly seemed so trivial.

"He's just a guy we arrested before getting here," she said. "Unrelated to the accident."

"Huh," Mitchell said. "He doesn't look happy."

"He had a bad day."

"Okay," Mitchell said. He looked around. "It's really dark here. You say the victim was wearing black? It's possible that the driver didn't see her at all at first."

"That's what I thought," Tanessa nodded.

"Okay. So here's what I need you to do—" His phone rang. He motioned for Tanessa to hang on and answered it.

"Yeah?" His eyes became more serious. "I see. Okay, thanks. Yeah, and Jacob Cooper, my partner as well. Okay." He hung up.

"Well," he said. "The victim just died in the ER. This is a homicide scene."

Tanessa looked at him, the words slowly making sense. The girl was dead. The same girl she had held, had reassured, telling her everything was going to be okay, was now gone. Tanessa might have been the last person to talk to her.

She realized Mitchell was still talking. "She wasn't carrying any identification, so it's possible her purse or handbag is still somewhere here. I want to find out who she was as soon as possible—"

"Her name was Tamay," Tanessa said. Her own voice sounded faraway. "She was a waitress in a local bar."

"Oh?" Mitchell said. "Okay, that's helpful. Good work. Let's see if we can find her purse."

Tanessa numbly gripped her flashlight and turned it on. She saw Sergio do the same, looking under a parked car. Good idea. It might have been thrown underneath one of the cars. She bent herself, and looked under a small Toyota.

She had caressed Tamay's forehead, moving aside one of her numerous braids.

Nothing under the car. She moved to the next one.

Who had done all those braids? Tamay? Her mother? Her friend? Someone who had now lost a dear part of his life forever?

The next car had nothing under it as well. She kept on looking.

Had Tamay felt any pain when she died? Had she been scared? What was her evening like before the car hit her? Was she just returning from a shift, taking orders from drunk customers, occasionally returning to a table to find out they hadn't left a tip? Or maybe she'd had a nice evening, spent it with her boyfriend, cuddled in front of the television?

"I don't think it's that far, Tanessa," Mitchell called after her. She realized she was already fifty feet from the accident site. How had she gotten so far? She stood up and turned away, looking into the darkness.

The tears came quickly, filling her eyes, clouding her vision. Her lower lip quivered, as it always did when she cried. Damn it! Not now. Later, later. If Mitchell or Sergio saw her like this she would die.

"Found it!" she heard Sergio shout. She wiped her eyes, tried to take a deep breath, but suddenly an image of Tamay blinking as Tanessa held her cheek popped into her mind, and a fresh tear trickled from her eye. She was a mess. Mitchell would never let her forget this. It would become an example of why she wasn't fit for the job. He'd never wanted her to be a cop, had begged her to reconsider, and now he would have a fantastic reason to keep on telling her to quit. He'd say she was too sensitive for this job, would rally Richard and Mom to the cause, and... and...

"Hey, Tanessa," she heard him say behind her.

"I'll be right there," she said. She could hear the shaking in her voice, knew Mitchell heard it as well. There was a pause. He was about to hug her, she knew, tell her it was all right. And later, he'd talk to her about it. Again and again and...

"Officer Lonnie," he said, breaking the silence, "I need you to drive over to the gas station on Pine Hollow Road. The car drove away in that direction. Maybe the gas station's security tape caught something."

"Okay," she said, confused.

"I'll drive," Sergio said.

"No, Officer Bertini, I need you to join me. We need to go door to door, ask people if they saw anything. Tan... Officer Lonnie will join us as soon as she gets back."

"Sure," Sergio said. "Hey, Tanessa, get me a cup of coffee when you're there, okay?"

"No problem," she said, her voice steadier, not looking back at them.

They walked away. She breathed deeply, wiped her eyes, and marched quickly to the patrol car, her eyes downcast as she got inside.

"Hey!" Kenneth said in a whiny voice.

"Shut up!" Tanessa snapped at him, her voice shrill. "Just shut the fuck up!"

He shut up. She started the car and drove away, leaving Mitchell and Sergio behind as they approached one of the houses.

She had never loved her brother more than in that moment.

―――

It was another boring night at the gas station, and Derek was thumbing through the last issue of *Car and Driver*, trying to calculate how many shifts it would take him to be able to afford any of those cars. The wage he was getting, about a gazillion shifts. Maybe even more.

The door rang, and a lady cop walked up to him and asked for a key to the bathroom. He glanced at her. Her face was blotchy and red, her eyes swollen. Her hair was a bit messy. He gave her the key, and returned to his magazine. Maybe if he got a raise, it would just take a billion shifts. He'd have to do the math later.

Ten minutes later she came back and handed him the key.

"Thanks," she said.

He raised his eyes as he reached for the key, and his breath caught. For a moment he thought it wasn't the same cop.

Her hair, now combed and pulled back, was chocolatey brown and completely smooth. A strand left out of the ponytail tumbled playfully on her forehead. Her skin was a sort of rich white, completely unblemished. He wondered how he had imagined it to be red and splotchy before. He was obviously mistaken. Her eyes… oh God, her eyes. They would follow him in his dreams for years to come. Almond-shaped and green, they reminded him of a deep, sparkling lake.

She smiled at him. This was the highlight of his entire year.

"Do you have a security camera somewhere?" she asked.

Security cameras. For a minute he had a hard time remembering what those were. Then he understood. Security cameras! Of course they did!

"Um… yeah! Sure I do! Lots!" he said, somehow feeling that the number of security cameras would please her.

"Any of them pointed at the road?"

He would point them all at the road if it made her smile again. He would install dozens of security cameras, all pointed at the road. There was one pointed at the road, he recalled. Happy day.

"Uh… Yeah! Absolutely!"

"Okay. I need to see the feed from the past…" she checked the time. "Ninety minutes."

"Okay."

He took her to the back room. He was in love. His friends always made fun of him, telling him he fell in love with anything that had breasts. Now he saw that they were right. All his previous loves were nothing, a mere crush. This was the real thing.

He showed her the console with the camera feed. It displayed a split view of several spots in the gas station. One of the views was pointed at the road. He fiddled with the console's controls a bit, nervous at the way she stood so close to him. He could smell her scent, reminiscent of springtime and cinnamon and sunlight. Finally, he managed to get the screen to display the view of the road. He rewound the feed back ninety minutes. The time on the screen was 01:43:00.

"Fast-forward a few minutes," she said.

He quickly followed her instructions. In seven minutes, between 1:43 and 1:50, only two cars went by. It was a very quiet road, this late at night. He felt like apologizing for the measly amount of cars. Then he wondered if perhaps she wanted fewer cars. Maybe fewer cars were a good thing. What should he say?

A third car moved across the road, and the cop said, "Stop. Rewind it a bit, and pause on the car."

He did, trying several times until he managed to get it just right. The frame was paused, and he noticed the car's right front light was broken. Was that what she was looking for?

"What kind of car is that?" she asked herself quietly, frowning.

"That's a Toyota Camry," he blurted.

"Yeah?" she glanced at him. "You know cars?"

"Oh, yeah," he said, his heart soaring. They would get married one day. They'd have a boy and a girl. They'd name the girl Amanda, after his mother.

"Awesome." She smiled at him, her eyes lighting up. How could a pair of eyes take his breath away like that? "What's your name?"

"Derek," he said.

"Derek, I'm Officer Tanessa Lonnie. You were really helpful. You just assisted us with a homicide case."

"Really?" he asked. He required nothing else of life.

"Really. Can I have that file?"

He didn't even charge her for the USB stick, though she insisted on paying for the three cups of coffee. And when she drove off, he stood by the glass door and watched her vanish into the night.

————

While Mitchell and Sergio went door to door questioning cranky people about something they hadn't seen, Matt Lowery, the crime scene technician, got to the scene and began to photograph it. Jacob got there ten minutes later and, after Mitchell filled him in, began to canvas the houses on the other side of the street.

The answers they got ranged from shrugs to angry rants about the time to curious questions. No one had seen anything useful. Two women had heard the crash, but by the time they got to the window, the car was long gone. They hadn't noticed there was anyone hurt on the road.

Mitchell sighed as the last door was slammed in their face. He turned to look at Jacob, who was just turning away from another door. Jacob shrugged.

"I think we're done," Mitchell told Sergio, who nodded sadly. It was a bust, and Mitchell was a bit disheartened.

He shoved his hands in his pockets, feeling the little square velvet box that hid deep within his left one. It had been there for the past three days.

It was an engagement ring.

He'd bought it in a moment of recklessness. He had been dispatched to check out a burglary scene in a jewelry store. The thieves had broke in, taken whatever jewelry was available, and run. There were still a couple of odds and ends in one of the glass display cases. One of them was a small delicate ring with a tiny, beautiful diamond sitting on top. Mitchell was not one who cared about jewelry, but when he saw that ring his breath caught. It evoked the image of Pauline almost instantly. The owner had been very eager to sell him the ring, and Mitchell made sure he got a receipt. He suspected the owner intended to include the ring in his report to the insurance company.

Now, he was waiting for the right moment, and kept the ring on him at all times. Pauline occasionally had unpredictable cleaning sprees, and Mitchell didn't want her to find the ring by accident.

He walked over to Matt, who was scraping something from the bent lamppost.

"What do you have?" he asked Matt.

"Car paint, I think," Matt said. "It's green."

"Green, huh?" Mitchell said. "So we're looking for a green car with square lights."

"I think so."

"What do you reckon happened? Does our patrol officers' theory hold?"

"Yeah," Matt nodded. "There are some tire tracks which definitely indicate that the car drove over the victim a second time as it was getting away."

"How drunk would the guy have to be?"

Matt glanced at Mitchell sharply. "As far as I can tell, the car kicked into reverse, turned around and drove straight forward toward the victim without hitting any of the cars parked around it. A drunk would have a hard time pulling that off."

Mitchell's heart grew cold. "Are you saying that it was… intentional?"

"That's how it seems to me," Matt said.

"Why?"

"You're the detective, you tell me," Matt said. "Maybe the driver panicked, wanted to get rid of the victim, make sure she couldn't testify against him in court."

"Can you tell the make of the car, from the color and the tire marks?"

Matt shrugged. "Maybe. Can't promise anything."

Tanessa's patrol car drove toward them, the front lights temporarily blinding them both. She parked the car and got out. Her face was grim, but in control. Mitchell felt a surge of relief. His sister had seemed on the verge of cracking when she'd left, and he knew well that she could never forgive herself if that happened in front of him. She was clearly calmer as she walked toward him, holding something small in her hand. A USB stick.

"The video feed from the gas station," she said.

"Oh, good," he said, taking it from her. "We'll look at it later. Maybe we'll get lucky."

"I already did."

"Did what?"

"Looked at it," she said. "The car is a Toyota Camry. I couldn't tell what color, the monitor in the gas station was black and white."

Mitchell stared at her, impressed. He hadn't wanted Tanessa to be a cop. He and Richard had tried repeatedly to convince her to drop it. Now, he was beginning to wonder if she wasn't in the right line of work after all.

"A Toyota Camry? Are you sure?"

"Yeah. Its right front light was busted."

"And… are you positive about the car's make?" Mitchell was pretty sure that when people asked Tanessa what kind of car she owned, she answered, "A red one."

"I know what I saw, Detective," she said sharply.

"I'm sure you do," he said, backing off. Maybe she hadn't been so close to cracking after all.

"Officer Lonnie," Jacob said warmly as he joined them. "How are you?"

"Hey, Jacob," Tanessa said, smiling at him. "I'm fine. How's Marissa?"

"She's wonderful as always," Jacob said, smiling back. "Who's your friend in the car?"

"Just a guy we arrested," she said. "He shot his computer to death."

"Really?" Jacob looked impressed. "I should go and talk to him. I've always wanted to shoot my computer, but I thought it might be frowned upon."

"We know the make of the car," Mitchell said.

"And the color," Matt reminded him.

"Right! It's a green Toyota Camry."

"That's amazing progress," Jacob said, rubbing his hands. It was getting a bit chilly. "Let's alert dispatch. Maybe one of our patrol teams will see it."

Mitchell called dispatch and gave them the description of the car.

Two hours later, it was spotted.

NINE

The green Toyota Camry had been abandoned on Yosemite Way, not very far from the scene of the hit and run. It was spotted by the other patrol team on the graveyard shift. They saw the car parked haphazardly, two wheels on the sidewalk. As they got closer, they saw its right front light was smashed, the hood was completely bent, and the front window was cracked. There were smears of blood on the hood and on the front window. They quickly called it in.

A quick check with the DMV found that the Toyota belonged to a Rabbi Baruch Friedman. He had a criminal record, and his file wasn't one of the thinner ones. He had been incarcerated twice for drug-related offenses, and once for assault. He was "allegedly" a prominent member in one of Glenmore Park's most notorious gangs, The Hasidic Panthers.

Twenty minutes later, two patrol cars, one of them belonging to Tanessa Lonnie and Sergio Bertini, parked in front of Rabbi Friedman's house. Wearing bulletproof vests, their weapons drawn, three of them knocked on the front door, while Sergio waited by the back door in case Rabbi Friedman decided to take a hike.

He didn't. He appeared to be miffed at being woken up so early in the morning, and his irritation grew much more when he found out they were there to arrest him. He called them "Goyim" and "Amalek," and as the situation escalated he started shouting angrily in Yiddish, which none of them understood.

He was taken to the police department for questioning. His lawyer appeared, angry and bustling, at eight thirty in the morning, asserting that his client should be released immediately.

Mitchell and Jacob started to interview the rabbi at nine.

———

Both interrogation rooms in the department were pretty much the same: small and cramped, with the floor and the bottom half of the walls painted black while the ceiling and the top half of the walls were painted white; this created a very depressing and stressful yin-yang effect. A lamp hung above the small table, its bulb casting a harsh, blinding light. One of the walls had a one-way mirror, which reflected both the investigators and the unhappy person who was being interrogated.

Mitchell and Jacob sat in front of the rabbi, staring at him. He stared back. He was a wide man with cold blue piercing eyes, and a huge black beard which he constantly touched, as if trying to reassure himself it was still there. The rabbi's lawyer, who introduced himself as Mel Turner, was a skinny, agitated man, with a pair of round spectacles and a balding head. He rummaged in his briefcase, muttering.

"Rabbi Friedman," Jacob said. "How nice to see you again."

"Detective Cooper," Friedman said. "Who is the little *pisher*?"

"That would be my partner, Detective Mitchell Lonnie. I'd mind my tongue if I were you, Rabbi. You're in trouble."

"What trouble, Detective? Why do you keep barging into my home, scaring my wife and my children?"

"Because" Jacob said evenly, "you keep breaking the law, Rabbi."

"Feh. I broke no law. I want to go home." He caressed his beard gently.

Jacob's voice became frosty. "You were seen running over a young girl in your car, Rabbi. Twice."

This made the rabbi pause and frown. He leaned back.

"Her name was Tamay. She's dead," Jacob added.

"What car?" the rabbi asked.

"Your car."

"What car, you *Shmegegge*? I have four cars registered to my name. What car are you talking about?"

"A green Toyota Camry," Jacob said. "Its license plate is—"

Friedman snorted, smiling behind his huge beard. "I sold it."

Jacob raised his eyebrows. "It's still registered in your name."

"Yes, yes. Some man walks by as I am driving my car, sitting at a red light. He offers to buy my car for six thousand dollars. Cash. I say, sure. He pops his suitcase, counts six thousand dollars, gives me the money, I give him my keys and he drives away. I was going to take care of the registration later."

"That's very convenient, Rabbi," Jacob said, narrowing his eyes.

"Ach! What's convenient?" Friedman asked, tugging at his beard, nearly ripping it off. "Waking up at four in the morning? Being handcuffed like a criminal?"

"My client has told you he doesn't own the car," Turner said. "Unless you have a witness who can positively identify him driving the car, I think we're done here."

Jacob ignored him. "Where were you tonight, between one thirty and two thirty?" he asked Friedman.

"Asleep, in my home, of course. With my wife."

"That's not a very strong alibi," Mitchell said.

"Oh," Friedman said, his voice dismissive, "the young *schmuck* can talk! How nice. Listen, Detective. I didn't drive this car, I sold it two days ago. What do you want me to say?"

"I will drag your wife here, Rabbi," Jacob said. "I will question her in a different room, and if her story is different, we will have a problem. As you would say... *Gevalt*."

"Your Yiddish is crap, Detective," Friedman said, his voice low and angry.

"This is an outrage," Turner said.

"Shut up," Friedman told him.

"Rabbi, you don't need to answer any more questions—"

"Shut up! Shut up, you shyster! Be quiet!"

Turner closed his mouth, a hurt look in his eyes.

"Fine," Friedman spat. "I was not at home. You happy now? I was out. But I didn't drive that car. I sold it."

"Okay," Jacob said. "Where were you?"

"At the Pussy Factory."

The Pussy Factory was a well known strip club in Glenmore Park. It was said that all the rich and powerful went there occasionally. It was said that the strippers made more in tips in one night than a police officer made in a month. It was said that the owner had dealings with the Yakuza. A lot of things were regularly said about the place, and it was anyone's guess which of them had an inkling of truth.

Rabbi Friedman said he had been there between eleven and three in the morning. He told Jacob to call them. He said they would remember him.

They did.

"Yeah, he was here," the shift manager told Jacob on the phone, his voice groggy as if he had been woken up by the call. "Rabbi Friedman? He's a regular. I saw him last night."

"Are you sure?"

"How could I not be? The guy made such a fuss about some cheese in his burger. He said it wasn't kosher. Can you believe it? This guy's a so-called holy man, a rabbi for Christ's sake, and he spends four hours in a strip club, gets two lap dances, and then starts worrying about kosher?"

"That… that is extraordinary," Jacob said, doing his best to keep the smile out of his voice.

"Burgers have cheese in them, am I right? We never need to worry about what's kosher. You know why, Detective?"

"Why?"

"Because this is a fucking strip club!"

"So you're sure he didn't leave before three?"

"Yeah. Gisele gave him another lap dance, just to calm him down about the whole kosher thing. He gave her a hundred-dollar tip. Shoved it right down the front of her thong. Called her *bubala*."

"*Bubala*, huh?"

"Yeah. She finished the lap dance around quarter to three, so I don't know. Maybe he left straight after."

"I might need a statement from Gisele."

"Sure, drop by tomorrow evening. She starts at seven."

"Okay, thanks."

"Sure," the man said, and hung up.

"Looks like the rabbi is telling the truth," Jacob told Mitchell.

———

The rabbi did not want to talk to a sketch artist; he just wanted to go home to his wife and children. He carried around his hurt pride like a scepter, brandishing it at will. Mitchell and Jacob tried to remain patient. Or, if Mitchell had to be honest with himself, Jacob tried to be patient, while Mitchell did his best not to hit Friedman's bearded face.

"A woman is dead, Rabbi," Jacob said, for what felt to Mitchell like the hundredth time.

"Ach, what do you want from me? Every time a woman dies, I need to do something about it?" Friedman sat by Jacob's desk, shoveling *kreplach* into his mouth. Jacob had ordered the *kreplach* from a Jewish restaurant Detective Hannah Shor knew. It was the only reason Friedman was still there.

"She was hit by your car," Jacob said. "You sold it to someone. We need to know what he looked like."

"I don't know what he looked like! What do you want me to say? He looked like a goy. I wasn't driving the car."

"We know that. We would be glad if you could help us find the man who did."

"I can't. I don't remember." Another *kreplach* was swallowed by the cavity within the black beard, never to be seen again. Mitchell sank into happy fantasies in which he set the rabbi's beard on fire.

"Okay," Jacob said. "If you don't remember, there's nothing we can do about it."

"That's right."

"I hope," Jacob said slowly, "that a search warrant for your house and office will provide us the information that we need."

"Eh?" Friedman's left eyebrow rose.

"Well, maybe there's a paper about the sale somewhere in your house. Or maybe it's in your office."

"There is no paper."

"Well, I want to make sure," Jacob said. "I think the judge will agree that it's the right thing to do. A woman died, after all."

"Ach! You police! Why can't you leave me alone?"

"We just want to find the man who hit the girl."

"Fine! I'll talk to your artist!" Friedman said, and began to mutter in Yiddish.

While Jacob called the artist, Mitchell went over to the evidence room and signed for Tamay's handbag and its contents. He returned to the squad room and went through the box. The purse had held a few basic cosmetic products, a phone, and a small purse with some change and a driver's license. He examined the license for a few seconds. Her full name was Tamay Mosely. She had been smiling slightly when the picture was taken.

Tanessa had gone to break the news to Tamay's parents, and had updated Mitchell about it that morning. Tamay didn't have a car of her own; she had used her parents' car occasionally. Mitchell thought to himself it was a pity she hadn't driven home last night.

He sighed and put down the driver's license, then picked up the phone, which was mainly what he was interested in. He had requested the night before that the phone be charged for a few hours, so he could check it in the morning. He saw with some satisfaction that it had a full battery. Even better, it had no screen lock and, with only a swipe, the device's many secrets were available to his fingertips.

It was a well-known fact in the squad that if you really wanted a thorough check of someone's digital life, Mitchell was your guy. He had a knack for locating and cross-referencing social network accounts and e-mail accounts, extracting endless information about the person's friends, habits, and secrets. With Tamay's phone and his own computer, he could now start to process her life.

She was an incredibly popular girl. Her Facebook account, which she mostly ignored, had over three thousand friends. Most of the action in her digital life revolved around Twitter and Instagram, and she had nearly ten thousand followers on each. He quickly found out that she had been a singer in a moderately successful indie rock band called *Black Bees*, which regularly played at The Wild Pony, the bar where she worked. Glancing through her phone's photo gallery, he noticed a guy who appeared in her selfies lately, mostly hugging her, probably a boyfriend. He also found a few partially nude photos she'd taken of herself, which he did his best to ignore, uncomfortable with the invasion of her privacy.

He heard Friedman yelling at the sketch artist in the background. "No! A bigger nose! What is the matter with you? I can draw better than this!"

Mitchell filtered the commotion out, diving deeper. Tamay's list of contacts was more interesting. These were the people she was really in touch with, as opposed to the thousands of social networks friends and followers. There were about four hundred names there, but recent call logs and message logs mapped out about fifty whom she had been in regular contact with. These were probably friends, other employees in the bar, and family. He made a note of the names, underlining the most prominent ones. He matched them with their social network profiles, checking out their posts, looking for anything that intersected with Tamay's posts. There were some photos of her singing on stage, some comments of adoration. Her boyfriend seemed to be at almost every gig she had. Some deeper digging gave Mitchell the answer as to why that was: he was one of the bartenders at The Wild Pony.

Now both the sketch artist and the rabbi were shouting. Jacob was trying to broker peace. The sketch artist had been offended somehow, something about his artistic merit. Friedman was threatening to walk out the door.

Mitchell knew there was no point in trying to help. This was just the kind of thing Jacob excelled at, and Mitchell should focus on what he did best. He put on his headphones, played an album by Franz Ferdinand to block out the noise, and kept on digging.

Her texts and private messages came next. Some tame sexting with the boyfriend. She had Snapchat, and he assumed the juicier content happened in there. Messages to and from her band mates. She messaged with her mother as well, though not with her father. Some promotional messages: a sale at a random online store, a used car salesman offering a hot deal on a car, a message claiming it could help her stop smoking within two weeks.

Her e-mail had some fan mail, and he took his time reading those. Fans could be obsessive—they could, potentially, be deadly—but he saw nothing that seemed alarming. Other than that, it was pretty much the usual: e-mails of confirmations of subscriptions and users, the occasional spam mail that somehow sneaked through the ever-watchful filters. Nothing seemed relevant. Her sent mail was not very illuminating either. He only read four months back. Her e-mail archive went back years, but when you were rooting through someone's digital life you had to know where to stop.

He lifted his eyes, saw Friedman and Jacob shaking hands. The sketch artist was gone, hopefully having managed to draw something that satisfied the rabbi. Would the sketch be helpful? Would it perhaps match one of the faces Mitchell had just seen in the thousands of online photos he'd gone through?

Something was bothering him. He had seen something that snagged in his brain. It itched in his mind, like a mosquito bite in the subconscious. What was it? He scanned the topics of her last e-mails, trying to pinpoint whatever it was that had raised the alarm. No. It wasn't an e-mail.

He frowned, his hand playing distractedly with the ring box in his pocket. It felt foreign to his touch, almost as if it belonged to a different life. He scanned the private messages again.

The last message was from Tamay's boyfriend, asking if she was awake. She wasn't. She never would be again. The message before it was from the car salesman. Mitchell suddenly noticed the time stamp of the message - 01:15 a.m. A message from a car salesman in the middle of the night? Mitchell opened it and scanned it once more, his mind finally registering what should have been obvious from the first second: There was an image of the car the salesman was advertising. It was a green Toyota Camry.

It was the vehicle that had run over Tamay Mosely twice only thirty minutes after the message had been sent.

———

Some hours later, Mitchell realized he and Pauline had scheduled a date for the evening—dinner at their favorite restaurant, Raggio Di Sole. This date, planned a week in advance, was supposed to have started five minutes ago. He jumped out of his seat and dashed out of the squad room in a state of acute panic.

He couldn't find his car, and whirled around in the parking lot in desperation. Once he found it, he realized he had left the car keys on his desk. He took off in another hysterical dash, berating himself. He barged back into the squad room, nearly knocking Hannah down, grabbed the keys, and zipped out of the room again.

Finally, inside the car, he pulled out of the parking lot way too fast and almost ran over an old woman, who angrily thumped his hood with her cane.

There was traffic. Of course there was traffic. He began forming excuses in his mind. He could blame rush hour. That was his best bet. With a bit of luck, he'd encounter an accident or a blocked road, which he would be able to maneuver into his excuse.

He reached the restaurant twenty-five minutes past the time they had set. He explained breathlessly to the hostess he was joining a table reserved for Pauline. The hostess said that though the table had been reserved, Pauline had not yet arrived. Mitchell took a moment to process the information. Finally, he asked where the table was.

Pauline arrived three minutes later, her face flushed, and apologized repeatedly for being late. Apparently there was a lot of traffic. And an accident.

Mitchell said that it was fine, and reproachfully added that next time she could leave work a bit earlier. After all, there was always traffic around this time of the day.

"So, where did you disappear to in the middle of the night?" Pauline asked, after the waitress had taken their orders.

"A girl was hit by a car," Mitchell said. "She died."

"Oh, no!" Pauline said, covering her mouth. "How did it happen?"

"Someone hit her, then drove over her again when he fled the scene."

"Oh my god! Was he drunk?"

"Don't really know yet. We think not," Mitchell said. "It seems intentional. There's a really weird detail…" He hesitated, then pushed on. "Apparently he was trying to sell the victim a car. And then, for some reason, he ran her over with that very car."

"Why?"

"We don't know."

"Did you catch him?"

"Not yet."

"Then how do you know that he was trying to sell her the car?"

Mitchell told her about the message. He'd spent the afternoon trying to track down the person who'd sent Tamay the message. The number that the man had used was disconnected, and was unlisted. Mitchell had begun searching for assault and murder cases that were related to used car sales, thinking maybe this was some sort of pattern of criminal behavior. A used car salesman had been stabbed in Glenmore Park five months before, because of a faulty vehicle he'd sold. But that didn't seem to be relevant to the case, and the perpetrator was behind bars. Nothing else even came close.

Eventually, Mitchell had sent an e-mail to Abram Simmons, a detective he knew in the Boston Police Department, asking if he had heard of any similar cases in Boston or anywhere nearby. It was a long shot, but Boston was a big place, and if this really was a pattern maybe it had started there.

He told Pauline about it, hoping maybe something would occur to him as he detailed the case thoroughly. He often discussed his cases with Pauline. He knew other detectives had problems in their relationships because they refused to talk about the job with their spouses. Jacob had told him about it once, saying Marissa often complained that she felt as if she wasn't part of a significant portion of his life.

It was only as they were eating dessert, drinking their third glasses of wine, that Mitchell suddenly recalled the ring in his pocket. This was the perfect place for it, but he suppressed the urge to pull it out. They had just talked for over an hour about a girl who had been murdered.

It seemed like a poor prologue for a marriage proposal.

TEN

Mitchell was alone in the squad room the following morning. Jacob had gone to talk to Tamay's boss at the Wild Pony, but Mitchell preferred to keep on searching the crime reports. He was already on his third cup of coffee, yet his eyelids kept drooping as he scanned report after report, looking for any missing links.

He jumped when the phone rang, then answered it. "Detective Mitchell Lonnie."

"Lonnie, " a gruff voice said. "This is Detective Simmons, from the Boston PD."

"Oh, hey, thanks for getting back to me," Mitchell said.

"Sure, no problem. So someone tried to sell this girl… Tamay, a car. Then later ran her over with the same car?"

"Yeah, I was wondering if you ran into a similar crime. Maybe an assault that happened when someone was trying to buy or sell a car, or—"

"Yeah, yeah, I get it. I didn't see anything like that about a car, but I have a really weird coincidence for you."

"What is it?" Mitchell asked, doodling on his notepad. He wrote down *Used Car* and *Coincidence*, and then drew a small snake wearing a shoe.

"I have a man who was trying to sell a young woman a gun, and then later she was shot with the same gun."

Mitchell's doodling hand paused. "Really?" he said.

"Yeah. I'll send you the case, you can check it out for yourself. A woman named Aliza Kennedy was shot to death on her way to work. The gun that was used to shoot her was found in a nearby dumpster. It was a Beretta PX4. Later, it turned out that someone was trying to sell her a Beretta PX4."

"Are you sure it was the same gun?"

"No, but it's too much of a coincidence."

"Maybe," Mitchell said, but he felt doubtful that it was related to his case. "Thanks for letting me know, I'll check it out."

"Yeah, absolutely," Simmons said. "I'll keep my eyes open for any car-related crimes."

A moment later, the e-mail from Simmons popped up in Mitchell's inbox. It was a scanned document of all the case paperwork. Mitchell opened the document on his computer and read it. There were several images from the crime scene. A young woman lay dead in the street, her shirt drenched in blood. There was a picture of the dumpster, the gun tossed inside—in clear view, as though someone didn't care if it was found. According to the report, no fingerprints or any other trace evidence were found on the gun. Mitchell skimmed over the case's details. Finally, he found what he was looking for. It wasn't a simple gun transaction gone wrong, as he had previously assumed.

Aliza, the victim, had received a message half an hour before she was shot: *As we discussed, attached is a picture of the Beretta that I have for sale.* The attached image was of a Beretta PX4. Aliza had replied, *You have the wrong number. I'm not interested in purchasing a gun.* There were no further replies from either of them. The phone number had been traced to a disposable phone, which was disconnected.

Mitchell searched for Aliza Kennedy, and found some images of her easily enough. She had been twenty-two when she was murdered. She was Caucasian, blonde, with a perfect smile and a sweet, innocent face. She was uncommonly beautiful.

He opened Tamay's Instagram page and looked at her pictures. One thing was clear: she was also young and incredibly beautiful.

Had Tamay really wanted to buy a car? She had never responded to the message with the Toyota's image. Was it also a wrong number?

Both girls had been killed in the street. One going to work, one coming home from work.

Both phones, disposable and disconnected.

Mitchell looked up, his mind whirring, as Jacob walked into the squad room.

"The boss is a dead end," Jacob said. "Also, I think he has a horse fetish. The entire place is covered with pictures of—"

"Jacob, check this out," Mitchell said. "I think I got something."

Jacob came over to Mitchell's computer, and Mitchell showed him Aliza's murder case, pointing out the similarities. Jacob grabbed a chair and sat down in front of Mitchell's computer, reading the entire report twice. Mitchell remained silent, knowing his partner hated distractions when reading. Finally, Jacob leaned back and frowned.

"Maybe this guy makes a living selling stuff," Mitchell said, trying to formulate an idea. "Except when he encounters young women, he—"

"He didn't *encounter them*," Jacob said. "He sent them messages. At least in Aliza's case, it looks as if she wasn't even searching for a gun to buy."

"Yeah, but—" Mitchell stared at the ceiling. "This is really strange. He found out where they were. And somehow he had their numbers. Maybe he was tracking them through their phone somehow—"

"You kids and your technology," Jacob said. "He didn't find out where they were. He got them on a route they took regularly, between work and home. He was stalking them."

Mitchell felt an idea beginning to form, something that would make this puzzle complete. "A route they took regularly," he said slowly. "At a place or time where there were no people to see. And he was trying to sell—"

"It was never about selling anything," Jacob said, his voice low. "It was about sending them an image of the murder weapon. An image of the way they were about to die."

Mitchell stared at Jacob. Something clicked inside his mind. He suddenly realized what had eluded him two weeks before, as he'd stared at Buttermere Pond. Of course! How could he have been so blind!

"Oh, God," he said. "Hang on, I need to check something." He got up and strode out of the squad room, his jaw clenched tight. As he walked, puzzle pieces snapped together in his brain, forming a clear and horrible image. He kicked himself for not noticing the connection earlier. Aliza and Tamay weren't the only ones.

At the evidence room, he asked for Kendele Byers's phone.

The cop in charge found the phone quickly and handed it over, passing over the form Mitchell was supposed to sign. Mitchell ignored the form and turned on the phone, checking Kendele's last messages.

A message from a tourist agency, advertising a lake trip, with an image attached. Except it wasn't an image of a lake. It was a picture of a pond—Buttermere Pond. In which Kendele Byers had been drowned.

Kendele Byers had gone jogging four times a week, always at five in the morning. *Like clockwork*, her friend Debbie had told them. What you might call a routine, like going to and from work.

Aliza Kennedy.

Kendele Byers.

Tamay Mosely.

There was a serial killer in Glenmore Park.

ELEVEN

Jacob sat in Captain Bailey's office, waiting patiently. The captain rummaged through the papers on his desk, muttering to himself.

"No rush, Fred," Jacob said. "There's just a serial killer out there, looking for his next victim. No biggie, he can wait."

"Shut up for a second. I swear I had the report right here…"

Jacob stared at the captain's desk. *Right here* was quite vague. The desk was a paperwork disaster of epic proportions. It would probably be easier and cheaper to burn the entire thing to the ground than to try organizing it.

"Forget about the damn report, Fred. I'll print you a new one. Look, we need to discuss who's leading the case."

Bailey stopped throwing papers around and eyed Jacob. "You were in charge of both murder cases, and you're the senior detective in the squad. Is there a reason you think someone else should be leading this case?"

"Well…" Jacob hesitated. "This is a serial killer case, and I have no expertise with serial killers. And it comes to mind that you were once involved in a serial killer case. And you're the captain of this squad, so…"

"First of all," Bailey said, raising a finger, "It wasn't really a serial killer, just a gang member trying to eliminate the competition of the other gang. And we botched the case, nearly losing it during trial. Second, let's face the truth. You're a better investigator than I ever was. You're in charge of this case."

Jacob nodded. False modesty was something other people did. Jacob knew the captain was right: Jacob was the better investigator.

"Don't worry," Bailey said. "When you catch the guy, I'll be sure to zip in and take the credit."

"That's very reassuring," Jacob said. "Listen, uh… what about the FBI? I suppose we should involve them."

"I agree," Bailey said. "I'll call Christine Mancuso. She's an FBI agent, and I know her quite well. I'll ask for the FBI's help with the profiling."

"Okay, but…" Jacob hesitated for a moment. "I don't want them to come here and take charge—"

"Don't worry about it. Mancuso can be trusted."

"Okay. Thanks, Captain."

"Now, go catch me a serial killer, before he kills someone else."

Jacob got up and left the office, reassured. He looked at the squad room, at the three other detectives sitting at their computers. They all appeared busy, but he was certain they had listened to the entire conversation between him and the captain. The captain's office door might look sturdy, but it carried sound as if it were made from silk.

"Okay, listen up," he said. The three detectives turned to look at him.

"As you all know, Mitchell figured out that we have a serial killer in Glenmore Park, and it's his fault that you're pulled off your own cases." Jacob grinned. "We need to catch this guy before he kills anyone else. Because of the case's severity, the chief has allowed us some extra resources. Hang on…"

He got out of the room, grabbed the rolling whiteboard from the hallway and pushed it into the room.

"Ta da," he said. "Don't say that we've spared any expenses."

Bernard whistled. "A third whiteboard. I bet even the Feds don't have a fancy whiteboard on wheels."

"And it's reversible," Jacob said, flipping the board. "See? Like I said, budget is no issue in this case. Okay, we need to get working. It's now… eleven a.m. We have the whole day ahead of us. Bernard, Hannah, did you read the reports?"

"Yeah," Hannah said. "And Mitchell filled us in."

"Good," Jacob nodded. "In all probability, the killer doesn't have any close connection to the victims. He isn't Tamay's boyfriend, or Kendele's abusive father. So we'll focus on the *how*. How did he find our victims? Did he simply walk around, looking for young beautiful women? Not likely. He had their numbers, and he was well aware of their routines. And these days, unfortunately, he can stalk women without even getting out of bed, as long as he has a phone or tablet. Mitchell, I want you to start working on our victims' social networks. Tamay, Kendele, and Aliza. Look for any connection, any shared friend, anything that would hint at the way the killer found the three women."

Mitchell nodded, his face somber.

"Hannah, I want you to figure out if there's anything we can do with the phone numbers. We already know that each was used only once, and they were all disconnected immediately after. According to the cellular providers, in each case the messages were sent from within one mile of the scene of the crime. Can we track where the phones were bought? Were they bought together? If so, how many other phones were bought by the same individual? We'll probably have some help from the Feds, so talk to Captain Bailey and he'll get you someone you can talk to over there."

"Okay," Hannah said, making some notes in her notebook.

"Bernard," Jacob glanced at the big man. Bernard was not going to like this. "You're going to Boston."

Bernard groaned.

"I need someone there to go over the cases, with the help of the Boston PD. Mitchell talked to someone. A detective…?"

"Simmons," Mitchell said.

"Right. Talk to him. If you need some political leverage to get them to help you, talk to Captain Bailey."

"Okay," Bernard said, sighing heavily.

"Let's get to work," Jacob said.

"Hang on," Hannah said. "What about the whiteboards?"

"We'll get there," Jacob said. He knew they had hours of frustrating work ahead of them. Most leads would probably turn out to be dead ends. Filling up whiteboards was satisfying, made everyone feel as if they were accomplishing something. Better save that task for a bit later, when the adrenaline began to fade.

Mitchell turned to his screen, and Hannah picked up the phone.

Jacob walked over to Bernard's desk. "Sorry," he said.

"Carmen is going to kill me," Bernard said. "Rory is sick, and she needs me close in case there's an emergency. Do you know what she'll say when I tell her that I'm now going to Boston every day?"

"You're not going every day—"

"Jacob, we both know that this is not one trip. I'll be there every morning for the foreseeable future, right?"

"Boston's a nice city," Jacob said brightly.

"Maybe you should go," Bernard suggested.

"Look, I need someone experienced there. Someone who can make things happen. I can't send the two young ones there; they'll get lost in minutes."

"We can hear you, you know," Hannah said, her phone in her hand.

Jacob grinned at her, then turned back to Bernard. "You know this is the only way."

"Yeah, yeah. I'll just tell Carmen that it's all your fault. Don't be surprised if she seems like she hates you next time we meet."

"Tell Carmen that Hannah couldn't go because she's still not old enough to drive a car."

A balled-up paper hit Jacob on the back of his head.

"See what I need to go through here?" Jacob said. "I wish I could go. I really do."

Bernard shook his head, a small smile on his lips, and grabbed his keys from the table. Jacob slapped him on the shoulder and went over to Mitchell's desk.

Mitchell was the only detective with two monitors on his desk, supplied to him after a special request by Captain Bailey. He had at least five different windows open on them, and was switching between them, clicking links, his eyes roaming the screens intently.

Watching Mitchell doing his thing made Jacob dizzy. The fact that there was no one better than Mitchell at searching and cross-referencing things online was well-known. Less well-known was the fact that Jacob could barely open his e-mail account, and even that wasn't always a walk in the park.

Jacob knew he was falling behind, that technology was more important than ever in his job. A day would come when being good at interrogation and having a sharp instinct wouldn't be enough for a detective. When that day came, Jacob knew, he would find himself behind a desk. He sighed. Time to start calling people.

He left himself the most undesirable task of them all: calling Tamay and Kendele's friends and family, asking questions, trying to figure out if anyone knew about a stranger who'd approached either of them, or if any of them had complained about a stalker, online or in real life. In Tamay's case, he would talk to people who had just lost a person they loved. There would be a lot of grief and anger in those talks, and he knew he would end the day exhausted and sad.

But being a detective was never easy.

———

Jacob took a bite from the slice of pepperoni pizza in his hand, staring at the phone. He had spent the last three hours on the phone, and he was already depressed. Tamay's family were in complete shock, and talking to them got under his skin. Her friends were in various states of grief as well. Later they would all get angry, start demanding the killer be brought to justice. Anger, Jacob could handle. But right now their grief just made him sad.

"So… the phones," Hannah said, standing next to him.

Jacob turned to face her. "Yeah?"

"I called a dozen places in the area that sell disposable phones, and got pretty much the same answer. The numbers are not issued in advance. In fact, a customer can put in his own number to replace the number issued to him. Then I checked online, and realized that anyone can buy a phone and have it delivered to any address within twenty-four hours. I talked to Agent Mancuso, and she said pretty much the same thing. She said they'll conduct their own investigation with the numbers I gave her, but she wasn't very hopeful. I don't think there's anything we can do with those phone numbers."

Jacob nodded. This didn't surprise him. He'd already known most of what she'd just told him, but it never hurt to double-check.

"Okay," he said. "I think it's time for the whiteboards."

Hannah's face brightened up a bit.

"Left whiteboard," he said, pointing at it. "I want the crime scenes. Diagrams, maps, tape a few of the crime scene photos as well. I want us to get a sense of how he picks his locations. I want timelines on the right whiteboard, as detailed and thorough as possible. The exact time the message was sent, our estimated time of death, when the body was discovered… anything that comes to mind."

"What about the third whiteboard?"

"I'll do that one. One side will be detailing our victims. Photos, basic details, immediate acquaintances… that sort of thing. The other side of the board will be dedicated to suspects."

"Do we have any suspects?"

Jacob sighed. "Not yet, not really, but hopefully we'll have some by the end of the day."

Hannah nodded and went over to the left whiteboard. Jacob sent some of the victims' photos to the printer, and then stood by it, watching the faces of dead young women slowly slide out of the printer's maw. They were all so young. He sighed heavily.

"Detective Cooper?" a sharp voice said behind him. "How is the investigation progressing?"

Jacob tuned around. Chief Veronica Dougherty was a striking woman, and quite intimidating as well. She was well-known for her unique body language, which often warned of an incoming outburst. When her hands went up to her curly hair, fluffing it, it meant one should get to the point. When she began to nod curtly, it was a sign she was getting impatient. And if she raised her eyebrows, the person talking with her was usually doomed. Currently she stood with one hand clutching the opposite wrist, a posture that signified she wanted to hear good news.

"It's going quite well!" Jacob said, his brain frantically collecting every shred of political wisdom he had. "All of us are investigating the uh… leads, and some indicate patterns that um…"

"Chief Dougherty." Captain Bailey's voice rang across the room. He stood in the doorway of his office. "Please come in. I'll give you a full report."

She nodded curtly and crossed the room to enter the captain's office, closing the door behind her. Jacob sighed in relief. There were some things he simply had no idea how to handle.

His phone rang, and he glanced at the screen. Bernard.

"Yeah?" he answered.

"Jacob? Listen. I'm sitting here with Detective Simmons, and we managed to find two similar cases."

"Okay," Jacob said. "Shoot."

"The first one is a woman named Yvonne Richie. She was killed with an ice pick just hours after buying it in a local store."

"Was there a message?"

"No, but the messages the other victims received all seemed like someone was trying to sell something, so I thought it was worth mentioning."

"Okay. What's the second case?" Jacob took the photos from the printer and began taping them to the whiteboard, the phone held between his ear and his shoulder.

"A woman named Isabella Garcia was stabbed to death in an alley near her work in January. She had an image of a knife sent to her just before she was killed, like an adver-tisement. Just the same as the others."

"Did they recover the knife?"

"No," Bernard said. "And no one heard her scream, even though it was day. No witnesses. It turns out she went down to that alley to smoke eight to ten times every day."

"Okay," Jacob said. "Send me the second file."

"Don't you want to have a look at the first one?"

Jacob hesitated. "I trust your instincts," he said. "Do you think it's relevant?"

There was a pause. "No," Bernard finally said.

"Okay. Send me the second file, please."

"Sure. Listen, Jacob. The Boston PD wanted to take over the investigation."

"Uh-huh. Can Detective Simmons hear me right now?" Jacob asked.

"No."

"Like hell they'll take over," Jacob said. "The clueless assholes have had someone murdering women in their city for months—since January, maybe even longer! And they found nothing."

"They claim they have precedence," Bernard said. "They had the first case."

"Okay, I'll handle it," Jacob said.

He ended the call and knocked on Captain Bailey's door.

"Yeah?" He heard the captain say from inside.

He opened the door. Captain Bailey and Chief Dougherty sat across from each other, both looking at him.

"We have a probable fourth victim," Jacob said. "Killed in Boston seven months ago. Stabbed to death. Same MO, with the message."

Captain Bailey nodded. "Thanks for the update, Detective," he said.

"Uh… the Boston PD wants to take over the case. The say they have precedence."

The chief's eyes widened, and Jacob hoped she was aiming her rage at the Boston PD, and not at him. "I'll handle it," she said, standing up. She walked out, and stopped by Jacob. "Let me know if you need anything else," she told him, and left the squad room.

Jacob went back to his desk and opened his mailbox. The e-mail from Bernard was already waiting for him. He opened it and began to read the report of the Isabella Garcia case.

He read it three times, taking notes in his notebook. The third time through, he noticed something unusual in the autopsy report. Gabriella had long curly hair, and she'd had a haircut only a day before her murder. This made it much easier to see that one clump of her hair was shorter than the rest. Inspection under a microscope found that the hairs were cut with different scissors than the ones used by Gabriella's hairdresser. No further note of this was mentioned in the entire case file, and Jacob felt like punching the detectives in the Boston PD. He picked up his phone and dialed the ME's office.

"Hello?"

"Annie, it's Jacob Cooper."

"Hey, Jacob. Tamay Moseley's autopsy isn't done yet," she said immediately. "It'll take a few more hours—"

"No problem," he interrupted her. "I just wanted to ask something specific. Did Tamay have some of her hair cut off just before or after the murder?"

"What do you mean?"

"I mean… was there some hair missing? A piece that was a noticeably different length than the rest? Probably cut with…" He glanced at Isabella's autopsy report. "Blunt scissors?"

"Let me check. I'll get back to you."

"Thanks." He put down the phone, then printed out Isabella Garcia's photograph and stuck it to the whiteboard next to the three other victims. "Mitchell, Hannah," he said. "This is Isabella Garcia. She's probably our earliest victim. I've forwarded the case files to your e-mails."

The detectives both nodded. Jacob took another look at Isabella's face. Would they find any other victim? He could already see Isabella Garcia's Facebook page opening on Mitchell's left monitor; the right monitor displayed her murder report. Jacob wondered briefly if Mitchell could really pay attention to both windows simultaneously.

His phone rang and he answered immediately.

"You were right," Annie told him. "One of Tamay's braids had been cut off using a blunt blade. How did you know?"

"It's a serial killer, Annie," he said. "One of his other victims had her hair cut as well. I think it's part of his MO."

She was silent for a moment. "Any other victims in Glenmore Park?" she asked.

"Kendele Byers."

"So Kendele had part of her hair cut as well."

"Probably."

"And I didn't notice it."

Some people didn't give themselves any slack. "You did an amazing job there, Annie. The body was severely deteriorated when we found it—"

"Not the hair, Jacob. I should have spotted it." She sounded as if she was about to resign there and then.

"You're an incredible medical examiner, Annie. I don't know what we would do without you."

"Shut up, Jacob. You're just trying to make me feel better."

"What's wrong with that?"

"I need to get back to my autopsy. I don't want to botch this one as well." She hung up.

Jacob sighed.

The killer was keeping mementos from his victims. He had actually stopped the car after running over Tamay for the second time to cut a braid of her hair. If Jacob had any doubts that this was a serial killer, this fact pretty much dispelled them.

He got to work again, filling up the whiteboard with basic facts about the victims. Then he began to make calls to Isabella Garcia's family and friends.

An hour later, a man walked into the squad room. Jacob immediately noticed his shoes: brown, expensive-looking, and brand new. His hair was completely white, and he was dressed in a gray suit. His face was vaguely familiar, but Jacob couldn't quite place him.

"Sir?" he said, hurrying forward, trying to block the man's view before he noticed the boards. "This area is off limits—"

"The chief let me in," the man said calmly.

Jacob paused, frowning, trying to figure out who this was. Someone from the Feds, maybe? Or… oh. He suddenly felt like a fool. Not a feeling he was a stranger to.

"Mr. Mayor," he said. "I'm sorry, I was just—"

The chief bustled in. "Mr. Mayor," she said. "I'm glad you could make it. Right this way, please." She led him into Captain Bailey's office. Jacob saw Hannah grinning at him.

"Like you would have handled it any better," he grumbled.

"I know what the mayor looks like, just saying," she said. "But memory fades with age, so…"

"Shut up," he said.

He noticed a new e-mail in his inbox and opened it. It was a short video from a CCTV camera Bernard had sent him. The camera was positioned near the spot where Aliza Kennedy had been shot. The video showed a man rushing away from the scene. He didn't look anything like the sketch they had. Jacob forwarded the e-mail to Hannah.

"Hannah," he said. "Can you find a good frame from the video I just sent you, where the guy's face can be seen clearly? I want it printed for the suspects whiteboard."

"Sure thing," she said, opening the clip.

He made a few additional phone calls, with no results, before Hannah handed him three printouts. One was from the video he had sent her. The second was the sketch Rabbi Friedman had helped with. The third showed a shadowy profile of someone sitting in a car.

"This one is from the video that Officer Lonnie obtained," Hannah said, pointing at the third printout.

"The man in the car might match the sketch," Jacob said, narrowing his eyes. "But the third guy is different."

"Just different hair and beard," Hannah said. "It's probably a disguise."

"Yeah, maybe," Jacob said. He got up and flipped the whiteboard. He then taped the three printouts to it, and took a step back. Could it be the same guy? It was hard to tell.

He went over to the timeline whiteboard and looked at it. The killer had struck at least four times. Isabella Garcia had been murdered six months before. Aliza Kennedy had been murdered three and a half months after. Kendele, according to the time of the text message, was murdered on July 21st, ten weeks after Aliza. Tamay had been killed six weeks after Kendele. Maybe there were missing cases, maybe not, but the pattern seemed clear. The killer was accelerating. The clock was ticking.

He glanced at his watch and groaned. When had it gotten so late? There were no windows in the squad room, but according to the time it was already dark outside.

He dialed Marissa.

"Hello?"

"Hey, hon," he said. "Listen—"

"You're running late," she said. There was no anger in her voice, just a hint of sadness.

"Yeah."

"When will you be back?"

"Uh… very late, I suspect. You'll probably be sleeping when I get home."

"Did you have dinner?"

"We'll probably order something," he said.

"Do that. Don't start forgetting to eat again. A workaholic husband is one thing, but I don't want you getting skinny."

"What do you mean?" he asked, smiling. "I already am skinny."

"Sure you are, Jacob. Don't fall asleep driving home."

"Bye, hon."

"Bye."

He ended the call and stuck the phone in his pocket, then noticed Captain Bailey standing near the coffee maker.

"Making a pot of coffee?" he asked.

"I need to be helping somehow," Bailey said.

"I could definitely use some," Jacob said, and sat down. There was another e-mail from Bernard, just a quick update. Everyone in the Boston PD had suddenly gotten a lot less helpful. He was having trouble accessing their files.

"Hey, Captain," Jacob said distractedly, "Once you're done with the coffee, Bernard could use some help from you and the chief. Looks like Boston PD got the memo that they're not going to be in charge, and they seem to be feeling a bit childish about it."

"I'll handle it," the captain said.

Jacob heard Mitchell's voice in the background, and realized he'd hardly heard his partner talk since morning. When Mitchell was doing online research, he always became deeply absorbed, not noticing what went around him, talking to no one. Now he was on the phone, talking to Pauline, having the same conversation Jacob had just had with Marissa. Jacob wondered if Hannah was about to call anyone. As far as he knew she had no one in her life, but who could tell?

His phone rang again. Matt this time. "Hey, Matt," he said.

"Hi, Jacob. Listen, we finished processing the Camry."

"What did you find?"

"We found several hairs and a few fabric threads," Matt said. "And one set of fingerprints that matched Rabbi Friedman, who's in the system."

"Okay."

"I don't know about the fabric yet; we're running tests. Let's talk about the hair."

"Let's," Jacob said.

"So… we have two groups of hair. One is probably Friedman's; it matches his hair color and it was his car. The other hairs are much darker, and the strands are thinner. They don't look like a good match for the rabbi, and apparently his wife and kids all have lighter hair."

"How do you know?"

"I sent one of my guys over there. Friedman wasn't happy."

"I'm sure," Jacob grinned.

"So these hairs might belong to our guy. I sent them to the lab for DNA testing."

"Okay, good."

"Not so good. They're hair shafts—no roots—and the shafts usually don't contain nuclear DNA. Nuclear DNA is the type we need to match against CODIS. We're testing them anyway, but it's a long shot."

"I have full faith in your skills, Matt."

"Faith is not the issue here. We either have nuclear DNA, or we don't. If we get lucky, we might still find some nuclear DNA in the hair. And when I say we, I mean the Feds."

"You sound tired."

"It's been a long day. And it's not over yet."

"Yeah, no kidding," Jacob said. "Thanks, Matt."

———

Mitchell was vaguely aware of everything going on around him, but he pushed it all out. His mind was deeply focused on the four women.

Isabella Garcia, Aliza Kennedy, Kendele Byers, and Tamay Mosely. Each woman had thousands of virtual strands online—social network profiles, forums, e-mail accounts—and he was diving through the ocean of information, trying to submerge himself in the lives of all four women, looking for the connections.

It was easy to get lost in trivial details. Two of the victims liked the same movie, or shared the same Internet meme, or a video of a funny goat. He ignored the noise, looking harder.

They each had hundreds of connections. Tamay had thousands of fans, Kendele had dozens of clients, Aliza and Isabella had numerous social media friends and followers. He tried to gauge which was more important, which was worth noticing. The names blended in his mind; when he tried to list them, the work became monotonous, slow and useless. What was a list of names worth? No, he had to *feel* them. The victims' digital lives were complete things, not lists of names, of likes, of comments. Each of them was a real thing, that should be treated as a whole.

The first connection was easy to spot, and he discovered it quickly. All the victims had followed supermodels and modeling agencies via the different social networks. None of them were models, but they were all interested in the modeling world. Could the killer have found them at a fashion show, or a fashion world event somewhere? He tried to look for events they had attended. Aliza did go to fashion shows, and posted about them regularly in her Instagram feed, but he saw no indication of the same behavior in the other three. Still, it was a possible connection, and he made note of it.

There were hours where he simply clicked link after link, scanning their posts and their friends' posts, switching between the four victims constantly. When pizza or coffee came his way, he ate and drank, the taste a faraway thing.

Then, when he was just about nodding off in front of the screen, his concentration fading away, something snagged his mind. He was looking at Kendele Byers's Twitter account, examining the handles she followed. There was one named *@AtticusHof*. He frowned, and then recalled that a week before he'd been calling all the people in Kendele's contact list on her phone, trying to fish for any clue. She had an Atticus there as well.

He opened the list of all the calls he'd made. There— Atticus Hoffman. Mitchell remembered him. He was an agent who represented models. He had said Kendele asked him to represent her, and he refused.

Mitchell reached for Tamay's phone, which lay on his desk. He opened her contact list and scrolled until he found it. *Huffman Modeling*. She'd misspelled the agency name. He compared the number to the one he'd called the week before, just to be sure. They matched.

"Jacob," he said aloud. "I think I found a suspect."

He glanced at the time, exhausted. It was half past midnight.

TWELVE

When Atticus Hoffman woke up in the morning, he wished for death.

This was not something new. He wished for death quite a lot. He wished for death after eating too much, he wished for death when he had a cold, he wished for death when there was a traffic jam. But lately his death wishes were becoming somewhat more sincere.

This was mostly Dana Hoffman's fault. She was his wife—or, to be a bit more precise, his fifth wife. Soon to be his fifth ex-wife. She was the reason he was waking up on the floor of his office, in clothes he'd worn the night before, with the acute taste of vomit in his mouth and one of the worst hangovers in his entire life.

Dana had kicked him out of their apartment two days ago, after she'd found out he was fucking Maribelle. He suspected the real cause for her anger was not that he was fucking someone else, but that he was fucking someone younger. She'd chased him out with a broom and a bread knife, swinging them both like a deranged gladiator. He hadn't even had time to pack any clothes. When he could finally return home, his clothes would probably be cut to ribbons. It wouldn't be the first time, either; his second wife, Jessica, had done that when they broke up. And Ingrid, his third wife, had once burned all of his underwear.

Well, that would teach him not to marry the models he represented. Of course, he hadn't learned the previous four times, so there was no real reason to assume that this time the lesson would stick.

He shakily got up and opened his desk drawer. There was an emergency whiskey bottle, just for occasions like this one.

Ah, it was empty. Worst morning ever. He went back to wishing he was dead.

Someone was thumping on the door—though, frankly, it felt as if they were thumping on Atticus's skull. He did the only thing he could think of: he curled into a fetal position and waited for it to stop.

It didn't stop. There was yelling as well: "Open up! Police!"

Had Dana sent them? Had she told them about the cocaine stash he had in his office? Ha! The joke was on her; he'd snorted the entire thing the day before. He stumbled over to the door and flung it open.

Gah! Bright light! Atticus felt like Gollum as he stumbled back, yelping, the sunlight searing his eyes. *It burns! It burnnnnnns!* Two men entered the office and closed the door behind them, and the room sank into its previous darkness. Atticus breathed in relief.

"Whatchuwant?" he asked, trying to focus. These weren't regular policemen. They wore tasteless cheap suits. One of them, a bald guy with cold blue eyes, flipped open a badge.

"MY NAME IS DETECTIVE COOPER. THIS IS MY PARTNER, DETECTIVE LONNIE. ARE YOU ATTICUS HOFFMAN?" he said, each syllable squashing Atticus's brain.

"Yes," Atticus whimpered. "Yes. Please, stop shouting." He opened the drawer in the desk again. Ah, sweet painkillers. Perhaps he should just take two dozen, end this terrible day?

He took two, swallowing them without water.

"Mr. Hoffman," Detective Cooper said, clearly trying to talk a bit more softly. "We're here to ask you a few questions."

"Okay."

"Your wife said you would probably be here."

"Okay."

"She asked us to shoot you if you don't cooperate."

"Okay."

"She asked us to shoot you if you do cooperate, as well."

"Yeah, that sounds like her," Atticus said, closing his eyes.

"Mr. Hoffman, did you represent Tamay Mosely?"

Atticus frowned, trying to think. "Hang on," he muttered. He turned on his computer, the glare from the screen driving virtual nails into his eyes. Oh, the suffering. "How do you spell that?" he asked.

"T... A... M... A... Y..." the younger detective, Lonnie, said. He was beautiful, Atticus realized. He wondered if the detective would be interested in some modeling gigs.

He typed in Tamay's name, and her picture appeared. "She came here a few months ago, and I said I'd keep my eyes open," Atticus said, reading his notes. They said *Quite fuckable. Would not open her legs. Suggested nude modeling and she refused.* "But I never found a job for her."

"How about Kendele Byers?" Cooper asked. "Did you represent her?"

"She's the one who died, right? You people asked me about her already," Atticus said, typing in her name. Kendele's picture showed up. The notes said *Not pretty enough. Suggested nude modeling and she refused.* "I couldn't find anything for her. She wasn't a good match for modeling."

"Why not?" Lonnie asked.

Atticus shrugged. *Because she was too ugly,* he wanted to say. "Not everyone fits the profile we're looking for."

"Mr. Hoffman, where were you last night?"

Atticus cleared his throat. "Here."

"By yourself?" Lonnie asked.

"That's right."

"All night?" The detective pressed.

"Yeah."

"What were you doing?" Lonnie asked.

Drinking and crying. "Working," he said. "I had a lot of work."

"Mr. Hoffman, Tamay Mosely was hit by a car last night."

"That's terrible," Atticus said, trying to manufacture the horror he assumed he was expected to feel. "So… uh… young." He thought for a moment. "And innocent," he added brightly.

"Innocent of what?" Cooper asked.

How the hell was he supposed to know? It was just something you said about people. "Oh, you know. Just generally innocent."

"A lot of women you've represented have died lately," Cooper said.

"I didn't represent the first one." Atticus said, starting to feel defensive.

"She was in your database."

"That's right. I'm the only modeling agent in town. If any girl in Glenmore Park wants to model, she ends up here."

"Do you by any chance represent a woman named Aliza Kennedy?"

Atticus checked. "Nope."

"How about Isabella Garcia?"

"Hang on… No. Who are they?"

"Some women from Boston."

"Then why would I represent them? There are perfectly good modeling agencies in Boston, Detective."

"Does anyone else have access to your lists?"

"My secretary."

"Anyone else?"

"No."

"Did you give your lists to anyone?"

"Absolutely not. If I did, I'd be out of a job. Knowledge is money."

"Could your secretary have given them to anyone?"

"If she had, she'd find herself sleeping with the fishes," Atticus said. Both detectives stared. "That was a joke," he explained. "I didn't really mean it. I would have fired her. I don't… I don't kill secretaries. Or anyone else, for that matter."

In retrospect, maybe that hadn't been a very good joke to tell detectives who were investigating the death of some model wannabes. But the hangover was taking its toll, and Atticus was feeling quite impatient.

"Mr. Hoffman, would you mind accompanying us to the police station, to answer a few more questions?" Cooper asked.

"Well," Atticus said. "That depends."

"Depends on what?"

"Are you arresting me?" he looked at both detectives, trying to gauge their reaction. The Cooper guy, he was cool. No expression whatsoever. His eyes, Atticus thought, were as cold as a supermodel's cunt. But Detective Lonnie's face changed, just a bit, and Atticus knew all they had were theories and veiled threats.

That was fine. He had fled just two days before from a crazy woman with a broom and a knife. He could handle two detectives.

"No, Mr. Hoffman," Cooper said. "We just want to ask a few questions."

"Well, if you're not arresting me, you're free to ask your questions… but do it here, please. And maybe we can wait until my attorney gets here."

Detective Cooper sighed heavily.

That's right, asshole, Atticus is no pushover.

"Very well, Mr. Hoffman," Cooper said. "We just need to have a look through your things."

"What?"

With a short, dismissive flick of his wrist, Cooper tossed a paper on the table. "A search warrant," he said.

"What are you looking for?" Atticus asked, picking up the warrant.

"Some disposable phones," Cooper said. "Some strands of hair. A wig. Those kinds of things."

"I'm calling my lawyer," Atticus said angrily, reaching for the phone.

"Please do, Mr. Hoffman. But while we're waiting, our men will begin executing the warrant," Cooper said. Detective Lonnie walked to the door and opened it; to Atticus's horror, four policemen came inside, and began to methodically empty and upturn everything in his office.

Life, Atticus thought as Lonnie started messing with his computer, was just a big pile of stinking crap.

He wished he was dead.

———

When they got back from Hoffman's office, Jacob and Mitchell walked straight to Captain Bailey's office. They hadn't found anything at Hoffman's, except for the list of the clients he represented. Mitchell had copied that, along with all the clients' details. Hannah and Bernard were at Atticus's house, performing a similar search, but Mitchell had a feeling they wouldn't find anything either. The killer was incredibly careful, leaving no trace behind. If Atticus was indeed the killer, he wouldn't have anything incriminating simply lying around.

Mitchell knocked on the door and opened it without waiting for a response. He was instantly sorry. Both the mayor and the chief of police were inside the office, and they were talking animatedly to Captain Bailey, who sat behind his incredibly cluttered table, looking exhausted.

"Sorry," Mitchell quickly said. "We'll come back."

"No, no," Captain Bailey said, his eyes lighting up. "Come in, Detectives. We could use your input in this discussion."

Mitchell was no expert politician, but he knew how to translate the last sentence. What the captain had just said was essentially, *Please back me up in whatever I say, and nod when I talk*.

"Mr. Mayor," Jacob said, nodding at the man. "Chief." He entered the room in an easy manner and grabbed the only other empty chair. Mitchell was left standing, feeling acutely out of place.

"Okay," Jacob said. "What are we talking about?"

"A press conference," Captain Bailey said.

"Ah."

"The chief has just informed me that this case has reached the governor's ears," Fred Bailey said. "Apparently, our esteemed mayor convinced the governor that the Glenmore Park PD should remain in charge of the investigation."

"Really?" Jacob asked, raising an eyebrow. "Wouldn't the Staties want to take charge?"

"They might," the mayor said, his voice firm. "But I can be persuasive. The governor instructed the state police to give us their full cooperation. The chief assured me that Glenmore Park PD is completely capable of handling this case."

"I'm sure she did," Jacob said calmly.

The chief would love for this case to stay in her department's hands, Mitchell knew. Assuming they could catch the killer.

"Anyway, we were discussing—"

The door banged open again, and a young woman in a gray suit walked into the office. She looked around, and said to Jacob, "You took my chair."

"I'm very sorry, Miss," Jacob said, remaining seated. "Uh… And you are?"

"Zoe Bentley," she said. "I'm the forensic psychologist."

"Zoe will be working with us on this case," Captain Bailey said. "She was sent by the FBI. Mitchell, can you get two more chairs, please?"

Mitchell walked back to the squad room and grabbed two chairs; he rolled them into the captain's office and sat on one of them. Zoe sat on the other. Mitchell found himself staring at her. She couldn't have been more than thirty. Her nose was a bit crooked, like an eagle's beak, but somehow it actually made her face strangely alluring. Her hair was cut at about shoulder-length, in a careless manner, and he could almost imagine her cutting it herself in front of a mirror.

She had a peculiar expression on her face, as if she truly was an eagle, examining its surroundings alertly, looking for prey. When she looked at him, he almost flinched. He felt as if she could see everything going on inside him. His thoughts, his feelings—hell, even his spleen.

"Zoe, can you please update Detectives Cooper and Lonnie about your thoughts regarding the killer?" Captain Bailey said.

She nodded curtly. "Yes. I went over the case files yesterday. There are some clear traits which you've probably noticed. The traceless crime scenes, the planning, the ritual of sending the message of the murder weapon—they all indicate high obsessiveness."

"Isn't that typical with serial killers?" Jacob asked.

"Not necessarily," she said. "The murder victims are all beautiful young women, and I suspect he enjoys his control over them."

"In what way?" Jacob asked.

"He probably enjoys that he manages to kill his victims despite the fact that they supposedly know how they are about to die half an hour before it actually happens. That's what the messages are about."

"But they don't actually know it," Mitchell said. "He masks the messages. They mostly look like someone who sent a message to the wrong number by mistake."

"Yes." She nodded in agreement. "But the victims have the information in their hands. He likes the superiority of the situation. In his eyes, the victims have all the relevant information, and still they walk right into their death." She cleared her throat and seemed to think for a moment. "I'm worried about the decreased time elapsed between the murders. He seems to be accelerating. His carelessness is another indication of that. He didn't bother hiding the car used to kill Tamay Mosely. Serial killers often become careless when they accelerate. It's a manifestation of their increased self confidence. Fear of being caught stops holding them back."

She spoke in a tone that people typically used to explain how a toaster works. There was no hesitancy there, no doubt. She was so incredibly sure of herself, and Mitchell found that this grated on him a bit. Criminals were not predictable; serial killers were even less so. That was what made them so damned hard to catch.

"We need to assess if we're really dealing with a psychopath," she said.

"I'd say that much was a given," Mitchell said.

"It's very likely. Stalking, the search for control, a low sense of empathy, an issue with women. These are all indicators of psychopathy. If so, he would likely have a history of violence. We would be looking for someone with antisocial tendencies in his everyday life. However, he can clearly plan quite carefully, which indicates high intelligence. It's possible that he manages to function in society quite successfully just by mimicking the behavior of others."

The mayor cleared his throat. "We want to have a press conference," he said. "We were discussing when and how it should be done."

Mitchell glanced at Captain Bailey, who was regarding the mayor and the chief with distaste. Clearly, the captain was not part of the "we" who wanted the press conference.

"Why a press conference?" Jacob asked. "The killer doesn't know yet that we've connected the dots. We should wait a few more days, try to gather as much information as we possibly can."

"People should be alert," the chief said. "And if the killer sends a woman a text message, we want her to call the police."

It was a good point. If alerting the public would save lives, it was best to do it as soon as possible.

"He isn't going to strike tomorrow," Captain Bailey said. "We have a few days. A press conference will make him more careful, push him to hide his tracks better."

"As far as I can see, he's left no tracks," the mayor said. "I don't want another citizen to get hurt."

"A press conference might make him strike sooner," Zoe said. "This is a man who likes control. He'd want to show everyone that he's the one who calls the shots, not the police."

"That might make him careless," Mitchell pointed out. "Perhaps he'll make a mistake."

He could feel the temperature in the room dropping. The captain and Jacob both looked at him angrily. He had broken ranks, betrayed his allies.

"That's a good point," the mayor said warmly. "We'll break the news to the public this afternoon."

"Very well," Captain Bailey said, and turned to the chief. "You should let the dispatchers know. The public will get hysterical. They'll be swamped with calls."

"I'll talk to them," she said. "I want a summary of everything we know about this killer on my desk in two hours."

"Detective Lonnie will take care of it," Bailey said. "He's great at writing summaries."

THIRTEEN

anessa had been surprised at how quickly she adjusted to the graveyard shift. She'd thought it would be terrible, going to sleep in the morning, waking up in the afternoon, staying up all night. A teenager's life during spring break, but with less dancing and alcohol, and more arresting prostitutes and answering complaints about noisy neighbors.

Waking up in the afternoon still felt wrong. Her head always felt as if it had been submerged in sand while she slept, and her eyelids were heavy and gritty. She knew from experience that a cup of strong coffee in front of the TV, followed by a warm shower, helped her metamorphose from a shriveled mummy to a human being.

She sat down with her mug of life-reviving coffee and turned on the TV. The chief appeared on screen, talking on the front steps of the police department. That was enough to make Tanessa rub her eyes, sit up straighter, and turn the volume up.

"—two women in Boston, and two more in Glenmore Park," the chief was saying. "We have established that these heinous crimes were committed by one individual."

Tanessa listened in amazement as the chief explained about the serial killer running loose in Glenmore Park. Apparently, the police force was doing all it could to catch him. That didn't seem to include Tanessa, who up until that moment had not known anything about a serial killer at all.

She dialed Mitchell.

"Hey," he answered. "You're up."

"There's a serial killer in Glenmore Park?" she asked him.

"Oh, you're watching the press conference," he said, but she hardly heard him, because the chief had just listed the names of the killer's victims. The name *Tamay Mosely* rung in her ears, and images of the broken girl lying on the road popped into her mind. She recalled how she'd caressed the girl's cheek, how she had told her it was going to be all right.

"Are you on the case?" she asked, her voice tense.

"Yeah. Jacob is lead. All the detectives are involved."

"I want to help."

"Sure. Uh… Keep an eye out for anyone that seems suspicious during your patrols, and—"

"Don't bullshit me, Mitchell. I want to help."

"What do you want me to do, Tanessa, ask the chief to promote you to detective?"

The chief was explaining that the killer was targeting young women, and that if anyone received an image from an unknown source she should immediately dial 911, to inform the police.

"What's this about?" Tanessa asked. "The messages."

"Tanessa, I really can't talk about ongoing cases. Not even with—"

"Cut the crap, Mitchell."

Mitchell sighed. "He sends his victims an image of what he's about to use to kill them," he said.

"Jesus."

"Yeah."

"So Tamay… Tamay Mosely," Tanessa swallowed hard. There was a lump in her throat. She recalled the girl's braids. Hundreds of braids. "Did she…"

"She had a message with an image of the Toyota Camry in her phone."

The chief was now leaving the press conference, refusing to answer any more questions. Tanessa kept staring at the TV, thinking of the girl she had seen die.

Only ten minutes later she realized she had never hung up. The phone was discarded in her lap.

The shower did not help her feel better this time.

———

He was watching the press conference. At first, a wave of panic shot through him. *They knew.*

But then he realized he was more angry than worried. They were talking about him. They were calling his deeds "heinous" and "brutal." No one mentioned the care with which he acted, making sure he left no trace to follow. They said all the victims were young women, but they didn't say they had been beautiful. They mentioned the texts, alerting the public, letting them know that someone was sending something. They never mentioned the elegance in the text. The *anticip…*

…ation.

They were not telling his story, and this was a story that should be told. He had always known that eventually someone would connect the dots. He'd known it would come. He'd waited for it.

He *anticipated* it.

Now it was time. But the public should hear the full story. Not the one sided, vague police version. No. They should hear from him as well.

He opened his browser, and found the *Glenmore Park Gazette*'s site. He located the e-mail addresses of two reporters. One was named Steve Pollard. The other was named Ricky Nate.

He flipped a coin. Heads for Ricky, tails for Steve.

He didn't check the outcome. Instead, he covered the coin with a small yellow Post-it lying on the table.

Anticip…

According to his articles, Steve Pollard seemed like a serious man who checked and double-checked all the facts, reported everything objectively, and never hid anything from the public. Ricky Nate seemed like a woman who reported on sensational stories, looking for the juicy bits, exposing the dirt on everything and everyone.

Who would tell his story?

He left the coin covered for fifty minutes.

…ation.

Finally, he could bear it no more, and he lifted the Post-it.

Ah.

———

Mitchell sat across from Pauline in the kitchen, drinking his morning coffee. The night before, he had gotten home at two in the morning, after long hours spent going through the list of models and model wannabes from Atticus Hoffman's computer, checking them out, trying to find links between them and the murder victims, attempting to predict the murderer's next victim.

It was impossible. Glenmore Park wasn't such a large place. Many of the models were acquainted with one of the victims, or had shared friends with one of them. They all knew Atticus, of course. Mitchell knew he'd have to spend the day calling them, interviewing them. It was not a task he was excited about.

"There's an article about your serial killer," Pauline said, swiping her finger along her tablet. She was eating some granola. She hadn't really spoken to him all morning; she was apparently pissed off, though he couldn't fathom why.

"Yeah," he said, tiredly. "I'm sure there are a lot of articles."

"He sounds like a really creepy psycho," Pauline muttered. "Sending messages to the victims, with the murder method? That's fucked up."

Mitchell stared at her in shock. He snatched the tablet from her hand.

"Hey!" she shouted at him, but he ignored her.

The public wasn't supposed to know that the messages were the murder method; that was information the department had held back on purpose. He scanned the article quickly, his heart sinking in horror. It was all there. The article included the actual text messages, as well as detailed descriptions of the images. It also mentioned that all the victims were "unusually beautiful." The article even gave the killer a name: *The Deadly Messenger*. What the hell was going on?

He checked the name of the reporter. Ricky Nate.

"Here," he said, shoving the tablet into Pauline's hands. This was his fault. He should never have supported the press conference idea. Jacob and Captain Bailey had obviously known something like this would happen. He got up and began pacing back and forth in their tiny living room, then pulled his phone from his pocket. He browsed to the *Glenmore Park Gazette* site, found their phone number and called it.

"Glenmore Park Gazette," a young, feminine voice answered "This is Neomi, how can I help you?"

"I need to talk to Ricky Nate."

"I'm sorry, Ricky's not here yet. Can I take a message?"

"This is Detective Mitchell Lonnie from the Glenmore Park PD. I need to talk to her urgently. Can you give me her number?"

"The private phone numbers of our reporters are confidential," she answered. "If you'll leave a message, she'll call you as soon as—"

"It's about the serial killer. I need to talk to her now."

"As I said, the private phone numbers of our reporters are—"

"Okay, listen," Mitchell said, losing the little patience he had. "Write down my badge number. Call the department. Verify that I'm really a damn detective, and then have Ricky Nate call me to this number."

There was a moment of silence, and then the woman asked for his badge number. He dictated it, and she hung up. A few minutes later his phone rang, and he answered immediately.

"Hello?"

"Detective Lonnie?"

"Ricky Nate?" Mitchell paced around the coffee table.

"That's right." The voice sounded feminine, but low and throaty. Mitchell knew that many men found this kind of voice sexy. He just wanted her to cough out whatever was lodged in her trachea.

"I'm Detective Mitchell Lonnie from the Glenmore Park PD. I'm calling about the article you wrote."

"I was about to call you myself," she said.

"Call me?" he felt confused. "Who told you about me?"

"No! I meant call the police. Let you know that the killer had contacted me."

Mitchell felt as if all his hair stood on edge. "What?" he hissed "When did that happen? How?"

"He sent me an e-mail last night," Ricky said, her voice completely calm. "He described the messages he sent. He also mentioned that he took care to make sure that his victims were all incredibly beautiful."

"Why didn't you tell us about this last night?"

"Oh, it was quite late. I thought it could wait until morning," she said.

He wanted to shove his hand through the phone and strangle her. He knew very well why she hadn't called. She hadn't wanted the police to stall the article.

"I need a copy of that e-mail," he said. "And I need to talk to you."

"What a coincidence." She sounded as if she was smiling. "I need to interview you."

"We'll see about that," he said, his voice sharp and angry. "How soon can you get to the police department?"

"I'll be there in an hour."

"Good. I'll see you there." He hung up the phone, fuming. He grabbed his small briefcase and walked out, trying to think how he should approach Ricky Nate.

He didn't realize until he got to work that he hadn't said goodbye to Pauline.

———

Ricky Nate was young; Mitchell pegged her as no more than thirty. She was brown-skinned with a warm bronze undertone that emphasized her dark eyes. Her hair was pulled back haphazardly into a curly ponytail. She sat across from the detectives in the interrogation room and regarded Mitchell and Jacob with a small smile. Mitchell hated her instantly. There was something patronizing and mocking in her entire demeanor. He despised the feeling that someone was looking down on him.

"So, Ms. Nate—" Jacob said.

"Ricky," she interrupted him sharply.

"Ricky," he said, his rhythm unwavering. "When did you receive the e-mail from the supposed killer?"

"Yesterday at eleven p.m," she said.

"And why didn't you inform us?"

"Like I told your friend, it was late. It didn't seem urgent. I thought I'd wait until morning."

"You received an e-mail from a serial killer, and it didn't seem urgent to call the police?" Jacob raised his eyebrow. "You and I have different perceptions about what's urgent."

She shrugged. "It's not like there's information there you didn't already have," she said.

"We should be the judge of that," Mitchell snapped. "You just didn't want us to stop you from publishing the article."

"Stop me?" she looked at him, clearly amused. "How would you have done that, Detective? Isn't the First Amendment a thing in this country anymore?"

"That's bullshit and you know it. We could have—"

"Ricky," Jacob said loudly, cutting Mitchell off. "Did you have any other contact with the killer?"

"I replied to his e-mail with some questions," she said. "And he didn't answer."

"Had he ever contacted you before?"

"No."

"Are you sure? It could have been a random message on your phone, or an e-mail from a different address—"

"I receive a lot of messages, e-mails, and tweets every day, Detective," Ricky said. "Of course it's possible that one of those was the killer. But if it was, he never identified himself as the killer before, and never mentioned the serial murders."

"Any idea how he got your e-mail?"

"It's available on the *Gazette*'s website," she said. "That's probably how. Or maybe he somehow obtained one of my business cards. They have my e-mail as well. My e-mail is not a very well-kept secret. I'd be a crappy reporter if people had a hard time reaching me."

"Is this the e-mail he sent you in its entirety?" Jacob showed her a printout of the e-mail she'd forwarded to them.

She glanced at the printout. "That's right."

"He doesn't identify himself as the killer here, either," Jacob said.

Mitchell glanced at his own copy. It was unsigned, and fairly brief. It stated what the messages to the victims were, described the images, and quoted the texts, followed by that creepy sentence about beautiful victims. It had been sent from a temporary mailbox site.

"No," she agreed, "But he details all the messages, and says that he only selected beautiful young women. The fact that he's the killer is implied."

"How did you know it wasn't a crank call?"

"I have my sources," she said. "And I'm not going to expose them. Once I had the messages in hand, it was easy enough to validate that they were genuine."

Mitchell wondered if her sources were on the Glenmore Park police force, or Boston's. She probably had sources in both, he thought angrily.

"If the killer approaches you again, please let us know immediately," Jacob said.

"Well…" She grinned at him. "We could both help each other, you know. I can promise to let you know as soon as he contacts me, and you can give me an interview."

"Go to hell," Mitchell said feeling a sudden pulse in his forehead. "You'll let us know, or you'll be charged with accessory to murder."

"Fine," she said, her voice clipped and sharp. Her patronizing look disappeared, replaced with fury.

"Thank you, Ms. Nate," Jacob said.

She left in a huff. Jacob glanced at Mitchell, his blue eyes disappointed. "What's wrong with you?" he asked.

"I don't know," Mitchell muttered, knowing very well what was wrong. He felt guilty for causing this. "She got under my skin."

"You don't want the press to be hostile," Jacob said. "She might look like a snotty woman who's just out to spite you, but she's a reporter. You don't fuck with reporters."

FOURTEEN

Detective Hannah Shor was following a trail of hair—the hairs found in the Toyota Camry that had been used to kill Tamay Mosely.

Matt had sent all the hair to the lab for diagnosis, hoping they might contain some rebellious nuclear DNA, so they could find a match via CODIS. The mayor, or perhaps even the governor, had pulled some strings, and their sample had been pushed to the front of the line. And, lo and behold, one of the strands *did* contain some nuclear DNA.

It matched a woman named Beatrice Smith, who lived in West Virginia. She had been arrested twice for theft, three times for prostitution, and once for drugs found in her possession. No one had any idea what her hair was doing in the car. It did not sound likely she was their serial killer, especially considering the fact that she had been incarcerated at the time Aliza Kennedy had been murdered. Jacob had theorized that the Toyota Camry had been hers before it was Rabbi Friedman's, but a quick investigation found that the Toyota had only had one other owner, a Glenmore Park resident.

There was only one conclusion: Beatrice had ridden in the car as a passenger at some point. Rabbi Friedman vehemently denied ever driving around with a prostitute from Idaho. He was, in fact, fairly specific in his denial; apparently, driving around with prostitutes from someplace other than Idaho might be a different story. He also said, when shown her mugshot, that he didn't recognize her.

Hannah had decided to talk to Beatrice face to face.

She might have tried using the phone in any other case; Idaho was not exactly nearby. But, hey—unlimited resources, right? She booked a flight.

She was assisted by the local police in Nampa, Idaho, who escorted her to a rundown trailer in which Beatrice was known to serve customers. Beatrice—or Clover, as she was known in the area—refused to go to the police station. She reluctantly agreed to talk to Hannah in her trailer.

Now Hannah sat in the cramped space, the smell of sex and sweat clogging her nostrils. All the trailer windows were curtained by a pink cloth, and the light was dim and bluish. A small mini-fridge stood in the corner, an assortment of bills and a small picture of a family tacked on it with magnets. Hannah had politely refused to sit on the bed, knowing if her pants rubbed the bedsheets by accident, she'd throw them away. She sat on a small stool instead, while Clover sat on the bed.

Clover was incredibly pale and thin. She wore almost no makeup except for very light mascara on her eyelashes. She wore a loose, faded blue t-shirt and a pair of black yoga pants. Her black hair was cut short.

"I ain't never been to Massachusetts," she said. "I don't know where Glimmer Park is at."

"Glenmore Park," Hannah said. "Have you ever seen this man?" She showed Clover the sketch they had of the killer.

"Naw."

"How about this man?" She showed her a picture of Rabbi Friedman.

"A religious Jew, huh? I know someone who specializes in those, maybe you should ask her. I never seen him."

"Did you ever ride in this car?" Hannah showed her a picture of the car.

"I rode in hundreds of cars. I've had sex and given blow-jobs in hundreds of cars. Yeah, I might've been in this car, who knows?"

"We've found your hair in the front seat of the car."

"Sure, whatever."

"This car was used to run over a girl and kill her."

Clover did not seem to be shocked by the news. "That sucks," she said. "I ain't never run over a girl in any car."

Hannah sighed. It was a long way to come just to find a dead end, but that was the way of detective work. She began thinking about the flight back. She hoped she'd manage to sleep a bit on the way. She was tired as hell. They'd been working around the clock for days, and it was wearing them thin. She looked around at the trailer once more, then stood up and inspected the picture stuck on the mini-fridge more closely.

"That your family?" she asked.

"Yeah."

"Mount Rushmore, huh?"

"Yeah," Clover shrugged. "I guess everyone goes there at some point."

"I've never been," Hannah said.

"Your time will come."

"You had really long hair," Hannah said. "It goes all the way down to your waist in the picture."

"It was even longer after I showered," Clover said. "It took me hours to brush it."

"Your hair is really short now, though."

"Yeah. I don't like when customers pull it when they fuck me from behind. I'm not a damn horse."

The little details always penetrated deepest. Hannah bit her lip, trying to dispel the upsetting images in her mind. "So you cut it."

"Yeah."

"Did you by any chance sell it?"

"Yeah, sure, how did you know?"

Bingo. "Do you have the name of the place you sold it to?" Hannah asked.

"I have their phone number," Clover said, pulling out her phone. She located the contact, then showed it to Hannah, who carefully copied it to her own phone.

"Thanks," Hannah said, standing up. "I think that's all I need."

"Cool. Glad I could help," Clover said, opening the door of the trailer for Hannah.

"Uh... Listen, Clover..."

"Yeah?"

"I think you keep that picture for a reason, you know? Maybe to remind you of better times? You know, there are people who can help."

Clover nodded thoughtfully. "Yeah. That picture? My dad took it on a family trip, when I was seventeen. I was addicted to crack, and two weeks before that vacation I had just given my first blowjob for a twenty A few days later I was raped. There was a party, and I was unconscious, but I was bleeding when I woke up. I told my mom and she asked me not to say anything to my dad before vacation, because he was under a lot of stress. You know why I keep that picture?"

"Why?" Hannah asked, her voice barely above a whisper.

"Because I like Mount Rushmore. Goodbye, Detective."

The trailer door closed behind Hannah with a click. She should have felt victorious; she had a lead. But at that moment, she only felt sad and useless.

———

He decided to go shopping.

He had already selected his next target. Such a beautiful young girl. He'd watched her the day before, returning home from work. A lowly job, for such a special girl. It was unfathomable. Was he the only one who could see how special she was? How much anticipation she could inspire?

It was time to choose the murder weapon. He knew what he was looking for; he had decided upon it shortly after killing Tamay. That had been such a noisy death. And the way he had lost control and run into that lamppost? It was the closest he had ever come to screwing everything up.

No. This time it would be a quiet death.

But even knowing what he was looking for, there were so many options to choose from! He stood in front of the various samples, touching each one, trying to figure out what would be best for his next endeavor.

He liked shopping.

"Can I help you?" a feminine voice asked. He turned around. Ugh. He would never touch this one. Those pimples, those glasses. Terrible.

"Yes," he said. "I would like some help."

Can you please help me choose a murder weapon? He wanted to say. *I need something that can kill.* He nearly laughed out loud at the thought.

"I really have no idea what to choose." He smiled at the homely woman, thinking of his next victim with anticipation.

———

The trail of hair was now really easy to follow. It was practically a highway of hair.

Hannah had called the phone number of the woman Clover had sold her hair to. That woman had given Hannah the wig manufacturer's name, and managed to find the receipt for the date of the shipment that contained Clover's hair.

Since the wig manufacturer was in Nebraska, Hannah decided to first make sure the hair didn't come from a wig that belonged to the rabbi's wife. If she was anything like many Orthodox Jewish women, Mrs. Friedman had several wigs in her possession. Hannah called Jacob, and asked him to check if it was possible the hair belonged to Mrs. Friedman. A couple of hours later, a very testy Jacob Cooper called her back to say that it did not match any of Mrs. Friedman's wigs, and did she want to hear what he just went through to ascertain this? Hannah told him that she did not.

The wig manufacturer was a bit trickier. They didn't want to share. She had to get the local district attorney over there to issue a search warrant, and then had to enlist the local police to assist with her search. It was a hassle. Any other time, it would have taken weeks, maybe months. This time, one phone call to Captain Bailey, and she was knocking on the wig manufacturer's front door with a search warrant and four patrol officers in uniform to back her up.

She saw a lot of hair and hair-related paperwork in there.

It took her almost all day to understand the way they filed their paperwork, to track the shipment with Clover's hair, to figure out which wigs it was probably used for. She would never have managed it if it weren't for one of the clerks that worked there. She was a bright girl, and helped Hannah connect all the dots. Hannah suspected the girl had a crush on her.

There were over fifty wigs that might have used Clover's hair, and no real way to narrow that number down. The wigs were then sold to several wig distributors, because apparently that was a real job.

Two days. It took her two days to trace those wigs. Two days of calling costume shops, cancer treatment centers, wig salesmen. Thirty-seven of the wigs were traced to various men and women around the country. Five wigs were still on the shelves of various stores. Eight wigs had been sold to unknown individuals whom Hannah could not locate.

Of the thirty-seven names she had, she managed to make sure that thirty-one had tight alibis for at least one of the murders, if not more. That left six names. One of them was an eighty-year-old woman; one was a woman who was going through severe cancer treatments and could barely lift her own purse, let alone strangle and bury Kendele Byers. Three of the remaining four names belonged to middle-aged women; the last was a fifty-year-old man. She filed them under "unlikely suspects."

All she was left with were the eight missing wigs. One had been sold in Boston. It seemed wise to start there.

It took the owner of the costume shop an incredibly long time to find the receipt for the damn wig. It had been bought along with thirteen other wigs, four fake beards, and three fake mustaches. The entire sum of the purchase was $3,452.

It had been paid in cash.

The owner remembered the purchase. It wasn't every day a customer forked over three thousand dollars in cash. However, he couldn't tell Hannah a single thing about the customer, besides the fact that he had a ridiculously thick wad of cash. Apparently, the cash had erased from his memory any trace of the customer's appearance. He gave Hannah a catalog in which he marked all the wigs, beards, and mustaches that the customer had bought. One of the other wigs matched the hair in the sketch that had been made with Rabbi Friedman's help.

Using the catalog and the previous description from Rabbi Friedman, the police sketch artist created several dozen images of how the killer might look with the different props. They now had a mugshot book of how the serial killer could look.

Bernard had finally finished investigating the crimes in Boston, and was back in Glenmore Park. He and Hannah started interviewing relatives of the murder victims, showing them the mugshot book.

Tamay's boss identified one of the pictures. He said a man similar to the one in the pictures had been in the pub twice, just a week before Tamay had been killed. The man had seen Tamay's band perform, and stayed until the bar closed. They'd had to ask him to leave. Yes, he was sure this was the guy. He was a bit different than the picture, but the hair was unmistakable.

Kendele's friend Debbie pointed out one of the other sketches, saying she was sure that guy had been in the restaurant several times.

It was good enough. They had sightings of the suspected killer, and a plethora of sketches that might match him.

FIFTEEN

Candace Wood had been a police dispatcher for over six years. She loved her job, and was pretty good at it, too. She liked the action and the satisfaction of helping people. She adored most of the people who worked with her, the other dispatchers and the cops.

Two weeks ago, the public had learned there was a serial killer in Glenmore Park, whom the press had dubbed The Deadly Messenger. Now Candace was seriously considering a change of work. She had never thought human beings could be so hysterical.

Maybe she could become a kindergarten teacher, like her cousin. Sure, Candace had always felt she would rather shove chili peppers up her own nose on a daily basis than become a kindergarten teacher, but could it really be that bad? Thirty screaming five-year-olds—running everywhere, pulling each other's hair, and crying—sounded just fine right about now.

The public had learned that the killer was sending messages with images of the murder weapon to his victims. And now, the public had a new hobby: driving Candace insane.

The phones never stopped ringing. People got messages all the times. And e-mails as well. Because sure, up until now, the killer had communicated by messages, but who said he couldn't communicate by e-mail?

This day was already one of the worst. She'd had to calm down a man who said he received an image of a very sharp-looking knife. That did sound worrisome, until it turned out he had received the message from his wife, who was thinking of buying the knife for his father's birthday. "Is it likely that your wife is the serial killer?" Candace had asked him.

"You never know," he'd replied.

Then over the next couple of hours she'd talked with dozens of people who'd received images from spammers, associates, and friends. With each call she had to go through the same interview process. It always turned out to be nothing. Her head began to pound.

But the best call had been yet to come. Because the best call came from a completely hysterical woman who said the killer had sent her a picture of his penis.

Candace was sure she had heard wrong. She asked the woman to say that again.

She had heard right.

The woman explained that it was definitely from the killer, because she didn't recognize the number.

Did the woman perhaps give her phone number to someone she didn't know lately, Candace wanted to know. Perhaps someone she was dating?

Yes, she had. The night before. After she had sex with him.

How, Candace questioned patiently, did the woman think the killer was planning on killing her with his penis?

Well, that was the police's job to find out, wasn't it?

Candace had discussed this afterwards with the other dispatcher, Kelsey. Kelsey speculated that maybe the dong in question was long enough to wrap around someone's neck. Candace suggested that maybe it was irregularly heavy, or incredibly sharp. A really sharp dong could do severe damage.

They nicknamed him the "serial dong killer." They drew sketches on the whiteboard. Then Chief Dougherty came in.

They erased the sketches.

It was just a few minutes past midnight when the phone rang again. It was the end of her shift. The dispatcher who would replace her was just sitting down, and Candace nearly let her answer the call. But, on a whim, she decided to take it. Who knew, maybe the serial dong killer had struck again.

"Nine one one, how may I help you?"

"H… Hello?" the frightened voice of a young woman said. "I… I just received a message on my phone. And they said on the news that the killer is sending messages and… and…"

"Yes ma'am," Candace said, trying to remain patient. "What is your name?"

"Ivy. Ivy O'Brien."

"Okay, Ms. O'Brien, what does the message say?"

"It doesn't say anything. There's just an image of a rope on a table."

"I see. And is the message from someone in your contact list?"

"No. I don't know this number."

"What's the number?" Candace asked. The woman dictated the number. Candace looked it up. It was unlisted.

"Ms. O'Brien, when did you get the message?"

"Uh… Fifteen minutes ago, but I didn't notice it at first. I was watching TV."

Candace realized she was tensing up. This was not like the other calls. Still, she kept her voice calm and professional. "Okay, Ms. O'Brien, I'll send a patrol vehicle to your home just to be safe. Are the doors to your house locked?"

"Yes." The woman whimpered. "Do you think it's him?"

"I doubt it, but it's always best to make sure," Candace said. "Is there a room with a lock in your house?"

"Yes."

"Okay," Candace checked the phone number the woman was calling from. It was a mobile phone. "Go to the bedroom and lock the door. I want you to take the phone with you and keep talking to me, okay, Ivy? My name is Candace."

"Okay, Candace."

"What's your address Ivy?"

"It's 27 Sharon Drive"

Candace muted the call and switched to the radio. "Attention, all units, I have a possible ten-five hundred at 27 Sharon Drive." Ten-five hundred was the agreed-upon code for a message from the serial killer. They didn't want to alert the killer in case he listened to police frequencies.

Tanessa Lonnie's voice replied. "Four fifty one, responding."

"Four fifty one, what's your ETA?"

"Dispatch, ten minutes."

Candace bit her lip. If this was the real deal, they were cutting it close. "Four fifty one, we are seventeen minutes after initial contact."

There was a moment of silence, and then Tanessa answered. "Dispatch, I copy. We'll get there as fast as possible." She sounded worried.

Candace hoped they could make it much faster than ten minutes.

She switched back to the phone call. "Ivy, are you in the room?"

"Yes."

"Good. The patrol car is on its way. Don't leave the room until I tell you to, okay?"

"Yes." The girl was crying, her voice terrified.

"Ivy, everything will be okay. You have nothing to worry about."

"Okay."

She did not sound reassured.

———

He was already in the house. He'd wanted to be sure he could get inside before he sent the message. Sure enough, the girl had left the window in the kitchen unlocked, as always. He'd slid inside, making no sound at all, leaped down from the kitchen counter to the floor, and hid. Only after he was in position had he sent the message.

He glanced at the time; twenty minutes had gone by. He quivered with anticipation. Did his victim feel it too? He twisted the nylon rope in his hand. The woman in the store had assured him it could hold very heavy weights, and was easy to knot. He examined the noose for the hundredth time. It seemed tight. He smiled. Anticip…

…ation.

The fun was about to start.

———

Ivy O'Brien sat on the bed, shivering. Should she check the door again? No. She'd checked it twice. Would it even stop him? It was just a wooden door. She looked around for a weapon. Any weapon. There was nothing. Why had she thrown away that vase her mother had bought her? At the time, its flower pattern had turned her off, but it was long and narrow, and would have made a good weapon. She could have used it to keep him at bay.

What was that? Had she heard a creak? It was an old house; sometimes the floor creaked. She was used to ignoring those sounds. But now the small sounds became ominous. Was he slowly walking closer to the bedroom door? She curled into a ball, shuddering, and held the phone to her ear.

"Candace?"

"Yes, Ivy?" Candace's reassuring, firm voice answered her. Candace would not have been so helpless. Candace probably had a gun in her bedroom. Ivy did not believe in possessing guns. She had always been adamant in her belief that gun laws should be much stricter. How stupid her beliefs felt now.

"Are the police here yet?"

"Any minute now. Don't worry."

"I'm scared."

"Everything will be all right, Ivy. No need to be scared. He won't be able to get into your locked bedroom."

"Okay, I…" The words died in her throat.

The bathroom door.

It was closed. Had she closed it at some point? She almost never closed it.

The realization sunk in. He was here. He was in the bathroom. There was no lock on her side of the door.

"Ivy?"

Candace's voice sounded far away. Ivy's heart fluttered, her mind clouded. He was here with her.

"He's here!" she said, choking. "I need to go!"

"Ivy? Ivy, wait!"

The phone tumbled to the floor as Ivy leaped from her bed toward the locked bedroom door. Her hands clutched at the key, shaking. Another creak, much louder than before. She knew what it was: the bathroom door opening.

He was coming. Oh God... Oh God.... ohgodohgo-dohgod...

The key clicked. She flung the door open and stumbled outside, whimpering.

———

Tanessa glanced at Sergio. He moved slowly toward the front door, his gun in his hand. Tanessa drew her own gun, the cold metal reassuring in her palm. She walked toward the back door, as they'd agreed beforehand. Her senses were alert for any noise. Had the killer already entered the house? Candace had reassured them that Ivy was still alive, locked in her bedroom, when they'd parked the car.

She heard a thump from inside the house. A small scream. Both she and Sergio bolted forward, each to his assigned position. She reached the back door in six steps. Shook the handle; it was locked. She took a step back, preparing to kick the lock open, hoping to hell she'd manage to do it before it was too late. She took a deep breath...

The door burst open. A dark figure ran at her. She raised her gun, and nearly pulling the trigger, when the light hit the figure's face. It was a young woman, a terrified look on her face. She almost ran into Tanessa, and screamed in horror. Realization dawned in her eyes.

"He's inside!" she screamed. "He's still inside!"

Tanessa heard something crash. Sergio, kicking in the front door? She hesitated for a moment. Should she stay with the girl and protect her? Or should she back up her partner?

She pointed at the patrol car. "Inside!" she barked at the terrified girl "Lock the doors!"

The girl nodded and ran to the car. Tanessa held her place, listening carefully for any sound, until she saw the girl get into the car. Then she moved into the house, pulling out her flashlight.

The house was dark. Had the killer killed the electricity? No. She could see a light from a room down the corridor. She saw another flashlight beam—Sergio. She aimed the light at his feet to avoid blinding him, and saw him nod at her then point to the corridor. She nodded back.

With Sergio in front, they crept toward the light coming through the half-open door. When they reached it, Sergio kicked the door open and pointed his gun inside.

"Clear," he whispered.

She walked in after him. It was the girl's bedroom. The bathroom door was shut. They both approached it. Tanessa put her back against the wall beside the door. Sergio gently twisted the doorknob, then kicked the door open and pointed the gun and flashlight inside.

"Clear," he said, louder this time.

They searched the rest of the house. It was empty. The killer wasn't there.

———

He approached the girl, his heart beating wildly. She was fast asleep, her rich brown hair spread out on the pillow like a halo. She was facing away from him, but when he towered over her he could see her profile, her small nose, her angelic closed eyes. She really was beautiful. So innocent. So clueless.

He quivered with excitement. So close!

He hefted the rope, carefully bringing it closer.

When he abruptly tightened it, her eyes flew open. But no sound emerged from her mouth.

SIXTEEN

Tanessa and Sergio leaned against the patrol car, watching as a medic inspected Ivy. She'd been hyperventilating so badly that Sergio had called an ambulance.

"What do you think," Sergio asked Tanessa. "Was the message from the killer? Did we stop it?"

Tanessa shrugged. "I have no idea," she said. "It doesn't look like the rest of the messages. It has no text at all. Also, well…"

"What?" Sergio asked.

"She doesn't exactly match the type. Of the victims." Tanessa squirmed uncomfortably. She knew, as a woman who was widely considered outrageously beautiful, that it was not her place to call another girl homely. After all, beauty was in the eye of the beholder, and what mattered was what was on the inside and so on and so forth. Fine, yeah.

But beauty had some standards, even if those standards were crappy and unfair. Ivy was not beautiful. She was far from it. She had a long, sharp nose, and thick, neglected eyebrows. Her teeth were uneven and slightly yellow. She was clearly overweight. Tanessa wasn't judging, and God knew she was lucky to have her mother's genes, but, well…

Up until now, the killer had only killed beautiful women. Not beautiful on the inside. Beautiful on the shallow, discriminating outside. Then again, maybe the killer had a different taste. Or maybe he thought women should be treated equally, no matter how they looked.

"Yeah, but it's a weird message," Sergio said.

Tanessa nodded. Had she saved a life tonight? She wanted to believe that. But it was strange that such a careful killer would simply decide not to show up because he saw a patrol car. It was strange that he would choose to break a very clear pattern. Was he simply messing with them? She wondered if she should call Mitchell. Maybe he'd want to question Ivy.

"Four fifty one, dispatch," her radio rattled.

She pressed the PTT button. "Go ahead," she said.

"Are you still at 27 Sharon Drive?"

"Affirmative."

"There's a reported breaking and entering at 17 Roxbury Drive. A neighbor saw a man climb out a window. It's just two blocks from your location."

"Dispatch, no problem, we're on our way."

Roxbury Drive was indeed just a short distance from Ivy's home, and they reached it in three minutes. They found number 17 easily, parked in front, and got out of the car.

The house was small and a bit shabby-looking. The front yard was unkempt, with weeds growing everywhere. The windows were dark. A dusty white Pontiac was parked in the driveway, so Tanessa figured the residents were inside, probably sleeping. Sergio touched her arm softly. One of the house's windows was wide open.

"Do you think they didn't wake up from the noise of the burglary?" Tanessa asked.

Sergio shrugged. "It's possible. I once answered a morning call, for a burglary. The residents woke up to find the burglars had taken almost all the valuables in the house. Their phones were lying on their night tables, just by their heads, and the burglars took those, too."

"Ugh. Creepy."

"Come on."

They approached the front door. Sergio knocked on it firmly. They waited.

There was no sound. He knocked louder, his fist clenched. "Open up," he said. "Police!"

There was no movement from inside the house. They circled the house, glancing through the windows, and eventually reached a window that looked into the bedroom. Though it was dark, Tanessa could see the silhouette of a woman, lying on the bed, the angle of her body very wrong.

They ran back to the front door. Sergio kicked it open— *Second time in one night,* Tanessa thought— and they entered the house, guns ready. Tanessa turned on the light.

"This is the police," Sergio said loudly. There was no sound. They both hurried to the bedroom, switching on the light as they walked inside.

A young woman lay on the bed, her eyes wide, her body still. There was a rope tied around her throat. As Tanessa ran to her side, horrified, she could easily tell it was the same type of rope as the image Ivy had received.

———

Mitchell parked his car by the ambulance. He was the last guest to arrive to this morbid party. There was a patrol car nearby, as well as Jacob's car and the crime scene unit van. He walked toward the front door, where Tanessa and Sergio stood with somber looks on their faces. Mitchell looked at his sister closely. Her eyes were empty; her shoulders slumped. She seemed deflated somehow, as if this night had taken a heavy toll. *She isn't built for this line of work*, he thought, once again. *It will end up breaking her.*

"Sergio." He nodded at the cop, who nodded back. Mitchell looked at his sister. "Tanessa. What happened here?"

Sergio answered. "A neighbor called at oh-forty. He saw someone leave the house from that window over there." He pointed, and Mitchell glanced over. It was a narrow horizontal window, through which Mitchell could see a small kitchen. Violet stood inside, photographing something. "We arrived at the scene at oh-fifty. We found the resident, a woman named Skyler Gaines, dead in her bedroom, a rope around her neck."

Skyler Gaines. The name triggered something in Mitchell's brain. Where had he seen that name? Then he recalled. She was on Atticus Hoffman's list, another model wannabe. He had talked to her briefly, but couldn't remember what she had said. There was a recording of that phone call back at the station.

"We administered emergency CPR until the medics arrived a few minutes later, but they pronounced her dead on-scene," Sergio said.

"Everyone showed up incredibly fast," Mitchell said, frowning.

"We were answering a call two blocks from here," Tanessa said in a hollow voice, her eyes avoiding his.

"Could the neighbor give a description of the burglar?"

"He said the guy was dressed in black and wearing a mask. He thought he was tall."

"Okay…" Mitchell looked at both of them. "Dispatch told me this could be our serial killer. Was there a message on the victim's phone?"

"No," Tanessa said. "Uh… Maybe, I don't know. We didn't look. But Ivy… the other call… she had a message—"

"I don't understand," Mitchell interrupted her. "What other call?"

"A woman named Ivy O'Brien called dispatch at oh-five," Sergio said.

Tanessa turned away, looking at Violet through the kitchen's window.

"She received a message, with an image of a rope," Sergio continued. "The rope matches the one found on the murder victim's neck. We answered the call at Ivy's, but there was no one there."

"Where is she now?"

"At home," Tanessa said, turning to face him. "We called the other patrol to monitor her house."

"I see," Mitchell nodded. "Thanks, Officers."

He signed the crime scene logbook in Tanessa's hand and walked inside. Jacob was in the bedroom, along with Matt and Annie. The body of Skyler Gaines lay on the bed, looking empty-eyed at the ceiling. She was dressed in blue silk pajamas with the top two buttons undone. She had been beautiful, Mitchell saw immediately. Despite the grim mask of death, it was easy to see the delicate, perfect features of her face.

The room was in disarray, with the bedsheets crumpled in one corner of the bed and a pillow lying on the floor. A small pile of books was scattered by the night table and, discarded next to them, the girl's phone. Mitchell guessed the books and the phone had been struck during a struggle, and tumbled off the small night table. Annie was carefully checking Skyler's hair. Jacob crouched by her side, examining the bed.

Matt was snapping photographs of the room. Mitchell approached him. "Matt," he said, "I want to check her phone for messages. Can you please process it?"

Matt nodded and put down the camera. Turning toward his kit, which was lying on the floor, he said. "Gloves, Detective. Don't mess up the crime scene."

"Here," Jacob said, passing Mitchell a pair.

Mitchell slid the gloves on. "What do you think?" he asked Jacob. "Do you think it's him?"

"Too soon to tell," Jacob said.

"Did Tanessa tell you about the message on the other woman's phone?"

Jacob nodded.

"Do you think it could be a wrong number?" Mitchell asked.

"A wrong number that just happens to belong to a woman who lives two blocks from the murder victim?" Jacob asked. "Doesn't sound likely."

"Maybe he's messing with us."

"Could be. Let's not let him. We should approach this just like any other murder. Follow all the leads. Examine all the evidence."

"Yes, but… There's context here, Jacob. We can't just ignore—"

"We don't know that it's him yet." Jacob said sharply.

"This girl was on Atticus's list," Mitchell said. "Is he still…"

Jacob nodded. "The surveillance team is still on him. I just talked to them. He's sleeping in a motel on the other side of the city."

They had decided to trail Atticus after the previous murder. He didn't match the sketches they had, but he'd still been their number one suspect.

Not any more, it seemed.

"There," Annie said.

Mitchell turned toward her. She was holding a section of the victim's hair. It was much shorter than the rest.

"He cut her hair," Annie said. "This matches the pattern of the previous killings."

"Then there should be a message on her phone," Mitchell muttered.

"Here, have a look," Matt said, handing him the phone. "I got a set of fingerprints from it."

Mitchell took the phone, and checked it. The earliest message was from six hours before. It was a message from Skyler's Mom, reminding her that it was her aunt's birthday. No image from the killer. Mitchell frowned, scanning the earlier messages. Perhaps the killer had sent it earlier this time...

His eyes caught a familiar name. Ivy O'Brien.

"Jacob," he said. "Check this out. Skyler and the woman who got the message were friends." He showed the phone to Jacob.

"Huh," Jacob said. "That's interesting. Maybe they switched phones? So her friend had Skyler's phone and vice versa?"

"No one does that," Mitchell muttered. "That's like... switching underwear."

Jacob stared at him.

"What?" Mitchell said. "A phone is private."

"I am never touching your phone again," Jacob said.

"Yeah, whatever."

"I'm done here, Detectives," Annie said. "This woman died in the past hour. You can see a few red spots in her eyes; those are petechial hemorrhages, which are consistent with death by strangulation. There's some blood and skin under her fingernails, but I wouldn't get your hopes up—there are scratches on her neck that seem to indicate she clawed at her own neck, trying to remove the rope. I doubt it's the killer's. I'll send them for testing, of course."

"Okay. Thanks, Annie," Jacob said.

"Yeah, thanks, Annie," Matt blurted.

Annie blushed, looking away from Matt. "Sure," she said, and quickly left the room. Matt looked after her longingly.

Mitchell sighed. "Matt, is there anything you can tell us?" he asked.

"What? Oh… no. Not yet. I'm just getting started."

"I think we should talk to Ms. O'Brien," Jacob said.

Mitchell nodded heavily.

———

Ivy was still shaken up from the night's ordeal. She glanced out the window once again, making sure the patrol car was there. She felt completely exhausted. After the medics had calmed her down, helping her to control her breathing, she had excused herself and gone inside, bursting into tears as soon as she closed the door behind her. The lock on the front door was broken; the cop had bashed it in when he barged inside. The door wouldn't close properly, and finally she propped a chair against it to hold it closed.

She'd gone to the bathroom, in which no killer had ever hidden, despite her fears. She washed her face, hiccupping and sobbing as she did so. She missed Tom. They'd broken up two months before, because… well because of many reasons, most of which could be summed up with the fact that he was an asshole. But she needed someone to hold her and hug her right now, and Tom could have done that.

The cops had promised her someone would be watching her home until morning. They'd also suggested taking her to the police station. Maybe that was a good idea, she thought. There was no way she was falling asleep after tonight.

Someone knocked on the front door. She sighed and glanced at herself in the mirror. Ugh. Terrible. Her eyes were blotchy and red, her hair a mess. There was another knock. She went over and looked through the peephole. Two men in cheap suits stood on the doorstep.

"Yes?" she asked, not opening the door. It was all a ridiculous charade. The lock was busted. Anyone could walk in.

One of them, a man with a fedora, flipped a badge in front of the peephole. "Detectives Cooper and Lonnie, Ma'am. Mind if we come in?"

She pulled back the chair and the door swung open.

She led them to her small kitchen, where she made them coffee. They gratefully accepted the mugs, and the three of them sat around the small, round table she had bought at a garage sale two years before.

"Do you know if it's him?" she asked them. "The serial killer? Is he the one who sent me the message?"

"It's too early to tell," said the one with the fedora, who had turned out to be bald once he took it off. Detective Cooper, she remembered. "Would you mind if we ask you some questions?"

"Not at all," she said. She was happy for the company. As long as the detectives were here, she was safe from thoughts about lurking killers.

"Do you know a woman named Skyler Gaines?" Detective Cooper asked.

"Of course I do," she said, surprised. She definitely hadn't thought this would be their first question. "She's a good friend of mine."

"When was the last time you talked to Skyler?"

"Uh…" she tried to think. "Two days ago, I guess. Why? What does Skyler have to do with this?"

"We understand that Skyler wanted to be a model."

"Yes, she does," Ivy smiled. "She's really beautiful. She has the perfect face. And her body? I mean… she's probably the most gorgeous woman I know."

"Did she ever manage to find a modeling job?" Detective Cooper asked.

"Not yet," Ivy said. She didn't tell them about the hospital. No point in telling them that. Why were they asking about Skyler, anyway?

"Don't you want to ask me about the message?" she asked.

"We'll get to that," Detective Cooper said, his face serious. "Did Skyler tell you if she met anyone unusual lately? Perhaps she saw someone following her? Was she approached by a stranger online?"

"Nothing that comes to mind," Ivy said slowly. Something wasn't right here. "What's wrong with Skyler? Is she in danger? Did she get a message too? Is she…" she froze, her mouth open. *We understand that Skyler wanted to be a model*, the detective had said. *Wanted*. Past tense. A slip of the tongue. Shaking, she pulled out her phone and dialed Skyler.

The other detective, Lonnie, leaned over and plucked the phone gently from her hand, disconnecting it. He looked at her. His eyes were incredibly sad, and she knew for sure Skyler was gone. She burst into tears.

"I'm really sorry for your loss," Detective Lonnie said softly.

"How did she… how…" Ivy tried to ask, her words unintelligible between the sobs and hiccups.

"She was murdered," Detective Lonnie said.

"By that… that killer?"

"It's too soon to say."

Ivy shook her head and closed her eyes, feeling the need to scream, to hit someone, to break something. This night had been too much—first the fear, then the loss. She couldn't handle it. She couldn't!

She felt a hand wrap around her own. She opened her eyes and saw Detective Lonnie was watching her with his big, sad eyes.

"I know what you're going through," he said, "but it's really important that you try to concentrate and answer some questions. To help us catch the man who did this to Skyler." His eyes were like soft pools of sorrow, and she knew he really could feel her pain. He must have experienced something like it himself, sometime in the past. Slowly she calmed down, feeling like his hand gave her strength.

"She was so full of life," Ivy said, wiping her eyes. "So happy. She was just getting over some really tough crap, and… and…"

"What tough crap?" the other detective asked.

"Oh, nothing really. She wanted to be a model. She was really beautiful, you know? Anyway, she called this modeling agent, set up a meeting. And when he saw her, he told her she was too fat to be a model. Can you believe that? The girl barely had an ounce of fat on her entire body."

The detectives nodded, listening. She talked on, looking at Detective Lonnie. He was really easy to talk to.

"Well, she decided she should go on a diet. It was really aggressive, and she used those dieting pills they sell at the store. I kept telling her she shouldn't, that it was bad for her." Ivy searched for the approval in Detective Lonnie's eyes. He smiled a small, understanding smile, and she felt encouraged. She hadn't told Skyler to stop, really. She had wanted her friend to become a model, and it had looked like the pills were working. But she liked to think she would have stopped Skyler, if she had known what would happen. And that was the important thing, right?

"She took too many, I think," she said. "She ended up in the hospital. She nearly died. I helped her get better. I visited her every day, until she was ready to come home. She said she could never have gotten better without me." The tears started trickling down her cheeks once more, as she slowly got lost in the drama of her own story.

"That's so sad. You're a true friend," Detective Lonnie said. "Ivy, is there any reason that anyone would think that your phone number was actually Skyler's?"

"What do you mean?" Ivy asked, confused.

"Have you two switched phones, or maybe she gave someone your phone number instead of her own?"

"No," Ivy said, frowning. "I can't think of any…" But then she thought of a reason.

Because there had been that day when she saw that advertisement online—the brand new modeling agency, looking for models to represent. She'd thought of Skyler. But she'd been afraid that, if she told Skyler about it, Skyler would start self-medicating again to get thinner and improve her chances.

So Ivy had filled out the form herself, putting in Skyler's details, and attaching some pictures of her friend as well. Except when she put in the phone number, she'd used her own instead of Skyler's. She didn't want them to call Skyler and tell her to get a bit thinner. She thought if they wanted to hire Skyler, Ivy could break the news to her. She was just protecting her friend from the horrible mental toll the modeling world could impose.

She told the detective, and he listened attentively.

"But it was just an ad," she shrugged. "And they never got back to me, so I guess they weren't interested. Is it important?"

The detectives looked at each other. Was it her imagination, or did Detective Lonnie's hand tensed a bit, clutching her own a bit more tightly?

"Well," he said, "it's best if we follow all leads. Do you have the URL to the website?"

"No," she said. "I just clicked an ad."

"When did you see that ad?"

"Three or four weeks ago, I think. On Instagram."

"Can you show me your computer?" His hand let go of hers, and she suddenly realized how warm her own hand had become. It felt nice.

She took him to her computer. He opened her browser, and to her horror, opened the history tab. In her panic, she nearly pushed him away from the computer and unplugged the damn thing. Now he would see that three days ago she had browsed to a porn site, had watched the clip with the firemen. He'd realize she went to porn sites twice, sometimes even three times, a month. What would he think of her then? Her eyes filled with tears once more, this time tears of humiliation and embarrassment.

He scrolled past the link to the firemen video clip, didn't even glance at it. He also didn't pause at the nude pool video. In fact, he didn't seem to notice anything, until suddenly he froze and stared intently at the screen.

"What's that?" he asked, pointing, and her heart plunged. Now he'd noticed. Now he… Oh, hang on.

"I don't know," she said. "I don't recognize this. That's weird, it doesn't even end with dot-com. What's RU?"

"That's a Russian website," Detective Lonnie said, and clicked the link.

The modeling agency form opened on the screen.

"That's it!" Ivy said, relief washing over her. "Well, if they're a Russian modeling agency, it's no wonder they never called back."

"Yeah," Mitchell said. He copied the URL and sent it to his own e-mail. Then he got up and smiled at her. "Thanks for all your help, Ivy." He pulled a card from his pocket and handed it to her. "If you remember anything else, I would be happy if you call me."

She suddenly really hoped she would remember something else.

As the detectives were leaving, she grabbed Detective Lonnie's hand. "Detective," she said. "Will the killer be back for me?"

He looked at her, and said, "No, Ms. O'Brien. The killer will never set foot in here."

And she knew he was telling her the truth. She could see it in his eyes.

SEVENTEEN

Mitchell and Jacob were the last to join the meeting. Mitchell had only been in the chief's office twice before, and it wasn't an experience he relished. Everything in that office spoke of meticulous order, to the point of obsession. The few sheets of paper on her desk were sorted in a single pile, none of them even marginally sticking out. The rest of the desk was completely empty except for a keyboard and a mouse, both shiny and clean. Keyboards and mice were not typically so clean. Mitchell had once upturned his own keyboard and shaken it, and the things that fell from within the cracks and crannies between the keys still haunted him. Nevertheless, he was certain if he did that to the chief's keyboard, not even a crumb would drop. The walls were covered with framed certificates and honorary what-nots.

The chief had made sure they had enough chairs for everyone. Jacob sat on the left-most one, leaving Mitchell to sit between Jacob and Zoe, the forensic psychologist, with Captain Bailey on her other side. Mitchell realized Zoe smelled of shampoo, and he was quite sure it was the same shampoo Pauline used. This, as well as the past sleepless night, made him feel a bit unfocused.

"So," the chief said, her voice sharp and angry. "We have another dead girl."

They all remained quiet.

"I understand that dispatch did get a call, so please explain what happened."

"The wrong girl called," Jacob said. "The killer sent the message to the victim's friend."

"Why?" The chief looked at Zoe.

"It sounds like he was—" Zoe began.

"He did it by mistake," Mitchell interrupted her impatiently. "He had the wrong number." He explained what they had found out.

"So the killer used a modeling ad to get the victim's details?" the chief said.

"That's what it looks like," Jacob said, nodding.

"Can we find out anything from the site? Get a search warrant to look at the host's database? Maybe locate the killer via his credit card?"

"The domain is Russian, and probably so is the host," Mitchell said. "That's definitely intentional. He wanted to make sure it would be tough to trace him through it."

"Can we take it down? Maybe call the Russian host? Explain this to them?"

"Why would we want to?" Jacob asked.

The chief stared at him. "I'm sorry?"

Jacob looked back at her, his eyes calm. "We have the first real lead," he said. "Serial killers are incredibly tough to catch, and now we have a real advantage: we know how he locates his victims."

"But we don't know who's registered on the site," Captain Bailey pointed out. "So how does it help us?"

"We can supply a victim," Jacob said.

The room became deathly silent. If a fly had sneezed at that moment, Mitchell would have been able to hear it wipe its nose.

"That's… interesting," the chief finally said. "And dangerous."

"It's our best move to catch the killer," Mitchell said. He and Jacob had discussed it beforehand. They had both agreed it was a good idea, and they should advocate strongly for it. There was no other way. Mitchell had some ideas of where they could look for the right bait. The state police would probably have policewomen trained for such honey traps, women who could look the part. Or maybe the FBI.

"How would we be able to make sure he takes the bait?" Captain Bailey asked.

"The killer stalks his targets, and he probably starts with social networks," Zoe said. "All the victims had an Instagram profile with some images. I can try and create an Instagram profile that matches patterns in those profiles. I've noticed that all of his victims pose in specific ways that might have gotten his attention."

"Beyond the fact that they're all beautiful, the victims look different from each other," Bailey pointed out.

"Yes," Zoe agreed. "But there are still some patterns. They all have selfies of themselves in bars, some with multiple men. The killer might be targeting women that he thinks of as promiscuous."

"You've just described every Instagram account of any young woman ever," Mitchell said.

"They all have photos with close-ups in which they look downward," Zoe carried on, ignoring him. "The killer is probably attracted to this pose, thinking of it as submissive."

"How can you be sure?" Mitchell asked, frustrated by Zoe's matter of fact voice.

"I can't," she said, looking at him with a raised eyebrow. "I'm mostly guessing. But I'm pretty good at guessing."

"Okay," Mitchell said, deciding to drop it. "I really think it's worth a try. We need to check around, find a cop that's good-looking enough to grab the killer's attention. Maybe state police can help us or…" he slowed down. He suddenly realized everyone except Zoe were looking at him strangely.

"What?" he finally asked.

"We already have a really good-looking cop," the chief said.

"Really?" Mitchell frowned. "Great. Who do you have in…" the rest of his sentence dissipated as realization sank. He turned to Jacob, who was looking back at him, his blue eyes reflecting nothing but innocence; Mitchell realized his partner had known where this would go all along. He was stunned at the betrayal.

"No," he said.

"Mitchell—" Bailey began.

"No!" he said, louder. "She just joined the force a few weeks ago. She's not experienced enough. It's too damn dangerous. I will not allow it. I—"

"Detective Lonnie!" The chief snapped, her voice slicing his words to shreds. He shut up. "Officer Lonnie is perfectly capable of making up her own mind. I will be the only one to decide if this is too dangerous. I remind you that only a few seconds ago you were very enthusiastic about the idea."

Yeah, Mitchell thought. But that was because he had never realized his sister would be the bait.

―――――

Success, it turned out, was way more addictive than Ricky Nate could have ever imagined. When she had started working at the *Gazette*, fame hadn't been foremost in her mind. She mostly worked there because the thought of telling her mother she had been right, and a degree in journalism really had been a waste of time and money, made her nauseous. But the reporters at the New York Times didn't have the *Glenmore Park Gazette* in their CV. It wasn't exactly a stairway to the world of journalistic acclaim.

Until the article about The Deadly Messenger. Her life had changed overnight. Her words had been quoted in dozens of incredibly respected magazines, both online and offline. She'd received e-mails from important people who probably hadn't been aware of her existence the day before. Her mother had called to tell her that Uncle Richie in Boston had read her article and was very impressed.

The day after the article was published was by far the happiest day of her life. Three days later, when she realized the phone calls and e-mails had stopped completely, and her article hadn't been referenced for over twelve hours, she crashed.

She had to get more of that.

Problem was, success was not a drug easily purchased. She couldn't walk up to a guy on a shady corner, pull out a twenty-dollar bill, and ask if he had some triumph and fame.

She had to get it the hard way. She tried writing the killer several times, hoping he would respond, but her fourth e-mail was returned to sender, the e-mail address no longer in existence. She tried to milk all her contacts at the police, but most had nothing to tell her, and those that did kept quiet. She did a follow-up on Tamay's family, and was moderately successful—she was quoted in two medium sized online news sites—but this wasn't the pure thing she had felt before. She needed to do better.

She showed up at Skyler Gaines's funeral. She would never have done it a month before. She had always hated journalists who hounded the grieving parents or widows, refusing to give them space to mourn. But that had been before she became an addict. Now, she needed the story. If she had to invade the privacy of a mourning family, it was a small price to pay.

It was heartbreaking, really. Skyler's mother was clearly shattered, staring blankly at her daughter's casket, completely oblivious to the condolences she received from the people who surrounded her. The father tried to be strong, until he suddenly burst into a fit of loud sobs that echoed in the large chapel.

Ricky kept trying to format what she was seeing and feeling into dramatic, emotion-inducing sentences. *Skyler Gaines was plucked from her loving family's embrace*— No. Plucked evoked thoughts of chickens. *The Deadly Messenger has struck again, stealing Skyler from her loving*— Oh, for God's sake, what was she, in third grade? Some real passion was required here.

Maybe make it more personal. *As I watched Skyler's parents weeping, I couldn't help wondering...* Not bad. Not bad at all. What couldn't she help wondering? About mortality? Motherhood perhaps? She definitely had something there; she just needed to keep at it.

A woman sat beside her, crying, constantly wiping her nose with a limp paper handkerchief.

"I'm sorry for your loss," Ricky told her quietly.

"Thanks," the woman said, blubbering.

"Are you related to the deceased?" Ricky asked.

"No, I'm just her friend," the woman said. "We were very good friends."

"I'm sure you were," Ricky said distractedly, trying to think of a poetic way to describe all the flowers around the coffin.

"He was going to kill me as well," the woman said.

"I'm sorry, what?" Ricky asked, turning toward her in shock.

"The killer. He sent me a message."

Ricky was prepared to dismiss the woman as a lunatic, or attention-starved—she knew what that was like— when the woman pulled out her phone, fiddled with it, and showed the screen to Ricky. Ricky blinked at the image of the rope. It definitely looked foreboding.

"He sent it to me only a few minutes before he killed poor Skyler," the woman said, sniffling. "I think he was coming for me next. But the police showed up."

"Really?" Ricky said, her heart racing. "Do you want to talk about it?"

———

They all knew there was no time to waste. The time between each murder was getting shorter. Two weeks between the last murders. They probably had no more than ten days until the killer would strike again.

Captain Bailey called Tanessa, waking her up. Waking up a few hours after a graveyard shift was a nightmare in itself. When she found out Chief Dougherty wanted to see her, it became even worse. Except it turned out the chief didn't want to chew her ear about anything she did in particular. This was not, contrary to what Tanessa had thought, about the doughnut box incident. No, the chief just wanted to ask if Tanessa would be willing to be bait for a deadly serial killer.

That was all.

Sure, Tanessa said, the image of Tamay's face burning in her mind. She'd be happy to help.

Zoe Bentley, Tanessa, and Mitchell were tasked with creating an Instagram profile to bait the killer. They decided to use Tanessa's own profile, which had images of her from the past year, though she'd neglected it lately. They removed any image which had any connection to the police. Then Zoe began to figure out how Tanessa should pose for the new pictures. What she should wear. Where she should take them. They scanned the profiles of the previous victims. All his victims were between eighteen and twenty-two. Tanessa was twenty-five, but Zoe said it was fine. They'd just lie about her age.

Mitchell was getting on Tanessa's nerves. He kept asking her if she was sure she wanted to do this. He mentioned their parents a couple of times. He talked about how dangerous it was.

Did they really need Mitchell for this? she asked Zoe.

It turned out they didn't. Mitchell was politely told to fuck off.

Meanwhile, Captain Bailey and the rest of his detectives planned Tanessa's cover. Agent Mancuso from the FBI drove over to consult and help. She stressed that there were two important things to pay attention to. One, the killer should be oblivious to the fact that this was a trap. He should see no police presence anywhere. Two, they had to make sure the killer would attack Tanessa from close range. If he chose to shoot her with a sniper rifle, for example, the trap would be left empty, and the bait might end up dead. No. They needed him close enough that the police escort and Tanessa could catch him, while preferably Tanessa should stay alive.

Mitchell, who had walked in on the discussion, was getting very loud. He suggested things like bulletproof vests, a detail of over a dozen people watching Tanessa's every move, and an apartment that had its windows boarded up. Agent Mancuso asked who this guy was. Jacob explained that this was Detective Mitchell Lonnie, who by happy coincidence was the bait's brother.

He was politely told to fuck off a second time.

It took most of the day, but they finally located a small apartment within two hundred feet of a flower shop. She would live in the apartment, and work in the flower shop. This way, they kept her time in the open to bare minimum. The flower shop was on Clayton Road, which was one of the busiest streets in Glenmore Park. There was always another person on shift, sometimes two. It was highly unlikely the killer would strike there. He'd have to strike her at home, or on the route between the flower shop and the apartment.

The killer was clearly stalking his targets, learning their routine. They came up with a simple routine for him to follow: Tanessa would leave "home" at eight and go to the flower shop. She would return home at five thirty, and open the bedroom window in the apartment to "let some air in." Then she'd close the window around eleven, and go to sleep.

There was a drainpipe near the bedroom window. They hoped the killer would try to get into her apartment that way. There was one cop in the apartment, and one cop across the road watching the drainpipe and the window. While she walked to the flower shop, they had someone watching her every step, armed with a sniper rifle. There was a camera aimed at the front door, another one on her window, and two cameras inside the apartment, all their feeds sent directly to dispatch.

Tanessa felt it was too much. The killer would send her a message, after all. They would know beforehand that he was coming for her. Zoe didn't agree. She pointed out that the time between the message and the murders might get shorter, just like the time between murders was becoming shorter. The killer seemed to be getting impatient. It was best to be prepared.

Tanessa's phone was tapped; every message she received appeared directly on a monitor in the dispatch center. Dispatchers were instructed to pay attention to that monitor. Nobody wanted the message to go unnoticed when the time came.

Bernard and Hannah were tasked with talking to all the women on Atticus's list of models and wannabe models, yet again, to make sure none of them had registered on the killer's site. As it turned out, three of them had.

Twelve hours later the three women all posted on Facebook, Instagram and Twitter that they were going away for a short while. One of them was taking a surprise vacation. One was visiting a sick relative. The third was going on a business trip.

The three women were relocated to a safe, unknown location, escorted by heavily-armed bodyguards.

The police could only hope there weren't any women who had registered on the site and weren't on Atticus's list.

Tanessa moved into her new apartment that evening, then her details were added to the killer's website.

The trap was set. It was time to see if the predator took the bait.

EIGHTEEN

He kept glancing at his laptop, trying to postpone the moment. Anticipation. Was there anything better? And now the entire city brimmed with it. They all wondered when and where he would strike. Who would he choose this time? Young women all over Glenmore Park slept uneasily, wondering if they were next. Others thought of their sisters, daughters, girlfriends, wives, neighbors. Who would it be? It was not exactly anticipation they were experiencing, of course. It was dread.

But every coin had two sides. His anticipation was so much stronger because of their dread. And finally, finally! It was almost like the first time: him postponing the moment, half because he wasn't sure he could go through with it, half because the anticipation drove him into a frenzy of excitement he'd never felt before. Her dread as she realized what was about to happen, the fear in her eyes, exciting him even further. He'd been chasing that moment ever since.

The first time was special. And when you were young, everything was more exciting. Now, he had to make an entire city dread him to feel the same.

But it was wonderful.

Was it time to select his next victim? Surely he could postpone it only a bit longer?

Anticip…

He stood up, prepared a cup of coffee. Not too much sugar; he was slowly cutting back. When he'd been young, he would drink coffee with two spoons of sugar. Two! Now he was down to half. He sipped slowly, imagining the caffeine mixing in his blood, increasing his excitement even further. Finally, he finished the cup, washed it in the sink, dried it carefully with a towel.

…ation.

He gave in, sat at the laptop, and turned it on.

He had fourteen to choose from. Someone new—good. He'd check her out later. After all, he pretty much knew who it was going to be. He had followed her for a while already. She went to the gym every Thursday, taking a shortcut through that alley. Who wouldn't? If she went all the way around, it would take her ten minutes more. So what if the alley was dark, and narrow, and long, with many places for someone to hide. Ten whole minutes! Wasn't it worth it? He smiled as he opened her details. She was gorgeous. He browsed to her Instagram profile, to look at her pictures yet again.

The smile died away.

She was going to visit a sick relative. She didn't know when she would be back. His fist crashed inches from the laptop. Damn it! What about routine? Didn't she care about her routine?

How could he plan anything if people broke their routine? Half the anticipation revolved around the planning. He gritted his teeth. Fine. He would choose someone else.

He skimmed through the profiles. Some didn't live in the city, although his ad was targeted at residents of Glenmore Park. Some didn't feel right, either too old or not pretty enough. They had to be pretty, like *she* was. One was too young. He opened the details of the new girl.

Well, now.

This one. She was something else. Looked a bit too old. He glanced at her age. Twenty-one. Huh. Well, young women kept trying to look older and more sophisticated than they were. He looked at her for a while. Those lips… that smile… perfect color, tender but somehow sexy as well.

Just like *her* smile. He looked for her Instagram profile, opened it. Scrolled through it a bit.

In the small apartment, the killer smiled. He'd found his new target.

———

"Can you believe that woman?" Mitchell was clearly enraged, his voice too loud in Tanessa's ear. She turned the phone's volume down a bit and took a sip from her coffee mug. She'd drunk a lot of coffee in the past forty-eight hours. After more than two months on the force, her body was completely accustomed to night shift. Suddenly flipping to day shift was a lot harder than she'd thought it would be.

"Mitchell, what are you so mad about? She's a journalist. That's what they do. They report the news."

"She says we were at the wrong house! She makes us sound like incompetents!"

"Well… we *were* at the wrong house," Tanessa pointed out, turning the volume down a bit more. Her brother was giving her a headache.

"Yes! Because the killer made a mistake! The killer is incompetent, not us!"

"Well, that doesn't sound like a very good news story. *Incompetent killer still on the loose* sounds a lot less newsworthy than *Incompetent police save the wrong girl*," Tanessa said. "Besides, she probably didn't find out about the website, so she thinks that the killer misled us."

"She's going to get us taken off this case," Mitchell muttered.

"I doubt it. She's just one reporter."

"Well, I'm going to question her again. I want to know where she got the info."

"Fine, you do that. Meanwhile, I need to go and sell some flowers," Tanessa said.

"Yeah, okay. Take care."

She hung up, grabbed her purse, and took off. Despite herself, she felt her body tense as she left the apartment. She glanced over her shoulder constantly while she locked the door.

As she walked to the flower shop, she had to force herself to avoid looking around, searching for *him*. Either he was watching her or he wasn't. If she kept looking for him, he might realize this was a trap. She had to walk as if she had no cares in the world. *Tralala*, young Tanessa going for her shift at the flower shop, blatantly ignorant of the psycho killer who might be stalking her. It drove her insane.

Her phone beeped, making her heart leap. She checked the display. It was just Richard, her other annoying brother, messaging to check up on her. She got her breathing under control and replied that she was fine but, if he didn't mind, she'd rather he simply called instead of sending her a message.

Messages were suddenly a foreboding thing. A message could potentially contain an image of the murder weapon which would be used to kill her.

She reached the flower shop, *Hummingbird Blossoms*, and walked inside. George, the owner, welcomed her with a smile. She smiled back and glanced around the shop. She couldn't help it. They were working under the assumption that the killer wouldn't strike in the flower shop.

What if the killer wasn't informed?

It was a small shop. The front room had a tall wooden counter with a cash register, and other than that there were only flowers. Thousands of flowers. The bursts of bright colors and the strong, sweet smells that intermingled in the air played havoc with Tanessa's senses, which were used to darkness, dim colors, and the scent of the patrol car's interior. She was constantly in a state of sensory over-load, breathing short breaths to avoid inhaling too much, or staring at the bare floor to rest her eyes. This was a problem in her cover that they hadn't anticipated, and it was now too late to change it. Once again, she could only hope the killer wouldn't strike while she was in the shop. Hopefully in a few days she would get used to it.

"Help me get the front up?" George asked.

"Sure," Tanessa said.

Each morning, when George opened the shop, he'd organize a colorful display of flowers on the sidewalk. He'd place them in large black buckets on a small table, and around the table on the ground. The result was a small mound of colors, easily the most eye-catching thing on the entire street. As Tanessa and George carried the buckets of flowers outside, she noticed him glancing at her several times, frowning.

She looked at him curiously. He was fifty-ish, his hair white, his skin a pale pink, his eyes beaming happily around. If Santa Claus had had a cousin, he'd have looked like George. She wasn't sure how much he knew, but he wasn't entirely ignorant. The flower shop hadn't really been looking for extra hands, and George somehow knew Captain Bailey. Had Captain Bailey told him she was a cop? Did he know she was bait?

They finished organizing the display and walked back inside. She was sweeping the floor when the door was flung open. Without her even realizing it, her hand went to her side, where she typically kept her Glock while on duty. But there was no gun there. Her heart pounded as a young man entered the store, walked over, and asked what kind of flowers were best to say *I'm sorry*.

The anticipation and fear were driving her out of her mind. She wished the killer would strike already.

———

All day, Pauline had been dreading the moment the apartment door would open. She'd called in sick that morning, knowing she was in no shape to work. When the door finally opened, she was nearly relieved. The waiting game was over.

Mitchell walked inside, his face deep in thought, his forehead in the constant frown that had been her companion for the past month. It had been even worse for the past week, ever since his sister started acting as bait for the serial killer. He was constantly tense, snapping at her for no good reason, occasionally staring into nothing, ignoring her completely.

"Hey," he said distractedly, as he saw her standing in their living room. "Sorry I'm so late."

He was, in fact, comparatively early. It was only half past nine in the evening. He usually came home after midnight these days, crawling into bed beside her while she was already asleep.

He appeared to notice her face. Her red eyes, swollen from endless crying.

"What's wrong?" he asked, worry and care in his voice, and his concern nearly shattered her to bits. He walked forward to hold her, and she took a small step back, raising her hands. He stopped, puzzled.

"I'm leaving," she said. "I'm sorry."

She could see the incomprehension on his face, his brain trying to parse the information in a way that would not mean what it actually meant. Perhaps she was quitting work. Or perhaps she was leaving for a short trip to Paris, would be back within a week.

"I don't think we should be together," she added, to dispel the confusion. Bring in the hurt. "We're too different, Mitchell. It won't work."

"But it is working," he said.

"No," she said. "It isn't. Not for me."

He seemed completely stunned and, not for the first time, she wondered how someone who tracked criminals for his living, deciphering the smallest clues, could be so blatantly blind.

"I don't understand," he said. "We should talk about this."

She shook her head, her throat clenched tight, the words refusing to come out. It was too late to talk. Yes, she should have talked, a month ago, or three weeks ago, when she had realized that she wasn't happy anymore, that she hadn't really been happy for a long time. But he was never there; he was always at work, chasing the serial killer, and she'd been left alone with her thoughts. And when they did talk lately… it was always about the case. Every conversation they had, tainted by grisly murders, panty-sniffing perverts, hookers, drug dealers, domestic abuse. She had been innocent once, had truly believed that people had beauty within them. But innocence and ignorance apparently went hand in hand, and now she felt and knew different.

"Pauline," he said. "I love you. I want to make this work."

His eyes were so sad and hurt. Not the sadness everyone thought they saw in him, the sadness he claimed was a product of eyebrow maintenance. Real sadness. His entire face crumpled in true loss. And she nearly relented, nearly said okay, maybe they should go to couples therapy, try to spend more time together.

But it was too late, wasn't it? There was a third entity hovering above this conversation. Someone else.

She had met Paul at work. He came for a standard check, his teeth perfect and white. He began flirting with her, and asked her name. When she'd told him, he burst out laughing, said there was no point in talking further. They couldn't possibly hook up. A couple named Paul and Pauline should not, under any circumstances, be a thing. She loved the way he laughed, the way he joked about everything, taking nothing too seriously. She had never thought of herself as someone who could be unfaithful, but with Paul it became clear that it was about to happen despite her self-perception. And she'd made a decision.

"It won't work," she told Mitchell, a tear trickling down her cheek. It was a wonder there were any of those left. She'd been crying the entire day, as she scrolled through their pictures on her laptop, as she packed, as she tried to write half a dozen letters that would explain how she felt, crumpling up the paper each time.

His face changed, the ever-sorrowful eyes narrowing angrily, his jaw clenching hard.

"Fine," he said. "Fuck off, then."

And she did.

NINETEEN

The hot shower after a workout was probably Janice Hewitt's favorite time of the day. The sensation of the powerful torrent of steaming water on her exhausted muscles easily surpassed any other earthly joy. This was why she typically showered for twenty minutes, and sometimes—when the day was really tough—even half an hour.

But every shower had to end eventually. She sadly turned off the water and stepped out, wrapping herself with a towel. She walked to the bedroom and approached the bed, where she had prepared a clean set of clothes beforehand. On the nightstand, her phone was blinking; she picked it up and glanced at it, her hand already reaching out to pick up her underwear.

Her hand froze in mid-air.

There was a message from an unknown number waiting for her. It was an image of a large chainsaw placed on a small table. Underneath, three words. *See you soon.*

She glanced around her, her heart beating wildly. The bedroom door was ajar, and through it she could see into the corridor. She moved aside, pressing her back to the wall so as to see the entirety of the corridor. There was no movement. She looked at the image again, making sure she had seen correctly, then dialed 911.

The call didn't go through. She tried again, achieving the same result. Something was wrong with her phone.

Her breath was shaking slightly as she slowly crept out of the bedroom, down the corridor, to the front door. Her eyes kept glancing around, searching for any sign of movement. Her entire body was tense, ready to bolt. She reached the main door and peeped through the peephole. She could see the hallway of the apartment building. It was empty. She hesitated for a minute, then unlocked the door, and pulled it.

It wouldn't budge. She pulled it harder. Nothing. The door was stuck.

She forced herself to breathe deeply. She had to act quickly, time was moving fast. Her mind whirred, processing the last few minutes. The man who had sent her this message thought she was trapped in the house with her phone disabled. She had to outmaneuver him somehow, and fast. Before he showed up with a chainsaw in hand.

Her laptop! She dashed to the living room. The laptop was there, on the coffee table. It was already on. Wasn't there a way to contact the police via chat? She was sure there was. Her fingers flew over the keyboard, typing furiously. She entered the Glenmore Park Police Department site and scanned it. There was no chat, only a "Contact Us" link. Damn.

She searched wider, looking for "Police chat USA." Okay, there were quite a few there. Apparently she could chat with the police in Arlington, Texas. Good enough. She clicked it. The chat window opened.

This is the Arlington police online assistance, how can I help?

She thought for two seconds. She had to get this right.

I live in Glenmore Park, Massachusetts. I just received a message from a murderer, and he's about to kill me. I am trapped in my home, my phone doesn't work and the door won't open. Please help.

She waited for a moment, praying that whoever it was in Arlington would take her seriously.

This is the Arlington, Texas Police chat. We don't respond to calls from Massachusetts.

Of course. Nothing was ever easy. *Please*, she typed. *Just call the Glenmore Park PD. Let them know. I can't reach them. I have no time. He will kill me.*

After a second, the response appeared: *What's your address?*

She breathed in relief. She typed in her address. Then she waited. Something in the house creaked. He was there with her, she was sure of it. She was running out of time.

They're on their way.

Good. Now it was time to—

A figure dressed in black stepped into the living room, a chainsaw in its hand. Janice screamed and stood up. The towel wrapped around her unfastened and dropped to the floor.

The man with the chainsaw stepped forward.

─────

Officer Neal Fuller was thrilled to realize their patrol car was the first on the scene. All units had been called to a possible attack by the serial killer the press had dubbed The Deadly Messenger. Details were scant, since dispatch hadn't gotten a lot of information from the caller.

It was an apartment building. Five floors, no elevator, and the slight whiff of pee around the bottom stairs. It all vaguely registered as he dashed up, jumping two stairs at a time, knowing there was no way Markus, his partner, could ever keep up. After all, Neal was twenty-two, fresh from the academy, and in great shape. Markus was forty-three, with a beer gut and a knee that acted up occasionally.

Neal zoomed up the stairs, adrenaline kicking in to help him run faster than he had ever done before. He was breathing heavily as he reached the top floor, and he knew he should wait for backup, but he also knew it was an emergency and there was no time. He rushed to the door and thumped on it.

"Police!" he shouted.

There was a high-pitched scream from inside. Neal tried the door. It was unlocked, but for some reason it wouldn't budge more than an inch. Something was blocking it.

He took a step back and threw himself at the door. There was the sound of wood splintering, and he felt something give. From inside, a woman shouted for help. He could hear a man shouting something as well. He hit the door again, and the thing burst open. Neal nearly lost his balance as his body kept moving forward into the apartment.

There was a large room on his left. A man, dressed entirely in black and wearing a ski mask, was facing him. Behind the man, Neal could see the screaming woman, naked, cowering on the couch.

Neal's gun was already aimed directly at the man's chest.

"Don't shoot!" the man screamed, his arms in the air. "Don't shoot!"

Neal's finger was on the trigger, pressing ever so lightly. He almost fired, already tensing for the gun's recoil.

"I'm unarmed!" the man shouted. "Don't shoot!"

"On your knees!" Neal screamed. "Hands above your head! Do it! Now!"

For a moment the man hesitated.

"Now!" Neal shouted again.

The man fell to his knees, raising his hands high above his head and Neal was on him, pushing him to the floor, cuffing his hands behind his back. As he cuffed the man, Neal saw what was lying on the floor: a chainsaw. The sick fuck had been about to kill the woman with a chainsaw. Neal kicked the man, who fell to the floor with a scream. The woman whimpered in fear.

"It's okay!" Neal told her, trying his best to look only at her face and failing miserably. "We got him!"

The woman fumbled at the floor, where a white towel lay discarded. She clumsily wrapped herself, shaking.

"Please!" she said. "Just get him out of here!" She hid her face in her hands.

Neal realized Markus was standing behind him, ogling the woman.

"Help me out here," he said, pulling the man to his feet.

"You don't understand—" the man began.

"Shut up!" Neal shouted, shaking him roughly. "Shut the fuck up!"

They manhandled the man downstairs, ripping the mask from his face in the process. He was young, no more than twenty-five, his forehead sweaty, his face fearful. He tried to talk once again, and Markus shook him roughly. He stayed quiet after that.

Neal grinned at Markus as they dragged the suspect out. He thought of his mother. Perhaps this weekend his family would be talking about Neal, and not about damn Peter and his successful business. This time, Neal would give his mother a reason to be proud.

There was a reporter outside. How the hell had they heard about this already?

"Officer?" The reporter rushed at him. "What happened?"

"We got him," Neal said, drunk with victory, already imagining the newspaper in his mother's hands. "We got The Deadly Messenger."

TWENTY

"There's something wrong with all this," Zoe told Mitchell.

He looked at her blankly. His eyes itched from lack of sleep, and he felt disconnected from the whole thing. They'd caught the killer. Yay. All he wanted was to go back home and lie on his bed, staring at the ceiling, like he'd done pretty much the entire previous night. Recalling his past conversations with Pauline, trying to find hints he'd missed, anything that indicated she was about to leave.

"Mitchell, are you listening to me? I don't think it's the guy."

"He sent a message with a murder weapon to his victim. He was literally caught attacking her with a chainsaw. He's the guy, Zoe."

"He was not caught attacking her. I just talked to the cops who arrested him, and—"

"Zoe, he's the damn guy! Let this go!" He didn't realize he was shouting until he noticed everyone in the squad room staring at him.

Zoe bit her lip, then went back to sit at the makeshift desk they had provided for her. She grabbed some papers and stared at them, her face red.

"Look," Mitchell said, taking a deep breath. "Jacob is on his way over here, and then we'll interrogate this guy, and get a confession from him. Do you want to join us in the interrogation?"

Zoe remained silent, facing away from him. Mitchell sighed, and sat at his desk. He stared at his dark monitor, drained, and thought about the engagement ring. He should return it. He briefly wondered what would have happened if he had proposed in the past weeks, instead of constantly postponing it, waiting for the right moment. Would Pauline have said yes? Would she still be with him? It was not the first time these thoughts had occurred to him. Nor the second. They'd been spiraling in his brain over and over, a merry-go-round of self-loathing and sadness.

Jacob entered the squad room, smiling.

"I understand that we have a good reason to celebrate!" he said. He'd been in Boston when the arrest transpired, examining the places where the serial killer had previously hit.

Both Mitchell and Zoe turned to face him. His smile drained from his face.

"What's wrong?" he asked.

"I don't think it's the guy," Zoe said.

"Why not?" Jacob asked. "I understand that the M.O. is identical."

"It isn't," Zoe said. "When the police walked in they found the guy in the living room, the victim still alive, the chainsaw on the *floor*."

"Maybe he had some technical problems," Jacob suggested. "A chainsaw can be a tricky thing to use."

"This killer always plans ahead," Zoe said impatiently. "Do you really think he wouldn't have made sure that he could turn on a chainsaw? Besides, the way he was dressed—completely in black, and a white hockey mask?"

Jacob furrowed his brow. "That's what he was wearing?" he asked.

"Yeah! Does this sound right to you?"

"What's wrong with that?" Mitchell asked sharply. He knew damn well what was wrong with it. It was completely off. But he clung to his conviction as if he believed it. Just like he had believed everything was all right between Pauline and him until the moment of truth.

"Seriously?" Zoe glanced at him contemptuously. "A white hockey mask? It's a prop! It's something that someone would wear after watching *Friday the 13th*! Do you really think that this guy would do that?"

"Who knows what he would do?" Mitchell said. "He's a psycho! Maybe he always wanted to be just like Jason when he grew up!"

Zoe shook her head. "Whatever. Do you know what the message he sent said? It said *see you soon*. This is not a serial killer. This is a serial killer wannabe."

"So what do you think?" Jacob asked Zoe, his eyebrow raised. "A copycat?"

"Maybe," Zoe said. "But he's not the guy, I'm almost certain."

"Well," Jacob said. "Let's talk to him and find out."

———

Danny Stevenson was scared, aching, and nauseous. He'd thrown up in the patrol car, to the cops' immense displeasure, but had done nothing to alleviate the queasy feeling in his stomach. That was partly due to the punch in the gut he had received earlier. The bastard cop had fists of steel. Danny felt as if something had been dislocated.

He looked around him. The room was stark, the furniture almost nonexistent. One simple metal table and three chairs, the one on which Danny sat, and the two on the opposite side of the table. His hands were still in handcuffs. Until they'd reached the police station, his hands had been cuffed behind his back. Once they'd entered this room, they had removed the handcuffs, pulled his arms roughly forward, and locked them again. They had tightened the cuffs too much, and his hands were slowly turning red. He moved his fingers, trying to get the blood flowing. It hurt. Everything hurt. His eyes filled with tears of pain and fear.

How had such a simple, elegant plan become such a mess? The whole point was that Janice wouldn't be able to call the cops! That was why he'd blocked outgoing calls on her phone in the first place. And he still couldn't understand why—

The door opened, and two men and a woman walked in. The woman carried a small folding chair. She unfolded it and sat in the corner, looking at him as if he was a garden slug on her doorstep. The two men sat in front of him.

The bald man began talking, reciting the sentences Danny knew so well from movies and TV shows. He had the right to remain silent. He had a right to an attorney. Danny tried to speak once, but the bald man simply raised a finger, as if to hush him, and kept reciting Danny's rights. When he was done, he pushed forward a piece of paper and a pen. Danny stared at them. The same words were written on the paper, and the bottom had a line for a signature.

"What's this?" he asked.

"Sign it," the bald man answered.

"But what is it?"

"It just clarifies that you've been read your rights and that you understand them."

Danny clumsily picked up the pen and signed the paper with his left hand, his right hand hanging uselessly in the air.

"You're left-handed?" the bald man said.

"Yeah, so what?"

"So nothing," the bald man said. "I'm Detective Jacob Cooper. This is Detective Mitchell Lonnie, my partner, and that's Zoe Bentley, from the FBI. What's your name?"

"D... Danny. Danny Stevenson." Danny said and looked at Detective Lonnie. The man stared at him with blank, empty eyes, as if Danny was nothing. This was almost more disconcerting than the hostile looks he was receiving from Detective Cooper and Bentley.

"Danny," Detective Cooper said. "Would you care to tell us why you tried to kill Janice Hewitt?"

"I didn't! I swear! You got it all wrong! Janice is my girlfriend! It was just a prank!" Danny said, a hysterical note crawling into his voice.

The surprise on the detectives' faces was palpable. Clearly this wasn't what they were expecting. Well, he had tried to tell it to the cops who had arrested him, but they had threatened to tase him if he said another word, so he'd shut up.

"Janice is your girlfriend?" Detective Cooper repeated.

"Yes! You can call and ask her!"

"This was a… prank?"

"Yes! Janice and I… that's what we do! We prank each other! We're famous for it!"

"Attacking your girlfriend with a chainsaw is not exactly my idea of a prank," Detective Cooper said.

Well, that was hardly surprising. The old detective probably thought a whoopee cushion was the best prank ever. Danny shook his head. "I never attacked her. Look, here's what I did. It was supposed to be really simple. Janice does these really long showers after a workout. While she was showering, I installed a small application that blocked her phone from making outgoing calls, and placed a small wedge under the front door. Then I hid in the apartment, in this disguise with my chainsaw, and sent her the message—"

"You admit you sent her the message," Detective Lonnie interrupted him.

"Yeah, sure. I mean, that was the entire point. I wanted her to think that this serial killer was coming for her." Danny almost smiled. Things were looking up. Surely they'd understand their mistake. How he and Janice would laugh about this later…

"This is your idea of funny?" Detective Cooper stared at him, his eyes wide, his nose crinkling in disgust.

"Sure," Danny shrugged. "Not just me. I mean, Janice thought it was hilarious, too."

"What do you mean?" Detective Lonnie asked.

"Well, I showed up, and she screamed so loud, I nearly went deaf. And then I took off my mask, and she saw it was me. We both laughed so hard!"

"You were wearing the mask when the cops showed up," Detective Cooper pointed out.

"Well… yeah. I mean… Janice thought it would be funny to have sex like that. So she asked me to put on the mask. And then you guys showed up."

"She was screaming for help," Detective Lonnie said.

"It was just part of the fantasy! Look, just call her. She'll tell you! You've got it all wrong!"

The detectives glanced at each other.

"I'll be right back," Detective Cooper said. He stood up and walked out of the room.

They sat in silence. Danny was feeling better, though he still hurt all over.

"Can you loosen the handcuffs, please?" he asked. "I can hardly feel my hands."

Detective Lonnie stared at him as if he hadn't said anything. As if he wasn't even there. Something was wrong with this guy. Danny glanced at Bentley. She was looking at him thoughtfully, but did not appear as if she were about to help with the handcuffs. Something in her eyes scared the shit out of him. He felt as if she could stare into his brain and read his memories. Danny shuddered and waited.

Finally, Detective Cooper walked in, and sat down.

"I'm afraid I have some bad news," he said. "Janice's sister answered the phone. She said that Janice was currently in shock, and she couldn't come to the phone. The trauma of being attacked by a serial killer was too much for her, that's what she said."

Danny smiled. He'd underestimated the old detective. This was a guy who could see the opportunity for a good prank when it showed up. "Nice," he said. "I mean… really funny. So, she told you, right?"

The detective lifted an eyebrow. Danny waited.

"As I said, I only talked to the sister," the detective said.

Danny blinked. He didn't understand. Did the guy really think… and then the pieces fell into place. He suddenly recalled how Janice had asked him to put on the mask. How she'd shrieked even when the cops were in the apartment. How she hadn't stopped them when they had taken him away. Danny had thought it was because she didn't want to run outside wrapped in a towel.

The police hadn't shown up by mistake. She had somehow managed to contact them. She had known all along that it was him; he hadn't fooled her for even one second.

That bitch. He wanted to kill her. He wanted to kiss her. It was the most brilliant double prank she had ever played.

"She's messing with me," Danny told the detectives. "She knew all along. That's why she's acting as if I'm the real killer. She's the one pranking me!"

"I've had enough of this," Detective Lonnie snarled, and slammed his hand on the table. "You sent the message! You attacked Janice with a chainsaw! You are the one who killed Skyler Gaines, Tamay Mosely, Kendele Byers—"

"No! It was just a stupid prank!"

"We'll find the evidence, Danny! We have eyewitnesses who can identify you! You'll be lucky if you don't get the death penalty, Danny!" Detective Lonnie leaned over the table, his eyes wide and red, spittle flying from his mouth. The man was clearly deranged.

Danny suddenly thought of dirty cops who tailored evidence to the case, cops who hit a suspect until he signed whatever confession they wanted. Would he end up in jail? Getting the death penalty? It was just a prank!

Detective Cooper seemed more or less reasonable, as well as Zoe Bentley. They were both looking at Detective Lonnie as if they were surprised by his outburst. Danny just had to keep his mouth shut until Janice or his attorney showed up. He turned to look at Detective Cooper.

"I'm not saying another word until I get my phone call," he said.

———

"What the hell happened in there?" Jacob asked Mitchell furiously once they were out of the interrogation room. "I've seen rabid dogs act more sensibly than you! Of course he lawyered up! Even Mother Theresa would have asked for her attorney after your outburst!"

"I know!" Mitchell spat back angrily. "I just couldn't take it anymore! Have you ever heard such bullshit?"

Jacob stuck his finger in Mitchell's chest. "Yes!" he said. "Yes, I have! And so have you! People give us bullshit there every day. It's the bullshit room, and we're the number one bullshit consumers! That's our job, to listen to bullshit, and then figure out what's actual shit and what isn't. Now here's what I want you to do. I want you to go home, and sleep off whatever the hell it is you're on. Stay away from this guy until you get it together, got it?"

Mitchell thought he might punch Jacob, or just tell him to fuck off, but Zoe joined them. She gave him a look that made him feel like a three-year-old who'd had a temper tantrum because he didn't want to eat his porridge. He turned around and walked away, furious.

Damn Jacob. Who the hell did he think he was? As if *he* hadn't lost *his shit* with that pedophile case they'd had a year and a half ago. Mitchell had had to pull him out of the room before he killed the suspect. So yeah, he got angry, made the suspect a bit defensive. Bernard and Hannah did it all the time in the interrogation room—good cop, bad cop. It got results every now and then, didn't it?

He barged into the squad room, banging the door against the wall, and sat down at his desk. He wasn't sure what he wanted to do, but his mind felt hazy with rage. He had to calm down, had to think it through. He had never lost his temper like that before, and he knew very well it had nothing to do with the damn case. He needed to talk to Pauline, to understand what had happened. Maybe he could still fix this. He'd bought an engagement ring only a few weeks ago. This girl was the love of his life; he couldn't let her go without a fight!

"Hey, Mitchell, the word about the arrest is out," Hannah told him from her own desk.

"What?"

"Yeah. Check it out. I just sent you a link."

Mitchell opened the e-mail she'd sent, clicked on the link. It was the *Glenmore Park Gazette*. The headline read *Police Arrest Suspect in Deadly Messenger Case*. Mitchell read it through in disbelief. How had they heard already?

There. One of the cops who'd arrested Danny Stevenson had actually talked to a reporter. Idiot. But who had tipped the reporter in the first place? He glanced at the reporter's name. Ricky Nate. Yet again. The woman was a vulture. There it was, the rage again. He shut his eyes.

Danny Stevenson was not the serial killer. Mitchell didn't need Zoe to point it out. He'd known it as soon as he'd heard about the arrest. A bumbler caught with his chainsaw on the floor? Letting the victim contact the police, moving slowly enough to let them get there *while his victim was still alive*? Of course he wasn't the deadly, careful serial killer. But was he telling the truth, or had he really been trying to kill his girlfriend?

He'd said that he and his girlfriend pranked each other, that they were famous for it. Weird way to put it. He hadn't said they were known for it, as if all their friends knew about it. He said they were *famous.*

Mitchell was vaguely aware that pranks had infested the internet lately. You couldn't go a day without someone sharing a video in which some guy pranked his friend, or mother, or sister. Watch how I convince my brother his dog died. Check it out as I run at random people in the street, dressed as a rubber chicken. Click this video, in which I tell my girlfriend I cheated on her. Hilarious.

Mitchell began searching. He searched for "Funniest pranks." Scanning the results, he decided "Funniest pranks USA" was better, as apparently Russians loved pranks. He watched dozens of mind-numbing videos. He found himself full of hatred toward the human race. This was what they'd become? A bunch of bipeds with a can of whipped cream and a condom full of water?

He searched for "couple pranks English." The third video he clicked hit home.

Danny and Janice had a whole YouTube channel, with more than fifty video clips. In disbelief, Mitchell began to watch them.

It all started with something completely random. Danny had put a huge amount of chili powder in Janice's sandwich, and replaced her glass of water with vodka, filming the entire thing. Har har, the hilarity. Janice decided it was time for payback, and put tear gas in Danny's deodorant spray. Then there was a prank with flour, and a prank with two dozen rubber spiders… they were all bland and badly filmed. The number of views wasn't very high—several thousand, which in Mitchell's opinion was several thousand more than they deserved.

The first video that had gone viral was a prank in which Janice had somehow rigged Danny's jogging shorts and underpants to tear while he was running. The viewers received several seconds of Danny's bare butt, lightly pixelated, before he noticed anything was wrong. This video had more than half a million views. The following video had Danny pouring a bucket of freezing water into the shower as Janice was taking one. She barged out, screaming, again with some minimal pixels covering her privates. A million and a half views.

They had become better at devising pranks in which nudity was involved. Mitchell suspected some of the pranks were staged. When they played a prank in which there was no nudity, the views dropped to less than a hundred thousand.

As he went back to the video list, his heart dropped. A new video had been uploaded. He clicked it.

By that point, the filming and editing was pretty professional. The video started with Danny explaining to the viewers what he was about to do. He was about to convince Janice he was The Deadly Messenger, and she was his next target. He showed the viewers the disguise, and the chainsaw. Then there was a shot of the bedroom. Janice walked in, wrapped in a towel. She picked up her phone and glanced at it. Then she froze and looked around.

Mitchell paused the video and went back for a second or two. There. He paused the video again and stared at the screen. You could just see Janice's mouth stretch a bit. A small smile. She knew it was a prank.

The video went on. Danny moved in the apartment with a GoPro camera on his head, wielding a chainsaw. He entered the living room, where Janice sat in front of her computer. As he walked in, she looked up, and then *clicked the mouse and nudged the laptop to face Danny*.

She did it incredibly fast; Mitchell wouldn't have noticed if he wasn't paying attention, because the next moment she was standing up, screaming. The towel fell from her body, which was once again pixelated. Maybe she actually had pixels where her nipples and privates were supposed to be. Mitchell was convinced she let the towel drop on purpose.

Then the image froze, and switched to Janice—grinning, talking to her web camera. And she explained it all. How she instantly realized the chainsaw in Danny's message was lying on his friend's table. How she decided to prank him back, calling the police on him. How funny!

Mitchell wondered if it had crossed her mind that the cops might shoot Danny in the heat of the moment. Probably wouldn't have changed anything even if it did. She was too pleased with her clever prank to stop.

Now the video went on, the laptop's webcam filming the rest. Danny putting the mask on when Janice asked him to, her screaming for help, the cops barging in to arrest him. Then a final sequence where Janice's friend answered Janice's phone, and said Janice was too traumatized to talk to the cops right now. No, of course the killer wasn't her boyfriend, what sort of nonsense was that?

Because, ha ha, it was even funnier if Danny was left to stew in jail for a couple of hours.

Mitchell got up and walked to Hannah's desk.

"Want to join me on an arrest?" he said. "Jacob's busy."

"Sure," she said, standing up. "Who are we arresting?"

"The most recent victim."

TWENTY-ONE

Captain Jack Marrow had been a captain for a very long time. Too long. He suspected this was due to the similarity of his full title to Disney's favorite pirate captain. He was a walking pun.

He believed he was a very good officer. He had done his job as captain of the patrol squad in Glenmore Park as well as one could. Frankly, he was ready to move on. For one, a rise in rank would stop Captain Bailey's insistence on offering him grog, and saying "shiver me timbers" every damn time they met.

When the serial killer's case unfolded, Captain Marrow did his best to involve himself with it. His first big break had occurred when Tanessa Lonnie, who was under his command, had become bait for the serial killer. Captain Bailey had insisted Officer Lonnie and her detail should be under his supervision. Captain Marrow had flatly refused, demanding to be in charge of the sting operation since Tanessa Lonnie was one of his officers. The chief had sided with Marrow, and from that moment he'd had the pleasure of showing up at all meetings pertaining to the case and offering his advice.

Now, to his endless joy, it appeared his own officers had arrested the serial killer. Not Captain Bailey's slow-witted detectives, but Captain Marrow's determined troops. He had nearly danced a victory jig in his office when he'd heard the news. He called his wife to inform her they were going out to celebrate that evening in a restaurant. No, not at Pierrot's, did she think he was made of money? They could go out to eat simple steak and fries; there was no better way to celebrate. He then called Tanessa Lonnie to inform her the sting operation was over, they had caught their man. He contacted Tanessa's security detail as well, to spread the good news.

Two hours later, the chief called and asked him to come over to her office. As he was walking over, he tried to think of the best way to explain humbly that his officers had merely done their job as he himself had taught them. He entered her office, where Fred Bailey was already sitting, a look of disappointment on his face. Captain Marrow did his best to hide his victorious smile as he sat by Bailey, who for once did not call him "Matey."

The chief began filling Marrow in. They hadn't arrested the serial killer; they had arrested a prankster. There was a video of one of his cops shaking the suspect violently while he was already in cuffs. The press had already notified the public that a suspect had been arrested, apparently quoting one of Marrow's own moronic cops.

Captain Marrow didn't need to try and hide his smile any longer. There was no smile to hide.

They had to begin with some damage control. Captain Bailey would organize a press conference. This was not a complete disaster. After all, the prankster should have known better, and it was safe to believe public opinion would favor the police. And they still had the ongoing sting operation. Hopefully, the killer would take the bait soon. The forensic psychologist was quite sure he would try to kill again within a day or two. In fact, the news of this arrest might prompt the killer to act faster.

Captain Marrow had once gone on a roller coaster called The Plunge, to disastrous results. The feeling in his gut on that terrible day did not even come close to what he experienced at the moment when the chief mentioned the sting operation.

Could the chief hang on for a second? he asked. He just had to make an urgent phone call. Or two.

———

It was a busy day in the Glenmore Park police dispatch center. It had started in the morning, with the phone call from the Arlington Police dispatcher, who said a woman from Glenmore Park had contacted him and said someone was about to kill her. This quickly led to the arrest of the suspected serial killer. Half an hour later there had been a sewage spill downtown, which led to dozens of furious calls. The dispatchers had a hard time explaining the concept of "emergency" to the angry citizens who wanted someone to come and get the shit off their lawn immediately.

Then, at some point, a rumor had begun to show its face. The rumor was that one of the dispatchers had been bribed by a reporter named Ricky Nate. Allegedly, this dispatcher contacted Ricky Nate every time a serious call regarding the serial killer reached the center. There was talk about an investigation by internal affairs. There were numerous guesses about the dispatcher's identity. These guesses didn't really revolve around the moral capacity of this or that dispatcher, and instead were mostly based upon old grudges. Certain dispatchers who for some reason were *never* available for shifts on Christmas Eve were suddenly under a lot of scrutiny by their peers.

At three p.m., Detective Mitchell Lonnie arrested Janice Hewitt for giving false testimony to the police and obstructing justice. The first thing Janice did once she'd been arrested was demand her phone call. No one knew who she called, but it wasn't her attorney.

Half an hour after Janice made the call, all hell broke loose. Dispatch began receiving hundreds of calls. Some were angry fans of the pranking couple, who demanded that the innocent couple be released at once, so their hilarious shenanigans could carry on. Some were crank calls: complaints of robbers armed with bananas, giraffes sighted running around the city, dark gritty voices threatening to shoot the moon with laser beams. These were probably the couple's pranking buddies, dropping everything to come to their friends' assistance. One caller wanted to report a murder. When asked who the victim was, he answered "free speech." It was safe to assume he was very pleased with himself.

While this was unfolding, an investigator from internal affairs showed up. He "just wanted to look around."

The atmosphere was becoming quite tense.

It was no wonder, then, that when one of the monitors displayed a new message sent to Tanessa's phone, no one noticed it at first. When one of the dispatchers finally glanced at it, seven minutes later, events were already underway.

———

Tanessa was surprised by how relieved she felt when Captain Marrow called to tell her the killer had been arrested, and their sting operation was no longer needed. She didn't really realize how tense she'd been for the past week and a half, until all of a sudden she could unwind. She was embarrassed when a small tear materialized in her left eye. She quickly wiped it and turned to George, who was making a bouquet of Queen Anne's lace, phlox, and cosmos.

"Hey, George?" she said, her voice wavering a bit uncertainly.

"Yeah?" he said, his brow furrowed like it always was when he was trying to get a bouquet just right.

"I'm uh… done. I mean, I'm not coming back tomorrow."

"Oh," he said, raising his eyes to look at her. "Really? That's a shame. I was getting used to having you around."

They smiled at each other. Once again, she wondered how much he really knew.

"I really enjoyed working with you," she said.

"Likewise. I think you have a great eye for flowers," he said. "Though, frankly, the way you use the pruning shears makes me want to take cover."

"I think I'll still end my shift, if that's okay," she said. She realized she was reluctant to leave this man too abruptly. He was a bit strange, but over the last few days they had bonded a bit over tales about his travels in the far east, and over her stories about her childhood.

"Sure. We can even grab a cup of coffee afterward, if you want," he suggested.

"That would be nice," she said.

A few hours later, a man entered the store in a great state of agitation, and asked for their largest bouquet. Tanessa suspected this was a man who had been caught cheating. He was biting his nails constantly, glancing at his phone, and once he let out a small moan as if suddenly remembering that his life was on the brink. Tanessa finally provided a bouquet which appeared to satisfy him, and he paid and left. She noticed that her phone, which was sitting on the counter, was blinking. She tapped it, and glanced at the message.

It was from an unknown number, and there was no text. It was an image of a samurai sword, leaning against a wall under a window through which Glenmore Park's vista could be seen.

Tanessa tried to understand what she was seeing. Realization came fast. They hadn't caught the killer; he was still roaming free. This was a text from him. Her security detail was gone. She was all alone, her only defense a small 9 mm Smith and Wesson in her purse, which was in the back room. She turned to go get it, and the store's front door opened.

The man who walked in was wide-shouldered, and pale. He had thick blond hair and wore gray sunglasses. Her mind matched his face and hair almost immediately to one of the sketches they had.

It was him. He had taken the bait. He had come to kill her.

He marched forward, a bit too quickly to be a casual customer. Tanessa saw that one hand was shoved into his pocket, but the other was hiding something behind his back. And then, before she even had time to process it all, he stopped in his tracks and swung his arm forward.

If she hadn't recognized him from the sketch, if she had hesitated for a millisecond, it would have been too late. The sword swung toward her neck with breathtaking speed, but Tanessa was already moving, her hands shoving her body away from the counter, her head tossed back. She would have sworn she could feel a small breeze as the sword missed her throat by no more than a hair. The blade kept moving, creating a perfect arc in the air. Unbalanced by her sudden movement, Tanessa lost her footing and crashed backward, her hip hitting a low shelf behind her, pain blooming in her side.

"George, get out of here!" she yelled.

She was now on the floor, with the counter between her and the killer. She glanced around for something, anything, to use as a weapon. She grabbed a flowerpot from the low shelf just as the killer rounded the counter, his face a mix of rage and confusion. She threw the pot at him.

She was lying on the floor, and the angle was difficult for a good throw. The pot barely grazed the killer's arm, smashing behind him. He took three steps forward and thrust the sword at her. She rolled aside, hearing the blade clanging on the floor, was relieved it had missed her—then she felt the sharp pain in the side of her neck. The sword hadn't missed completely.

The killer appeared to have a problem. There wasn't a lot of room behind the counter to maneuver the sword; the space between the counter and the back shelves was too narrow. He tried to thrust the sword into her stomach, and she rolled aside again, this time his clumsy move missing her completely. He was now roaring angrily as he lifted the blade up, seemingly intending to chop her like fire-wood. Reflexes took over, and her leg kicked hard, hitting him in his left knee.

He howled in surprise, falling backward. Tanessa took the opportunity to pull herself up, using the shelf. She felt dizzy and lightheaded. Her shirt was soggy, clinging to her body—blood. It was wet with her blood. Had George managed to run? How long since the killer had entered the store? It felt like hours, but it couldn't have been more than a few seconds.

The killer got up as well. He was blocking her way out; the counter was on her left, the shelves on her right. Behind her there was a bare wall. She was trapped. The only way out was to jump over the counter, so that was what she did. Or, at least, that was what she tried to do. She was weak from blood loss, and her body hurt like hell. She managed to half-jump, half-fall over the counter and onto the floor.

The world was getting dark as she tried to get up, her limbs refusing to obey her commands. She could see the figure of the killer advancing—now much slower, calmer, knowing he had won, savoring the moment. She would kick him again, buy some more time… except her foot wouldn't budge.

And then, an explosion. The killer swerved to the side, the sword dropping from his hand. There was another explosion, and the sound of something smashing. The killer moved fast, bolting through the front door just as a third explosion filled the air.

George stood above her, holding a pistol. Her pistol.

"Did you get him?" she muttered.

"Yes, but I don't think he's hurt badly," George said, and then pressed his fist into her neck. Tanessa screamed in pain.

"Sorry, I just have to keep pressure on it," George said, his voice urgent. "I called the police. Help is on its way. Hang on, Tanessa, everything is going to be okay. Can you hear me? Hang on, it's going to be just fine."

She had said the same words not long ago, she thought hazily. To a girl named Tamay. What had happened to that girl?

She couldn't remember. She couldn't even remember why her neck hurt so much.

TWENTY-TWO

He shook as he drove, fear intermingling with rage. Was this it? Would today be the day they would catch him?

Perhaps. Perhaps not.

Not knowing was frightening… but exciting as well. He grinned—a manic grin, half snarl, half laughter. Beaten by a florist. Shot in the belly by a goddamn shopkeeper. How had this happened? He had been prepared! He'd followed the girl for days, practiced his sword swing for hours, making sure he had the range right, that he could move fast enough to surprise her. There was no way she could have dodged his slash.

Except…

She'd known who he was.

It wasn't just suspicion triggered by the message he sent her. No. There had been recognition there. Not a sliver of hesitation. Somehow, despite the fact that he had been in disguise, despite the fact that he had taken every precaution, never coming near her, she had instantly known he was there to kill her.

How?

HOW?

He smashed the steering wheel in frustration, smearing it with blood. His blood. The memory of the girl—the delicate, tiny girl, kicking him with the force of a mule—came back. Who was this Tanessa Lonnie? Had he really done his research well? She'd seemed to be just another empty-headed girl, working in a flower shop, dreaming of being a model. How had she been so fast? Where had she found that strength?

He took a deep breath. He would think about it later. For now, he had to make sure he didn't get caught, and he didn't die of blood loss. He probed his wound gently; the pain nearly blinded him, and the car swerved left, then right.

Careful, dammit! He should avoid attracting any attention. He'd been hit in his waist, but it was difficult to gauge how severely. He had a few more blocks to the motel; he could check the damage there.

If the police were raising roadblocks, at least they hadn't blocked his route. This wasn't a huge surprise. He had planned his route well, choosing small streets with little traffic, in the time just a bit before rush hour really started.

Maybe he should have broken through the girl's window, caught her alone in her apartment. But he hadn't wanted to rely on her opening that window. Besides, he'd gone through a window last time. Repetition was a great way to get caught. That was why he'd entered the store only five minutes after sending the message. He needed to stay unpredictable.

It had seemed so perfect when he'd heard on the news about a suspect being arrested. Originally, he had planned on killing Tanessa a couple of days from now. But once he'd realized that the police thought they had the killer in custody, he'd known it was the time to act. Catch them unaware, as they were giving their victory speech.

Hadn't turned out so well after all. He was getting dizzy.

He had to get to the motel.

———

Tanessa smiled as Mitchell appeared in the doorway of the hospital room. His face reminded her of a day, long ago, when they had been riding their bicycles side by side and she'd crashed into a tree. He had blamed himself, thinking he'd been riding too close to her. As she had cried, he'd knelt by her and tried to make sure she was fine, apologize, and berate himself all at once, resulting in a hysterical, nonsensical monologue.

"Are you okay?" he asked, half-running to her small hospital bed.

"Sure," she said, her voice slurred. They had given her some pain killers, which she suspected were intended for suffering horses. "It's just a scratch. It hurts more when I nick myself shaving my legs." *Listen to the witty patient, joking with her brother.* She had planned this joke for twenty minutes, just to sound casual, as if nothing was wrong. She had one more up her sleeve.

"They just told me," Mitchell said. "He attacked you in the flower shop?"

"With a sword," she said. "A samurai sword. What a geek."

"Damn it, Tanessa, I'm so sorry—"

"It's not your fault."

He didn't argue, but she could see in his face that he was blaming himself. God only knew why. He'd done all he could to stop her.

"Where were you hit?"

She turned her head a bit to show him the stitches on her neck. The movement hurt like hell, and for a moment her casual smile twisted in pain. She let out a small hiss, biting down on the scream that threatened to emerge. If the blade had cut a few millimeters deeper, she would have died, the doctor said. Another tidbit she'd prefer her brother didn't hear. She put her smile back on.

"The guy who operated on me?" she said. "Doctor Frankenstein. I swear to God. I saw villagers amassing outside the operating room with pitchforks and torches. I could seriously picture him screaming, *It's alive!*" That was joke number two. She hoped Mitchell wouldn't stay much longer, because it began to be difficult to maintain this façade.

"We'll get him, Tanessa, I promise you."

"Don't be so dramatic, Mitchell, I know you will," she said. "Say, where's Pauline?"

"She, uh… She said she'd get here as soon as she could."

"Okay, no rush."

Mitchell glanced back at the doorway. "You know there's a cop outside," he said.

Tanessa nodded. "Yeah, Noel. He got Tanessa detail for today."

"Tanessa detail?" Mitchell looked confused.

"Chief's orders. Apparently your forensic psychologist said that the killer might try killing me again." Her voice cracked for the first time. She cleared her throat as if it was nothing, and said, "He isn't a guy who takes no for an answer." She felt frustrated. When her jokes weren't prepared in advance, they were always lame. Mitchell was the witty one in the family.

The doctor walked in. Tanessa hadn't been exaggerating; he did look like a mad scientist. He was bald except for two tufts of gray hair on the sides of his head, and he wore thick, black, round spectacles on an absurdly long nose. His eyes, magnified by the thick lenses, were constantly open wide, as if he was in shock, and his outfit was rumpled and disheveled as if he had rolled it into a ball just before wearing it.

"*It's alive*," Tanessa whispered to Mitchell, wiggling her eyebrows.

"How are you feeling?" the doctor asked. There was no trace of a German accent in his speech. Disappointing.

"Just fine," she said. "How much longer will I be here?"

He shrugged, as if determining the length of her hospitalization was beyond his job description.

"You'll have to come back during visiting hours," he told Mitchell.

Obediently, Mitchell said goodbye, promised to come the following day, and left. The doctor checked her vitals and left as well. She was alone.

She didn't want to be alone.

Because when she was alone, the fear kept her company. She saw in her mind the killer standing above her, looking down at her from behind his gray sunglasses, his blade flying fast toward her. Once again, she realized how close she had come to dying, despite all the precautions they had taken. Once again, she was filled with the terror of facing a killer, knowing she was on her own.

She fought the urge to call Noel in, like a small child telling daddy she couldn't sleep because of the monsters under her bed. She tried to force the dark images away, thinking of books she loved, of movies she wanted to see again. She listed her top favorite songs. But a face wearing dark shades barged over and over into her mind, the happy thoughts dissipating like thin clouds.

With no one to see her, Tanessa curled under the hospital's blanket, her body shaking.

―――――

Mitchell's brother, Richard, was yelling at him on the phone. Richard had inherited their mom's short temper, and talking to him was sometimes like talking to a pile of dynamite sticks while juggling three torches.

"… I told you, you should have stopped this!" he screamed. "Now look what happened! She almost died, Mitchell!"

"Well, what did you want me to do, Richard?" Mitchell asked, his voice getting louder as well. "Tie her to a chair? She wouldn't listen to me!"

"Then you should have talked to your captain! Using Tanessa as bait was an amateurish hack job! Where is she?"

"She's recovering from surgery in the hospital, but visiting hours are over and—"

"Visiting hours! Jesus. I'm going there right now," Richard said. He would, Mitchell knew. He'd storm in, and threaten to sue anyone who'd stop him. Richard was a rising defense attorney, and threatening everything and everyone with lawsuits was his favorite hobby.

"Listen, Richard, could you call Mom and Dad and let them know? I'm trying to catch the—"

Richard let out a hysterical forced laugh. "Call Mom? Mitchell, this is your screwup. You call Mom. I'll call Dad." He hung up.

Mitchell stared at the phone, his emotions in turmoil. He should have stopped this. He should have tried harder, at least. The sight of Tanessa lying in that hospital bed, trying to act brave, was heart-wrenching. And his heart was wrenched enough as it was. He was ready for some good news.

"Mitchell." Captain Bailey walked in. "How's your sister?"

"Officer Lonnie is fine," Mitchell said. Tanessa had forbidden him to use the word "sister" within the police department.

"Okay. The chief just ordered Danny Stevenson and Janice Hewitt set free," Bailey said. "I thought you'd want to know."

"What?" Mitchell felt as if he was about to kill someone. "Why did she do that?"

"Well, for one, neither of them is our serial killer," Bailey said. "They're just a couple of pranksters."

"They obstructed justice! They purposefully filed a false—"

"In addition to that," Bailey said, his voice rising to quash Mitchell's complaints, "the police department is swamped with calls from reporters, bloggers, and pranksters. Dispatch can't do their job with that going on. This is why we didn't respond as quickly as we should have when the killer sent your sister the message."

Mitchell closed his mouth, dumbfounded. His fault. Always his fault.

"The department is receiving some very bad press," Bailey continued. "The chief says it makes us look as if we have no sense of humor."

"Sense of humor?" Mitchell said, his voice high pitched. "Seriously?"

"Look," Bailey said sharply, "if this could help us catch the guy, I'd have your back. But holding that dumb couple in jail is just pure spite, plain and simple. We're letting them out."

"Fine!"

Bailey put a hand on Mitchell's shoulder. "What's going on, Mitchell?"

"Tanessa—"

"Don't give me that bullshit. You were acting like a zombie with a chip on his shoulder before your sister was attacked. You've lost your focus. My dad would say that you're walking like a drunk man in a field of strawberry pies. What is going on with you?"

Mitchell's face went blank. "I'll be fine," he said, his voice straight. "I'm just tired, that's all."

"You can take a vacation day or two. Bernard can fill in for you until—"

"I'll be fine, Captain. Thanks."

Bailey looked as if he was about to say something else when Jacob burst into the squad room.

"Come on," Jacob told Mitchell. "We have to go."

"What's going on?" Bailey asked.

"Did you see the message that Tanessa received from the killer?" Jacob asked. "It's a samurai sword leaning against a wall. There's a window above it."

"I saw," Bailey said.

"Through the window you can see a cellular antenna tower, and Peterson's Mojo," Jacob said. Peterson's Mojo was the tallest building in town. It was a slick office building that had been built by Mayor Peterson fifteen years earlier, just after his wife left him and married a senator. He'd named it Glenmore's Hub, but since everyone assumed the building was designed so tall to compensate for something, Peterson's Mojo was the informal name that had stuck.

"I just came from Matt's lab," Jacob said. "For the last hour we've been trying to triangulate the location of the room in which the picture was taken. It was tricky, because there are a lot of cellular antennas, but we're pretty sure we found the right one."

Mitchell stood up, putting on his jacket, his heart beating fast, as a smile appeared on Jacob's face.

"We have the killer's address," Jacob said.

TWENTY-THREE

It was a bit after ten in the evening when Mitchell parked the car on the curb by the small shabby apartment building in Hillside Drive. He and Jacob stepped out of the car and looked around. The street lights were all either flickering or broken, but even in their meager light it was possible to see the chaos on the building's walls. Crude signatures in black spray paint marred nicer graffiti signatures in pink, green, and blue, and those were clearly sprayed over a badly-drawn graffiti imitation of Pink Floyd's *The Wall* album cover. The original color of the building couldn't be seen.

Looking up, Mitchell could see the neglected, peeling, soot-covered wall. The graffiti on the bottom of the wall was the building's most elegant feature.

Two squad cars were parked on the sidewalk just by the main entrance. One officer—a guy named Ron or Rob, Mitchell wasn't entirely sure—stood by the door, gun in hand.

"What's going on, Officer?" Jacob asked, walking briskly toward the man. "Did you get him?"

"They are just about to break down the apartment door, Detective," Ron/Rob said. "I was stationed here in case he tried to make a break for it."

"Any back door to the building?"

"No, sir, but there is an emergency stairway." The cop pointed toward the right side of the building. "If he goes down those stairs, they'll radio me."

Jacob didn't seem happy with this arrangement, but said nothing. Instead he strode into the building, with Mitchell close behind.

They heard shouting from upstairs, and then the loud, sharp sound of a door breaking. They rushed up the stairs, leaping over two and three stairs at a time, guns drawn. Mitchell reached the third floor seconds before Jacob. He saw the open door, its lock broken. Someone shouted "Clear!" from inside the apartment.

Mitchell nearly rushed inside, but Jacob grabbed his arm.

"Those cops in there are tense, trigger-happy, and looking for a killer," he said. "If you pop up behind them in plainclothes, holding a gun, one of them might shoot."

Mitchell could see the sense in that. He waited with Jacob by the door. After a few seconds they heard someone shout, "All clear! There's no one here!"

"Damn it," Jacob muttered. "They should have scouted ahead first."

Mitchell felt a wave of disappointment and lethargy wash over him. "He'll probably see the patrol cars outside and vanish," he said. "We blew our chance."

"We'll see," Jacob said and called out, "Detectives Cooper and Lonnie here! We're coming inside!"

The apartment was small, incredibly dirty, and almost devoid of furniture. There were two small rooms, one bathroom, and a kitchen. One of the rooms had an old mattress on the floor. The other room had a small, rickety wooden table and a folding chair in the middle of the room, plus a TV standing on a small prefab stand in the corner. The window that had appeared in the message to Tanessa was in the makeshift bedroom. The three officers lingered around the apartment, unsure what to do, the anticlimax of the whole thing etched deeply into their faces.

"I'm not sure this is the right place," one of them said sullenly.

"What were you expecting?" Mitchell asked. "A stock of weapons? A coffee mug with the inscription *Best Serial Killer Ever*?"

"I don't know," the unhappy cop answered. "Pictures of the victims or something?"

"Oh, I know what you mean," Mitchell said. "Pictures of the victims with their eyes cut out. A full-sized image of one of them, drawn in blood and feces. Something like that?"

"Yeah, I guess," the cop said, ignoring Mitchell's sarcastic tone.

"You watch too many movies," Jacob said. "Get those patrol vehicles away from the building. Any serial killer coming back from a trip to the supermarket would disappear if he saw those cars waiting for him."

The cops left the apartment.

"Okay." Jacob sighed. "I guess we should get Matt and his crew over here. At the very least, I hope to get some fingerprints and DNA samples from this dismal apartment."

———

Hannah was exhausted. It had been one of the crazier days for their squad, and she hadn't been spared. She'd just spent four hours going door to door around the flower shop, looking for anyone who'd seen anything. Two witnesses had actually heard the commotion and seen a man run out of the flower shop and get into a car that quickly drove away. However, their descriptions of the man and the car were so hazy and conflicting that merging them into a coherent statement was practically impossible. Hannah was used to witnesses describing events differently, but having one of them say the car was a blue Ford and the other one saying she was sure the car was red had nearly made Hannah scream.

Jacob had called to update her that they had found the apartment where the killer had been staying, but he wasn't there. George, Captain Bailey's florist friend, said he was certain he had hit the killer, and blood spatter in the flower shop corroborated this. Was the killer dead in his car somewhere in the city? Had he gone for help? Bernard was checking with all the private clinics, nurses, doctors, and vets around the city, searching for a man who had turned up with a bullet wound. So far, no luck.

It was getting very late, and Hannah decided to go home for the night. Images of her bed beckoned to her. The paperwork and the hundreds of yet-unchecked leads could wait until tomorrow. She grabbed her handbag and walked toward the squad room door. And then, of course, the phone on her desk rang.

She nearly let it go to voicemail. After all, they had almost missed her. It was late. She *really* wanted to get to bed.

She answered the phone. "Hello?"

"Hello, is this the Glenmore Park Detective Squad?" a feminine voice asked.

"That's right."

"Hi, I'm Officer Veronica Marsen from the state police. Who am I talking to?"

"I'm Detective Shor," Hannah said, impatient. "What's this about?"

"It's about the shooting that occurred today at the flower shop. As you know, we are working with your department on this case, and I wanted some updates regarding this development for our reports."

"Yeah, sure."

"What was the name of the woman who was hurt?"

"Officer Tanessa Lonnie," Hannah said.

The woman on the other side paused for a moment. "Officer… yes. Of course. We are talking about the officer that… Hang on, I have this report here…"

"Tanessa was the bait," Hannah said. "Listen, can we do this tomorrow? It's really late."

"Yes, of course. I'm really sorry. I just have a few more things for my report, and I was assured your full cooperation, so…"

"Fine," Hannah nearly spat. "What else?"

"I understand that the shooter escaped?"

"The shooter? You've got it wrong, Miss Marsen. The killer was the one who was shot. He attacked Tanessa with a sword."

"Oh! I don't know why the initial report didn't mention that! Okay. So the killer was shot and ran away, and Officer Lonnie… that's extraordinary. Don't you have a Detective Lonnie on the case?"

"Yeah, sure—that's her brother. He's…" Hannah stopped mid-sentence. "What did you say your name was again?"

"Officer Marsen. I think I have all the details I need. Goodbye!" The line went dead, and Hannah was left gripping the phone, her blood running cold.

Officer Veronica Marsen. The woman might as well have called herself Officer Nancy Droop. There was no way in hell the Staties were so clueless regarding the flower shop shooting. The chief updated them constantly.

Who had she talked to?

———

Matt Lowery carefully dusted the window, the powder scattering down on the sill. Three black ovals materialized near the left side of the pane. The ridges of at least two of the fingerprints were plain to see. A *plain arch* and a *spiral whorl*, his mind registered distractedly, classifying the fingerprints. The third looked like a plain arch as well, but he couldn't be sure, as it was badly smeared. He put the powder and brush back inside the fingerprinting kit that lay by his feet, and grabbed the camera from the table. He took two photographs of the prints. Then he grabbed the tape from the kit, and carefully applied a strip to one of the fingerprints. He lifted the tape, which now contained the print, from the window, and stuck it on a small card. He did this twice more. Then he wrote "N. Facing Window" on all three cards. He added those to the nine other cards he had already collected from the bathroom. Assuming this really was the place where the killer had been staying, he hadn't tried to wipe the place clean. They'd already found several hairs in the shower and on the mattress as well. The apartment was bound to contain endless DNA samples to check against CODIS, even if the hair amounted to nothing.

He sighed, stretching to his full 5'1". Plenty of work today, and this apartment was as boring as a crime scene could be, especially considering the fact that a serial killer had probably lived here.

Violet was in the kitchen, extracting samples from the sink and the cupboard handles. The television set probably had a few prints as well. If the apartment had been wiped clean, they'd have tried to get some fingerprints from the wooden table and the chair, or perhaps from the bathroom wall. But since the person living here had been so accommodating, Matt was prepared to call it a night. He glanced at the time. Nearly midnight.

"Violet!" he called. "How much longer?"

"Just a few more minutes!" she called back from the kitchen.

He looked around one last time and was about to leave the room when he noticed something. The floors of the entire apartment were covered in dust, food stains, and random dirt. However, just by the mattress there was a small section of the floor that was a bit cleaner. He knelt by it, trying to trace it in his mind. It was triangular, one side aligned with the mattress' edge. Someone had moved the mattress recently, and it had dragged the dust and dirt with it. Matt pulled the mattress aside. There was nothing behind it. He lifted it up, and saw nothing out of the ordinary—just more dirt.

Up close, he examined the floor tiles under the mattress; one seemed loose. He pulled out a sharp pocket knife and stuck it in the space between the tiles, lifting the loose one.

There was a small round hole in the mortar under the tile, and it held something. Using a pair of tweezers, Matt carefully pulled it out.

It was a dusty, sealed nylon bag. It contained a lock of red hair.

TWENTY-FOUR

There was a tense silence in the squad room when Mitchell walked in, a bit late. Usually they'd drink coffee, banter with each other; Bernard would moan about his lack of sleep, Jacob would thump his keyboard and complain about the computer. But that morning there was nothing but dark looks and an undercurrent of anger.

"What's going on?" he asked, not really wanting to know.

"Check out the *Glenmore Park Gazette*," Jacob said.

Mitchell felt heavy and drained as he sat down in front of his computer. He opened the browser, and slowly typed in the three first letters of the *Gazette*'s URL; the browser completed the rest. The main page popped up, a picture of *Hummingbird Blossoms* in the top article. The headline was *Deadly Messenger Evades Police Trap*.

It got worse. There was a picture of Tanessa. The article mentioned that she had been used as bait. It hinted that this plan was ill-conceived, and that Tanessa had been chosen because of her family relation to Detective Mitchell Lonnie, one of the primary detectives on the case. The article then mentioned Mitchell's arrest of Danny Stevenson and Janice Hewitt as suspects in the case, stressing that in fact they had merely played a harmless prank. The reporter's name was, of course, Ricky Nate.

Mitchell stood up, feeling dizzy. His body was shaking, his teeth grinding. He knew he was about to explode, and a faraway part of his brain screamed at him to get out of there, drive home, let loose there, where it was safe. But he ignored that meek suggestion.

"Damn it!" he screamed, and kicked at his chair, which rolled across the room and banged against the wall. He picked up a mug from his desk, still half full of coffee, and threw it at the same wall, the mug crashing to pieces and leaving a huge stain.

"Relax, Lonnie!" Jacob yelled at him, leaping from his chair.

"How? How did she find out all that?" Mitchell yelled at him "Who told her?"

"I did."

Mitchell turned around and stared at Hannah. She looked back at him, her face red.

"You?" he said, his voice sharp. "Why?"

"I didn't know she was a reporter. She said she was from the State Police. She fooled me, Mitchell. I'm sorry."

"You told her that using my sister as bait was my idea?"

"Of course not," Hannah said sharply. "That was her own notion. But I told her that Tanessa was used as bait, and that she was your sister."

"How could you be so stupid?" he asked.

Hannah didn't even flinch. Her face stayed completely blank as she kept staring at him. But Mitchell had known her for a long time, had gone to the academy with her. The flicker in her eyes told him this was not something she was about to forgive anytime soon.

"Fuck you, Lonnie," she said. She stood up and walked slowly out of the squad room. Bernard looked at him with disgust.

"You're a real asshole, Mitchell," he said.

Mitchell looked at Bernard tiredly, suddenly wishing he could rewind the past thirty seconds. He glanced at the wall, at the coffee stain trickling down to the floor where the mug shards were scattered.

"I know," he said. He stuck his hands in his pockets. His right hand knocked against something hard. Pauline's engagement ring, in his pocket ever since the day he had bought it. He felt as if he were suffocating, as if he were being pulled in all directions at once. He strode out of the room and went down the stairs, through the department's exit, and into the car. He stared at the steering wheel for what felt like an eternity, and then drove home.

———

Jacob had served enough years in the force to know when a cop was no longer functioning. As far as Jacob was concerned, Mitchell had become completely useless. Jacob wasn't sure what had triggered it, and for now he didn't care. Later, he would call Mitchell and try to help him out, as a friend. But as a detective, he had to focus on the fact that there was a killer on the loose and a reasonably good trail to follow. He grabbed the keys from his desk and stood up.

"Where are you going?" Bernard asked.

"Door to door in the killer's apartment building," Jacob answered.

"If he really lived there," Bernard said.

"Well, I talked to Matt this morning. He found a lock of hair hidden in the apartment. This matches our killer's MO, so for now I'm assuming this was an apartment he stayed at."

"Oh, okay," Bernard said. "Does it belong to one of the victims?"

"Matt said that it seems to match Kendele Byers's hair, but he couldn't be sure. He said there was something strange about the sample, and that he needed more time to figure it out." Jacob shrugged. "Anyway, I'll take our sketch book and see if anyone saw our killer walking around. Perhaps I'll strike gold. Who knows, maybe he asked his neighbor for a cup of sugar without wearing a disguise. That would be nice."

"Hang on; I'll come with you," Bernard said.

The detectives stepped into the car, Jacob relinquishing the driver's seat to Bernard. As they drove to Hillside Drive, Jacob became lost in thought, wondering yet again where the killer had gone. He'd been wounded during the fight in the flower shop, that much was certain. Did he get help?

"You called doctors yesterday, right?" he asked Bernard.

"Yup. Doctors, nurses, vets, retired doctors, medical students… It was a damn long list."

"Find anything?"

"Not really. No one that admitted to taking care of a man with a bullet wound, anyway."

"Hm."

"Say, what's wrong with Mitchell?" Bernard asked.

"I don't know," Jacob said, his voice sharp and final.

Bernard didn't push the issue.

They reached the apartment building. It looked even shabbier in the daylight, the sun emphasizing the places where the plaster had peeled off the walls completely, exposing the bare bricks. One of the window panes on the first floor had been broken; rather than fix it, the tenants had simply boarded the window up.

"Do you want to split?" Bernard asked.

"Nah, let's do them together," Jacob said. "There are only three floors."

They started at the third floor, where the killer had been staying. No one answered the first door they knocked on, and the other apartments were opened by hostile residents who made it perfectly clear they had never heard anything, seen anything, or smelled anything that could be of interest to the police. If the killer had asked them for some sugar, they weren't about to share. The second floor was pretty much the same.

An old woman opened the first door they tried on the bottom floor. For an instant, Jacob was sure he knew her from somewhere. Then he realized why she was so familiar. She looked just like Sophia from *Golden Girls*, a TV series he used to watch with his wife every week when he was much younger. She had a round blob of gray hair and obscenely large glasses, behind which sharp eyes stared out at them. She was dressed in something that could have been a dress, a gown, or a tablecloth; it was hard to tell. It was blue, and spotted with the occasional flower. She was comically tiny, less than five feet, her hands and feet small as a child's. Since Bernard was almost six feet tall, she looked up at him like someone staring at a bird flying in the sky.

"Yes?" she asked.

"Ma'am, I'm Detective Bernard Gladwin," Bernard said, flipping open his badge. "This is my partner, Detective Cooper. We wanted to ask—"

"Detectives, huh?" she said. She looked at Jacob. "Nice fedora."

"Thank you, ma'am," he answered. "We wanted to ask you some questions about a man who lived here not long ago."

"Yeah?" she frowned. "Come in, I was just making tea."

"We really don't want to come in, we just wanted to ask—"

"Well, I'm not about to stand out here in the hallway and answer questions, so you might as well come in, drink some tea, and eat apple strudel." She turned around and walked inside, leaving the door wide open. Bernard hesitated for a moment and then walked in, followed by Jacob.

Her apartment stood in complete contrast to the way the building looked outside. It had recently been freshly painted; the walls were white and clean. All the furniture looked well taken care of, though old. A rocking chair and a sofa stood around a small round wooden coffee table on an intricately-patterned red and green Persian carpet. All the walls were hidden by immense bookcases containing hundreds of books, except for one wall which was covered by framed photos of numerous kids. Her grandchildren, Jacob guessed.

"Sit down," she said. "I'll be right back."

Right back turned out to be a quite flexible concept, as the woman moved at a pace that seemed to ignore the existence of time. Jacob didn't check, but it felt as if serving them tea and a freshly-baked apple strudel took her about two days. She breathed through her nose the entire time, her face a mask of deep concentration. Finally, they each had a cup of lukewarm tea and a plate with a small slice of strudel.

"I love strudel," she said. "You know what's the secret to a good apple strudel?"

"No," Jacob said. "What is it?"

"The recipe," she said, and laughed. Or at least he thought she laughed. It sounded as if someone was torturing mice. He had a feeling it wasn't the first time she had told this joke.

"Ma'am, we are looking for information about a man who used to live here not long ago," Bernard said. "He lived on the third floor."

"Oh?" she said.

"We wondered if you had seen him."

"Maybe. I see people going up and down the stairs, occasionally. What did he do?"

"We're not sure," Jacob said. "But we would like to question him."

"I see." She glanced at his plate. "Don't you like the strudel?"

Jacob cut a small piece with his spoon and put it in his mouth. It was, in fact, delicious. He chewed it carefully and swallowed. "It's very good," he said.

She nodded, satisfied. "So," she said. "What do you want to know?"

He pulled the folder with all the sketches out of his briefcase and handed it over to her. "There are some sketches there," he said. "We wanted to know if you recognize any of these men."

She opened the folder and looked at the first sketch. "That's a nice sketch," she said. "Did you draw this?"

"No," Jacob said. "It was a sketch artist."

"My granddaughter Bella goes to art school," she said, looking at the sketch. "She's very talented. She draws."

"That's nice," Jacob said.

"She draws on the computer," the old woman said. "She's very smart."

"Can you look at the rest of the sketches, please?"

She flipped a page. "This one is also very nice," she said.

Jacob began wondering if she thought he was one of her grandchildren, showing her the picture he had just painted.

"Have you seen this man?" he asked her, but she didn't answer right away.

Jacob glanced over at Bernard, who was leaning back, sipping from the small cup of tea. His fingers could barely squeeze through the teacup's handle. He looked as if he was playing with a kid's plastic tea set. He didn't seem restless at all, but then again Jacob had never seen Bernard restless. The man had the patience of a Galapagos turtle.

Jacob, however, was getting impatient. They were wasting time. This woman was just looking for company; she hadn't seen anyone. He leaned forward to take the folder from her hands, but she flipped another page and finally spoke again.

"Oh," she said. "I thought you said you were looking for a man who lived here recently."

"That's right," Jacob said.

"Well, you're wrong."

He blinked. "I'm sorry?"

"He lived here, but not recently. They moved away twenty-five years ago."

"No, ma'am, we're looking for someone who lived here until a week ago. If this sketch reminds you of someone you knew long ago, it's just a coincidence—"

"I'm old, Detective, but I'm not senile," she said, her voice becoming sharp. "Pete Stokes lived here with his family for almost fifteen years. The sketch doesn't remind me of him. The sketch is him. Or at least, him as he looked thirty years ago." She flipped the folder back at him, open at a sketch of the killer wearing a toupee of smooth black hair combed to the side, and a large fake mustache. "That's Pete Stokes. But he was a nice man. I'm sure he didn't do anything wrong."

"How old was Pete when he lived here?" Jacob asked.

"About fifty, I think," she said, leaning back in her rocking chair. "He was always very polite. And he did live in the apartment on the third floor, so you got that right."

"Which apartment?" Jacob asked.

"Apartment 15. The one the cops broke into yesterday," she looked at them, her face crinkling with a smile that exposed way too much gums. "What? Did you think I didn't know? With the noise you people made?"

Jacob and Bernard glanced at each other. Bernard raised his eyebrows as if to say this was a dead end; she was talking about a man who would now be seventy-five, maybe eighty years old.

Jacob turned toward the old woman, his mind suddenly whirring.

"What family?" he asked.

"I'm sorry?"

"You said he lived with his family. Did he have a wife?"

"Yes. A wife and a son. I used to exchange recipes with his wife, Meggie. She could appreciate my baking," she added, glancing at their still-unfinished strudels.

"How old was the son when they left?" Bernard asked, leaning forward. He was getting it.

"I'm not sure. He left for college a bit before, I think," she said. "When they left he must have been about… twenty. Maybe twenty-one."

"What was his name?" Jacob asked, his fingers tightening around the plate.

"His name was Jovan. Jovan Stokes. Such a sweet boy."

TWENTY-FIVE

Mitchell arrived late to work, and entered the squad room in the midst of a meeting. It was nearly noon. He was hung over, and tired after hardly sleeping the night before. There was lonely drinking, and there was lonelier drinking. Then he had almost drunk texted Pauline, but he was pretty sure he'd decided not to do so, which was probably his proudest recent achievement.

As he entered, everyone turned to look at him, though Hannah quickly looked away, disgust on her face. Even without their previous exchange, he knew he had earned the disgust. He wore the same clothes as the day before, he was unshaven, and, judging by the taste in his mouth, his breath stank. He wasn't even sure why he had come to work. Jacob, who stood near the rolling whiteboard, looked at him and raised an eyebrow. There were no chairs available. Mitchell's own chair was taken by Captain Bailey, so he leaned against the wall.

Jacob started talking. "As I was saying, according to this woman, twenty five years ago a man named Pete Stokes lived with his family in apartment fifteen. His son's name was Jovan Stokes, and we're almost sure that he's our guy."

Mitchell stared, blinking, feeling sick. While he'd been acting like a whiny brat, throwing fits and getting drunk, feeling sorry for himself, the rest of the squad had exposed the identity of the serial murderer. If he'd had to put a finger on the lowest point in his career, this was it.

What the hell was wrong with him? He'd always managed to keep his life and his work apart, he had always been professional. Why was he screwing up like this?

"The woman positively identified one of the sketches as Pete Stokes," Jacob carried on. "And told us that father and son were very similar. We aren't sure if Jovan Stokes purposefully chose one of the disguises to match his father's looks—"

"Dressing up like his dad?" Zoe said, raising her eyebrow. "That's a little Freudian."

"Sure, I guess," Jacob said. "In any case, we've managed to retrieve some info on Jovan Stokes." He pointed at a picture taped to the whiteboard. In it, a man of about forty with short-cropped, light brown hair stared seriously at the camera. He had a small mustache and a beard, both trimmed carefully. His eyes were also light brown, his lips tight and pale. He looked as if he was constantly angry. "Jovan Stokes. Born in 1968 in Glenmore Park. He was a brilliant kid, top of his class. His family was quite poor—his dad worked in construction, and his mother was unemployed. When he graduated high school, he managed to get a scholarship and enrolled in the Boston University School of Medicine. He was one of the top students there as well. The image you see here was taken from his driver's license. We believe that he has shaved his beard and his mustache since then. While studying in Boston, he met a woman named Wanda Johnson, and he married her in 1995. They've been married for eighteen years."

Jacob paused and glanced at the whiteboard. There was a timeline drawn on the bottom. He pointed at its base. "On July 14, 2013, both Wanda Stokes and Jovan Stokes did not show up to work. No one has seen either of them since."

"Are they both involved in the murders?" Hannah asked.

"Not likely," Jacob said. "According to our friends in the Boston PD, two days after Wanda disappeared her sister, Sylvia Johnson, filed a missing persons report. She claimed that Wanda was about to divorce Jovan, and that she would never have disappeared with him. The most likely scenario right now is that Jovan Stokes killed Wanda soon after she told him she wanted a divorce. Their shared bank account was emptied a day before the couple vanished. They had about two hundred thousand dollars in the account." He let that sink in. "No one has seen or heard from Jovan or Wanda Stokes since July 2013. It is probable that Jovan has false papers, and is nearly always in disguise," Jacob said. "There's a large gap in which we aren't sure what he was doing, but then on February 10, 2015, Isabella Garcia was murdered." He pointed at the timeline again. "So we have him in Boston at that time. Later, he moved to Glenmore Park—"

"He could have been here all along, and simply driven to Boston to murder there," Mitchell pointed out.

Jacob nodded. "That's true."

"Did anyone talk to the landlord of the apartment?" Captain Bailey asked. "He'd be able to pinpoint the exact date, and give us the name Jovan Stokes used. Maybe some additional information."

"The previous landlord died from cancer three months ago," Jacob answered. "The new landlord—that's his daughter—is still trying to figure out her inheritance. Apparently the deceased left a mess. What she could tell us was that she could find no lease for the apartment, and that she remembers her dad saying that the rent for the place had been paid in advance, in cash."

He paused, waiting to see if any more questions popped up. Then he moved to point at a picture of a lock of red hair. "This hair was found hidden inside the apartment. Originally, we thought it was Kendele Byers's; it seemed to match her hair color. However, Matt found out that the hair is, in fact, much older."

"How much older?" Captain Bailey asked.

"Matt is working on an estimate, he said that it's at least ten years old, though it's probably even older. Assuming that Jovan Stokes only moved to his childhood home recently, our current assumption is that this lock of hair was placed there when his family originally lived there."

"An old victim?" Mitchell asked.

"Again, we have no way to be sure. It might belong to a victim, or a friend he had." Jacob shrugged. "Anything's possible. We intend to follow this lead and see where it takes us. For now, we're focusing all our efforts on Jovan's past. Bernard and Hannah will be going back to Boston, to work with Bernard's buddies at the Boston PD on Wanda Stokes's missing persons case."

Bernard did not seem especially thrilled to meet his so-called buddies again. He wrinkled his nose as if confronted with a particularly ripe sample of French cheese.

"The rest of us will be trying to extract additional information here. There are numerous people who've had contact with Jovan over the years, and perhaps some of them might shed some light on his actions."

"Okay," Captain Bailey said. "I'm meeting with the chief later, and I'll update her on our progress."

With the meeting clearly finished, everyone began to move around. Mitchell was about to ask Zoe for his chair, when Captain Bailey said, "Detective Lonnie, join me in my office, please."

It was an irregularly official request, and some part of Mitchell's heart sank. He followed the captain to his office.

Captain Bailey sat down behind his desk of chaos. Mitchell looked around. All the other chairs had stacks of papers on them.

"You can move those papers there." Captain Bailey pointed at one of the chairs.

Mitchell picked the stack of papers up, and after a moment of hesitation laid it gingerly on one of the piles on the table. Bailey grunted and moved the papers to a different stack. Apparently, Mitchell had disrupted his carefully managed filing system. Mitchell sat down.

"You're off the case," Captain Bailey said, not bothering to soften the blow. "Chief's orders."

"Because of the article in the Gazette?" Mitchell asked. "Captain, you know I just did what needed to be done."

"It definitely contributed," Captain Bailey said, frowning. "As did the hundreds of blogs and vloggers who trashed us for arresting Janice Hewitt and for trampling the First Amendment."

"But this has nothing to do with the First—"

"Damn it, Mitchell, you act as if you just got here from Canada! You arrested someone for making us look like a bunch of idiots. Of course everyone will say it's a First Amendment thing. It doesn't matter if she filed a false complaint, or if she nearly got her boyfriend shot by the cops. She's the hero here, sticking it to the man. You're the villain who doesn't care about freedom of speech. Did you see how many views she has on her last video? Over twenty-five million. You've practically made that woman's career."

"Fine, I'll stay in the office, then. Try and track this Jovan from—"

"Mitchell, I don't want you on this case either. You've lost your focus, and you're acting like an asshole. Did you throw your mug at the wall yesterday?"

"Who told you that?" Mitchell asked, fuming.

"No one told me. Your friends have your back," Bailey said, waving his hand dismissively. "But there was a big stain on the wall, and fragments of your mug on the floor. I don't know if you realize, but I was once a detective as well, and I didn't need to take DNA samples to know what the hell happened!"

Mitchell shut his eyes.

"I want you to take a few days of vacation. Go visit your sister. Spend some time with your girlfriend. Calm the hell down."

"I don't need a vacation. I can get myself together. I can help."

The captain's eyes narrowed. "Don't make me suspend you, Lonnie. I will."

Mitchell opened his mouth to argue again, and then closed it. Beyond the haze of rage and indignation, he knew it was all his fault.

"We're done here," the captain said, his voice calmer, but final. "Send your sister my regards."

———

Jovan Stokes got out of the shower and walked slowly back to his bed. The weak light from the bedside lamp illuminated the small motel room. Someone had decided to go with a bright green color theme when they selected the sheets, wall to wall carpeting, and furniture; the result was less than inspiring. It didn't matter. Jovan wasn't really paying attention to the room's design; it was just a place to sleep.

When he sat on the bed, his entire body shuddered. The worst was over. After the shooting, he had sewn and bandaged his wound himself, nearly fainting at the pain. Now his body felt as if it had gone through shock. He was weak and dizzy, and had a slight temperature. He'd bought some painkillers and was taking them sparingly, trying to get used to the pain. It wasn't going away anytime soon.

He wasn't sure what he should do.

For the past two years, he'd had a plan. He was chasing a moment, a memory, a feeling. A second of pure joy that he had once experienced, long ago. Nothing mattered, except for that moment. For more than twenty years he had lived numbly, his life dreary and boring. Incidents of pleasure, happiness, or even sadness were few and far between.

And then, one day, he had suddenly remembered there had been, once in his life, something else.

But now he wasn't sure he'd ever reach that moment. His plan had encountered an unexpected obstacle. It had nearly cost him his life.

Tanessa Lonnie. She was the first to struggle in any meaningful way. And he hadn't seen it coming.

Maybe he had to move on, choose his next victim, keep with the original plan. Yes. That was what he should do.

He turned on his laptop, knowing the anticipation would make him feel alive again, give meaning to his actions. He waited for the anticipation.

Nothing.

It was as if something was broken inside him, and for a second he panicked, wondering if somehow he had hurt his head when he was shot, if he had maybe suffered some brain damage.

But no, there was a much simpler explanation. He did not want to move on. Because moving on wasn't keeping with the original plan. The original plan was to select a victim and to stick with her, drawing out the anticipation, finally killing her. This plan was supposed to get him closer to that original moment of joy. But now one of his victims had gotten away.

He opened Tanessa's file and stared at her. She was so similar to *her*. A lot more than the others.

Had she really known who he was? How? And how had she moved so fast?

He opened the local news site, wondering if they had added anything to their original, vague report of a shootout in a flower shop.

He stared at the screen.

Tanessa Lonnie.

A cop.

Bait.

A brief moment of rage and fear. The police had almost caught him! They must have figured out how he found his victims! And then they had created this bait, a woman who would snag his attention. Tanessa Lonnie, the sister of one of the detectives who was investigating the case. He shook angrily, nearly hurled the laptop at the wall. And then he paused, as he felt it once again.

Anticipation.

———

Tabitha Mermenstein had been the principal of Glenmore Park High School between 1981 and 1988, which meant she had been the principal when Jovan Stokes had attended there. Jacob hoped she would be able to tell him something that would shed some light on the suspected killer. As he sat in front of her in her living room, he fidgeted a bit, finding himself slightly nervous.

When Jacob had gone to elementary school, the deputy principal, Ms. Bell, had hated him. He'd had a knack for getting himself into fights, and often ended up in her office. There she would yell at him for what felt like hours, as he sat with his eyes downcast, trying his best not to cry. There was a rumor that if she ever caught you with head lice, she would shave your head in the gym while the rest of the class watched. To this day he wasn't sure if this rumor had an inkling of truth in it. He had definitely never participated in such a ghastly ritual. But as a child, sometimes his head itched after he'd gone to bed, and he would lie awake for hours, horrified, certain the next day would be his day of shame.

Tabitha Mermenstein looked *exactly* like Ms. Bell. She had long, gray hair tied into a braid to which no head lice would ever dare come close. Her eyes would have made a hawk feel like perhaps it needed eyeglasses; all the better to spot kids fighting, or random head lice wandering about. Jacob realized that, for the first time, he was quite happy with the knowledge that he was entirely bald.

Of course, he would have to stop thinking about head lice if this interview was to progress in a satisfactory manner.

"What's this about, Detective?" Tabitha asked, her voice clear and formal. She had offered him water when he'd come in, but that was as far as her hospitality went.

He cleared his throat. "Ms. Mermenstein, you were principal of Glenmore Park High School between the years 1983 and 1987, right?"

She thought for a moment. "Yes, that is correct."

"During those years, there was a student named Jovan Stokes. Do you perhaps remember him?"

She made a small snorting noise which did not seem to align with the rest of her demeanor. "Detective, there were about seven hundred students at Glenmore Park High School every year. To assume that I remember any of them thirty years later is frankly quite absurd."

"Of course," Jacob nodded. "But I would be happy if you try and recall anything about him nevertheless. He appears to be a major suspect in our investigation."

"Which investigation would that be?"

"I'm not at liberty to say."

"Well, I'm sorry, but you've wasted your time coming here. I can hardly recall the teachers who worked for me in those years."

"Do you think that one of the teachers that taught him would remember him?"

"I would not presume anything."

This woman was a barrel of laughs. Jacob sighed. "Do you have the yearbooks for those years?" he asked.

"Of course."

He waited for a few seconds. She didn't move. "Can I see them?" he asked.

She nodded curtly and got up, then went over to a tall bookcase and started scanning one of the shelves. "He graduated in 1987?" she asked.

"That's right."

She pulled out a book, yellow with age, and sat back down on her couch. Jacob held out his hand, but instead of handing the book over, she started flipping the pages.

"There," she suddenly said, and gave him the book. It was open to a page full of senior portraits, with names below the images. In the third row, on the left, was a picture of a boy with short, brown hair. He was smiling inanely at the camera. The name under the picture was, indeed, Jovan Stokes. Jacob could see the similarity to the picture he had of him.

"Are there any other pictures of him?" he asked, flipping the pages. Pictures of school club activities, faculty members, and additional portraits filled the pages.

"Possibly," Tabitha said. "If he was involved in school activities, it's likely there are additional pictures of him there."

"Can I take this book with me?" he asked.

"Of course not."

He smiled a tight-lipped smile. "Let me rephrase that question," he said. "I can come with a warrant, and take all of your yearbooks. They'll be stored in the evidence storage room in the police department. You'll be able to get them back in a few months, but it would require some paperwork, and I understand that it's a long process. Or you can loan me this book, I'll photocopy whatever I need from it, and return it within two weeks."

She looked at him, narrowing her eyes. He didn't lower his gaze, nor did he feel the urge to cry. It occurred to him that somewhere along the way, he had grown up, and he didn't even believe anyone's head had ever been shaved in the school's gymnasium.

"Fine," she spat. "But I want it back as soon as possible."

"Thank you," he said, and flipped the pages to the book's beginning. He frowned. "Who's that?" he asked.

She craned her head to see what he was looking at. It was a full-page image of a female student, smiling at the camera. She was clearly very beautiful, with red hair and dark eyes. Jacob felt a deep feeling of déjà vu, like he had seen this girl before.

"That's Gwen Berry," Tabitha said. "She disappeared in the middle of the school year, and was never found. I remember that someone wanted to print *In Memoriam* under the picture, but we weren't sure if she was dead or had simply run away, so we ended up just putting her picture on the first page. It was a dedication of sorts."

"Yeah," Jacob said, staring at the image. He knew where he had seen this girl before. In a bunch of dead women's pictures. She had Kendele's hair and Tamay's eyes. She had Skyler's nose. And she had Tanessa's smile.

"Thank you, Ms. Mermenstein," he said distractedly. "You've been a great help."

TWENTY-SIX

Zoe stared in frustration at the ever-growing mountain of information on her desk. It definitely didn't help that it was a small folding table, whose original purpose was to stand in a kitchen, or outside during a barbecue. When she had joined the task force, Captain Bailey had thought it best if she sat in the squad room with the rest of the detectives. That had sounded like a good idea to Zoe as well, but then she realized no one was about to provide her with a reasonable workspace. They'd put up the folding table in the corner of the room, just next to the coffee machine, so whenever someone felt like coffee he'd walk over and stand above her, looking over her shoulder. Two times in the past week, coffee had been spilled on her table and pages, to the tune of profound apologies from the careless detective. She really missed her own desk, back in Boston. Where she had the luxury of laying *three* pages side by side, and still had room for her computer screen, inbox, and a cup of coffee. Occasionally she returned there to work for a day or two, just to regain a shred of sanity.

Ever since they'd found out Jovan's name the week before, she'd been constantly provided with things that had something to do with him. Some, like the precious yearbook Jacob had retrieved, were invaluable. Other things, like his birth certificate, a newspaper clip from 1977 mentioning his neighborhood, or the printout of a picture in which he appeared in the background sipping from a red cup, were just noise. Now people kept supplying her with things that related to Gwen Berry, his presumed first victim, as well. Trying to construct a profile from all this info was like trying to construct a thousand-piece puzzle after it had been mixed with twenty other puzzles. It was slow, mistake-prone work, and mostly theoretical.

It was also the most exciting case she had ever worked on. She felt extremely lucky to be involved with this case, folding table and all.

She was working on finding connections between Gwen and Jovan. They'd had a math class together, that much Zoe had established. Gwen had been a popular girl, according to her mother, whom Jacob had interviewed the day before. Jovan, from the scarce details Zoe had extracted, was quiet, and so far they hadn't managed to find anyone who really knew him. The few people they'd managed to find who had gone to high school with him either didn't remember him, or remembered him as a figure in the background. He had received a scholarship for excellence, so she assumed he was a brilliant student, though they hadn't acquired the paperwork submitted for the scholarship yet. They needed more people working on this case, and had asked for some assistance from state police and from the FBI. But for some reason the request for more manpower was delayed.

Someone cleared his throat behind her. She recognized it as Captain Bailey, and turned around. He stood by the entrance to the squad room, three people behind him. For a moment she felt relief. Finally! More people. Then recognition hit. No, damn it, not—

"Jacob, Zoe, this is Lieutenant Bob Talbot, from the state police."

"How do you do," Jacob nodded from his desk.

"This is Detective Jacob Cooper, and I believe you know Zoe Bentley," Captain Bailey said.

Talbot nodded at Jacob, then grinned at Zoe. "Yeah," he said. "We've met."

They had. Zoe had been assigned to help the state police create a profile for a serial rapist who had been terrorizing Hyde Park. Bob Talbot was the lead investigator on the case. When she finally submitted the report, he skimmed it and put it aside, saying he didn't think it matched the person they were looking for. The arrogance in the way he had said that had enraged her, as had the fact that he kept staring at her breasts.

She'd said some things. She suggested his pre-frontal cortex failed to regulate the stupid part of his brain. She'd also mentioned cave men mentality. And she had been reprimanded and removed from the case. It later turned out she'd been dead right about the rapist. If they had listened to her, two additional rapes might have been prevented. But that didn't matter, and Lieutenant Talbot hadn't seemed inclined to admit he had been wrong.

"The governor and the chief of the state police have decided that further involvement of the state police in this case is necessary, with deeper involvement by the FBI," Captain Bailey said. The failure of their sting operation must have triggered this, Zoe thought. "From now on we'll be working with Lieutenant Talbot and his men. He'll be leading the case, and coordinating with the FBI."

Zoe looked at Jacob. The detective's face was calm and impassive, almost as if he didn't care.

"Thank you, Captain Bailey," Talbot said. "I'm happy to be working with your team."

"Detective Cooper will be able to fill you in on our progress," Captain Bailey said.

"Absolutely, I'm looking forward to it. I understand that you've been investigating Jovan Stokes's background," Talbot said, looking dismissively at Jacob. He was almost sneering. Zoe wanted to throw her chair at him.

"Yes," Jacob said.

"What progress have you made tracking his digital signature?"

"I'm sorry?" Jacob said.

"Did you try to trace him online? Pinpoint his IP? Maybe find some patterns in his online behavior?" Talbot asked.

"We only have very minimal information regarding his online activity," Jacob said.

"I thought you had a website that he created, and that he had sent an e-mail to a local reporter," Talbot said. "Additionally, you know for a fact that he has entered the Instagram profiles of all his victims, probably several times each."

"That's true."

"It should be enough to start," Talbot said, and turned to Captain Bailey. "Where can my men and I stay while we're tracking Jovan?"

"I'll find you a room," Bailey said. He seemed tired.

"Thanks. For now, I want your men to assemble a detailed list of all the Instagram profiles of the victims, as well as any woman we know has registered on Jovan's site. I need someone to get me that reporter's e-mail account. And I would be happy if someone figured out where Jovan bought that sword. I assume it wasn't sold at Walmart."

"Lieutenant," Zoe said. "They're understaffed as it is, and their effort is focused on reconstructing Jovan's first murder. I need all the—"

"No need," he interrupted briskly. "We believe our focus should be on tracking him online. This isn't the 20th century anymore, Bentley. People leave digital traces everywhere. I'm sure, as a consultant in the Bureau, that you're well aware of it. If you've got the right task force, which we do, you can find anyone without leaving your office."

"Jovan Stokes was very careful—" she began.

He interrupted her again. "Thank you. I believe that we won't be needing your help anymore. You're off the case. I've already discussed this with your superiors"

She had known it as soon as she'd seen his face. He wasn't the kind to forgive and forget. He was practically smirking as he dismissed her from the most important case of her career. She took a page from Detective Cooper's book and made her face blank and calm, pushing down the turmoil she felt. There would be time for anger later.

"Very well. Thank you, Lieutenant," she said. She noticed the flicker of irritation on his face. What did he expect? Did he think she would beg him to let her stay? Or did he want her to throw a fit, call her superiors, realize he was telling the truth?

Captain Bailey led Talbot and his men out. Zoe was left to stare at the mound of useless paperwork on her desk.

A shadow loomed over her. Jacob. Probably there to make himself a cup of coffee.

"It's a shame," he said. "I was feeling we were getting close."

"Yeah," she said morosely.

"It's too bad that all of the detectives in the squad are assigned to work with Talbot," Jacob said.

"I know! It really sucks! I think he's wrong to ignore what we have," she said angrily, biting her lip.

"Yes," Jacob said, pouring himself a cup of coffee. "But all of us are working with him now. Me, Hannah, Bernard. All of us."

"I know that, Detective. I was here. I heard," she said sharply. The man was getting on her nerves.

Jacob cleared his throat. "If only there was someone who could work with you on Jovan Stokes's past," he said.

"There isn't, so there's no sense in harping on it," she said, frustrated.

He stared at her.

"It was nice working with you, Detective," she said after a moment, feeling as if he expected her to say something.

"For God's sake," he said. "Detective Lonnie is available to work with you."

She looked at him. "Oh," she said.

"That's what I was trying to hint at."

"Right."

"I didn't really want to be the one to tell you to disobey your superior officer," Jacob elaborated. "So I tried to be subtle. Mitchell is on a sort of forced vacation. I'm betting he'd be happy to assist you."

"Uh-huh. I see what you mean now," Zoe said, feeling her face redden.

"Let's hope they won't ask me about it," Jacob said. "My plausible deniability is shot to hell. You've been extraordinarily unperceptive. My daughter listens better than you do, and she's a teenager."

"Yes. I know. I was thinking of something else."

"Do you need anything else? Do you want me to call him for you? Or can I go and act as if I don't know anything about this now?"

"I… I think I can take it from here," she said, standing up. She blinked and smiled. "Thank you, Detective."

He smiled back at her and went back to sit at his desk, sipping from his cup of coffee.

Tanessa seemed pale, Mitchell noticed, with black pouches under her eyes. Though she'd recently been released from the hospital, it was clear his sister was far from well. Nevertheless, she lit up when he appeared on her doorstep, pulling him in and bustling off to the kitchen to make them both cups of coffee while shouting pleasantries at him. He looked around the living room. It was drowning in a flowery flood, splashes of colors everywhere. Bouquets had been sent to Tanessa in droves, and it was obvious his sister had run out of containers long ago. Some of the lucky bouquets were in vases, but the rest were either in various plastic bottles that had been filled with water, or simply discarded on shelves to wither in dry, waterless oblivion. The smell of flowers in the room was overpowering, and Mitchell briefly wondered if there was enough oxygen in the air to sustain human life.

Tanessa walked in with two mugs, and handed one to him. He sat down on her couch and she sat next to him, her body facing his.

"I see you got some flowers," he said dryly.

"Yeah, crazy, right?" she laughed. "Most are from George—that's the guy in the flower shop. But there are a lot from the department as well. That one there is from

Captain Bailey, the smaller one next to it is from Captain Marrow, and the huge one on the table is from the chief. I guess that's what happens when you get hurt in the line of duty."

Especially if you got hurt because of your department's colossal mess, Mitchell thought.

"People should really pay attention to what they're sending though," Tanessa carried on. "I mean… That calla lily bouquet? That's for weddings! And those roses and tulips over there are classic valentine flowers, I don't know what the person who sent them was thinking. And, seriously, if you send a bouquet made entirely of California poppies it just looks boring! And this bouquet is clearly meant for funerals, which is just kind of creepy."

"You've become a flower snob," Mitchell remarked.

"Yeah, well, you work in a flower shop for a week, see how you turn out," Tanessa said, punching him lightly in the shoulder and spilling some coffee on the couch. "Aw, shit."

"Well, you shouldn't have worked as bait in a flower shop in the first place," Mitchell muttered.

"Oh, give it a break, Mitchy," Tanessa said. "I can take care of myself."

"Really?" He glanced at the stitches on her neck.

"Yeah, really!" she said, her voice getting sharper. "Didn't I graduate the police academy? Didn't I make several successful arrests already? Didn't I break Bill—"

"Dellinger's nose back in middle school," Mitchell interrupted her. "I know, you always mention him when we argue about this. You accidentally broke a guy's nose and—"

"It wasn't an accident! I head butted him in the nose on purpose!"

"Fine, fine," Mitchell said, tired of the same argument.

They sat for a second in silence, then Tanessa cleared her throat. "Say, where's Pauline? She called to make sure I was all right, but she never came to visit."

Mitchell took a deep breath. "Pauline and I broke up," he said.

"Oh no!" Tanessa's face crumpled. "What happened?"

"Apparently, we're too different from each other," he said.

"Oh, Mitchell, I'm so sorry."

"Yeah, well." He shrugged as if he were over it. This forced vacation was just making it worse. He'd begun to check Pauline's Instagram and Facebook profiles every day, trying to figure out if she was missing him, or if she was seeing anybody else. Another new hobby he'd recently developed was browsing old Instagram photos in her account, photos in which they both appeared, trying to figure out if her smile was real or fake. When this picture had been taken, had she already decided to leave him? That selfie at the beach, did she take it while thinking they were drifting apart?

"Well, if that bitch doesn't realize you're the catch of a lifetime, she's not good enough for you anyway," Tanessa said, her voice angry. Mitchell smiled wanly. He was beginning to suspect he wasn't really the catch of a lifetime. Pauline was, and he'd blown it.

"The officer outside your door seems… bored," Mitchell said, changing the subject. The cop had been half asleep when Mitchell showed up.

"Can you blame him?" Tanessa said. "Watching my door for eight hours? I'd go insane."

"Maybe, but he won't do any good if Jovan shows up here," Mitchell said. "They should relocate you somewhere safe. Just until we catch him."

"What if you don't, Mitchell?" Tanessa asked him, her voice low. "What if he just disappears? How long do I stay in hiding? A month? A year?"

He was about to answer when his phone rang. He checked the screen. It was an unrecognized number. He nearly didn't answer, but Tanessa had already gotten up and gone back to the kitchen. She was probably getting some chocolate.

That was Tanessa's answer to all of life's problems. Chocolate. He answered the call.

"Hello?"

"Hi, uh… Mitchell?" a feminine voice said.

"Yeah, who's this?"

"It's Zoe Bentley."

"Oh!" he was surprised. "Hi!" He almost added *Why are you calling me?* but stopped himself. "Is this about the case?" he asked instead.

"Well… sort of. I've been reassigned. I'm no longer on the case."

"Oh, okay," he said, frowning. "I'm not involved anymore. You should tell Jacob, he's the lead detective."

"He knows," she said. "He's no longer the lead detective. There's an ass… a lieutenant from the state police who's leading it now."

"I see," Mitchell said. "So… did you call to say goodbye?" He felt confused. They'd exchanged no more than a hundred words the entire time she was working with him, and she'd somehow still managed to irritate him a few times.

"No. Listen, the guys that are now leading the investigation are taking it in a completely different direction, and I want to keep pursuing Jovan's background. I'm acting on my own here."

"Okay," Mitchell said. The conversation felt surreal. Sometimes it was just best to lay things flat on the table. "Zoe, why did you call me? What do you want?"

"I want you to work with me on this," she said.

"Oh," he said.

Tanessa came into the living room holding a bowl full of M&Ms in one hand, and two chocolate bars in the other hand.

"Sure," he told Zoe. "Where do you want to meet?"

TWENTY-SEVEN

As far as Mitchell was concerned, there was only one place in Glenmore Park to get Indian food, and that was Bhopal's Indian Eatery. To be fair, there were only two Indian restaurants in the city, and Delhi's Cuisine was infamous for serving food that was spicy to the point of inferno, so there wasn't a lot of competition. Still, Bhopal's Indian Eatery served very good food, and Mitchell loved to go there. Pauline hadn't liked Indian food, so they'd never gone there together, a detail that was very much in his thoughts as he gave Zoe the address.

She was waiting for him outside, dressed in a thin black coat and tight jeans. He realized it was the first time he'd ever seen her out of her gray suit. It made her look much younger, as did the embarrassed smile on her face.

"I didn't want to walk in without you," she said. "I'm not sure why. I didn't want to be the girl sitting alone at a table for two."

"Okay," he said, and stopped in front of her. There was that smell again. Pauline's shampoo. He blinked, trying to dispel the jumble of emotions that hit him when he smelled that scent.

"Let's go in," he said, clearing his throat.

The sharp, spicy smells that hit them as soon as they opened the restaurant's door obliterated any lingering effect of the emotional shampoo scent. The red and orange colors of the eatery were a sharp change from the dark black and blue shades of the night sky outside, and Mitchell paused for a second to get his bearings. The waitress led them to their table, and they sat down. Zoe took off her coat to reveal a low cut white shirt, and Mitchell managed to locate huge reserves of willpower and keep his eyes fixed on her face. That was a problem as well, since her stare made him feel, yet again, as if she had X-ray vision that could easily bypass his skull and reach for his brain.

The waitress handed them menus and asked if they wanted to order drinks.

"Water, please, and *thali*," Zoe said, without looking at the menu.

"I'll have *thali* as well," Mitchell said. "And a pint of Julius, please."

The waitress took their menus and left.

"So… you like Indian food?" Mitchell asked.

"When it's good," Zoe said.

"Oh, it's very good here."

"I certainly hope so."

They sat in silence for a moment.

"I talked to Jacob," Mitchell said. "He sounded really surprised to hear that you called me."

"Yeah?" Zoe grinned.

"Jacob is never surprised at anything," Mitchell said. "He's three hundred years old. He's seen everything."

"Yes. He might have hinted that this would be a good idea."

"Okay. I'm not exactly sure what this is," Mitchell said. "I mean… the staties and the FBI took over, right? It sucks for us that we didn't get the guy, but it sounds like a lot of very talented people are now looking for him. They'll get him."

"Maybe," Zoe said. "Probably. But how long until they do? Two weeks? Three? Four? That could potentially mean two or three victims. The killer is getting impatient and impulsive."

"You can't know that."

"The frequency of the murders is accelerating, Mitchell. The memory of the murder is no longer enough; he has to commit them to feel the same thrill. He feels a compulsion to keep killing to chase that feeling."

"Maybe, but he could be feeling vulnerable right now, because he's just been shot," Mitchell pointed out. "So that might make him slow down."

"I find that very unlikely. His central drive is thrill-seeking. He won't become dormant just because he got hit. He survived it, didn't he? He'll want to experience the stimulation again, and there's only one way he can do that. By—"

"Stop doing that!" Mitchell snapped. "Cut it out with all the bullshit! What you just said could apply to any psychopath out there, and it means fuck-all. It doesn't get me closer to catching the guy—"

Zoe flushed, her eyes becoming angry slits. "This was a mistake," she said, and stood up.

"Look—" Mitchell began.

"Shut up, Mitchell, okay? I don't go shitting all over your job, don't go shitting over mine. I get that you have girl problems in your life or whatever, but taking it out on other women is frankly disgusting. And I don't think you're in any shape to find where you parked your car, never mind locate a serial killer!" She whirled around and walked out.

"Damn," he muttered. He realized the waitress was standing next to him, two servings of *thali* in her hands. "Just put them down," he said. "I'll get her back."

She seemed skeptical, but nevertheless put the dishes on the table as Mitchell dashed after Zoe.

"Zoe!" He caught up to her as she was unlocking her car.

"Fuck off!"

"Look… Can we start over? I'm sorry I… acted like an asshole. You didn't deserve that."

"Yes, you were very much an asshole. I'm going home."

"Look, you're right," Mitchell said, his voice earnest. "He's out there, and he's dangerous. There's no time to lose, and you and I can prevent another murder. Just… don't leave, okay?"

She turned to him. "Fine," she said curtly. "But you're paying for dinner."

"I was going to do that anyway," he muttered as they walked back to the restaurant.

They sat down and started to eat. Mitchell didn't say anything, letting Zoe cool off.

"It's not bad *thali*," she finally said.

"It's the best," Mitchell said.

"I've eaten better."

"Yeah? Where?" he asked, his tone challenging.

"In India."

"Oh." He felt deflated. This woman made him feel ridiculous at every turn.

"It's really fine, though."

Mitchell ate another bite. "So… Did Jacob tell you about Pauline?"

"Who's Pauline?"

"My ex. When you said I have girl problems, I just assumed…"

"Oh." She waved her fork dismissively "It's all over your face. You've been walking around like a lost puppy for about a week. I know a broken heart when I see one."

"Because you're a psychologist?"

"No," she said, her mouth twisting into a small smile. "Because I'm me."

He realized he was grinning at her. "Okay," he said. "So what's your plan?"

"Well… we've been researching Jovan Stokes's history, right? Why?"

"To understand him better, I guess," Mitchell said.

"Right. If we get why he kills the way he does, we might be able to predict where he hits next, right?"

"Theoretically." Mitchell was wary of angering Zoe again.

"I want to find out the connection between Jovan Stokes and Gwen Berry. She's what molded him, what turned him into what he is. She was his first victim, and it's likely that his entire M.O. is related to that first murder. Now, that idiot Talbot—"

"Who?"

"That's the new guy in charge of the investigation. He doesn't care about old crimes. He's focusing on the recent murders."

"Sounds like the smart thing to do."

"Don't start with me, Mitchell. Anyway, this is an abandoned angle, and I think it's important, so I was thinking we should check it out ourselves."

Mitchell ate his food, thinking about it. He doubted it would get them anywhere, but he could sure use the distraction. And the idea of working with Zoe Bentley was strangely alluring.

"Okay," he finally said. "It's worth checking out."

She smiled at him, and laid her hand on his wrist. Startled, he almost pulled his hand back. Her fingers were warm, soft. "We're going to make a great team," she said.

For the rest of the evening, they sifted through possible leads, of which there was a long list, trying to determine how to tackle the case. They finally decided to try and find people who went to school with Jovan Stokes and Gwen Berry, hoping to get lucky and find someone who really knew one of them.

———

In the following days, they came up with plenty of people who had known Gwen, and no one who remembered Jovan. Gwen, it turned out, had been popular, just like her mother said. Mitchell and Zoe met three different girls who claimed they were Gwen's best friend, and two ex-boyfriends. Since she had disappeared and was presumed dead, the memories were colored somewhat. They all remembered a perfect version of Gwen: loving, caring, couldn't hurt a fly, everyone loved her, beautiful, funny, smart… It was difficult to pry for a reason anyone would want her dead. One of the ex-boyfriends said he recalled she didn't really like dogs, but that hardly seemed like a motive for murder.

Then again, Zoe said, it was very likely Jovan had killed Gwen precisely because she had been beautiful, funny, and popular.

Jovan, as far as his schoolmates were concerned, was invisible. People remember their best friend in high school, the beautiful girl they had a crush on, the bully who harassed them, the guy in class who was the first to own a car… No one remembered the silent student who aced his tests.

It didn't help that Zoe was wrong—they didn't make a great team at all.

Detective partners developed a routine of questioning. Everyone knew the "good cop, bad cop" routine, but it was just one of many. Mitchell and Jacob were "cold cop, warm cop," with Jacob questioning about the hard facts, and then Mitchell taking control of the conversation, with his sorrowful eyes understanding and kind. Hannah and Bernard had a routine that could best be described as "human cop, Incredible Hulk cop," as Hannah performed the entire interrogation calmly until, at a moment of impasse, Bernard would explode with rage, extracting a confession from the terrified suspect.

Mitchell and Zoe had not yet developed a routine, and their natural chemistry was pretty much crap. At first, Mitchell thought they were simply like oil and water, two professionals who did not mix well. Later, he began to suspect a better analogy would be a dieting book and a chocolate cake, or running shoes and an elegant suit. Two things that actively negated each other and disrupted each other's efforts.

In one interview, a tearful woman told them how Gwen had confided in her that someone had been following her. Mitchell was holding her hand, leaning forward, his face full of compassion as she told them what a burden the memory had been all these years.

And then Zoe asked, her voice dry, why the woman hadn't mentioned it before. The spell was broken. The woman fumbled for an explanation, and finally said she wasn't sure she was remembering right. Then she recalled that she had to take her boy to a piano lesson. When Mitchell confronted Zoe, she said the woman was just inventing tales to feel important. Mitchell suspected this was true, but he asked Zoe to shut the hell up next time.

A few hours later, they were interviewing a man who thought he remembered Jovan. He was talking endlessly, just to fill in the silence. Whenever he stopped, Zoe repeated the last sentence he'd said, and he would start anew. But Mitchell grew impatient with the man's long, winding stories about cafeteria food and their strange-smelling history teacher, and he asked point blank what the man remembered of Jovan. After a second, the man said he didn't remember much, really. The rest of the interview was halting and pointless. Zoe said nothing when they left, but Mitchell could feel her judgmental vibes as they got into the car.

Some of the people they questioned had their yearbooks available. They were all happy to talk about Gwen's disappearance, contributing their own theories, which ranged from her eloping with a sailor to her being kidnapped by a secret cell of Russian spies. When pointed to Jovan's picture, some would blink and shrug, while others would frown and say hesitantly that they thought they remembered seeing him around. No one connected Jovan to Gwen.

"Let's try to zoom out a bit," Mitchell said. They were sitting in Raul's Cafe, taking a short break. Mitchell was sipping an Americano, while Zoe ignored her cafe latte and messed around with a cinnamon roll, which she was slowly taking apart with her fingers. Mitchell tried to concentrate on his thoughts, but the cinnamon roll massacre in front of him was distracting.

"Yeah, sure, okay," Zoe said. "Zoom out. What do you mean?"

"Let's stick to the facts. What do we think happened?" Mitchell asked, prying his stare from Zoe's sticky fingers.

"We think that Jovan killed Gwen, and kept a lock of her hair as a souvenir in his home," Zoe said.

"Are we sure that's what happened?" Mitchell asked. "Could he have killed a different redhead?"

"That's your department," Zoe said. "I just make up amusing psychological theories."

"Well…" Mitchell raised a finger. "We don't really know how old that hair is, nor do we have DNA proof that it was Gwen's. But it seems like the most plausible explanation. We have a missing redheaded girl. We have a serial killer who went to school with her. We have a lock of red hair in the killer's apartment which really seems to match her hair color. I'm sold on the Jovan killed Gwen theory."

"Me too," Zoe said, finally putting a piece of the roll in her mouth. "Okay, wess affume that Jova—"

"I can't understand a word you're saying," Mitchell interrupted. "Didn't your mother teach you not to talk about serial killers with your mouth full?"

Zoe chewed a bit, lifting her finger as if to claim the next sentence in the conversation for herself. Mitchell drank the rest of his Americano in one gulp. He was drinking a lot more coffee these days. He was hardly sleeping.

Finally, Zoe swallowed her bite, sipped noisily from her mug, and said, "Let's assume that Jovan killed Gwen."

"Right." Mitchell nodded. "But is that really interesting?"

"Yes," Zoe said. "It's the murder that molded him into—"

"Yeah, yeah, I get it. But apart from that. We have no witnesses, any evidence is gone, and even if we found out what happened, it probably won't help us find him now."

"Stop trying to cheer me up," Zoe muttered.

"Let's talk about the second murder for a bit, okay?"

"The second… you mean Isabella Garcia?"

"No. I mean his wife. He probably killed his wife, right?"

"Probably," Zoe said.

"Do you think he killed anyone between Gwen and his wife?" Mitchell asked.

"I don't know. Maybe. But suppose he didn't." Zoe thought for a moment. "We know that his wife disappeared, and then all those girls start dying. One after the other. And he's accelerating. Yes, I think he was dormant for all those years. I think he killed his wife, and she was his second victim."

"You can't do that," Mitchell said impatiently. "You can't conjecture a whole story without a shred of evidence, and then say that's what happened."

"Why not?"

"It's unprofessional."

"I think you're just unimaginative," Zoe said, her eyes twinkling at him infuriatingly. "Fine. Let's assume for a minute that his wife was his second victim, okay?"

"Great, let's." Mitchell said. "So why don't we investigate that murder?"

"Well…" Zoe seemed unhappy. "We agreed we'd investigate Gwen's murder, remember? Because it's what molded him into—"

"Zoe, I'm going to say something, and I need you to not get up and throw a fit, okay?"

Zoe nodded silently.

"I don't give a damn about what molded him, okay? I just want to catch the guy. I'm not shitting on your job. You're amazing, and you have great instincts, and you're probably right about everything, but we need to stop him. And investigating a thirty-year old murder won't do that."

"Okay," Zoe said. "So what do you want to do?"

"We're investigating in the wrong place," Mitchell said. "We should be looking in Boston, talking to people who knew his wife and him."

"Bernard and Hannah already did that."

"They never finished," Mitchell pointed out. "They got called back."

Zoe thought for a moment, licking crumbs off her finger. Mitchell stared at her mouth, transfixed. Finally, she leaned back and wiped her fingers on a napkin. "Okay," she said. "But if we're going to Boston, it's not because of all of what you just said. It's because when he killed his wife, that's when something truly woke up in him. That first murder was just a fluke. The second murder created his compulsion."

"Sure," Mitchell grinned. "Whatever rocks your boat."

TWENTY-EIGHT

Mitchell called Meredith Johnson, who had reported her sister Wanda missing when she disappeared two years earlier. Meredith said she could actually meet them that very evening. Zoe said they would take her car. They'd been using Mitchell's car in Glenmore Park, but Boston was Zoe's city and Mitchell didn't want to argue. He had a feeling that if he argued, Zoe would say he just didn't want to let a woman drive. And she'd probably back it up with psychology. No, it was probably better to take Zoe's car.

She switched on the radio, turning it to WJMN. Mitchell was about to say something condescending, but caught himself just in time.

Traffic was relatively sparse, and Mitchell realized he was slowly relaxing. Zoe was lost in thought, half smiling as she drove, her face distant. Mitchell watched her for a few seconds, surprised at how sweet she seemed when she wasn't staring at him with her eagle eyes. Her lips were pink and soft, and he caught himself wondering what it would feel like to kiss them.

"Oh, I love this song!" she suddenly said, and turned the volume up.

"What… *It's Gonna Be Forever*?" Mitchell asked, bemused.

"It's actually called *Blank Space*," Zoe said.

"Are you—"

"Shhhhh."

"Seriously? I mean—"

She turned the volume up a bit more. "Shut up!" she said, grinning, her head bobbing with the beat. She began to sing along, her features softening as she lost herself in the music.

As she got to the middle of the chorus, Mitchell burst out laughing.

"What?" she said playfully. "Do you have a problem with my voice?"

"Did you just sing 'Got a list of Starbucks lovers'?" he asked.

"Yeah."

"Awesome."

"What? Those are the words."

"Oh, definitely," Mitchell nodded, his face suddenly serious. "Starbucks lovers."

"Yeah! They're like… y'know. Cheap lovers. Like the coffee you get in Starbucks. A guilty pleasure."

"U-huh."

"You didn't even know the name of the song!" Zoe said.

"No, no, you're definitely right. You know what I think? I think you should go to a karaoke bar and sing this song. In front of a large crowd. You sing it really well."

"Are you messing with me?"

"Absolutely not! Just make sure you sing the line with the Starbucks lovers."

"Those are the words!"

Mitchell burst out laughing again.

They fell silent, listening to the music for a bit.

"So… How'd you end up a cop?" she asked.

"Well… my father was a defense attorney," Mitchell said. "So I guess I was exposed to a lot of really depressing stories when I was young. Criminals who never got a second chance, cops who abused their role, and a crappy system that didn't really work. When Richard and I—"

"Who's Richard?"

"My twin brother," Mitchell answered. "When Richard and I grew up, we both kind of wanted to fix things. So

I became a cop, and he became a defense attorney, like Dad was."

"Are you guys close?"

"Richard and I? Yeah. He also lives in Glenmore Park. He's kind of pissed off at me right now."

"Why?"

"Because Tanessa got hurt."

"How is that your fault?"

"It is."

"Your brother sounds just as dumb as you are."

"I'm usually considered to be the dumbest of the siblings," Mitchell said cheerfully. "What about you? How did you become a Fed?"

"I'm not really a Fed; I'm just a consultant for the bureau."

"Whatever. You're still a suit. How did you become an FBI consultant?"

"Too much TV, I guess," Zoe said. "I always thought it would be really awesome, working for the FBI."

"And isn't it?"

"Sometimes. I don't know. I definitely like this case."

They became silent. Mitchell preferred not to talk about the case, enjoying the intimacy of their conversation. He didn't want Jovan Stokes to ruin it.

"Why did you and Pauline break up?" Zoe asked, and quickly added, "It's okay if you don't want to talk about it. Just tell me to shut up."

"No, it's okay," Mitchell said. "I have no idea. Apparently she thought we've been drifting apart for a while."

"And you didn't?"

"I was about to propose to her. I bought the ring and everything."

"Aw, crap. I'm sorry."

"Yeah."

Zoe put her right hand on his knee and smiled at him. "She sounds stupid."

"Yeah?" Mitchell said, his leg tingling at the touch. "Maybe. I don't know."

She took her hand off his knee and put it back on the steering wheel. The rest of the drive was quiet, and Mitchell found himself glancing at her every few minutes, just to look at her again.

———

When they reached Meredith Johnson's home, it was almost nine in the evening. Mitchell felt a pang of regret when the car stopped. He had enjoyed the calm ride, the complete release, his endless spinning thoughts slowing down to a casual pace. Now, as they looked at the red brick row house in which Meredith lived, he felt his mind accelerate again, a jumble of racing feelings and images screaming in his mind. Jovan Stokes attacking Tanessa, the police failing to protect her, guilt over his own failure—they all started whirring again. Looming above all this was a constant cloud of longing for Pauline.

"Shall we?" Zoe asked. She was frowning, looking at him, and he wondered if his feelings were so obviously written on his face.

"Yeah, sure," he said, and they got out of the car.

Meredith opened the door for them and led them to a small, cozy living room. It reminded Mitchell of his grandmother's home, which he'd visited almost every Christmas as a kid. Meredith herself was about fifty, with salt-and-pepper hair. Her face was plain and covered with pale makeup; her mascara and lipstick fought one another for dominance. Her eyes were large and blue, and it wasn't clear why she covered her face with so many colors that would attract attention away from them. They sat down, Meredith on a rocking chair, Mitchell and Zoe on the scarlet couch. For a moment they both tried to sit on the left edge of the couch, closer to Meredith. Then Mitchell shot Zoe a look, and she relented, letting him sit closer.

"Meredith, we wanted to ask you a few questions about your sister, and about Jovan Stokes," Mitchell said.

"Sure," she said. "The police suddenly took interest lately, after ignoring me for two years. They already asked me everything."

"Who did?" Mitchell asked.

"Two detectives came here a few days ago. A black guy and a skinny woman. They asked a lot of questions about Jovan," Meredith said.

Mitchell nodded, ignoring the stereotypes in which Meredith placed Bernard and Hannah. "Okay," he said. "We'll just—"

"Sometimes it helps to talk about things a second time," Zoe interrupted. "It might jog your memory a bit."

Mitchell cursed himself for not discussing their interview strategy with Zoe beforehand. They'd be tripping over each other again.

"Anything that would help to find Wanda," Meredith said.

"When did you realize that your sister had disappeared?" Mitchell asked.

"Well, she didn't reply to my phone calls," Meredith said. "We used to talk almost every day. And then I found out that she'd missed a shift at work, and they couldn't get a hold of her. She was a doctor, you know."

Mitchell nodded.

"I called Jovan, but he didn't answer either, so I went to their house and there was no one there."

"Did you have a key?" Mitchell asked.

"Yes. I let myself in. There was no one in the house."

Mitchell knew from the police report that they'd found most of Jovan and Wanda's clothes missing, along with some toiletries, their wallets, and their car keys. Both cars were missing as well. It all seemed to indicate that the couple had decided to leave in a hurry, though it wasn't clear why.

"So you called the police," Mitchell said.

"Yes," Meredith said, nodding. "And they came and looked around. And then they said it looked like they'd gone on vacation and had forgotten to mention it." She shook her head angrily. "I told them that Wanda would never have left with Jovan. She was in the process of divorcing him. The police just said that maybe they were patching things up. They were very impatient with me."

"I'm sorry," Mitchell said.

"After a week, when no one heard from Wanda, they looked a bit deeper," Meredith said. "They asked some questions, checked around a bit, and said they'd call if there was any progress in the case. But they never did."

A case like that, of a missing couple, would be very low on the police's priority list.

"I never heard from Wanda again," Meredith said. She said it calmly, her voice practiced, but underneath Mitchell heard a current of sorrow and longing. His fingers moved forward, about to touch Meredith's hand in compassion, when Zoe said, "Why did Wanda want to divorce Jovan?"

"He was… not a good man," Meredith said. "At first, Wanda was happy with their relationship. She was very focused on her career, and a life partner who didn't really stand in the way was just the thing she felt she needed. But later on things began to bother her. She caught him lying to her several times. And he could sometimes lose his temper, become quite aggressive—"

"I'm sorry," Mitchell said. "You said she caught him lying. Lying about what?"

"About all sorts of stuff. It seemed like he was lying for the hell of it. She once discovered that the names of half his co-workers were different from the names he told her. Or he'd make up a story about a patient that she later found out never existed. Just the weirdest lies."

"Did she think he was hiding something?"

"Well… yes. But most of the lies he told weren't covering for anything. They were just… lies."

"You said that he was violent sometimes," Zoe said.

"No, not violent. Aggressive. He was never really violent, but he would scream at her the most horrible things. Most of the times, he was simply cold, never demonstrating any affection. Eventually she wanted more." She became silent.

"Eventually she wanted more," Zoe repeated.

"That's right," Wanda said, but did not elaborate.

"Ms. Johnson, anything you can add will be a great help to our investigation," Zoe said.

"I'm not sure what you—"

"Did Wanda have a lover?"

Meredith drew back.

Mitchell wanted to strangle Zoe. He'd been so close to making a connection. Now the woman would become cold and distant. Another dead end.

He was about to try and salvage the situation, when Meredith said, "Yes."

"I see," Zoe said. "For how long?"

"A few months. It was another doctor at the hospital. A really lovely man. She wasn't proud of it, and she was about to tell Jovan."

"We'll need the doctor's name," Zoe said.

"Of course. His name is Barry Rose. I think I have his phone number written down. I'll go get it."

"In a minute," Mitchell said hurriedly. "We'd like to ask just a couple of additional questions."

"Sure," she nodded.

He prayed Zoe would shut up, and pushed forward. "Are you sure Wanda didn't simply run away with Jovan? Decide to start a new life with him?" he asked, trying to touch that raw nerve yet again.

"Of course I'm sure."

"Why are you so sure, Ms. Johnson? People move all the time."

"Wanda would never have left her job without telling anyone," Meredith said angrily, looking at the floor. "She was so responsible. And she'd never… she would have let me know. I'm sure she would have let me know. She would have called me…" Her voice cracked, just a bit. Mitchell leaned forward and touched her wrist lightly. She raised her eyes and met his compassionate stare.

"I'm sorry," he said. "Of course you're right. It isn't likely that she just left."

Her face crumpled, the words she'd wanted to hear for so long finally spoken. As tears ran down her cheeks, she told Mitchell about how close she and her sister had always been. How she was Wanda's bridesmaid. How Wanda had always protected her when their mother complained that Meredith never aimed high, that she couldn't find a nice guy, or a good job, or be more like her sister.

Zoe remained silent.

"I kept some of her things," she said, sniffling. "Once in a while I like to look through them."

Mitchell didn't recall Bernard and Hannah mentioning this. "Can we see them?"

"They're in a storage facility, with some of my stuff," Meredith said. "Not far away from here. I can call the man at the reception tomorrow, ask him to let you in to take a look."

"That would be very helpful," Mitchell said, and Meredith smiled at him with a tear-stained face.

———

Mitchell realized the problem as soon as they left Meredith's home. He was mentally preparing himself for the ride back to Glenmore Park when Zoe said her apartment wasn't very far. Of course, she lived here, it was only natural she'd want to go and sleep in her own bed. Except they'd driven to Boston in her car. He was about to ask if he could take her car to drive home, when she said she had a really comfortable spare bed in the living room.

"Uh, I didn't really pack…" he began, thinking of all the things he needed. A toothbrush was definitely at the top of the list.

"It's just one night, Mitchell," she smiled at him. "I swear, my sister sleeps at my place all the time, and she says the spare bed is better than the real bed in her home."

"Yeah, okay," he said after a second. He could always brush his teeth with his finger. God knew he'd done that more than once when he was in college. They stopped on the way to pick up some Thai food, and then drove to Zoe's home.

Zoe's apartment was a small, three-roomed space, sparsely decorated. The air felt a bit dusty, as apartments were bound to be after being left empty for a while. The living room was mostly a couch, a TV, and a small coffee table on which several books were lying.

"I have a fish," she said, unfolding the couch in the living room into a medium-sized bed. "And some plants. But I took them all to my friend's apartment when I joined the investigation. I didn't want to drive to and from Glenmore Park every day."

"Yeah, I get that," he said.

She got him some sheets from her bedroom, and then managed to locate an unopened toothbrush in her bathroom.

"I always buy a few," she said. "I usually throw away my toothbrush after a few months. I don't like it when it gets worn. It grosses me out."

They ate the Thai food in silence. Mitchell felt slightly uncomfortable while Zoe seemed completely at ease, chewing as she stared at a random spot on the wall. She ate her noodles with chopsticks, but Mitchell asked for a fork, thinking he should really try to get the hang of chopsticks some day. He felt like a caveman, pushing his fork into the cardboard box like a shovel, noodles constantly dropping from his fork back into the box. Arguably, cavemen didn't have Thai food, but they probably ate their takeout mammoths the same way. In contrast, Zoe distractedly picked up the noodles with the two thin sticks, opening her mouth delicately to eat, her mind elsewhere.

He went to brush his teeth. He wanted to shower, but didn't want to step into his worn clothes afterward, so he washed his face and his hair a bit in the sink instead. He had been told several times that his body odor was nice, and he supposed it was time to put that theory to the test yet again.

He lay down on the spare bed, and Zoe went to shower. He tried to close his eyes, feeling exhausted and sleep deprived, but his mind kept churning. It brought up images of Pauline, as it always did in the evening. He wondered for the hundredth time if she'd have stayed with him if he had proposed straight after he bought the ring. Probably not, but a small part of him believed she would have, and he kicked himself repeatedly for not doing so.

The sound of running water stopped, and in the darkness he saw Zoe, wrapped in a bathrobe, come out of the bathroom. The same familiar smell of Pauline's shampoo lingered behind her as she entered her bedroom. He breathed slowly and tried to relax, hoping sleep would come.

Thoughts about Jovan resurfaced. Would they find anything the following day? Perhaps Wanda's lover could shed new light on the case, or maybe there was a clue in Wanda's possessions?

The image of Tanessa lying there in the hospital popped into his mind again. She had tried to act brave, dismissing the entire thing, but he'd seen the pain in her eyes, and the fear. During the day Mitchell felt furious at Captain Marrow for calling off Tanessa's protection, but at night he would become consumed with guilt, certain it was all his fault for arresting the wrong couple, for creating a distraction. If George hadn't saved Tanessa, if she had been even slightly slower, she would have been dead. And it was all his fault.

Zoe's bedroom door opened and she walked into the living room. She was dressed in a long blue shirt that reached the middle of her thighs. She walked closer to him, her bare feet soundless against the floor.

"Hey," he said. She didn't answer. Instead, she leaned over him, lifting her leg over, straddling him. He could hear her breaths, short and fast, as she bent forward. Her lips brushed against his and opened slightly. He lifted his head a bit, his hands still at his sides, pressing his mouth against hers. She tasted fresh; her tongue darted forward just a bit to meet his. She bit his lower lip, and he realized he was holding his breath.

His hand grabbed the back of her neck, pulling her closer, suddenly craving the taste of her mouth, the touch of her tongue. His other hand caressed her back over the shirt, fingers light against her spine, the shirt silky and smooth. As he reached her lower back he realized she wore nothing except for the shirt, that she was sitting on him naked, and it drove him wild. Both his hands grabbed her ass, pulling her forward; her arm crept back, her fingers sneaking into his underwear.

Later, as she slept by his side, her hair tickling his ear, he felt completely calm for the first time in days. After a few minutes, he was asleep as well.

TWENTY-NINE

"This is the one." Jonas Roza, the manager of Roza Storage Solutions, stood in front of a blue metal door. It was one of a dozen metal doors in that row, and looked just like the others, but Mitchell didn't doubt Jonas's ability to distinguish one storage compartment from the other.

"Can you unlock it, please?" he asked.

The manager nodded, and bent to unlock the door. As he fiddled with the stubborn lock, Mitchell glanced at Zoe, who seemed fascinated by Jonas's efforts. Or maybe she just didn't want to meet Mitchell's eyes.

She hadn't been in the spare bed when he woke up, though he wasn't sure when she had left it. He'd slept deeply, and his phone had beeped for thirty seconds before it managed to penetrate his dreams and wake him up. Zoe had come out of her bedroom a few minutes later, already dressed, and asked him pleasantly how his sleep was. All morning, she'd acted as if the night before hadn't happened, talking with him about the case, and the best way to tackle their leads.

Mitchell followed suit, though he wanted to say something about it. But what? "You remember the sex we had last night?" Or maybe, "Hey, great sexing last night. Maybe we should have more sex in the near future." Any sentence he came up with sounded like something Austin Powers' slower brother would say.

Perhaps Zoe's attitude of leaving the night to linger only in their memories was better.

"There you go," Jonas said as he rolled the door up. "Knock yourself out. Call me once you're done." He turned and left, leaving them alone with Meredith's storage container.

It would have been nice if the storage contained only Wanda's things, preferably in boxes labeled *For serial killer clues, start here. This side up.* But instead the storage container was packed with what could only be called junk. Meredith was a hoarder. There were stacks of magazines, a rusty bike, a bag full of glass bottles, old fabrics, a broken chair, a tent... and that was just what Mitchell could reach. It got worse further back. There was an odd smell in the air, as if Meredith had decided at one point to store food in this container, and then forgotten about it.

They began pulling things out, searching for the boxes. They decided to create a small tunnel in the junk, cutting toward the back, after noticing that the far wall of the container was lined with boxes. After a few minutes, Zoe began to sneeze and cough.

"Dust allergy," she explained.

"You should stay back," Mitchell said. "I'll do this."

She shook her head, shut her mouth tight, and kept pulling bags and items out. But she got worse, and eventually she just sounded like a sneezing beat box. Finally, she walked out and sat on an old mini fridge, a look of frustration on her face. Her nose was as red as a tomato, her eyes were watering, and she coughed constantly.

It took Mitchell two hours, but eventually he located four boxes labeled *Wanda*. He prayed to the saint of storage containers that there weren't any more in there. He pulled the boxes out, and he and Zoe opened them and started to sift through their contents.

It was anyone's guess what Meredith's strategy had been when she decided what should go into the boxes. There were several books, as well as some clothes. In one of the boxes they found a bunch of CDs, mostly Johnny Cash.

Two boxes brimmed with papers, and those were much slower to sift through. Diplomas—both Wanda's and Jovan's—a bunch of bills, several printed medical articles, in two of which Wanda Stokes was mentioned as a contributor, some medical magazines… stuff and stuff and more stuff. Just random papery noise.

And then, stacked between an insurance policy and a thick pile of receipts, Zoe located an envelope that contained some Polaroid pictures.

They looked very old; the color was beginning to fade. One was of a small grove, the trees sparse. A second picture was of the same grove, further back. The third was the same. Six pictures of the same grove. They were not good photographs by any standard; some of them were a bit fuzzy, as if the camera hadn't been focused properly.

Zoe was about to put the pictures aside, when Mitchell grabbed her hand. It was the first time he had touched her that day, and for a moment he felt her tense, her breathing becoming rapid. Then she pulled her hand away.

"That grove," he said, ignoring the angry frown on her face. "It's in Buttermere Park."

"Where's that?" she asked.

"It's where Kendele Byers's body was found," he said.

———

It was a relatively pleasant day, and Buttermere Park was full of people. There were several joggers as well, despite the fact that a jogger had lost her life in this very park only a few months before. They jogged past Mitchell and Zoe, who walked briskly toward the grove. Mitchell had a dark duffel bag on his shoulder. It contained two shovels and a bottle of water.

They didn't really expect to find anything, but they felt they were following the best lead they had. Wanda's lover, it turned out, had moved to Texas. He spoke with Mitchell briskly on the phone, saying repeatedly that he knew nothing, claiming he had never known a woman named Wanda Stokes. A quick check found that he had been married at the time of the supposed affair, so his denial was easily explained. If needed, they would dig deeper into it, but for now they had a grove to investigate.

Kendele's burial site had been filled in, though there was a small memorial stone with several bouquets of wilted flowers and a framed picture of Kendele. Mitchell wondered where it had all come from, as Kendele hardly knew anyone in Glenmore Park. Sometimes people were just attracted to sadness. He could relate. He was relieved that none of her customers seemed to have left anything.

The pictures in the envelope were of a deeper part of the grove, though it was hard to determine where, exactly.

Mitchell and Zoe had hoped they'd locate the exact place by walking around, comparing the trees in the pictures to the ones around them. Of course, they hadn't accounted for the fact that trees tended to change with time. They had walked around for about forty-five minutes, seeing nothing similar, when Mitchell noticed something.

Most of the ground in the grove was carpeted with dead leaves, though there were occasional clumps of yellow flowers here and there. But at one spot, the trees were sparser, and numerous flowers grew there.

"That's weird," he said.

"What?" Zoe asked.

"Those flowers," he said. "I didn't see them anywhere else in the grove, did you?"

Zoe shrugged. "No, I don't think so, but this point is sunnier. Perhaps that's why they grew here."

"But where did they come from? They didn't just sprout out of nothing."

"The wind carried their seeds or something," Zoe said. "I don't know, I'm not a botanist."

Mitchell held the photographs in his hand, looking at them then at his surroundings. He walked slowly, circling the patch of yellow flowers. Suddenly one of the pictures clicked. He would never have noticed the similarity if he hadn't been actively looking for it, but it was the same place, beyond any doubt.

"This is the place," he said. He showed her the image. Zoe looked at it, and glanced around.

"You're right," she said.

"Do you think that Jovan planted the flowers here?" Mitchell asked.

"Fuck if I know," she said, and shrugged.

"If he did, and this is what we think it is, you were wrong," Mitchell said. "Gwen's murder was the important one in Jovan's life."

"Even I can be wrong occasionally, Mitchell."

One of the pictures focused on the ground. After studying the picture and the surrounding ground for several minutes, Mitchell pointed at one of the thickest patches of flowers. "This is it," he said.

They began to dig. It was just a random theory, of course, assuming the pictures marked a grave site. But it felt right.

The digging turned out to be a lot harder than Mitchell had thought it would be. He began to suspect that all the roots in the area had heard there was about to be a party in the grove. They invited all their rock friends, and converged in that very spot. He grew tired of sticking the shovel in the ground and hearing the noisy clang of a rock being struck. He also came to understand that when the shopkeeper had tried to convince them to buy some gardening gloves, he wasn't just trying to make a quick buck off of stupid city people. He'd been trying to prevent the blisters that now began to show up on Mitchell's palms.

"I once thought…" he said, breathing hard, "that gardening must be a very relaxing job."

"Why…" Zoe said, out of breath herself, "would you think that?"

"I don't know, really," he said. "Because they don't need to fill out paperwork, I guess. And handle criminals."

"Well," Zoe said, sticking her shovel in the ground and standing up, "if this is similar to gardening, I don't think I'm interested."

"Yeah," Mitchell nodded, his teeth jarring as he hit another rock. "Damn it!" he dropped the shovel and stretched.

"My back is killing me," he said.

Zoe simply nodded, looking tired. He looked at her. Her face was sweaty, a strand of hair matted on her forehead. A bead of sweat crept down her neck, where Mitchell had kissed her the night before. He wondered if he should do it again.

"I don't think there's anything here," Zoe said. "I think we should talk to the loverboy again, threaten to tell his wife if he doesn't cooperate."

"Just a bit more," Mitchell said. "I think I got to a spot where there aren't any roots."

"You said that three times already," Zoe said.

"This time it's true," he said. He picked up the shovel and began digging again. "So, last night…"

"Yeah?"

"It was nice." He found it easier to talk while focused on the ground.

"Yes, it was," Zoe said.

"Maybe we could do it again."

"I don't think that'll happen," Zoe said.

"Oh."

"No offense. But I'm working on some issues."

"What issues?"

"Personal issues."

"Okay," he said. His shovel hit a root again. He tried to chop it, but it didn't break. He bent, and uncovered the root with his fingers. Except it wasn't a root at all. "This looks like a bone," he said, uncovering it a bit more. It was smooth and gray.

Zoe joined him in the hole, helping him dig around the smooth object. It definitely looked like a bone, though he wasn't sure it was human. Finally they managed to remove enough dirt to be sure: it was definitely a bone.

Now they dug very carefully, searching. They uncovered two more bones.

"Do you think it's… her?" Zoe asked, her face pale.

"I think so," Mitchell nodded, "But we shouldn't touch anything else." He crawled out of the pit and called Captain Bailey. "Hey, Captain," he said when Bailey answered.

"Hey, Mitchell, how's the vacation?" Bailey asked

"It's… good. I think I found the remains of Gwen Berry."

There was a moment of silence. "I take it that you didn't spend your vacation on the beach," Captain Bailey finally said.

"Not exactly, sir."

"Where are you, Mitchell, and what are you talking about?"

"I'm in Buttermere Park, sir. Zoe Bentley and I followed some leads, and they led us to a place where someone buried what looks like a human skeleton."

"And are you sure it's Gwen Berry?"

"Reasonably sure, sir. Jovan Stokes had some pictures of this location in his possession. And it looks like he planted dozens of those flowers… what's their name? Uh…"

"California poppies," Zoe said.

"Right. California poppies. They're all over the…" His voice trailed away.

"Mitchell? Are you there?" Captain Bailey asked. But he sounded so very distant.

Tanessa's words flashed in his mind. *If you send a bouquet made entirely of California poppies it just looks boring!*

He pictured her room in his mind, the last time he was there. Dozens of bouquets, colorful splashes of different colors. And one big bouquet that consisted only of yellow California poppies.

He turned to Zoe. "Tanessa had a bouquet of those flowers sent to her," he said.

"What? When?" Zoe looked confused.

"I was in her home a few days ago. Someone sent her these flowers. Just these flowers."

Zoe considered this, her eyes worried. "Jovan sends messages to all his victims," she finally said.

"Could this be a message?" Mitchell asked urgently.

Hesitantly, she nodded. Mitchell realized he was still holding his phone, Captain Bailey's voice buzzing on the other end. He hung up and called Tanessa's number.

There was no answer.

THIRTY

Mitchell knew something was very wrong the moment he got up to the floor of Tanessa's apartment. The air was rich with the familiar and foreboding aroma of blood. His eyes caught a small brown smear on the floor next to Tanessa's door. He pulled his Glock from its holster and approached the door carefully. He heard Zoe behind him, finally catching up, breathing hard. He turned around, put his finger on his lips. Then he carefully twisted the door handle.

It opened, and he immediately saw the feet. He pushed the door wide open, exposing the body of Officer Riley Poe lying on the floor in a brown pool of dried blood, the chair Riley had sat on outside Tanessa's door tossed carelessly by his side. There was a lot to process. Was Riley alive or dead? When had this happened? How had this happened? Questions popped in Mitchell's mind and disappeared instantly. Nothing mattered right now. Nothing but the burning, terrible question: Where was Tanessa, and was she still alive? He heard a swift intake of breath as Zoe saw the cop, and could only hope she would realize that Jovan might still be there, that they had to keep quiet until they knew exactly what was going on.

He stepped carefully around the dried blood, his gun barrel leading the way. He could still smell the scent of blood, but it intermingled with the smells of the various flowers in the room. He glanced at the bouquets. The bouquet of California poppies was missing from the table it had stood on. Maybe it had simply rotted away, but Mitchell doubted it.

One by one he went through the rooms, making sure each was clear before moving to the next. If Zoe had been his real partner, he would have been able to count on her to watch his back. As things stood, he looked over his shoulder constantly to make sure no one was creeping up on him. Eventually he got to the bedroom, whose door was slightly ajar. He pushed it open with the Glock's barrel. The room was in disarray, the pillows and sheets crumpled on the floor. The bed itself was covered with rotting California poppies. Had Jovan brought them with him, or had he taken them from the living room? Again, the question blinked into his mind and disappeared instantly, his brain hardly registering its existence. He had trouble concentrating; he felt as if hundreds of bees were humming inside his skull.

He heard someone running behind him, and turned around, his gun aimed at the man's chest. It was Jacob. Mitchell lowered the gun.

"She's gone, Jacob," he said, his throat clenching. "Jovan took my sister."

———

Jovan Stokes felt as if he was on fire. He literally shivered with excitement as he paced around the small warehouse. He circled the room twenty, thirty, maybe even forty times, occasionally smiling or laughing to himself. Was it the thrill of the successful kidnapping? The feeling of victory as he took his victim despite her police protection? Or maybe it was because it was Tanessa Lonnie, whom he had tried to kill before and failed? Maybe that was the reason for the way his body was charged with energy?

He didn't know, but finally... *finally* he had managed to feel as he did that night, when he killed Gwen Berry.

It had been January, and the city covered in snow. It was freezing; anyone who stayed outside for more than five minutes would feel his snot frost up, his eyelids crusting with small icy particles, the skin of his face burning from the cold. Was it any wonder Gwen Berry had been glad when Jovan stopped to offer her a ride home in his dad's car as she walked down the street?

She was happy he'd happened to notice her. It never occurred to her that he'd driven by because he knew she would be walking there. Because she always walked down that street on Tuesdays at five in the afternoon, straight after cheerleading practice. It also never occurred to her that Jovan might still be angry, because three months earlier he'd asked her out and she had turned him down.

The streets were abandoned as he strangled her in his car. There was no one to see her struggling, her fingers clawing at his arms. No one there to hear her cough and choke. And finally, she stopped moving.

That was when the real miracle had happened.

After a minute, as Jovan calmed down, he had realized Gwen was still alive. She'd simply lost consciousness, but her chest still rose and fell, her pulse was still stable. There was no doubt in Jovan's mind that she had to die; she deserved it. But for some reason, he couldn't finish the job at that moment. Instead he drove out of town, to a remote field, and waited.

He waited for nearly two hours, his heart beating fast all that time, his teeth grinding with suspense, his breath shallow in anticip…

…ation. Waiting for the moment when she would wake up, for that moment when he would kill her again.

When it finally happened, when her eyelids fluttered open, and she realized who was leaning above her just as his fingers closed around her throat again, he felt a surge of excitement that he had never felt before. It was the greatest moment of his life.

It had taken him years to realize that nothing came close. He'd only finally understood this when he killed his wife, after discovering she was having an affair. When he stabbed her, over and over and over, he felt a sliver of what he had felt that day when he'd killed Gwen.

He had been trying to recreate that feeling ever since. But what had made that moment so exciting? He tried simply strangling a young woman to death, and though it was thrilling it didn't come close. No, he slowly realized over time that it was the anticipation, and the victim's dread. When he stalked his victims for days, practicing, planning, and dreaming of the moment of the kill, letting them know ahead of time that they were about to die… Then the thrill became something else. A surge of pure emotions. His dominance over them, his complete control, was intoxicating. It became truly sublime... almost like that very first time.

And now here was another unconscious woman at his mercy, her face so similar to Gwen's. For a moment he almost kissed her awake, a modern version of the Sleeping Beauty fairy tale. But no. Better to wait, and savor the anticipation.

He resumed pacing, his footsteps echoing in the empty space. He wondered at the future. He had clearly underestimated the abilities of the local police. Or perhaps there were higher authorities involved? FBI? Special Forces? For a second he stopped and glanced outside, half expecting to see an incoming chopper, black clad figures sliding down a rope. But no, there was no one—just the setting sun, casting its last rays of light on the nearby field. Would the police be able to follow him here? It was hard to tell. He thought he had hidden his tracks quite well, but maybe someone had seen him carry Tanessa out of her apartment building and toss her into the secondhand car he'd purchased just the day before. He knew they were getting very close. Could someone have identified him already despite the disguise, like Tanessa had done the last time they met?

Dread and anticipation, they went hand in hand.

He stopped next to the nylon-wrapped machine. The man who had sold it to him had taken care to wrap it well. After he'd left, Jovan had wanted to tear the wrapping off immediately, but he had stopped himself. Anticipation. Every time he passed by that machine his fingers tingled with the desire to unwrap his gift. Now, suddenly able to stand it no longer, he grabbed the wrapping and pulled it hard.

It came off easily, and he took a step back, inspecting his purchase. Would they be able to identify what it was? Locate the man who had sold it to him? If they did, they'd find the warehouse. The future was shrouded in uncertainty. He walked back to where Tanessa lay, her upper body propped up against the wall, and sat down on a small stool by her side.

Her breathing slowly became louder as her consciousness returned. When she woke up, she tried to scream through her gag several times, then struggled against her bonds, before finally becoming still and assessing the situation. She noticed him standing a few feet away, looking at her, and began to struggle again.

"You'll only hurt yourself," he told her. "I know how to tie a knot."

She froze, breathing hard and fast through her nose. She looked at him, then around her. She moved her head left and right, taking in the empty room. Her eyes stopped momentarily when she noticed the machine.

"What do you think?" Jovan asked, his voice shaking with excitement. "You like it? It has an important part to play in your near future."

She looked back at him, and he saw the dread in her eyes. It took him back to a day almost thirty years before. He knelt by her and raised his hand, which held a pair of scissors.

"Better do this now," he said. "It might be messier later."

She screamed into the gag as the scissors drew near her face. And then they snipped a lock from her hair.

THIRTY-ONE

Though it was already midnight on Thursday, the Glenmore Park police department buzzed with activity. Almost everyone who had a desk sat behind it, poring over reports, discussing the events with each other, coming up with plans. Riley Poe had been stabbed to death on Tanessa Lonnie's doorstep, but there was no time to mourn the loss of a comrade; Officer Lonnie had been kidnapped. This was a time to close ranks.

All departments converged, combining their resources. The traffic and patrol squads combed the streets, searching for Jovan Stokes. The FBI took over the two interrogation rooms and turned them into makeshift headquarters. Officially, they were now in charge of the investigation, with Agent Mancuso leading. Jacob and Captain Bailey walked in and out of those rooms constantly, coordinating their efforts with the Feds. Lieutenant Bob Talbot from the state police and his team of computer experts doubled their efforts, trying to trace Jovan's online activity. The detective squad and Matt Lowery's team went over Tanessa's apartment, checking every surface, every item, every thread, leaving nothing unturned.

Amidst all that, Mitchell tried to be useful.

Maybe some other detective could have managed to channel his fear and anxiety to help him focus on the case. It was easy for Mitchell to imagine Jacob in a similar situation, taking control of the investigation, becoming a better, sharper detective when a loved one's life was at stake.

Mitchell was not that detective.

He had a hard time concentrating. At times, he realized Matt or Jacob or Zoe was talking to him, repeating the same sentence over and over, with Mitchell nodding dumbly, not hearing a single word. He kept thinking of Riley Poe, lying in the entrance of Tanessa's apartment amidst a pool of blood. Kept thinking of that bed, covered with yellow California poppies. Jovan's earlier victims' names kept flashing in his mind, along with the knowledge that in all probability Tanessa was about to join that list very soon.

At one point he left the room in the middle of a debriefing, ran to the bathroom, and threw up. Then he sat in the toilet stall and shook like a leaf.

He finally found a place to hide: in front of his computer, watching footage from various security cameras around Tanessa's building, trying to spot anything relevant. The task was technical enough that he trusted himself to do it despite the torrent of fear and despair and guilt that flooded his brain almost constantly.

According to Matt, there were signs of struggle in Tanessa's bedroom, but none outside of it. There were plenty of scenarios, some less likely than others, but the prevailing one was that Tanessa had been incapacitated by Jovan and carried outside. It was unclear how he had done it, but he was a doctor, and it was more than possible he had managed to drug her. So far, no witnesses who'd seen Jovan or Tanessa had turned up, but a neighbor from next door, a mother of four, claimed she thought she heard some noise coming from the apartment. At the time she'd thought it was the TV, but once she realized her neighbor had gone missing it occurred to her that it might have been something else entirely.

It was a long night full of misery, grief, and anxiety. Dawn brought with it no relief.

———

Sometimes, Ricky Nate thought, there just wasn't enough coffee in the world.

She was on her third cup, and still her left eye refused to open all the way. Three hours of sleep was not enough for any human being to function. It was the dumb unveiling's fault. Her editor wanted her to write a seven-hundred-word piece on the unveiling of the new swan statue in front of the Broadway Shopping Center. Seven hundred words. About a statue of a bird whose neck was too long.

She'd tried to explain that something was going on, that there were hints from various people in the police department that The Deadly Messenger had struck again. Her editor had asked for a bit more. Just saying something was up was not a valid news story. *Something's Up, Thinks Our Reporter*, was not a very good front page headline, he said. So Ricky had spent the rest of the day—and evening—trying to get anyone to divulge some information.

She'd failed miserably. Her informer in dispatch would not speak with her again, afraid for her job. Various detectives, cops, and clerks did not even pick up the phone, and if they did, they barked "no comment" at her with such vehemence that her feelings nearly got bruised.

And then it was midnight. There was still a hole in the newspaper, and the statue unveiling piece needed to be written. She hadn't even seen the damn thing, but she figured if you've see one swan statue, you've seen them all. Never had a statue been described in such a sarcastic and bitter tone. As far as Ricky was concerned, it was the swan's fault she hadn't managed to get her information. She'd lain awake in bed for hours afterward, seething in frustration, certain that one of the competing newspapers would publish the article about the Messenger. Finally, around four in the morning, she'd managed to shut her eyes, only to hear the alarm chirp, letting her know it was seven o'clock and she had to get up and go to work.

She would call in sick, she thought. But there was still that thing with the deadly messenger, and perhaps there was a sensational story to write about it…

Her phone rang. She glanced at the number; it wasn't one she recognized. She answered in a croaky, morning voice. "Hello?"

"Is this Ricky Nate?"

"Yeah."

"My name is Jovan Stokes. I believe you call me The Deadly Messenger."

Her heart sped up. This was one of those moments that either made a reporter's career or broke it. All her exhaustion faded away, leaving her alert and tense.

"Why are you calling me, Mr. Stokes?"

"I really liked your articles so far, Ms. Nate."

"Thanks," she said, her voice quavering. Could she somehow get the police to track this call? She turned on her laptop. Maybe if she sent an urgent e-mail to someone in the department…

"I have another article for you to publish today, at one o'clock," the gritty voice said. She pictured the man whose image had been recently released by the police on the other side of the call.

"The *Gazette* is printed at night," she said. "And distributed in the morning. And tomorrow is Saturday, so we won't print it until Monday."

"We live in a remarkable time, Ms. Nate," he said, and she could almost hear the smile in his voice. "News is delivered twenty-four hours a day online. Publish the article on your website."

"What's the story?" she asked. Her laptop finished loading up. She opened the e-mail client.

"Do you remember Tanessa Lonnie? The cop they used as bait?" he asked.

"I… Yes."

"I have her."

"What do you—"

"Yesterday I kidnapped Tanessa. She's with me now, alive. I need you to publish two photos, which I'll send you shortly. But you have to publish them at one o'clock, and not sooner. If they're published a minute before that, I'll kill Tanessa. If you contact the police, I'll kill Tanessa. Do you understand?"

"Yes," she said. Her heart pulsed so fast it was practically vibrating. "What are the photos?" She finished writing a short e-mail, let her cursor hover over the "send/receive" button.

"You're the one who called me The Deadly Messenger," Jovan said. "It's a message."

The call terminated.

She stared at the laptop screen. The e-mail remained unsent.

She swallowed hard, and began searching her phone for Mitchell Lonnie's number. She found it under *Mitchell Lonnie - asshole detective*. She dialed the number.

He didn't answer. She cursed loudly. Did Jovan have sources in the police? Would he know if she simply dialed 911? She hesitated. Was it worth the risk? She trusted Mitchell Lonnie; Tanessa was his sister. Who else could she trust?

Her e-mail alert blipped. She had a new e-mail with attachments, the sender's address a jumble of characters. She opened it, and gasped.

The first attachment was a picture of Tanessa Lonnie. She sat against a wall, her feet tied, her hands behind her back, her face tear-stained. A red rag was stuffed in her mouth and held there by several layers of masking tape.

The second was an image of a strange-looking machine. It was made of metal, and seemed quite large, though Ricky had no real sense of the scale. On top of it there was something that looked like a large sink. It sat on top of a large box. A pipe shaped like the letter T connected the sink and the box, its third end protruding. The entire contraption looked quite silly, but in this context it became sinister, a machine used by a madman for unthinkable purposes.

Jovan always sent messages containing his murder weapons. Ricky didn't know what this machine was, but she had a suspicion regarding its use.

She opened a new message to Mitchell Lonnie, and attached the image of Tanessa to it. She wrote a couple of sentences: *Jovan sent this to me. Call me now*, and then sent the message.

Her phone rang within thirty seconds.

"Hello?"

"When did you get this message?" Mitchell sounded half-deranged, his voice growling and raw. Ricky had second thoughts about the person she'd chosen to contact.

"Jovan Stokes just sent it by e-mail," she said hurriedly. "He called me and said that he wants it published on our site at one o'clock. There's another image."

"What other image?"

"Some sort of machine. I think he intends to use it to kill her."

There was a moment of silence.

"I need you to come to the station," Mitchell finally said. There was a strange note to his voice. Relief. He'd thought Tanessa was dead, Ricky realized.

"Jovan said that if I contact the cops, he'll kill Tanessa immediately," Ricky said. "He might be watching me. Or maybe he has a source in the police."

"He has nothing, he's just bluffing," Mitchell said.

"Are you willing to bet Tanessa's life on it?" she asked.

There was a second of silence. "Send me both images," he finally said. "Do not do anything with them. Do not publish them unless we tell you to. If you don't do as I say, my sister's death is on you."

"I don't want Tanessa to die, Detective Lonnie." Ricky said, hurt. "Of course I'll do as you say. I have the phone number he called from. I'll send it to you as well."

"Okay," he said. For a moment she thought he was about to thank her, but instead he simply said, "We'll be in touch."

He was the second person to hang up on her that morning. Her body was screaming for action, but she knew she had done all she could to save Tanessa's life. Now it was time to write one hell of a story.

THIRTY-TWO

Mitchell's heart drummed in his chest. Alive. Tanessa was still alive. For the past few hours, he had begun to believe his sister was dead. He'd imagined himself telling Richard, their mom, their dad. Thoughts of a life without Tanessa had hounded him, nearly driving him into a sobbing fit. And now he knew she was alive.

He was suddenly driven, focused; he needed to do something to get his sister back. The entire detective squad was drowning in noise. He'd told the captain, who had updated the chief. Now there were three FBI agents in the room along with Agent Mancuso, as well as the four detectives, the captain, the chief, and Zoe. The small space was not intended for such a large crowd, and everyone was talking simultaneously.

"Okay, listen up!" Captain Bailey shouted, and the noise died down. Agent Mancuso nodded at the captain and left the room with the other agents.

"Here's where we're at," the captain said. "Zoe, Agent Mancuso, and I agree that in all likelihood, Jovan Stokes intends to keep Officer Lonnie alive until a few minutes after the article is published, at one o'clock. This is our assumption, but we can't rule out the possibility that he might decide to…" He hesitated, glancing at Mitchell. "…kill her before that, so we need to work as fast as possible."

Mitchell's leg tapped impatiently. They needed to move! What was with all the talking?

"He probably plans to somehow use this machine that he showed Ms. Nate to murder Tanessa, so we have to figure out what this machine is. Now, here's the thing: Jovan Stokes hinted that he has sources in the department. We don't know if it's true, but we can't rule it out. He stated clearly that if the police are involved, Tanessa will die immediately. So we need to keep this a secret. Only the FBI are involved, and we're not talking to anyone outside the squad."

"What about the state police?" Jacob asked.

"They're left out of the loop for safety's sake," Bailey said. "Here's what we do. The FBI are going to do their thing; we'll do ours. I'll coordinate between the two groups. Mitchell!"

Mitchell's heart jumped as his name was called. "Sir?"

"Try to find what you can on the number Jovan used to call Ricky Nate. He's been careful so far, but he might have messed up this time. Bernard, I want you to work on Tanessa's image, see if you can glean anything about her whereabouts. Jacob, Hannah, I need you to figure out what this damn machine is. Zoe, I want you to call Ricky Nate, get her to describe the entire conversation with Jovan, and see if you can figure out what he's thinking. Okay, let's go!"

Mitchell felt the room burst into action as he turned to his own task, the phone number. Ricky Nate had sent him the number. He called the district attorney, intent on getting an urgent warrant for the info on the number.

A few minutes later, he was still talking to one of the clerks at the district attorney's office, trying to explain that this was urgent beyond belief. The clerk repeated over and over that he understood, that they were working as fast as they could, but Mitchell felt like he didn't realize how critical it was.

"Got it!" Hannah suddenly said. All of them gathered around her screen, where numerous images of the same machine were displayed. "I got the answer on a Reddit thread," she said. "It's a commercial meat grinder."

Mitchell felt the blood drain out of his face, a wave of dizziness overcoming him. A meat grinder. The sick asshole. He felt a hand grabbing his arm, stabilizing him.

"Are you okay?" Jacob asked.

"Yeah," he said, though he felt as if he never would be.

"Okay," Captain Bailey said. "Either he found a commercial meat grinder somewhere in Glenmore Park, or he bought one. Bernard, Jacob, hit the phones. Figure out who sells those things, either new or secondhand. This looks like a damn heavy machine, so focus on anywhere within the state. Mitchell, try Ebay, Craigslist… whatever website you can think of that might sell these things. Hannah, try to figure out where in Glenmore Park you can get such a thing. Call all the butchers, supermarkets, and so on."

Mitchell returned to his phone call, opening a browser to start chats with Customer Support at Ebay, Craigslist, and Amazon. His confidence grew. They were progressing!

Two hours later, his confidence was shrinking again. The marks of fatigue and frustration were starting to show themselves on everyone. At one point, after a particularly frustrating chat with Ebay Customer Support, Mitchell picked up his keyboard and slammed it on the table, breaking it to pieces. It seemed as if they were getting nowhere and time was running out.

Zoe was helping Hannah make phone calls. They managed to peg two butcher shops in Glenmore Park in which there were commercial meat grinders. The owners sent them pictures of the machines, but they didn't seem to match the one Ricky Nate had sent Mitchell. Captain Bailey didn't dispatch anyone there yet. If Jovan Stokes planned to crash one of those butcheries, they'd have to ambush him. Sending a patrol over to those places too early would simply alert the killer, making him flee.

Mitchell finally got the warrant for the phone number. His heart in overdrive, he called the phone company. The entire call felt like it took hours, though when he glanced at the phone screen once he finished the call, he saw it had been just under twenty-three minutes.

"Captain!" he said. "The call was made from New Hampshire!"

At that same moment, Agent Mancuso barged into the squad room.

"We got him," she said. "He's in New Hampshire, at a warehouse."

The Feds had located a man who'd sold a commercial meat grinder three days before. The meat grinder was delivered to a warehouse in New Hampshire, about thirty miles from Glenmore Park. The Feds had contacted the seller, and received an image of the meat grinder. It matched.

There were no more commands to give. No phone calls to make. No websites to check. They all dashed to their desks, grabbing their car keys, their guns, their phones.

Mitchell grabbed his gun, then felt Captain Bailey put a hand on his shoulder.

"Detective Lonnie," he said, his hand holding Mitchell firmly. "I need you to stay here. We might need a man to coordinate the efforts with dispatch, and—"

Mitchell pulled his shoulder away in rage. "Sir," he said, feeling as if it were holding back a freight train. "This is my sister we're talking about."

"I know," Bailey said. "That's why I'm telling you to stay."

"Go to hell," Mitchell spat, feeling his face redden.

"Detective, if I have to, I'll put you in a holding cell," Bailey said sharply. "Don't make me waste any more time."

Mitchell took a step forward, but Jacob got between him and the captain.

"We'll bring her back, Mitchell," he said softly. "Trust me."

Mitchell looked at Jacob, gritting his teeth. Finally, his shoulders sagged and he nodded, his throat clenching. Captain Bailey nodded at him gravely and walked past him, his foot crunching over a discarded keyboard key.

———

Jacob drove the car, with Captain Bailey in the passenger's seat, navigating with a road map and his phone. They flashed past the other cars on the road, their speed constantly hovering around ninety.

"You can slow down," Bailey said, his voice strained. "We still have some time."

"We don't know that Jovan will actually wait for one o'clock," Jacob said, veering right to avoid running into a bus. "He might be grinding Tanessa as we speak."

"Don't say that," Bailey said.

"It is what it is," Jacob said. He felt sick. How would this day end? Would he be able to keep his promise to his partner? Or would he have to process another grisly murder scene? Images of possible scenarios flashed through his mind, and he wished he could turn off his imagination. When he'd been young, he had loved watching B movies littered with violence and gore. Now, as his imagination conjured images of Tanessa murdered in horrid ways, he regretted that pastime deeply.

The captain began talking to various people on the phone, trying to figure out their approach. Finally, after several phone calls, he turned to Jacob and said, "There's a bend in the road, about two hundred feet before the warehouse. Park the car there." He called Hannah and Bernard to tell them the same thing, then they drove in silence for a while.

"Do you think Jovan has a man on the force?" Jacob asked.

"No," Bailey shook his head. "I think he was bluffing. If he had someone, he wouldn't have walked into our trap in the flower shop. But he might be tracking Ricky Nate, or listening to police frequencies. There's no way to know for sure. Turn right here."

The car tires squealed as Jacob pressed the brakes, pulling off to the right. He felt the rear tires momentarily slide on the road as he wrestled with the steering wheel, straightening them in the right lane, narrowly avoiding a white Ford whose driver was honking furiously.

"If we end up in a ditch, we won't get Tanessa back!" Bailey roared at him. "Slow the fuck down, Detective!"

He slowed down to eighty, gritting his teeth.

Finally, they were half a mile from the warehouse. Jacob pressed the brakes and the car slowed to a reasonable pace. His muscles relaxed. Until then, he hadn't been aware of how tense his own driving had made him.

"There." Bailey pointed at two parked Chevrolets. "Stop there."

Jacob pulled off the lane, the car tires crunching gravel and dry leaves. He stopped the car just before the two Chevys. Six agents in body armor stood outside the cars. Agent Mancuso walked back and forth next to one of the Chevys, shouting into a shoulder mic. As Bailey and Jacob got out of the car, she stopped shouting, shaking her head.

"Only just managed to stop the damn chopper," she said, her voice hard and angry. "Idiots nearly flew in, exposing us."

Rows of trees stood on both sides of the road, and beyond them Jacob could see the occasional houses that spotted this area. It was a cloudless day, the sky was blue, and once Agent Mancuso stopped talking birds could be heard chirping. It was so calm, and ridiculously pastoral, considering the reason they were there.

Jacob took a deep breath, trying to focus. He was exhausted, and worrying thoughts gnawed at his heart.

"Do you think Mitchell will stay put?" Bailey asked.

"I have no idea," Jacob said.

Some cars passed by, and then another Chevrolet showed up and parked behind them. Three agents got out of it. A second later, Bernard's car appeared and parked behind them. Hannah and Bernard got out, and joined the group.

The agents and detectives advanced on the side of the road. They marched quickly at first, but as they reached the bend they slowed down. They were almost crouching as they circled the twist in the road, looking intently for the warehouse.

It was beyond some trees, in a slightly unkempt field. It was made of concrete, painted beige, with a rolling steel door in front. Further away, they could see a small house, and it looked as if the warehouse was part of the same property. They split into two groups that took both sides of the warehouse. Two agents with sniper rifles disappeared into the foliage.

Agent Mancuso got to the rolling door first, her gun already in her hand. As Bailey and Jacob joined her, she nodded at the locking mechanism of the rolling door. It was broken, leaving a small slit in the door's center. Someone had forced the door open. Jacob tried to peer through the lock, but couldn't see a thing. The space inside was dark, or maybe something was simply blocking the view.

The second group circled the warehouse and finally joined them. One of the agents shook his head, indicating that there were no other exits. They took the left part of the door, and the group led by Christine Mancuso took the the right. The problem with a rolling door was that it couldn't be opened with a kick. One of the agents, a six-foot tower of a man, bent down, preparing to pull the door open as the others tensed, raising their guns, fingers in the trigger guards. One of the agents held a flashbang in his hand.

The large agent pulled the door up, the metal curtain roll sliding with a metallic groan, the flashbang already tossed inside. Though he expected the explosion, the loud bang still made Jacob's heart jump. The warehouse interior flashed and the agents burst inside with the detectives following them, guns raised, their eyes scanning the open space frantically.

There was no one there. The meat grinder lay against the wall, its metal gleaming in a shaft of light that broke through the smoke. There was no Jovan, and no Tanessa.

———

Mitchell paced the room, occasionally pausing to glance at his screen, where Tanessa's photo was displayed. He felt like his nerves were about to snap. The only reason he'd agreed to stay was because he really didn't feel completely in control. His mind was cloudy, and he couldn't manage to follow a single thought through. He glanced at his watch again. They'd been gone for twenty minutes. They were bound to get there any moment. Jacob would call him as soon as it was all over, he was sure. He just hoped Jacob would have some good news.

"I don't like this," Zoe suddenly said. She sat by her desk, staring at the wall, a frown on her face. Her eyes were red and swollen. Mitchell assumed he looked even worse.

"Me neither," Mitchell said, pacing again. "I guess we'll get a phone call soon enough."

"No," Zoe said, shaking her head. "I mean… I don't think that Jovan plans on killing Tanessa at one o'clock."

"You think he already did it?" Mitchell looked at her.

"I don't know. That whole meat grinder thing? It doesn't feel right. It feels like he's pandering."

"Pandering?"

"Yeah. It's like something out of a horror movie. Why would he do that?"

"Why would he do anything?" Mitchell asked angrily. "He's a sick asshole! I mean… Why drown a girl? Why run over one? Why attack one with a sword? He's nuts, Zoe. Making sense of his actions is useless."

"I don't think you're right," she said. "All of his killings were more or less clean—"

"Tell that to Tamay."

"He was inside the car when he hit her. Gore isn't his thing. He just wants us to get worked up."

"He doesn't even know we have the photo," Mitchell said, leaning against the wall.

"He's not stupid, Mitchell. He knows that we have the photo."

"Whatever. He might just want to go out with a bang."

"It doesn't fit," Zoe said, thumping her table forcefully. "Jovan is obsessive. He never deviates from his plans. He sends a victim the image of the murder weapon, and then he kills her with the same weapon."

"What are you saying? That he sent something to Tanessa's phone? We have her phone, and she didn't get any new message from him."

"No, that would be stupid. He knows we have her phone."

"If you're right, he has Tanessa," Mitchell said. "He can just show her the murder weapon, and then kill her a few minutes later with it."

Zoe stared at the floor.

"Do you think that's what he'll do?" Mitchell asked.

"Maybe. I don't know."

Mitchell resumed pacing the room. Why wasn't Jacob calling?

"Even that's a deviation," he said after a while. "I mean… He already sent her the message with the sword. If he's that obsessive, he has to kill her with the sword."

"Yeah, but we have the sword in the evidence room," Zoe said. "I don't think he's obsessive to the point of utter stupidity. He won't storm the evidence room."

"Maybe he sent the meat grinder image to get all the cops to drive to that warehouse," Mitchell said, "and leave the evidence room unguarded."

"That sounds like a plot from *Die Hard*," Zoe said. "And it didn't work, right? Only the detectives left the station. No, I don't think he'll go for the sword. He'll probably show her a new image. Deviate just a bit from his original plan. It'll upset him, but—"

"He doesn't have to," Mitchell suddenly said. He rushed to his desk and started scrolling through his files on the computer.

"He doesn't have to… what?" Zoe asked.

"He doesn't have to deviate. He doesn't have to use the sword." Mitchell double-clicked an image and it opened on screen. It was the image Jovan had sent Tanessa. The sword, leaning against the wall in the room of his old apartment, under a window. Through the window, they could see Peterson's Mojo.

"There are two more murder weapons here," Mitchell said. "The window, and the building."

"You think he's going to throw her off a building?" Zoe asked.

"Does it fit?" Mitchell asked.

She hesitated a moment. "It fits," she finally said. "I think it does."

"We have to go," Mitchell said.

"Go where?" Zoe asked. "To Jovan's apartment or that tall building?"

"Peterson's Mojo is closer," Mitchell said. "But we'll alert dispatch. Get them to send patrol cars to both locations."

He grabbed his keys and gun, and bolted toward the door. Zoe looked at the image on the screen one more time, and then dashed after him.

THIRTY-THREE

anessa's head spun as Jovan pulled her out of the car. Her stomach was queasy. He'd injected her with something earlier. It hadn't knocked her out, but it made her weak and dizzy, and it was hard to concentrate. Where were they? It looked like a back alley somewhere, but she had no idea where, and her vision was a bit blurry.

He held her by the nape of her neck, his fingers gripping hard enough to hurt. She tried to struggle, but it was a pathetic attempt, and he simply squeezed harder, making her whimper with pain into the rag stuffed in her mouth. He pushed her forward toward a heavy white door, and she stumbled, nearly falling to her knees. He'd untied her feet, but her hands were still bound tightly behind her back. He pulled the door open and shoved her in, never letting go. His other hand held a gun.

There was a staircase, and for a moment she thought he was about to force her up the stairs, though she doubted she could climb even three or four of them without collapsing. Instead, he pulled her aside and she saw another large metal door. An elevator. He pressed the elevator's button. Tanessa tried to scream through the gag, but her scream was muffled, weak. Again, his fingers tightened, and he pressed the gun to her stomach.

"Don't make me shoot you," he said. His tone wasn't angry. If anything, it was ecstatic, energetic.

The elevator door opened. There was a man there. For a moment none of them moved. The man stared at them, wide-eyed. Jovan lifted the gun, and she heard two loud explosions that left a high-pitched whine in her ears. The man jolted backward, smashing against the back wall of the elevator, then slid down to the floor. Jovan pushed her inside, and pressed the button for the top floor.

She was nauseous from the drug he had injected her with, and when he'd shoved the gun barrel against her stomach, it had gotten worse. Now, as she stood above the man, a pool of blood spreading at her feet, she felt the bile rising. She choked as vomit clogged her throat and nose, her mouth blocked, unable to spit. Jovan cursed as he realized what was happening. He pulled off the masking tape that held the rag in her mouth and she coughed and spat on the floor, finally able to breathe again. She was bent toward the floor, the man Jovan had shot only inches away. He wasn't dead, a remote part of her brain realized, but he soon would be. He was losing blood very fast.

The elevator stopped and Jovan pulled her out. She noticed that they were both leaving smudged red footsteps behind them as they approached another door. Jovan pulled a key out of his pocket and stuck it in the lock. She wondered where he'd gotten the key from. He turned the key and opened the door.

A blast of chilly wind hit Tanessa in her face. As Jovan grabbed her by her arm and pulled her out, she saw the sky above them, the ledge not far away. They were on a roof.

Jovan locked the door behind them, and smiled. He still held her tightly; she could feel his fingers burrowing into her arm. To her surprise, he didn't move; he simply stood there for a while, doing nothing.

The chilly wind, and the fact that she could finally breathe regularly through her mouth, helped her to focus. What were they doing up here? Why didn't he just kill her and get it over with?

"Can you feel it?" he asked her. She stared at him, confused, saying nothing. She wasn't sure she could speak.

"I could drag this moment forever," he said. "It's even better than Gwen. It's… perfect."

They stood there for a few seconds, with Tanessa hoping he would give her just a bit more. Her strength was returning. She no longer felt the weakness in her arms or feet. She was still a bit dizzy. Just a few deep breaths more, and she'd have a chance at fighting him…

"Let's go," he said. He pulled her by her arm, dragging her toward the edge.

They reached the edge of the roof, and she could see the street below. Tiny, ant-like cars drove back and forth in the street. It was all so far down; she felt her dizziness return.

"Look at me!" Jovan barked. She did not turn her head. He grabbed her hair and pulled, making her scream as he forced her face toward him. He looked at her. Stared into her eyes. And then he smiled.

She kicked as hard as she could, hitting him in the knee. He screamed, his hand letting go, and she was free. She bolted away, stumbling back from the ledge, hearing Jovan curse behind her. She tried to formulate a plan as she ran toward the door. It was locked; there was no point trying to open it. There were some large pipes, more than three feet wide. Maybe she could hide behind one, kick Jovan again as he came for her. If she could manage to get the gun from him, or to incapacitate him somehow, she could—

Something hit her hard in the back of her head, and she collapsed, nearly blacking out. She felt him lifting her, vaguely saw the gun in his hand. Had he shot her? No, he'd just hit her with his gun. And now he was dragging her back to the ledge. She was out of ideas; her body felt weak again, and useless. She could only struggle helplessly as the edge of the roof got closer.

———

The man at the front desk hadn't seen anyone go past him, definitely not a man carrying a woman. However, he added thoughtfully, someone could have gone through the back door to the service elevator…

At which point Mitchell screamed at him like a madman, demanding to know the fastest route to the roof, shaking his badge in front of the man's face. They took one of the elevators to the top floor. It took ages to get to the top.

What if Stokes had decided to throw Tanessa from a window on one of the top floors instead of going to the roof? What if they were too late? What if they were at the wrong place? Mitchell's mind was buzzing. Zoe was standing by his side, her face grim. Why was she with him? She wasn't armed; she couldn't really help him with Stokes. It was too risky.

But it was too late to worry about that. She was here now. When the elevator finally stopped, Mitchell barged out of it, his heart feeling like an overblown balloon, ready to explode. He hurtled down the corridor, searching for the door to the roof. How would he be able to find it? There were doors everywhere. There were…

Bloody footprints. There was a service elevator on the wall to his right, and two sets of bloody footprints trailed out of it, leading toward a big door. Mitchell ran to the door and tried the handle. It was locked.

"Damn it!" He roared.

"Move," Zoe said behind him. She was holding a key.

"Where…?" he asked, moving aside.

"The man at the front desk. He said this door is always locked. He gave me the key while you were calling the elevator," Zoe said, fiddling with the lock. Mitchell stared at her. He had a vague recollection of Zoe talking with the man, exchanging a blur of garbled words he couldn't really grasp. Was he losing it? His mind wasn't really working properly. When was the last time he'd slept?

He heard the lock click, and he grabbed her hand before she could open the door.

"Stay behind me," he said. She obliged. He slowly turned the handle, and then kicked the door open.

Time moved to a crawl as he took in the scene in front of him. A man held Tanessa by the roof's edge as she struggled helplessly. He was pulling her arm, his other hand on her throat, tipping her toward the open air.

"Stokes!" Mitchell hollered, his voice loud enough to be heard over the wind. "Get your hands up!" He pointed his gun at Stokes, his finger wavering on the trigger.

Jovan Stokes whirled around, Tanessa's neck trapped behind his forearm as he held her against his chest. He had a gun in his hand, and he pointed it at Tanessa's head.

"If you shoot, I'll take your sister with me, Detective Lonnie!" Stokes said, a smile stretched on his face.

"If you hurt her, I'll kill you," Mitchell snarled. Blood pounded in his head. Tanessa stared forward, her eyes unfocused, blood running down her temple. Mitchell breathed short, hard breaths. This was about to end badly, he knew. "The police and the FBI are surrounding the building as we speak," he said, hoping it was true. "You have nowhere to go. There's no point in delaying this."

Stokes laughed. "Delaying this is the entire point, you moron!" he shouted back, a deranged grin on his face. "Can you feel it? Can you feel the thrill? The anticipation?"

"Is that what this was all about?" Mitchell heard Zoe ask loudly, from behind him. "Cheap thrills?"

"There's nothing cheap about them," Stokes said. "Put that gun down or I blow her brains out."

Mitchell slowly bent to the floor, and laid his gun down.

"It's all about holding off a moment," said Stokes. "About planning it, and thinking about it, and postponing it. The anticipation—"

"Oh, please!" Zoe yelled back. "Give us a break. Planning? You nearly wrecked your car when you ran over that girl. Postponing? Lately you can't go a few days without killing someone. You were so anxious to do it, you practically walked into our trap! You just enjoy killing women! Anticipation? Shmanticipation! You're just a killer who—"

"You don't know anything!" Stokes screamed, his face suddenly red with rage, turning his gun toward them. "I'm the fucking God of anticipation!"

He was distracted, and his arm was a bit loose. If only Tanessa could break free… but she seemed completely out of it, her eyelids shutting slowly. Mitchell's mind whirred.

"Put the gun down, Bill!" he shouted.

Stokes stared at him. "Bill?" he asked, frowning, tilting his head a bit. "Who the hell is Bill. My name is—"

"Bill Derringer," Mitchell said loudly.

Tanessa's eyes opened. Would she get the reference? Would she know what to do? She had to, or she was lost.

There was a moment of stillness as Stokes stared at Mitchell, trying to figure out what he was talking about. Tanessa seemed woozy, unsure. She wasn't up to it, Mitchell thought in despair, measuring the distance to Stokes. Would he be able to charge the man? It was worth a shot…

Then Tanessa dropped her head forward and smashed it back, hitting Stokes's face—just as she'd done to Bill Derringer, all those years ago.

Stokes screamed in pain, blood spurting from his nose, and Tanessa stumbled forward. Mitchell knelt, grabbed his gun, aimed, and fired three times.

His aim was bad; he was dazed, his body pushed way beyond its capabilities. Two shots missed completely. The third clipped Stokes in the shoulder. He whirled, his legs buckling as he tipped backward into the void…

And then his knees bent and he fell forward instead, crashing to the roof. Mitchell leaped forward, realizing he didn't have handcuffs with him. He could just shoot Stokes, get this over with. He pointed his shaking gun at the fallen killer.

"Mitchell, don't!" Zoe shouted.

"You're under arrest," he said, his own voice far away. "Put your hands over your head."

He knelt by Tanessa, who lay on her back, blinking.

"Are you okay?" he asked.

"I think so," she mumbled. "Thanks, Mitch."

"Sure," he said, sitting down. Two cops barged through the door and onto the roof, shouting, one of them aiming his gun at Stokes. Zoe began talking quickly to both of them, explaining. Mitchell couldn't really fathom what it was all about. He just held Tanessa's head in his lap and shut his eyes.

THIRTY-FOUR

Tanessa was watching TV when Mitchell dropped by. She was immensely relieved to see him. Staying with Mom and Dad was taking its toll, and she was one "Why don't you marry a nice young man" away from matricide. When her mother had asked her if she wanted to stay with them for a couple of days, she'd happily agreed. She hadn't wanted to sleep in her bed, where Jovan had grabbed her and stuck a needle into her neck. She hadn't wanted to be alone at all, in fact.

But now she recalled that her mother was not the nurturing kind of parent that Tanessa occasionally heard about. Her mother was the kind of parent who sucked out her children's energy and joy, to teach them about the misery of life. On the plus side, sleeping alone in an apartment from which she had been kidnapped began to sound quite attractive.

"Mitchell!" Tanessa heard her mother's sing-song voice intone as she opened the door. "How lovely to see you. You're here to see Tanessa? Of course. Why else would you come visit us?"

Tanessa gnashed her teeth. Mitchell came there almost every weekend. You never could win with this woman.

Mitchell entered the living room, smiling, sadness deep within his eyes. Real sadness, not the fake stuff he used in the interrogation room.

"Hey," she said.

"Hey." He sat down. "What are you watching?"

She shrugged and turned off the TV. "Nothing. How are you?"

"They want me off duty for a few more days," Mitchell said. "But I'm feeling much better."

"Ricky Nate called you a real American hero in her article," Tanessa said.

"That's me. Definitely an American." He looked at her. "What about you?"

"Oh, the usual," she said, smiling a thin smile. *The usual.* Nightmares, fits of crying, moments of intense anxiety. Just anyone's usual day, really.

"The feds are taking Jovan to stand trial in Boston," Mitchell said. "Too high profile for Glenmore Park, I guess."

Tanessa nodded. She didn't want to talk about Jovan Stokes.

"You asked about the guy in the elevator..." Mitchell hesitated.

"Yeah?" she asked, though she already knew the answer.

"He died yesterday. They couldn't save him."

Tanessa stared at the floor.

"This job, Tanessa... It takes a toll, you know?"

"I know," she said sharply. Damn it, she knew. She'd gone through a very intense education spree lately, just to learn this fact.

"But for what it's worth... you're really good at it," Mitchell said.

She lifted her eyes in surprise, meeting his stare. He wasn't smiling; his face was dead serious.

"Yeah?"

He nodded. "I'm afraid so."

She leaned forward and hugged him. "Thanks," she whispered.

———

Zoe sat patiently on one of the two chairs in the bare room. In front of her was a white table, and beyond it another chair. The room was lit by a bright, bare bulb. It was dirty, the walls gray. Everything pulsed with hopelessness and boredom, which was only to be expected in the Massachusetts Correctional Institution.

Finally, a guard walked him in and sat him in front of her. He wore the gray scrubs that all the prisoners there wore. He was unshaven, his eyes red. She was happy to see that prison life did not seem to agree with him.

"It's you," Jovan Stokes said.

"It's me," Zoe nodded.

"What do you want?"

She shrugged. "Just to talk."

"What's there to talk about?" he sneered.

"We haven't been properly introduced. My name is Zoe Bentley, and I'm a forensic psychologist," she said. "I was hoping that we could have a couple of conversations."

"Why?" Jovan asked. "So you can use me as your study material? Fuck off."

Zoe nodded. She'd expected this. She knew how to handle it. She stood up. "Just one question," she said. "How do you think it ends for you?"

He smiled and said nothing.

"We're in Massachusetts," she said. "There is no death penalty. You're about to receive life without parole, and you'll spend the rest of your days in this prison with nothing to live for, nothing to wait for, nothing to…" She drew out the sentence, half grinning. "…Anticipate."

The smile disappeared from his face.

"Maybe you think you'll be able to kill yourself. Let me promise you one thing: I'll have you put on suicide watch. You won't get a chance, Jovan, not one chance. You can't even anticipate that moment. No. The only thing you can anticipate are my short visits. If you behave, I'll even bring something nice to eat with me."

She could see the horror in his eyes as she obliterated his fantasy world.

"Goodbye, Jovan," she said, and turned to the door.

"Wait!" he said.

She opened the door and left, closing the door behind her.

"Wait!" she heard him shout. "Please!"

She smiled as she left the prison. She had the opportunity of a lifetime. And she planned to take full advantage of it.

She already felt the anticipation for her next visit.

———

INTERESTED in reading additional Glenmore Park books? Great! You can try:

Deadly Web - *One Night, Two Dead Victims. Killers Don't Patiently Wait Their Turn Before Committing Murder.* Get it on Amazon at:

WWW.AMAZON.COM/DP/B01G4AL7V0

Web of Fear - *Detective Hannah Shor is looking for a kidnapped twelve-year-old girl. But when the ransom note is posted on Instagram and goes viral, the situation spins out of control.* Get it on Amazon at:

WWW.AMAZON.COM/DP/B01M1YCII6

———

You can subscribe to Mike Omer's mailing list to receive a notification when future Glenmore Park books will be released at:

STRANGEREALM.COM/MAILINGLIST/

ABOUT THE AUTHOR

Mike Omer is the author of the Glenmore Park Mystery Series. He has been in the past a journalist, a game developer and the CEO of the company Loadingames. He is married to a woman who diligently forces him to live his dream, and the father of an angel, a pixie and a gremlin. He has two voracious hounds that *wag their tail quite menacingly* at anyone who comes near his home.

Mike loves to write about true people who are perpetrators or victims of crimes. He also likes writing funny stuff. He mixes these two loves quite passionately into his mystery books.

You can contact Mike by sending him an e-mail to:

MIKE@STRANGEREALM.COM

ACKNOWLEDGMENTS

Like every piece of drivel I manage to write on paper, this would never have become a novel without my wife, Liora. She is my developmental editor, my cheerleader, my most avid reader, my brainstorm partner. How do other writers write books without her? I must assume they have cloned her. Please stop cloning my wife.

Thanks to Christine Mancuso for providing invaluable comments which helped shape this novel into something coherent and engaging.

Thanks to Axel Blackwell and my dad for their extremely helpful beta reading input.

Thanks to Richard Stockford who answered all of my questions with the patience and diligence of a saint.

Thanks to Tammi Labrecque for editing this novel. Without her, half the words of this novel would have been *that* or *was*, and that would have been a confusing thing to read.

Thanks to all of the authors in Author's Corner, for being there every step of the way, giving me endless much needed advice, cheering me on, and helping me when I needed them the most.

Thanks to Shai Pilosof and Gil Wizen for figuring out with me what happens when a body is buried in a park for several weeks.

Thanks to my parents for both their invaluable advice and their endless support.

Made in the USA
Middletown, DE
04 May 2020